BIBLIOASIS INTERNATIONAL TRANSLATION SERIES

General Editor: Stephen Henighan

Sea Loves Me

Sea Loves Me

SELECTED STORIES

Mia Couto

Translated from the Portuguese by
David Brookshaw with Eric M. B. Becker

BIBLIOASIS
Windsor, Ontario

10 9 8 7 6 5 4 3 2 1

Stories in this volume first appeared in Portuguese in the collections *Vozes Anoitecidas*, published in Maputo, Mozambique, in 1986 by Associação dos Escritores Moçambicanos, *Cada Homem É uma Raça*, published in 1990, *Estórias Abensonhadas*, published in 1994, *Contos do Nascer da Terra*, published in 1997, *Na Berma de Nenhuma Estrada*, published in 2001, and *O Fio das Missangas*, published in 2004, all in Lisbon, Portugal, by Editorial Caminho, and in *Mar Me Quer*, co-published in 1998 by Parque EXPO, Lisbon, Portugal, and Editorial Njira, Maputo, Mozambique. Some of these stories first appeared in English in *Voices Made Night*, in 1990, and *Every Man Is a Race*, in 1994, both published in Oxford, U.K., by the Heinemann African Writers Series and translated by David Brookshaw, or in *Rain and Other Stories*, published in 2019 in Windsor, Ontario, Canada, by the Biblioasis International Translation Series and translated by Eric M. B. Becker.

Library and Archives Canada Cataloguing in Publication

Title: Sea loves me : selected stories / Mia Couto ; [translated by] David Brookshaw, Eric M.B. Becker.
Other titles: Short stories. Selections (2021). English
Names: Couto, Mia, 1955– author. | Brookshaw, David, translator. | Becker, Eric M. B., translator.
Series: Biblioasis international translation series ; no. 33.
Description: Series statement: Biblioasis international translation series ; 33 | Short stories in English; translated from the Portuguese.
Identifiers: Canadiana (print) 20200372645 | Canadiana (ebook) 20200372696 | ISBN 9781771963886 (softcover) | ISBN 9781771963893 (ebook)
Classification: LCC PQ9939.C68 A2 2021 | DDC 869.3/42—dc23

Selected and Edited by Stephen Henighan

Copyedited by Sarah Terry

Cover designed by Zoe Norvell

Book designed and set in LD Fabiol by Tetragon, London. Illustrations taken from a series of Mozambican postage stamps from the 1980s.

REPÚBLICA PORTUGUESA

CULTURA
DIREÇÃO-GERAL DO LIVRO, DOS ARQUIVOS E DAS BIBLIOTECAS

Funded by the Direção Geral do Livro, dos Arquivos e das Bibliotecas

PRINTED AND BOUND IN CANADA

Contents

The Fire and Other Stories

The Waters of Time and Other Stories

Sea Loves Me and Other Stories

The Fire

AND OTHER STORIES

Translated by David Brookshaw

These stories originally appeared in *Voices Made Night* (1990) and *Every Man Is a Race* (1994), published in Oxford, UK, as part of the Heinemann African Writers Series.

The Fire

The old woman was seated on the mat, waiting motionless for her man to return from the bush. Her legs suffered a double weariness: from the time-worn byways, and from the times trodden.

Her worldly goods were spread out on the ground: bowls, baskets, a pestle. Around her was emptiness, even the wind was alone.

The old man approached slowly, as was his custom. He had shepherded his sadness before him ever since his youngest sons had left on the road to no return.

My husband is shrinking, she thought. *He is a shadow.*

A shadow, yes indeed. But only of his soul, for he scarcely had any body left. The old man came nearer and draped his leanness on the neighbouring mat. He raised his head and, without looking at the woman, said:

—*I'm thinking.*

—*What is it you are thinking, husband?*

—*If you die, how shall I, alone, sick and without strength, how shall I bury you?*

He passed his skinny fingers over the straw mat on which he was sitting, and went on:

—*We are poor, all we have is nothingness. Nor do we have anybody else. I think it better that we start digging your grave now.*

The woman, touched, smiled:

—*How good you are, my husband! I was lucky to have you as the man of my life.*

The old man fell silent, lost in thought. Only later did he open his mouth:

—*I'm going to see if I can find a spade.*

—*Where are you going to get a spade?*

—*I'm going to see if they have one at the store.*

—*Are you going all the way to the store? It's a long way.*

—*I shall be back this side of night.*

All the silence remained hushed so that she might listen for her husband's return. When he came back, ragged tatters of dust were retaining the last rays of sun.

—*Well then, husband?*

—*It cost a lot of money.* And he held up the spade the better to show it to her.

—*Tomorrow morning I'll start work on your grave.*

And they lay down on their separate mats. Softly, she interrupted his drift into sleep:

—*But, husband . . .*

—*What?*

—*I'm not even ill.*

—*You must be. You are so old.*

—*Maybe,* she agreed. And they fell asleep.

The next morning he looked at her intensely.

—*I'm measuring your size. After all, you're bigger than I thought.*

—*Nonsense, I'm small.*

She went to the woodpile and pulled out some kindling.

—*The wood's almost finished, husband. I'll go to the bush to get some more.*

—*Go, woman. I shall stay here and dig your grave.*

She was already moving away when an invisible hand seemed to tug at her *capulana** and, pausing, but still with her back to him, she said:

—*Listen, husband. Let me ask one thing . . .*

—*What is it you want?*

—*Don't dig too deep. I want to be near the top, just below the ground, so that I'll almost be able to touch life a little.*

—*Very well. I shan't put much earth on top of you.*

For two weeks the old man busied himself with the hole. The nearer he got to completing it, the longer he took. Then suddenly the rains came. The grave filled with water. It looked like a brazen little puddle. The old man cursed the clouds, and the heavens which had brought them.

—*Don't talk silliness, you'll be punished for it,* his wife warned.

More days of rain, and the walls of the tomb began to cave in. The old man walked over and surveyed the damage. There and then he decided to go on. Soaked under a river of rain, the old man clambered in and out, his groans ever louder, the amount of soil he carried ever less.

—*Come on in out of the rain, husband. You can't keep on like this.*

—*Stop fussing, woman,* ordered the old man. From time to time, he would pause to see how grey the sky was. He was trying to see who still had more work to do, himself or the rain.

On the following day, the old man was woken up by his own bones, which were pulling him further into his aching body.

—*I'm in pain, woman. I can't get up.*

His wife turned to him and wiped the sweat from his face.

— *You're full of fever. It's because of the soaking you got.*

—*No, it isn't, woman. It's because I slept near the fire.*

—*What fire?*

---

* A dress worn by women, akin to a sarong.

His reply was a groan. The old woman got alarmed: what was this fire the man had seen if they hadn't even lit one?

She got up to take him his bowl of mealie porridge. When she turned round he was already up, looking for his spade. He grabbed it and crept out of the house. At every other step, he would pause to gather strength.

—*Husband, don't go out like that. Eat first.*

He made some drunken gesture of dismissal. The old woman persisted:

—*You don't know your left from your right. Rest a little.*

He was already inside the hole and getting ready to start work again. The fever punished him for his obstinacy, giddiness caused the sides of his world to dance before his eyes. Suddenly, he cried out in despair:

—*Woman, help me!*

He fell like a severed branch, a cloud rent asunder. The old woman ran over to help him.

—*You're very sick.*

Pulling him by the arms, she brought him to the mat. He lay there taking deep breaths. All his life force was concentrated there, distributed among those ribs which rose and fell. In this lonely desert, you slide into death as quietly as a bird folding its wings. It does not come with a violent flash, such as happens in places where life glitters.

—*Woman,* he said in a voice that left no trace, *I can't leave you like this.*

—*What is it you are thinking now?*

—*I can't leave that grave without a use. I must kill you.*

—*That is true, husband. You worked so hard to dig that hole. It is a pity it should remain empty.*

—*Yes, I'm going to have to kill you; but not today, for I have no body for it.*

She helped him to get up and made him a cup of tea.

—*Drink it, man. Drink to get better, for tomorrow you will need your strength.*

The old man fell asleep, and the woman sat down in the doorway. In the shadow of her repose she watched the sun, king of light, gradually drain. She thought about the day and laughed to herself about its contradictions: she, whose birth had never been registered, now knew the date of her death. When the moon began to light up the trees in the wood, she leaned back and fell asleep. She dreamed of times far away from there: her children were present, the dead ones and those still alive, the *machamba** was full of crops, her eyes slid over the green of it all. There was the old man in the middle, with his tie on, telling stories, lies for the most part. They were all there, her children and grandchildren. Life itself was there, unrolling, pregnant with promise. In that happy assembly, all believed in the truths of their elders, for they were always right, and no mother opened up her flesh to death. The noises of morning began to summon her out of herself, while she tried hard not to abandon her slumber. She begged night to stay so that her dream might linger, she begged this with the same devotion as when she had beseeched life not to take her children away.

She felt in the shadows for her husband's arm to give her strength in that moment of anguish. When she touched her companion's body with her hand, she saw that it was cold, so cold that it was as if, this time, he had fallen asleep far from that fire that no one had ever lit.

---

*   Small plot of land for cultivation.

The Day Mabata-Bata Exploded

S UDDENLY, the ox exploded. It burst without so much as a moo. In the surrounding grass a rain of chunks and slices fell, as if they were the fruit and leaves of the ox. Its flesh turned into red butterflies. Its bones were scattered coins. Its horns were caught in some branches, swinging to and fro, imitating life in the invisibility of the wind.

Azarias, the little cowherd, could not contain his astonishment. Only a moment before, he had been admiring the great speckled ox, Mabata-bata. The creature grazed more slowly than laziness itself. It was the largest in the herd, ruler of the horned fraternity, and it was being kept aside as a bride price for its owner, Uncle Raul. Azarias had been working for him ever since he had been left an orphan. He would get up when it was still dark so that the cattle might graze in the early-morning mist.

He surveyed the disaster: the ox turned to dust, like an echo of silence, a shadow of nothingness. *It must have been a lightning flash*, he thought.

But it couldn't have been lightning. The sky was clear, blue without the slightest smudge. Where could the bolt have come from? Or was it the earth which had flashed?

He questioned the horizon beyond the trees. Perhaps the *ndlati*, the bird of lightning, was still circling the skies. He turned his gaze towards the mountain in front of him. It was there that the *ndlati* dwelt, there where all the rivers are one, born from the same desire to be water. The *ndlati* lives concealed in its four colours and only takes to the air when the clouds bellow and the sky grates. Then it is that the *ndlati* rises into the heavens on the wings of its madness. High in the air, it dons its clothes of flame and casts its burning flight upon the creatures of the earth. Sometimes it throws itself to the ground, making a hole. It remains in the cavity and urinates there.

Once upon a time it was necessary to resort to the skills of the old medicine man to dig out that nest and retrieve its acid deposits. Maybe Mabata-bata had trodden on some malign vestige of the *ndlati*. But who would believe it? Not his uncle. He would want to see the dead ox, at least be shown some proof of the accident. He had already seen thunderstruck cattle: they became burnt-out carcasses, a pattern of ashes reminiscent of a body. Fire chews slowly, it doesn't swallow in one go, which is what had happened here.

He looked about him: the rest of the cattle had scattered into the bush in fright. Fear slid from the little cowherd's eyes.

—*Don't come back without an ox, Azarias. That's all I say: you'd better not come back.*

His uncle's threat blustered in his ears. That anxiety consumed the air he breathed. What could he do? Thoughts rushed at him like shadows but found no way out of the problem. There was only one solution: to run away, to travel the roads where he knew nothing more. To flee is to die from a place and, with his torn trousers, an old bag over his shoulder, what would he leave behind to regret? Mistreatment, running after cattle. Other people's children were allowed to go to school. Not he, for he was nobody's son. Work tore him early from his bed and returned him to sleep when there was no longer any trace of childhood left in him. He only played with animals: swimming the river clinging to the tail of Mabatabata, making bets when the stronger animals fought each other. At home, his uncle told his fortune:

—*This one, judging by the way he lives mixed up with livestock, will surely marry a cow.*

And everyone laughed, without a care for his tiny soul, his mistreated dreams. This was why he looked back at the fields he was going to leave behind without any regrets. He considered the contents of his bag: a catapult, some *djambalau* fruit, a rusty penknife. So little cannot inspire any remorse. He set off in the direction of the river. He felt he was not running away: he was merely starting out along his road. When he arrived at the river he crossed the frontier of water. On the other bank, he stopped without even knowing what he was waiting for.

As evening fell, Grandmother Carolina was waiting for Raul at the door of the house. When he arrived, she let fly with her anxieties:

—*So late, and Azarias hasn't come back with the cattle.*

—*What? That brat is going to get a good hiding when he gets back.*

—*Couldn't it be that something has happened, Raul? I'm scared, these bandits . . .*

—*Some fun and games have happened, that's what.*

They sat on the mat and had dinner. They talked about the matter of the bride price, the wedding preparations. Suddenly, there was a knock at the door. Raul got up, casting Grandmother Carolina a questioning glance. He opened the door: they were soldiers, three of them.

—*Good evening, do you want something?*

—*Good evening. We've come to inform you of an incident: a mine exploded this afternoon. An ox trod on it. Now, that ox belonged here.*

Another soldier added:

—*We want to know where its minder is.*

—*The minder's the one we're waiting for,* Raul answered. And he shouted:

—*These bloody bandits!*

—*When he arrives, we want to talk to him, to find out how it was that it happened. Nobody should go out towards the mountain. The bandits have been laying mines over there.*

They left. Raul remained, hovering round his questions.

Where's that son of a bitch Azarias gone? And was the rest of the herd scattered out there goodness knows where?

—*Grandmother: I can't stay here like this. I've got to go and see where that good-for-nothing has got to. He's probably let the herd scatter. I must round up the cattle while it's still early.*

—*You can't, Raul. Look at what the soldiers said. It's dangerous.*

But he disregarded her and went off into the night. Does the bush have a suburb? It does: it was where Azarias had taken the animals. Raul, tearing himself on the thorns, could not deny the boy's skill. Nobody could match him in his knowledge of the land. He calculated that the little cowherd would have chosen to take refuge in the valley.

He reached the river and climbed the big rocks. At the top of his voice, he issued his command:

—*Azarias, come back, Azarias!*

Only the river answered, disentombing its gushing voice. Nothingness all around. But he sensed his nephew's hidden presence.

—*Show yourself, don't be scared. I shan't hit you, I promise.*

He promised lies. He wasn't going to hit him: he was going to thrash him to death, once he had finished rounding up the cattle. For the time being he decided to sit down, a statue of darkness. His eyes, now used to the half-light, disembarked on the other bank. Suddenly, he heard footsteps in the bush. He stood on his guard.

—*Azarias?*

It wasn't him. Carolina's voice reached Raul's ears.

—*It's me, Raul.*

Curse that old hag, what did she want? To interfere, that's all. She might tread on a mine and blow herself up and, worse still, him too.

—*Go back home, Grandmother!*

—*Azarias will refuse to hear you when you call. He'll listen to me though.*

And she put her assuredness into effect by calling the cowherd. From behind the shadows, a silhouette appeared.

—*Is that you, Azarias? Come with me, let's go home.*

—*I don't want to. I'm going to run away.*

Raul began to creep down the rock, catlike, ready to pounce and seize his nephew by the throat.

—*Where are you going to run away to, child?*

—*I've nowhere to go, Grandmother.*

—*That fellow's going to come back even if I have to cudgel him back in little pieces,* Raul's guileful voice cut in quickly.

—*Be quiet, Raul. In your life you don't know the meaning of wretchedness.* And, turning to the cowherd:

—*Come, my child, I'll look after you. It wasn't your fault that the ox died. Come and help your uncle to herd the animals.*

—*There's no need. The cattle are here, alongside me.*

Raul stood up, unsure. His heart began to do a drum dance inside his chest.

—*What's that? The cattle are there?*

—*Yes, that's right.*

The silence became twisted and tangled. Azarias's uncle was not sure of his nephew's truth.

—*Nephew, did you really do it? Did you round up the cattle?*

The grandmother smiled, thinking of how the quarrels of the two of them would now end. She promised him a reward and asked the boy to choose.

—*Your uncle is very pleased. Choose. He will respect your request.*

Raul thought it better to agree to everything at that moment. Later, he would correct the boy's illusions, and his sense of duty as a cowherd would return.

—*Tell us your wish then.*

—*Uncle, next year can I go to school?*

He had guessed this would be it. There was no way he would consent to this. By allowing him to go to school he would lose a minder for his oxen. But the occasion required bluff and he spoke with his back to his thoughts:

—*Yes, you can go.*

—*Really, Uncle?*

—*How many mouths do you think I have?*

—*I can continue to help with the cattle. School is only in the afternoon.*

—*That's right. But we'll talk about all that later. Come on out of there.*

The little cowherd emerged from the shadows and ran along the sand to where the river offered him passage. Suddenly, there was an explosion and a flash which seemed to turn night into noon. The little cowherd swallowed all that red, the shriek of crackling fire. Amid the flecks of night he saw the *ndlati*, bird of lightning, swoop down. He tried to shout: *Who are you coming to get*, ndlati?

But he spoke not a word. It wasn't the river that drowned his words: he was a fruit drained of sound, pain, and colour. Round about, everything began to close in, even the river sacrificed its water's life, and the world engulfed its floor in white smoke.

—*Are you going to land on Grandmother, poor thing, so kind? Or have you chosen my uncle, repentant after all and full of promises like the true father who died on me?*

And before the bird of fire could decide, Azarias ran and embraced it in the passage of its flame.

How Ascolino
do Perpétuo Socorro
Lost His Spouse

VIVENDA da Santíssima Palha was the name on the sign by the side of the road. A path of sand led to the farm, a place which no longer knew the meaning of sweat and toil. In the middle, half hidden by mango trees, the colonial farmhouse measured itself against time. There, in the afternoon shade, Ascolino Fernandes do Perpétuo Socorro would relax on the veranda. Inheritor of the estate, he ruminated over memories, unhurried and without obligations. He recalled Goa, his native land. He rejected the Mozambican in him: *I am indeed an Indo-Portuguese, Catholic in my faith and in my customs.*

His dress was of the most formal kind, a suit of white linen, shoes of an identical whiteness, and hat of the selfsame colour. Ceremonious, correct, Ascolino embroidered his speech with the brocades of old Portugal which he admired so much. He decorated his repartee with adverbs for no reason or purpose. A long list of them introduced sentences which were spoken incorrectly and with a strong accent: *Notwithstanding, however, nevertheless, perforce . . .*

In Munhava he had established his domains, more dreamed-of than firmly fixed. He alone discerned the glory of being Goan, while separating the breeze from the flies during the long afternoons.

He bowed to his visitors, bestowing upon them long silences and green mangoes with salt. Dona Epifânia, his wife, was the one who served them, so thin that one was not even aware she was approaching. When the net doors flapped, one knew she was there. No one had ever witnessed any expression of love pass between them. Did they love each other? If so, they loved without their bodies. Ascolino suffered because of his wife's constant seclusion. He consoled himself, but without conviction. Epifânia, he was wont to say, is a clam. If opened, it dies, exposed to the air and to the tides. When the others noted his wife's absence, Ascolino would affirm:

—*Epifâne, most sacred spouse indeed. Notvitsanding, howevah, darty years of marriage.*

Five o'clock in the afternoon was a venerated hour, even more sacred than his wife. Whether or not there were visitors, the ritual was repeated. Vasco João Joāoquinho, faithful and devoted servant, would emerge from the shadow of the mango trees. He wore a khaki uniform which consisted of a tunic and neatly pressed trousers. He would approach, wheeling a bicycle. Ascolino Fernandes, with his eye for protocol, would salute both present and absent friends. The servant would hand him a little cushion which he would arrange on the bicycle frame. Ascolino Fernandes would climb on, taking great care not to dirty his trousers on the chain. With these preparations now complete, Vasco João Joāoquinho would mount the saddle, and with a vigorous shove begin the pageant. Their sally was made all the more difficult by the undulations in the sand. And the two of them, Ascolino and his bicycle chauffeur, would press on, bound for Meneses's liquor store, dispensing greetings as they went. The movements of both were correct, only their vehicle did not uphold the bylaws. On they would press, obeying the degenerate will of Ascolino, pedalling against thirst and distance.

On that afternoon the same scenery passed by with the same men inside it. Vasco chose the grassy parts of the track so the tires gripped better. Suddenly, the bicycle keeled over and both master and servant fell into the ditch. Ascolino lay motionless in the mud. Vasco picked up the bits and pieces, straightened the handlebars, and brushed down his master's hat.

Ascolino recomposed himself with some difficulty. He surveyed the damage and began to chide his servant:

—*What have you done, man? You have been spoiling our hat indeed. Who will pay for it perforce?*

—*Sorry, boss. I was trying to steer the bicycle clear of that mud back there.*

—*Are you not seeing, fellow? I am always telling you: do not brake so suddenly.*

And on they climbed again: Ascolino Perpétuo Socorro, his dignity restored, his hat battered, Vasco pedalling through the sunset. Overhead, the coconut palms lent sound to the breeze.

—*Try not to derail the velocipede again, Vasco, will you?*

Reeling through the sands, the servant pushed with all the strength of his legs. But the Goan's thirst could not wait for the minutes to go by:

—*Proceed post-haste, Vasco. Pedal harder!*

They arrived at the Bar Viriato, Meneses's store. The bicycle came to a halt by the cement-paved frontage. The master climbed off, brushing the dust off his clothes. He pulled out his pocket watch as he made his way towards his reserved table. Vasco did not enter the front part. Blacks, according to the custom of the time, were only admitted at the rear. In the back yard, watered-down wine was served. In the bar, in front, the quality was of a different order.

❧

Vasco João Joãoquinho took his time coming in. The others greeted his arrival and asked for stories about him and his boss Ascolino. Vasco always had a tale to tell, inventing amusing incidents. But he always lingered over the beginning while preparing the condiments of the adventure.

—*Well now, Vasco? What happened last night with your boss?*

Vasco considered his words, and chuckled as he thought ahead about the tale he was going to tell.

—*You won't believe this one about my boss . . .*

—*Come on, man! Tell us it.*

And he related the incredible incident of the previous night. Ascolino Fernandes, in the furthest depths of the middle of the night, had started his singsong with the "Fado of the Little Swallows." Vasco Joãoquinho imitated him, glass in hand:

> When a little swallow died
> All the little girls cried . . .

Ascolino sang the whole night through. The little swallows kept dying and his fury kept growing. Until he began to trumpet threats through the open window:

—*Now I'm going to throw the fan out.*

And down came the fan with a crash, hurled from the first floor. It smashed into smithereens on the ground, its pieces flying across the yard. Then another warning:

—*Now for the dishes.*

And down into the garden fell pieces of crockery. Gleaming splinters of glass exploded into a thousand moons in the yard of the farmhouse. Ascolino sang ever louder:

> When a little swallow died . . .

There was no sign of Epifânia. Maybe she was shut away in her room. Or perhaps she was crying in the way that only she knew how. The saddest sadness is that which is not heard.

—*I'm talking seriously, my friends, because I know all about sadness. Our race cries with its body. They don't. They're locked inside their tribulations.*

—*Listen here, Vasco, don't get off the subject. Go on with the story about your boss.*

Bits of furniture came travelling through the window. Vasco came over and begged:

—*Please, boss, stop all this.*

—*Get out of the way, Vasco.*

—*Oh, boss, don't go on, don't wreck the whole house.*

—*Whose house is it? Is it yours?*

—*But boss, have you seen all the junk down here?*

—*Get out of the way! Hurry! Now I am throwing the fridge machine.*

Terrified, Vasco left the yard. Taking a short step and then a longer one to avoid the broken glass, the servant went and hid in the shadows. There, sheltered by the darkness, he waited for the crash. Nothing. The refrigerator wasn't coming.

—*Boss?*

—*What is it that you are wanting? Nevertheless are you still annoying me?*

Then he began to sing fados again. He bellowed his song, the whole of Munhava was littered with little swallows. He interrupted his artistry and turned towards the inside of the house to insult Epifânia:

—*You don't care about me. It's just prayers from morning to night. This isn't a house for mortals. It's not a farmhouse! It's a church. The Cathedral of Santíssima Palha. Notwithstanding, I tell you what I am going to do: I am going to throw out all the furniture for praying, your crucifix, and the altar. Everything out, out of here!*

Then it was the turn of silence. Vasco Joāoquinho asked himself: is this an interval or the end of the show? Just as he thought it was all over, he heard the noise of a chair being dragged over to the window. It was then that the figure of the Goan appeared fully, from his knees to his head. His skinny hands tidied his unkempt appearance while he announced solemnly:

—*The furniture has all gone. Now it is my turn.*

And before Vasco could say anything, Ascolino Fernandes do Perpétuo Socorro threw himself down from the window. Ascolino's skinniness did not help his speed. He was more like a curtain than a body. When he landed, he didn't get so much as a grunt from the ground. Just a sigh, a little cloud of dust. Vasco, alarmed, ran over to help. He searched for signs of blood, of injury to the body. There were none.

—*Boss, did you damage anything?*

—*What anything? Help me out of the ground.*

He lifted his boss. When he had reached his full height, Ascolino surveyed the damage around him. Then he walked away through the darkness quietly humming his fado.

Everyone at the rear of the Bar Viriato laughed at the story. This time, however, Vasco Joāoquinho arranged his silence with an expression of sadness on his face.

—*Hey, Vasco, you always bring us such good stories, man.*

—*I didn't invent it. All of what I told you happened. But don't laugh so loud, he might be listening from over the other side.*

But nothing could be heard from the other side. Ascolino was hard at work on the whisky. Separated by only a wall, the other side was still a long way away.

Seated at his reserved table, Ascolino, relishing his own company, recalled Goa, Damão, and Diu and spouted adverbs. Notwithstanding, however.

—*Please to bring me another helping of visky.*

Meneses didn't even seem to see Ascolino. He poured out the orders while the sky gradually lost its light. Time slipped by between one glass and another. Ascolino drank with the confidence of a viceroy of the Indies. A finer quality Ascolino than the other Ascolino—the Indo-Portuguese superimposing himself on the Mozambican by means of alcohol. Only one anxiety remained, which had not been drowned by whisky: Epifânia. At this stage, his wife must be turning in her sleep, tossed between insults and exhaustion. Ascolino looked at the time; he didn't want to stop for the night on the journey home. Guessing his fears, a Portuguese said:

—*Don't hurry yourself, Fernandes. Don't hurry. Your lady's going to get angry with you anyway.*

Ascolino decided to ignore deadlines, to show he was a man and daring in his delay. If he was downtrodden in life, he excelled in the art of discourse.

—*Epifâne, she is already being aware of everything. Curry,* chacuti, sarapatel,* *all the good food there is, everything she has been cooking for us to eat upon our arrival. Epifâne, most sacred spouse.*

At another table, a group of soldiers awaited their chance. At this point they decided to issue their challenge:

—*Goa's gone. Indian motherfuckers; scum of the earth.*

But Ascolino, to their astonishment, did not show offence. On the contrary, he joined his assailants.

—*Yes sir, Indian motherfuckers indeed. Perforce, however, I am an Indo-Portuguese, defender of the Lusitanian fatherland against its enemies.*

The soldiers eyed each other suspiciously. But Ascolino took the affirmation of his Portuguese loyalty a step further. He climbed onto his chair and, swaying this way and that, held forth upon his heroic dreams. A crusade, yes, a crusade to reconquer the name of Goa for Portuguese usage. At its head, commanding the battalions, he, Ascolino Fernandes do Perpétuo Socorro. Behind him, soldiers and missionaries, ships loaded with arms, Bibles, and some little bottles of visky.

---

* Popular dishes in Goan cuisine.

—*This bloke's taking the piss out of us,* concluded one of the soldiers, the biggest one. He got up and walked over to Ascolino, getting the scent of his humours:

—*Crusades, what crusades? The only cross you carry is the cross your skinny little* caneco's* *legs make.*

It was not intentional, perhaps it was because he lost his balance, but Ascolino spilled a few drops of whisky on the other man's uniform. A fist flew through the air, tore through the orator's words, and Ascolino collapsed on the ground. The others seized the aggressor, dragged him away, and threw him out of the bar. Ascolino lay there on his back, in surrogate death, one arm raised and holding his glass. Meneses came to his assistance:

—*Senhor Ascolino, are you all right?*

—*I have been fallen flat.*

—*But how did it happen?*

—*Abruptly.*

They put the Goan back on his feet. He straightened his creases, and peered into the bottom of his glass. He looked round at the crowd and declared the crusade postponed.

In front of the bar, the Goan prepared his retreat:

—*Vashcooo, lessgo!*

While waiting for his chauffeur, he fumbled for his pocket watch, creature of habit that he was. Only this time he found the chain but no watch. Ascolino consulted his non-existent watch and remarked on the lateness of the hour.

—*Quickly, Vashcooo.*

He arranged the cushion on the bicycle frame before seating himself. The cushion was in place, it was just that Ascolino missed. He fell, tried again, and returned to the ground.

—*Vashcooo, switch on the light, switch off this darkness.*

---

* A derogatory term for a Goan in colonial times.

The servant aligned the dynamo with the wheel and gave the pedal a healthy kick. Ascolino was on his hands and knees looking for his own body.

—*Did my hat run away?*

Vasco Joãoquinho was also reeling. He picked up the hat and climbed on the bike. Then they both got ready, hindering each other in the process. Meneses enjoyed the spectacle from his window:

—*That* caneco's *stoned out of his mind. Full of whisky and punches.*

Vasco pushed aside pieces of darkness and other obstacles as they set off home. He pedalled along, ringing his bell, *cring, cring.* No longer could ravens be heard or herons seen. Night had levelled colours, erased differences. As they went on, the effects of the Scottish brew began to be felt even more strongly by the Goan, who abandoned his good behaviour once and for all.

—*I'm a pale-assed little* caneco, *a first-class one if you please.* And shouting with all his soul:

—*Long live Nehru!*

Some way further on, where the rice plantations end and the coconut palms begin, Ascolino exchanged his servant for his wife and began to call him Epifânia.

—*A woman doesn't ride behind. Get up in front.*

Vasco obediently gave up his saddle seat. The Goan, excited, grabbed his servant round the waist.

—*Hey, boss, get away with you.*

But Ascolino pressed forwards with sugary insistence. He tried to kiss his servant, who avoided him vigorously. As insistence increased, respect diminished. Vasco now pushed his boss aside:

—*Leave me alone, I'm not your woman.*

And another stronger shove sent Ascolino to the ground. Silence among the coconut groves. Only the ravens watched the scuffle inquisitively. The Goan lay spread-eagled on the ground. He asked for a light to see whether the stain on his trousers was puddle water, or whether he'd pissed in his pants. Vasco laughed. Ascolino began to raise himself, reeling, his nose nearly scraping the ground. Then, when finally upright, he examined the surrounding grass:

—*Vashcooo, they've stolen the Vivenda da Santíssima Palha!*

—*No, boss! We haven't got there yet, there's still some way to go.*

But Ascolino's mind was made up, and he retorted:

—*Vashcooo, we've lost the house. Perforce, you are going to look for it.*

The servant lost his patience and began to pull him along by the armpits. On tow in this fashion, Ascolino saw the road back to front, retreating crablike. Confusing his coming with his going, he pleaded:

—*Vashcooo, don't walk backwards. We are going back to Meneses's store.*

And as if going on ahead, he shouted his order:

—*Meneses, give me visky, and another helping for Epifâne, most holy drink. And* in a generous mood, he turned his head:

—*Order whatever you want, Vashcooo. And deduct it from your month's pay. You can drink on this side, there's no need for you to go to the back.*

Tired out with walking backwards, Vasco let go of him. Feeling himself horizontal, the Goan said his prayers and then took his leave:

—*Good night, Epifâne, most holy wife.*

But Vasco was no longer there. He went back to get the bicycle. Ascolino raised his head with difficulty and, seeing his servant loaded down, he hailed him:

—*That's it, bring my blanket to cover me with. And cover Epifâne too.*

Vasco, in despair, attempted a final warning:

—*I don't know, boss. If we don't get back tonight, and sleep here, your lady's going to kick up a big fuss.*

Ascolino agreed. The threat seemed to have had an effect. Propping himself on his elbows, the boss looked straight at his servant and said:

—*What's wrong, Epifânia? Are you sleeping in khaki trousers now?*

And without further ado, he fell asleep. So heavy was his slumber that Vasco failed to budge him.

Next morning, they were covered by a sheet of insects, leaves, and dew. Vasco was the first to arrive back in the world. He was surprised by the sound of a motor nearby. He looked around him, fighting the weight of his eyelids. It was then that he saw, in the near distance, the Vivenda da Santíssima Palha. Could it be that they had slept only a minute or two from home?

In the front yard, all the furniture had been piled up. There were men loading it all onto a truck. That, then, was the motor he had heard. Dona Epifânia was directing the operation like some supreme commander.

The servant hesitated. He looked at his boss, still given over to sleep. Finally, he made up his mind. Vasco Joãoquinho followed the familiar sandy path up to the house. When he got there, he realized what his mistress intended to do. She wanted to leave, to terminate her association with Ascolino without warning or explanation.

—*Senhora, don't go away, please.*

The mistress was startled. Then, recovering from her fright, she continued with her removal.

—*Senhora, we were late because of the beating the boss got back there in the bar.*

The servant's words had no effect. His mistress continued to give out her orders. But Vasco Joãoquinho didn't give up:

—*Senhora, it wasn't just the business of the beating. We were late because of an accident on the road.*

—*An accident?*

Epifânia, suddenly uncertain, began to think. She asked for proof of his truth. Vasco showed her the twisted hat. She looked at the stains and bit her lip. She chose her words carefully before asking:

—*Was he killed?*

—*Killed? No, Senhora. He's just lying in the road.*

—*Is he hurt?*

—*No, not at all. He's just sleepy. Can I go and get him?*

Words to be regretted, for once Epifânia had heard them she renewed her determination to leave and the furniture began to be loaded again.

Vasco retraced his steps along the road. Slowly, he returned to the place where he had left his boss asleep. When he got there, Ascolino was already stretching himself. Unable to take the light, he rubbed his eyes, unaware of the noise of the approaching truck. He sat up and his aching body shrank. The truck's horn startled him, and in one leap he landed in the ditch. The load passed slowly by, as if opposed to its journey. There before Ascolino's untutored eyes, his life was ebbing away, unrecorded and unnoticed. When the dust settled, Vasco could be seen standing glumly on one side of the road. On the other, Ascolino was climbing out of the ditch. As he looked, the truck continued further into the distance. Then, brushing the creases in his coat, he asked:

—*What's happening, Vasco? Are some neighbours moving from Munhava?*

—*They're not neighbours, boss. It's the lady, Dona Epifânia herself, who is going away.*

—*Epifâne?*

—*Yes. And she's taking everything with her.*

Ascolino looked askance, repeating:

—*Epifâne.*

He stood there churning over his thoughts, kicking at clumps of grass, untidying the scenery. The servant couldn't bring himself to look up. Then, suddenly, Ascolino spoke decisively:

—*Bring the bicycle, Vasco. We are going to pursue that truck. Quickly.*

—*But boss, the truck's a long way ahead by now.*

—*Quiet, you know-nothing. Load the velocipede, speedily.*

So the servant prepared the seats. On the frame, and without a cushion, sat the boss, while the servant sat on the saddle. And they began to cycle off down the road.

The groove made by the tires gradually unwove itself in the morning air. No longer could the noise of the truck be heard through the surrounding rice fields. Ascolino the viceroy led his impossible crusade to try and regain his lost spouse.

—*Pedal, pedal quickly. Perforce we must arrive early. When five o'clock strikes we must go back to Meneses's store.*

So You Haven't Flown Yet, Carlota Gentina?

1. Your Honour, let me begin

I ARE sad. No, I'm not mistaken. What I'm saying is correct. Or perhaps: we am sad? Because inside me, I'm not alone. I'm many. And they all fight over my one and only life. We go along reaping our deaths. But we only have one birth. That's where the problem lies. That's why, when I tell my story, I mix myself up, a *mulato* not of races but of existences.

They say I killed my wife. In real life, I killed one who didn't exist. She was a bird. I let her go when I saw that she didn't have a voice, that she was dying without so much as a complaint. What dumb creature was it that came out of her through the fissure of her body?

Very well, Your Honour, you, a doctor of the laws, have asked me to write down my story, and that's what I'm going to do, a little bit every day. What I'm going to tell you, you're going to use to defend me in court. But you don't even know me. Does my suffering interest you, sir? It doesn't matter to me either. Here I am talking away about this and that, but I don't want anything, I don't want to get out any more than I want to stay. These six years that I've been locked up in this cell have been enough for me to unlearn my life. Now, sir, I just want to be dying. To die is for such a long time, living is too short. I'll stay in between. On my way to death. Do you think that's funny? I'll explain: the dying are allowed to do what they want. No one laughs at them. They anticipate respect for the dead, they are pre-deceased. When the dying insult us, we forgive them for sure. If they shit in their sheets or spit on their dinner plate, we clean up after them, no questions asked. Please, Your Honour, help me. Fix it so that I can be dying, sub-dead.

After all, here I am in this prison because I decided to become a prisoner. That's the plain truth, no one pointed the finger at me. Sick of myself, I informed against me. I gave myself up. Maybe on account of being tired of waiting for a time that never came. I can wait but never get anything. When the future arrives it won't find me. When all is said and done, where am I? Isn't this time the place of my life?

I'm going to leave my thoughts to themselves, and get straight to the story. I'll begin with my brother-in-law Bartolomeu. The night he came looking for me, that was when disaster began to strike.

2. *Wings on the ground, embers in the sky*

Light was getting thin. Only a glassful of sky was left. In my brother-in-law Bartolomeu's house, they were preparing for the end of the day. He glanced round the hut: his wife bustled about, causing the last shadows from the oil lamp to flicker. Then his wife went to bed, but Bartolomeu was restless. Sleep wouldn't come quickly to him. Outside an owl began to hoot calamities. His wife didn't hear the bird warning of death, she was already in the arms of sleep. Bartolomeu said to himself: *I'm going to make tea: maybe that'll help me to sleep.*

The fire was still burning. He took a stick of wood and blew on it. He shook the crumbs of flame from his eyes and in the confusion dropped the lighted stick on his wife's back. The cry she let out no one had ever heard the likes of before. It wasn't the sound a person would make, it was the howl of an animal. A hyena's voice for sure. Bartolomeu jumped with fright: *What am I married to then? A nóii? Those women who turn into animals at night and go around doing witches' work?*

His wife dragged her burning pain across the floor in front of his distress. Like an animal. What a luckless life, thought Bartolomeu. And he fled from home. He hurried across the village to tell me what had happened. He arrived at my house, and the dogs were very excited. He came in without knocking, without so much as an "excuse me." He told me his story just as I am writing it down. At first, I didn't believe him. Perhaps Bartolomeu had mixed up his recollections when drunk. I smelled the breath of his complaint. It didn't smell of drink. It was true then. Bartolomeu repeated the story two, three, four times. I listened to it and thought to myself: *And what if my wife is the same? What if she's a nóii too?*

When Bartolomeu had left, the idea seized hold of my thoughts. And supposing I, without knowing it, were living with an animal-woman? If I had made love to her, then I had traded my human's mouth with an animal snout. How could I excuse such a trade? Were animals ever supposed to rest on a sleeping mat? Animals live and grow strong out in the corrals, beyond the wire. If that bitch had deceived me, I had become an animal myself. There was only one way to find out whether Carlota Gentina, my wife, was a *nóii* or not. It was to surprise her with some suffering, some deep pain. I looked around and saw a pot full of boiling water. I picked it up and poured the scalding liquid over her body. I waited for the scream but it didn't come. It didn't come at all. She just lay there crying silently, without making a noise. She was a curled-up piece of silence there on the mat. All the following day she did not move. Poor Carlota was just a name lying on the ground. A name without a person: just a long, slow sleep inside a body. I shook her by the shoulders:

—*Carlota, why don't you move? If you're in agony, why don't you scream?*

But death is a war of deceptions. Victories are just defeats which have been put off. As long as life has a purpose to it, it will build a person. That's what Carlota was in need of: the lie of a purpose. I played the fool to make her laugh. I hopped round the mat like a locust. I clanked cooking pots against each other and spilled the noise over myself. Nothing. Her eyes remained glued to the far distance, gazing at the blind side of darkness. Only I laughed, wrapped up in my saucepans. I got up, breathless with laughter, and went outside to give vent to my mad guffaws. I laughed until I was tired. Then gradually I was overcome by sad thoughts, ancient pangs of conscience.

I went back inside and thought she would probably like to see the light of day and stretch her legs. I took her outside. She was so light that her blood could have been no more than red dust. I sat Carlota down facing the setting sun. I let the fresh air soak her body. There, sitting in the backyard, my wife Carlota Gentina died. I didn't notice her death immediately. I only knew it when I saw the tear which had stopped still in her eyes. That tear was already death's water.

I stood looking at the woman stretched out in that body of hers. I looked at the feet, torn like the surface of the earth. They had walked so many paths that they had become like brothers to the sand. The feet of the dead are big, they grow on after death. While I measured Carlota's death I began to have my doubts: What illness was it that caused neither swelling nor cries of pain? Can hot water just stop someone's age just like that? This was the conclusion I drew from my thoughts: Carlota Gentina was a bird, of the type that lose their voice in a headwind.

3. Dreams of the soul awoke me from my body

I dreamed of her. She was in the backyard, working at her pestle. Do you know what she was grinding? Water. She was grinding water. No, it wasn't corn, or *mapira*,* or anything else. It was water, grains from Heaven.

I drew near. She was singing a sad song, it seemed as if she were lulling herself to sleep. I asked the reason for her work.

—*I'm grinding.*

—*Are those grains?*

—*They're your tears, husband.*

And then I realized: the origin of my suffering lay in that pestle. I asked her to stop but my voice could no longer be heard. My throat had gone blind. Just the *tonk-tonk-tonk* of the pestle, pounding, pounding, forever pounding. Then slowly I began to realize that the noise was coming from my chest, that it was my heart punishing me. Do you think I'm inventing this? Anyone can

---

*   A variety of local corn.

invent. But from this cell, all I can see are the walls of life. I can feel a dream, a passing whiff of perfume. But I can't grab it. Now I've exchanged my life for dreams.

It wasn't just tonight that I dreamed of her. The night before last, Your Honour, I even cried. It was because I witnessed my own death. I looked down the corridor and saw blood, a river of it. It was orphan blood. Without its father, which was my severed arm. Imprisoned blood like its owner. Condemned. I don't remember how it came to be severed. I have a darkened memory because of these countless nights I've drunk.

And do you know who it was that saved my spilled blood in that dream? It was she. She scooped up the blood with her ancient hands. She cleaned it, lovingly extracted the dirt. She put all the bits together and showed them the way back into my body. Then she called me by that name of mine which I have already forgotten because nobody calls me by it. Here I'm a number, my name is made of digits, not letters.

You asked me to confess truths, Your Honour. It's true I killed her. Was it a crime? Maybe, if that is what they say. But I sicken with the uncertainty. I'm not one of those widowers who buries his memories. They are rescued by oblivion. Death hasn't taken Carlota away from me. Now I know why: the dead are all born on the same day. Only the living have separate birthdays. Did Carlota fly? That time I spilled water over her, was it over the woman or the bird? Who can tell? Can you, Your Honour?

One thing I know for sure: She survived outside her coffin.

Those who wept at the funeral were blind. I was laughing. It's true, I was laughing. Because inside the coffin they were weeping at, there was nothing. She had fled, saved by her wings. They saw me laughing like this, but they didn't get angry. They forgave me. They thought it was laughter of the sort which is not an enemy of sadness. Maybe it was sobbing in disguise, the sweat of suffering. And they prayed. As for me, I couldn't.

After all, it wasn't a fully deceased dead woman lying there. Rather, it was a piece of silence in the form of a beast, that's what it was.

4. I shall learn to be a tree

Writing has made me tired of letters. I'm going to finish in a minute. I don't need a defence anymore, Your Honour. I don't want one. After all, I'm guilty. I want to be punished, I have no other wish. Not because of the crime, but because of my mistake. At the end I'll explain what this mistake was. Six years ago I gave myself up, I arrested me by myself. Now, I myself am condemning me.

I am grateful for everything, Your Honour. I took up your time, for no payment. You'll call me an ass. I know and accept it. But begging your pardon, Your Honour, what do you know about me? I'm not like others: I think about what I can put up with, not about what I need. What I can't manage has nothing to do with me. God's failing, not mine. Why didn't God create us already made? Finished, like an animal which, once it has been born, only has to grow. If God made us live, why didn't he let us rule our lives?

As it is, even when we're white, we're Black. With respect, Your Honour, you're Black too, let me tell you. It's a defect in the race of mankind, this race of ours which is everybody's. Our voices, blind and broken, no longer have authority. We only give orders to the weak: women and children. Even they have begun to be slow to obey. The power of a minion is to make others feel even smaller, to tread on others just as he himself is trodden on by his superiors. Crawling, that's what the job of souls is. If they're used to the ground, how is it that they can believe in Heaven?

Unfinished, incomplete, that's what we are, and we come to our end when buried. It's better to be a plant, Your Honour. I'm even going to learn to be a tree. Or perhaps a little clump of grass, for a tree wouldn't fit in here. Why don't those witches I was talking about try and be plants, all green and quiet? If that had happened, I wouldn't have had to kill Carlota. All I'd have had to do would be to transplant her; there would be no crime, no guilt.

I'm only afraid of one thing: of cold. All my life I've suffered from cold. Ague of the soul, not the body, that's what I get. Even when it's hot I still get the shivers. Bartolomeu, my brother-in-law, used to say: *Away from home it's always cold.* That's true. But I, Your Honour, what home have I ever had? None. Bare earth, without a here or a where. In a place like that, with neither arrival nor departure, you need to learn to be clever. Not the cleverness they teach you at school. An all-round cleverness, a cleverness with no fixed job in mind, no contract with anybody.

You can see from this last letter, Your Honour, that I've given up. Why am I like this? Because Bartolomeu visited me today and told me everything just as it really happened. Afterwards I realized my mistake. Bartolomeu came to my conclusion for me: his wife, my sister-in-law, wasn't a *nóii*. He got proof of this over several nights. He spied on his wife to see if she had some other nocturnal occupation. Nothing, she hadn't. She neither crawled round on all fours nor flew off like a bird. And so Bartolomeu was able to prove that his wife was a person.

Then I began to think. If my wife's sister wasn't a *nóii*, then neither was my wife. Witchcraft is a vice of sisters, an illness they are born with. But how could I have guessed it by myself? I couldn't have, Your Honour.

I am a son of my own world. I want to be judged by other laws, beholden to my tradition. My mistake was not that I killed Carlota. It was that I surrendered my life to this world of yours which does not rest easy with mine. There, where I come from, they know me. There they can decide what my goodnesses are. Here, no one can. How can I be defended if I can't obtain the understanding of others? I'm sorry, Your Honour: justice can only be done where I belong. When all is said and done, only they can tell that I didn't know Carlota Gentina didn't have wings to fly away with.

Now it's too late. I only notice the time when it has already passed. I'm a blind man who sees many doors. I open the nearest one. I don't choose, my hand merely stumbles across a latch. My life isn't a path. It is a solid stone waiting to become sand. Very slowly, I'm becoming at one with the grains of the earth. When they decide to bury me I'll already be soil. Seeing as I had no advantage in life, this will be my privilege in death.

The Whales of Quissico

He just sat there. That's all. Sat stock-still, just like that. Time did not lose its temper with him. It left him alone. Bento João Mussavele.

But nobody worried about him. People would pass by and see that deep down he wasn't idle. When they asked what he was doing, the answer would always be the same:

—*I'm taking a bit of fresh air.*

It must have really been very fresh when, one day, he decided to get up.

—*I'm off.*

His friends thought he was going back home. That he had finally decided to work and start planting a *machamba*. The farewells began.

Some went as far as to contest him:

—*But where are you going? Where you come from is full of bandits, man.*

He did not pay them any attention. He had chosen his idea, and it was a secret. He confided it to his uncle.

—*You know, Uncle, there's such hunger back there in Inhambane. People are dying every day.*

And he shook his head as if commiserating. But it had nothing to do with sentiment: just respect for the dead.

—They told me something. That something is going to change my life.
He paused, and straightened himself in his chair:
—You know what a whale is . . . well, I don't know how . . .
—A whale?
—That's what I said.
—But what's a whale got to do with it?
—Because one appeared at Quissico. It's true.
—But there aren't any whales; I've never seen one. And even if one did appear, how would people know what the creature was called?
—People don't know the name. It was a journalist who started spreading this story around about it being a whale or not a whale. All we know is that it's a big fish which comes to land on the beach. It comes from the direction of the night. It opens its mouth and, boy, if you could see what it's got inside . . . It's full of things. Listen, it's like a store, but not the ones you see nowadays. It's like a store from the old days. Full. I swear I'm being serious.

Then he gave details: people would come up to it and make their requests. Each one depending on what he needed, exactly so. All you had to do was ask, just like that. No formal requisitions or production of travel papers. The creature would open its mouth and out would come peanuts, meat, olive oil. Salt cod, too.

—Can you just imagine it? All a fellow would need is a van, he'd load the things, fill it up, drive it here to the city. Go back again. Just think of the money he'd make.

His uncle laughed long and loud. It seemed like a joke.

—It's all pie in the sky. There is no whale. Do you know how the story began?

He made no reply. It was a wasted conversation, but he kept up the good-mannered pretense of listening, and his uncle continued:

—It's those folk there who are hungry. Very hungry. They start inventing these apparitions, as if they were wizardry. But they're just figments of the imagination, mirages . . .
—Whales, corrected Bento.

He was unmoved. All this doubting wasn't enough to make him give up. He would go around asking, he would find a way of getting together some money. And he set about doing just that.

He spent the whole day wandering up and down the streets. He spoke to Aunt Justina, who had a stall in the market and with Marito, who had a van for hire. Both were skeptical. Let him go to Quissico first and bring back some proof of the whale's existence. Let him bring back some goods, preferably some bottles of that water from Lisbon,* and then they might give him a hand.

Then one day he decided to seek better advice. He would ask the local wise men, that white, Senhor Almeida, and the Black who went by the name of Agostinho. He began by consulting the Black. He gave a brief summary of the matter in question.

—*In the first place,* replied Agostinho, who was a schoolmaster, *the whale is not what it seems at first sight. Whales are prone to deceive.*

He felt a lump in his throat, as his hopes began to crumble.

—*I've already been told that, Senhor Agostinho. But I believe in the whale; I have to believe in it.*

—*That's not what I meant, my friend. I was trying to explain that the whale appears to be that which it isn't. It looks like a fish but it isn't one. It's a mammal. Just like you and me, for we are mammals.*

—*So we are like the whale? Is that what you're saying?*

The schoolmaster spoke for half an hour. He made a great show of his Portuguese. Bento stood with his eyes wide open, avidly taking in the quasi-translation. But if the zoological explanation was detailed, the conversation did not satisfy Bento's intentions.

He tried the white man's house. He walked down the avenues lined with acacias. On the sidewalks, children played with the stamens of acacia flowers. Just look at it, everybody mixed together, white children and Black. Just like in the old days . . .

---

* Term for cheap wine imported from Portugal in colonial times, and which was often watered down.

When he knocked at the wire mesh door of Almeida's residence, a houseboy peeped through suspiciously. With a grimace he overcame the bright light outside, and when he saw the colour of the visitor's skin, he decided to keep the door closed.

—*I'm asking to speak to Senhor Almeida. He already knows me.*

The conversation was brief, Almeida answered neither one way nor the other. He said the world was going crazy, that the earth's axis was more and more inclined and that the poles were becoming flatter, or flatulent, he didn't quite understand.

But that vague discourse gave him hope. It was almost like a confirmation. When he left, Bento was euphoric. He could see whales stretched out in rows as far as the eye could see, dozing on the beaches of Quissico. Hundreds of them, all loaded and he reviewing them from an MLJ station wagon.

With the little money he had saved he bought a ticket and left. Signs of war could be seen all along the road. The charred remains of buses coupled with the wretchedness of the *machambas* punished by drought.

Is it only the sun that rains nowadays?

The gas fumes produced by the bus in which he was travelling seeped in among the passengers, who complained, but Bento Mussavele was miles away, already visualizing the coast of Quissico. When he arrived, it all seemed familiar to him. The bay was fed by the waters from the lagoons of Massava and Maiene. That blue which melted away before one's eyes was beautiful. In the background, beyond the lagoons, there was land again, a brown strip which held the fury of the ocean in check. The persistence of the waves was gradually creating cracks in that rampart, embellishing it with tall islands which looked like mountains emerging from the blue in order to breathe. The whale would probably turn up over there, mingling with the grey of the sky at the end of the day.

He climbed down the ravine, his little satchel over his shoulder, until he reached the abandoned beach houses. In times gone by, these houses had accommodated tourists. Not even the Portuguese used to go there. Only South Africans. Now, all was deserted and only he, Bento Mussavele, ruled over that unreal landscape. He settled in an old house, installing himself among the remains of furniture and the ghosts of a recent age. There he remained without being aware of the comings and goings of life. When the tide came in, no matter what the hour, Bento would walk down to the surf and stay there staring into the gloom. Sucking on an old unlit pipe, he brooded. *It must come. I know it must come.*

Weeks later, his friends came to visit him. They risked the journey on one of Oliveira's buses, each bend in the road a fright to ambush the heart. They arrived at the house after descending the slope. There was Bento slumbering amid aluminum camping dishes and wooden boxes. A tatty old mattress lay decomposing on a straw mat. Waking with a start, Bento greeted his friends without any great enthusiasm. He confessed to having developed a certain fondness for the house. After the whale, he would get some furniture, of the type that can be stood up against the wall. But his most ambitious plans were reserved for the carpets. Anything that was floor, or looked like it, would be carpeted. Even the immediate vicinity of the house too, because sand is annoying and seems to move together with one's feet. And there would be a special carpet which would extend along the sands, joining the house to the place where the selfsame whale would disgorge.

Finally, one of his friends let the cat out of the bag.

—*You know, Bento: back in Maputo it's being rumoured you're a reactionary. You're here like this because of this business of arms, or whatever they're called.*

—*Arms?*

—*Yes,* another visitor chipped in helpfully. *You know that South Africa is supplying the bandits. They receive arms which come by way of the sea. That's why they're talking a lot about you.*

He began to fret.

—*Hey, boys, I can't sit still anymore. I don't know who's receiving these arms,* he kept repeating.

—*I'm waiting for the whale, that's all.*

They argued. Bento remained in the forefront of the discussion. Who could be certain that the whale didn't come from the socialist countries? Even the schoolmaster, Senhor Agostinho, whom they all knew, had said that all he needed now was to see pigs fly.

—*Hold it there. Now you're starting on a story about pigs before anyone's even seen the stupid whale.*

Among the visitors there was one who belonged to the cadres and who said there was an explanation. That the whale and the pigs . . .

—*Wait, the pigs have nothing to do with . . .*

—*Okay, leave the pigs out of it, but the whale is an invention of the imperialists to stultify the people and make them always wait for food to arrive from abroad.*

—*But are the imperialists making up this story of the whale?*

—*They invented it, yes. This rumour . . .*

—*But who gave eyes to the people who saw it? Was it the imperialists?*

—*Okay, Bento, you can stay, but we're going now.*

And his friends left, convinced that there was sorcery at work there. Somebody had given Bento medicine to make him get lost in the sands of that idiotic expectation.

One night, with the sea roaring in endless anger, Bento awoke with a start. He was trembling as if suffering a bout of malaria. He felt his legs: they were burning. But there was some sign in the wind, some sense of foreboding emanating from the darkness, which obliged him to get up and go outside. Was it a promise? Or was it disaster? He went over to the door. The sand had come away from its resting place and seemed like a maddened whip. Suddenly, underneath the little whirlwind of sand, he saw the large mat, the same mat he had laid in his dream. If it were true, if the carpet were there, then the whale had arrived. He tried to adjust his eyes as if to discharge his emotion, but giddiness over-turned his vision and his hands sought the doorpost for support. He set off through the sand, stark naked, tiny as a seagull with broken wings. He could not hear his own voice, he did not know whether it was he who was shouting. The voice came nearer and nearer. It exploded inside his head. Now he began to wade into the sea. He felt it cold, burning his tense nerves. Further ahead of him there was a dark patch which came and went like the throbbing heart of a hangover. It could only be that elusive whale.

As soon as he had unloaded the first items of merchandise, he would give himself something to eat because hunger had been vying for his body for a long time now. Only afterwards would he see to the rest, making use of the old crates in the house.

He thought about the work that remained to be done as he advanced through the water, which now came up to his waist. He felt lighthearted, as if anguish had drained his soul. A second voice addressed him, biting his last remaining senses. *There is no whale, these waters are going to be your tomb, and punish you for the dream you nourished.* But to die just like that for nothing? No, the creature was there, he could hear it breathing, that deep rumble was no longer the storm, but the whale calling for him. He was aware that he could hardly feel anything anymore, just the coldness of the water lapping at his chest. *So it was all an invention, was it? Didn't I tell you that you needed to have faith, more faith than doubt?*

The only inhabitant of the storm, Bento João Mussavele, waded on into the sea, and into his dream.

When the storm had blown itself out, the blue waters of the lagoon subsided once again into the timeless tranquility of before. The sands took their proper place once more. In an old abandoned house remained Bento João Mussavele's untidy heap of clothes, still warm from the heat of his final fever. Next to them was a satchel containing the relics of a dream. There were some who claimed that those clothes and that satchel were proof of the presence of an enemy who was responsible for receiving arms. And that these arms were probably transported by submarines which, in the tales passed on by word of mouth, had been transformed into the whales of Quissico.

The Tale of the Two Who Returned from the Dead

I T is a truth: the dead ought not to return, to cross the frontier of their world. They only come and disturb our sadness. We already know for sure: so and so has gone. We comfort widows, shed all our tears.

On the other hand, there are those dead who, having died, persist in coming back. This is what happened in that village which the waters had wrenched from the earth. The floods carried the village away, pulled up by its roots. Not even the scar of the place remained. Many were rescued. Luís Fernando and Aníbal Mucavel vanished. They perished beneath the waters, swept along by the river's furious current like a pair of fish. Their deaths had been taken for a certainty when, one afternoon, they turned up again.

The living asked them many questions. Then, alarmed, they called the militia. Raimundo appeared, he who carried his rifle as if it were a hoe. He was trembling with fear, and he could find no other words than:

—*Show me your papers.*

—You're mad, Raimundo. Put that gun down.

The militiaman gathered courage when he heard the dead men speak. He ordered them back:

—Go back to where you came from. It's no use trying anything: you'll be thrown out.

The conversation was not getting them anywhere. Estevão, who was responsible for guard duties, arrived on the scene.

Luís and Aníbal were allowed in so that they might explain themselves to the authorities.

—You're no longer on our list. Where are you going to live?

The two apparitions were offended by the manner of their welcome.

—We were swept away by the river. We ended up God knows where, and now you treat us like a couple of infiltrators?

—Wait, we'll have to speak to the director of social affairs. He is the only one who can deal with your case.

Aníbal became even more dejected.

—So we've become a case, have we? A person is not a divorce, a lawsuit. Nor was it that they had a problem: they just had their whole lives to sort out.

The official arrived on the scene. He was a tubby man, his belly inquisitive, peeping out of his tunic. They were complimented with the respect due to the dead. The official explained the difficulties and the extra burden they represented, as two dead people who had returned without warning.

—Look: they've sent us supplies. Clothes, blankets, sheets of zinc, a lot of things. But you two weren't included in the estimate.

Aníbal became agitated when he heard they had been excluded:

—What do you mean not included? Do you strike people off just like that?

—But you have died. I don't even know how you came to be here.

—What do you mean died? Don't you believe we are alive?

—Maybe, I'm not sure anymore. But this business of being alive and not alive had best be discussed with the other comrades.

So they went to the village hall. They explained their story but failed to prove their truth. A man dragged along like a fish only seeks air, he's not interested in anything else.

After some consultation the official concluded rapidly:

—*It doesn't matter whether you are completely dead or not. If you're alive, it's worse still. It would have been better to take advantage of the water to die.*

The other, the one with the tunic that played tug-of-war with its own buttons, added:

—*We can't go along to the administrative cadres of the district and tell them a couple of ghosts have turned up. They'll tell us we've got ourselves mixed up in obscurantism. We could even be punished.*

—*That's true,* agreed the other. *We did a political orientation course. You are souls, you're not the material reality that I and all the others with us in the new village are.*

The fat one added emphatically:

—*To feed you, we'd have to ask for an increase in our quota. How would we justify that? By telling them we'd got two souls to feed?*

And there the conversation ended.

Luís and Aníbal left the village hall, confused and baffled. Outside, a crowd had gathered to watch them. The two apparitions decided to look for Samuel, the teacher.

Samuel welcomed them to his house. He explained why they had not been included in the ration quotas.

—*The officials here aren't like the ones in other villages. They divert supplies. First they distribute them to their own families. Sometimes, they even say there isn't enough to go round, when in fact their houses are brimming full.*

—*Why don't you denounce them?*

Samuel shrugged. He blew into the embers to give the fire new strength. Red petals of flame spread the scent of light through the little room.

—*Listen, I'll tell you a secret. Someone did complain to their superiors. They say that this week a commission is coming to investigate the truth of such allegations. You should take the opportunity to explain your case to the commission.*

Samuel offered them a roof and food until the commission of inquiry arrived.

Aníbal sat his thoughts down at the rear of the house. He gazed long and hard at his feet and muttered, as if he were talking to them:

—*My God, how unfair we are to our body. What part of it do we take most for granted? The feet, poor things, which drag themselves along to hold us up. It's they that bear both sadness and happiness. But as they are far from the eyes, we ignore our feet, as if they didn't belong to us. Just because we are above, we tread on our feet. That's how injustice begins in this world. Now in this case, those feet are myself and Luís, scorned, plunged into the silt of the river.*

There was less light than a shadow when Luís came over and asked him what he was muttering about. Aníbal told him about how he had discovered his feet.

—*You'd do better to think of how we are going to show these folk that we are real people.*

—*Do you know something? In the old days, the forest used to scare me, so empty of people. I thought I could only live with others around me. Now, it's the other way round. I want to go back to where the animals are. I miss not being anybody.*

—*Do be quiet now. This is becoming like a conversation between spirits.*

The two stopped talking, fearful of their rickety condition. They began to fidget with things, to scrape their feet on the ground, as if trying to prove the substance of their bodies. Luís asked:

—*Can it be true? Might it not be that we really are dead? Maybe they're right. Or perhaps we are being born again.*

—*Who knows, brother? It could be any of these things. But what is not right is that you should be blamed, forgotten, struck off the list, rejected.*

It was the voice of Samuel, the teacher. He came over with some mangoes, which he gave to the two candidates for life.

They peeled the fruit, while the teacher continued to speak:

—*It's not fair they should forget that, whether you're alive or dead, you still belong to our village. After all, when we had to defend it against the bandits, didn't you take up arms?*

—*That's true. I even got this scar from an enemy bullet. Here, look.*

Aníbal got to his feet in order to show the others proof of his suffering, a deep groove that death had carved in his back.

—*Everyone knows that you deserve to be counted among the living. It's fear alone that causes them to keep quiet, to accept lies.*

Standing there like that, Aníbal clenched his fist as if to squeeze out his anger. Drops of the sweet-sad juice of the mango fell to the ground.

—*Samuel, you know about life. Don't you think it would be better if we left, if we chose another place to live?*

—*No, Aníbal. You must stay. You are bound to win in the end, I'm sure. After all, a man who leaves because he is beaten, no longer lives. He will find nowhere else to begin again.*

—*And you, Samuel, are you one of those who doesn't believe we are alive?*

—*Be quiet, Luís. Let Samuel here advise us.*

—*These people who bedevil you are bound to fall. It is they who do not belong here, not you. Stay, my friends. Help us in our plight. We too are not being considered: we are alive but it is as if we had less life, it's as if we were only halves. We don't want that.*

Luís got up and peeped out into the darkness. He walked round in a circle, returning to the centre, and, coming near to the teacher, said:

—*Samuel, aren't you scared?*

—*Scared? But these people must fall. Wasn't this why we fought, to get rid of such scum?*

—*I'm not talking about that*, replied Luís.

—*Aren't you scared that they will catch us here with you?*

—*With you? But do you really exist? Surely I can't be with people who don't exist.*

They laughed, got up, and left through the two doors of the house. Aníbal, before taking his leave, said:

—*Hey, Samuel! Long Live the Revolution!*

Three days later, the commission arrived. It was accompanied by a journalist who had become interested in the story of Luís and Aníbal. He had promised to investigate the affair. If the matter could not be resolved, he would expose the activities of the village officials in his newspaper.

The commission met for two days. Then the villagers were summoned to a general assembly. The room was packed out with people who had come to hear the verdict. The chairman of the commission announced its solemn conclusions:

—*We have closely examined the situation of the two individuals who arrived in the village, and have reached the following formal decision, namely that comrades Luís Fernando and Aníbal Mucavel should be deemed members of the existing population.*

Applause. The meeting seemed more relieved than happy.

The speaker continued:

—*But the two apparitions would be well advised not to leave the village, or life, or anywhere else again. We have shown clemency this time, but will not tolerate this behaviour next time.*

The meeting now applauded with real conviction.

Next day, Luís Fernando and Aníbal Mucavel began to see to the question of the documents that would prove they were alive.

Patanhoca,
the Lovesick
Snake Catcher

Patanhoca it was who killed the Chinawoman Missise, owner of the store in Muchatazina. Now as to the reason why he killed her, I can't tell you that. People talk a lot, each one according to their whim. When I asked, they gave me an answer. So I'm going to tell you the story. Or rather, pieces of the story. Torn pieces like our lives. We can join the bits but never complete the picture.

Some say it was nobody who killed her. She died just like that, from inside her body, on account of her blood. Others got as far as to see the wounds through which the poison entered the dead woman.

I don't want to present the truth, for I never knew it. If I invent, then it's life that's to blame. After all, the truth is no more than the *mulata* daughter of a dishonest question.

I'll start with Missise.

1. *The widow of distances*

Missise was a widow, a Chinese one, a woman of secrets and mysteries. Her shop was situated at the point where the roads end and all that is left are the unpaved tracks of the poor. There was no set time for opening and closing: her mood dictated this. It was she who decided what time of day it was.

Happiness stepped out of her life and forgot to return.

Sadness was a closed padlock on Missise. They even said it was Chinese bewitchment and that her far-off homeland, travelling in clouds of vapour, was tormenting her soul.

Nobody knew how she had come there, how she had abandoned her people. And China, as everyone knows, is a distance away. The journey is such slowness that a man has time to change colour. Her neighbours and customers wondered to themselves about her dead husband. And at night, whom did Missise share the cold with? Who was it who snuffed out her darkness?

When she had arrived in Muchatazina, she was still young. Pretty, say those who knew her then. The Portuguese came to visit her beauty on the sly. They failed to enter her favour, remained substitutes of nobody. The widow wrapped herself in a cloak of sourness, becoming ever more widowed. The Portuguese, rich ones even, would come out of there with heads bowed. They would pause in the garden, taking advantage of the shade of the many cashew trees. To distract their frustration they would tear the fruit from the branches. The cashew is the blood of the sun suspended, its fiery sweetness the juice we drink. Then they would walk away, venting their threats.

On Saturdays the widow would indulge herself in *bazookas*, large bottles of beer, first one, then another, and then more and more. She would finish when the beer had wetted all her blood. The store gave off brightness, the generator chugging away to push out that light. Fumes and mysteries would seep from the window, the Chinawoman's incense drugging the moons. It was at such times that the pain of this woman could be heard. Screams echoed in the corridors, her voice spiralled down a dark well. One night they distinguished words in her wailing:

—*My children! Give me back my children, murderer.*

So there were children after all? How could that be if no one knew of them? The neighbours listened in astonishment to her lament. The widow groaned, screamed, howled. They tried to go to her assistance, to wipe away her furies, but no one could get near. Shadow was ever-present. Death was the only garden round her house, enclosing her widow's despair.

2. *Patanhoca, the snake mechanic*

Patanhoca was a sad figure, robbed of life's good fortune. Something had torn his lips away, leaving his mouth with no above and no below. His teeth never unclenched. His mouth, because of the way it never blinked, was like a hyena's envy. Can a living creature keep his whole soul behind his teeth? Certainly this was Patanhoca's punishment. It was said he was the Devil who had come to Muchatazina. This was a lie. Who knows what the Devil's face looks like? Is it ugly? On the contrary, the Devil is as beautiful as can be, so as to deceive us into choosing backwards. A man like that is not tempted by women: he loves snakes, crawling animals, and things which don't demand beauty. The snake catcher had taught himself to be a bachelor.

Morning, evening, and other times too, Patanhoca would shut himself away with his snakes. A snake mechanic, he would scrape the rust off their scales and nurture their poisons. His was the art of those who have lost the skill of living, the Devil's lore. It wasn't even worth looking for the truth behind his life's condition. Did Patanhoca really know the secret of snakes? The answer has no document or testimony. But the doubters, if in fact there were any, were never heard.

When the evenings began to disperse the daylight, that was when he would go out, when darkness cradled the oil lamp. The paths were already pitch-black but Patanhoca would set his steps in the direction of the store.

When he arrived at his destination he put out the lamp and began the task of spreading his sorcery. His perch was there in her yard, he, an owl drawn towards the lights of Mississe.

What was Patanhoca's motive for always spending the night there? Were his lingerings just distraction? There was a reason, and that was love.

Shame manacled the snake catcher's passions. Looking was the only reward reaped from the shadows and the silences. To reveal the heart without showing the body, to dispense help and kindnesses: that is what João Patanhoca had decided to do in the secrecy of his life. Isn't a widow more alone than anyone else? Where is the arm to defend her?

That arm was Patanhoca. His powers kept thieves away from the store. Every night, so they say, he would set his snakes free around the house. So many of these snakes were there that the sand was poisoned under the blanket of night. You didn't need to be bitten. It was enough for somebody to step into the yard. In the morning, no one could enter or leave before the snake owner's prayers had given the go-ahead. His words swept the yard clean and abolished the frontier. All this, all this guard work, Patanhoca did without asking for anything in return. He would rivet his eyes on the widow, but they were no longer eyes. They were the servants of Chinese whimsies.

3. First night: the invitation

Then one night the widow opened the door. Was she naked? Or was it a play of light which eliminated her clothes? She waved to him. Patanhoca stayed where he was without revealing himself. Then she beckoned him. Her voice was a mother's:

—*Come out of the dark, come in!*

He did not move, guardian of fears, unschooled in matters of happiness. He had never had any. She called him again, this time more hoarsely. She went down the steps, and pushed forwards into the darkness. She tasted the smell of the mixtures and potions spreading their terror. She had never set eyes on such a smell before.

—*Get back inside, Mississe!*

This was Patanhoca's order. It was the first time he had spoken. The words came out spitting and scraping, without the shape lips could provide. The crickets fell silent, the night air stifled. The widow pretended she hadn't heard and went on without turning. Again Patanhoca shouted his warning:

—*Be careful! Snakes!*

Then she stopped. He came nearer, keeping to the dark side. He held out a little cloth pouch:

—*Warm up this tea: it's your medicine.*

—*No, I don't need it.*

—*What do you mean, you don't need it?*

—*All I want is for you to come and stay here.*

—*Stay where?*

—*To live here, together with me. Stay, João.*

He shuddered: João? His eyes closed, pained: can a word, such a trifle, do so much harm to a man?

—*Don't say that name again, Mississe.*

She advanced further, wanting ever more strongly to lean against his shadow.

—*João? It's your name. Why can't I say it?*

Silence gave the crickets their leave. Men and animals speak in turn, such is the law of nature.

Can a man weep? Yes, if you awaken the child he has inside him. Patanhoca wept, but he couldn't shed tears, for he had no lips.

—*Why don't you come back again?*

—*I'm Patanhoca, snake catcher. It's not just a name I was given. I've got a snout, not the face of a person.*

—*No, you're João. You're my João.*

He explained his sorrows, said his life was shattered and that when you want to pick up the pieces, it's always too late. The Chinawoman wearied of his lament:

—*Then let me out. Release me from this nightly prison, these terrors, these snakes encircling my life.*

In his fury he threw the little pouch to the ground and moved away from the circle of light to which he had brought his sadness.

4. Second night: the revelation

The next night, Patanhoca returned earlier. She was already seated on the steps, like a queen, smothered in perfumes. Her bangles robbed her of age, and made her skin glow. Patanhoca forgot to cover his shame in the darkness, and approached the woman from the back. He called her but she didn't flinch.

—*Missise?*

The widow looked up and he shuddered. There before him were her twenty years, there was the prize sought by all the hunters of desires.

—*Missise, you're chancing your luck. The snakes will bite you.*

She moved up one step and invited him:

—*Sit here, João. Let's talk.*

Back he stepped.

—*No. Speak from there, I'm listening.*

—*João, come nearer. I promise I shan't look at you. I'll speak to your back.*

He accepted. He remained coiled in his body.

—*Well then?*

—*There is no other man, nor will there be. Just you, you alone.*

—*Why did you ruin my life, Missise?*

—*Let's not talk about that problem, please.*

—*We must talk.*

She paused. The memory pained her, and it wasn't saliva she felt in her mouth anymore—it was blood pushing out her words.

—*You killed them, João.*

—*That's a lie, it was the snakes.*

Her nerves started to play on her, and her mouth stumbled in anger:

—*And who brought the snakes? Wasn't it you? I warned you, I begged you so many times: take them away from here, make them vanish into thin air. But you always answered that you were an artist. An artist of what?*

—*I was, I am. It was just on that night I was drunk. My secrets fled me, that's what happened.*

She cried, didn't even hide her face. The moon wreathed her tears. Pearls were born. The warmth of the real ones faded with envy. Clumsily, he tried to put right past insults.

—*And who were they? Children without any future. Mulato-Chinese, a race without a race. People make children in order to better them . . .*

—*Be quiet, Patanhoca!*

She raised both her body and her voice, the two suddenly mingled in one. She ran inside and slammed the door, sobbing. Patanhoca, standing, his hands together on his chest, apologized without effect. Missise's accusing voice reached him:

—*Everyone thinks you're good, but that's not true. They think you help me, with your snakes all around my night. I know, only I know the snakes are to hem me in. You want to imprison me forever, so that I won't run off with other men.*

He retreated slowly, hurting himself on her words. But that pain was almost good to feel and, from time to time, he dwelt on what she had said: *You are evil, Patanhoca. It wasn't you who chose the snakes, but they who chose you.*

He gave up and moved away, his soul reeling within. Jealousy of others, jealousy of the living, that was his wickedness. The others, whether they were handsome or ugly, could trade with each other by day. Only he didn't have the right currency. The others smoked, kissed, whistled, had a right to be greeted and bidden good day. Only he had nobody to grow tired of. That Chinawoman Mississe had stolen the fire which we can kindle in others.

5. Third night: the counsel of sleep

It was night, the last but one, and Patanhoca was still in his house. He lay on his mat ordering his thoughts: *It's true. I killed those two little children, but I didn't mean to. That night, drink confused my hands. I swapped the medicines round. But that Chinawoman got her own back on me.*

And he closed his eyes as if that crippling memory hurt him, she giving vent to her furies upon his head, smashing the bottle, cramming his flesh with glass. Blood and beer flowed in one and the same froth, her screams passed out on the ground where he was made night. Everybody thought he had died. Even she did, she who had left him, his wounds and his glass, to the night mist. She moved to a suburb of the city and opened her business.

He had crawled through the darkness, hands and voices protecting his thread of life and leading him along paths that he alone knew. He tried to forget the Chinawoman but he couldn't. He launched the boat of his life in other waters: the same current took hold of it.

He decided to move to her area, he trapped himself as if the hunter of his own destiny. He found her and saw that he had not yet been replaced. Mississe showed her suitors the street, even those who were rich and powerful. Could it be that she was waiting for him?

Fear and shame inhibited him from revealing himself. He appeared through his snakes, sent to dispel the threat of thieves. Whether she took her time to understand, Patanhoca never found out. She did not display any change, but continued, a widow without expectations. Did her calmness belie her?

Such were the questions the snake catcher of Muchatazina, João Patanhoca, pondered on as he laid his tiredness to rest. He fell asleep awaiting the counsel of dreams. He listened with attention to his visions. They told him the following: she had repented, forgiven him. He would be taken back, once again João, once again a name and a face. Once again loved.

6. The last night

Mississe had once more caused his heart to rejoice. She stood there in the cascade of light, extinguishing the stars. She alone glowed, her white blouse and skirt, her tousled hair dripping onto her shoulders. Patanhoca overflowed from his body: then it was true what the dream had said! She was prettifying herself to celebrate his return.

—*Tonight, João, let's have fun.*

He made no reply, he was afraid he might snarl and shame the João she was calling. With a movement of the head, she beckoned him towards the corridor:

—*Come in, João, let's drink.*

He climbed up the stone steps, shook the dust off his feet at the entrance, walked across the carpets, excusing himself at every turn. On a cupboard in the living room, a large photograph of their happiness was exhibited, a picture of them both and their two children commemorating life together.

He seated himself awkwardly. She served the glasses. It wasn't beer, but one of those wines that make you feel dizzy before you even drink it. He unravelled memories, sweet trifles flowed between them, from one glass to another. He began to lose his inhibitions, and drink dribbled shamelessly down his chin.

—*I'm going to stop drinking, Missise. I'm seeing the world go by at high speed.*

She wore a strange smile, which was too placid.

—*No, João. Drink your fill. I want you to drink. Afterwards, I have a request.* And, adversary of empty glasses, she filled another one. João was puzzled by the request, worried by that afterwards she promised. Hopes and fears crossed within him and he said what he didn't want, ever wanting what he did not say.

—*Missise: it wasn't the medicines that I swapped round. It was myself I swapped. Now, am I João or Patanhoca?*

She took his hands, made them one and spoke:

—*João, please, listen: go to your house and bring me that medicine you know about. I want to take it tonight.*

So this was the request? Or maybe it was a trap, hopes tricking him.

—*I can't, woman. I'm pissed; I have no legs to find my way with.*

—*Go, João. You know the way with your eyes closed.*

He looked around him: the linen tablecloth, the photograph, things from times that had fled them, they were there, silent witnesses to their disjoined lives. Mississe persisted. She got up and leaned her hot flavoured body against him, placing her hands on Patanhoca's sweating back. He felt uneasy, unable to take any more.

He got up abruptly, turned towards the corridor and went. He found it difficult to keep to the line of his route. At the end, almost repentant, he turned round:

—*But listen here: what medicine is it, Mississe? The snake vaccine?*

She didn't answer, remained with her back to him, clearing away the plates and glasses.

—*Do you know, Mississe? The only remedy, do you know what it is?* And he laughed, snorting loudly. She looked at him, saddened. How hard it was to look at that laugh he wore but which didn't belong to him.

—*Mississe, I'm telling you: the proper medicine is that wine we've just finished.*

—*It's late. Hurry up, João.*

He struggled down the steps and walked off into the night. She still seemed to say something he didn't understand; he shook his head, confused. Could it be that he had heard her correctly? Going back to China, was that what she had said? I yearn for the land about to be born? Ravings of a Chinawoman, he concluded quietly.

He smiled sympathetically. The old woman must be drunk, poor thing, she even deserved it. This is what João Patanhoca thought as he stumbled along the path. He felt pity for her. After all, she was the widow of a man who was still alive, he himself. And so many years had passed since she had last taken her lace blouse from the cupboard, so many years since she had spread the white tablecloth on her table for visitors.

The Barber's
Most Famous Customer

Firipe Beruberu's barber's shop was situated under the great tree in the market at Maquinino. Its ceiling was the shade of the crabapple. Walls there were none: which is why it blew all the cooler round the chair where Firipe sat his customers. A sign on the tree trunk displayed his prices. On it was written: *7$50 per head*. But with the rising cost of living, Firipe had amended the inscription to: *20$00 per headful*.

On the aging timbers there hung a mirror, and next to it a yellowing photo of Elvis Presley. On a crate, by the bench where the customers sat waiting, a radio shook to the rhythm of the *chimandjemandje.**

Firipe would weed heads while talking all the while. Barber's talk about this and that. But he didn't like his chit-chat to tire his customers. When someone fell asleep in the chair, Beruberu would slap a tax on the final bill. Underneath the prices listed on his sign, he had even added: *Headful plus sleep— extra 5 escudos.*

---

* A popular musical rhythm.

But in the generous shade of the crabapple tree there was no room for anger. The barber distributed affabilities, handshakes. Whoever let his ears wander in that direction heard only genial talk. When it came to advertising his services, Firipe never held back:

—*I'm telling you: me, I'm the best barber there is. You can walk anywhere round here, look into every neighbourhood: they'll all tell you Firipe Beruberu is the greatest.*

Some customers just sat there patiently. But others provoked him, pretending to contradict him:

—*That's fine salestalk, Master Firipe.*

—*Salestalk? It's the truth! I've even cut top-quality white men's hair.*

—*What? Don't tell me you've ever had a white man in this barber's shop . . .*

—*I didn't say a white had been here. I said I'd cut his hair. And I did, you take my word for it.*

—*Explain yourself, Firipe, come on. If the white didn't come here, how did you cut him?*

—*I was called to his house, that's what happened. I cut his, and his children's too. Because they were ashamed to sit down here in this seat. That's all.*

—I'm sorry, Master Firipe. But it can't have been a rich white. It must have been a *chikaka.**

Firipe made his scissors sing while, with his left hand, he pulled out his wallet.

—*Ahh! You folk? You're always doubting and disbelieving. I'm going to prove it to you. Wait there, now where is the . . . ? Ah! Here it is.*

With a thousand cares he unwrapped a coloured postcard of Sidney Poitier.

—*Look at this photo. Can you see this fellow? See how nice his hair is: it was cut here, with these very hands of mine. I scissored him without knowing what his importance was. I just saw that he spoke English.*

The customers cultivated their disbelief. Firipe replied:

---

*   A poor white.

—*I'm telling you: this fellow brought his head all the way from over there in America to this barber's shop of mine* . . .

While he talked, he kept looking up into the tree. He was keeping a watchful eye in case he had to dodge falling fruit.

—*These bloody crabapples! They make a mess of my barber's shop. And then there are always kids round here, trying to get at them. If I catch one, I'll kick him to pieces.*

—*What's this, Master Firipe? Don't you like children?*

—*Like children? Why only the other day a kid brought a sling and aimed it at the goddamned filthy tree, hoping to shoot down an apple. The stone hit the leaves and, mbaaa! it fell on top of a customer's head. Result: instead of that customer having a haircut here, he had to have a head shave at the first-aid post.*

Customers changed, the conversation remained the same. From out of Master Firipe's pocket, the old postcard of the American actor would appear in order to lend truth to his glories. But the most difficult to convince was Baba Afonso, a fat man with an impeccably groomed heart who dragged his haunches along at a slow pace. Afonso had his doubts:

—*That man was here? I'm sorry, Master Firipe. I don't believe a bit of it.*

The indignant barber stood there, arms akimbo:

—*You don't believe it? But he sat right there in that chair where you're sitting.*

—*But a rich man like that, and a foreigner to boot, would have gone to a white man's salon. He wouldn't have sat down here, Master Firipe. Never.*

The barber feigned offence. He could not have his word doubted. Then he resorted to a desperate measure:

—*You don't believe me? Then I'll bring you a witness. You'll see, wait there.*

And off he went, leaving his customers to wait with bated breath. Afonso was calmed down by the others.

—*Baba Afonso, don't be angry. This argument, it's only a game, nothing more.*

—*I don't like people who tell lies.*

—*But this one isn't even a lie. It's propaganda. Let's pretend we believe it and have done with it.*

—*As far as I'm concerned, it's a lie,* fat old Afonso kept saying.

—*Okay, Baba. But it's a lie that doesn't harm anyone.*

The barber hadn't gone far. He had walked no more than a few steps to talk to an old man who was selling tobacco leaf. Then the two of them returned together, Firipe and the old man.

—*This is old Jaimão.*

And turning to the tobacco seller, Firipe ordered:

—*You tell them, Jaimão.*

The old man coughed up all his hoarseness before attesting.

—*Yes. In truthfully I saw the man of the photo. It was cut the hair of him here. I am witness.*

And the customers showered him with questions.

—*But did you get to listen to this foreigner? What language did he speak?*

—*Shingrish.*

—*And what money did he pay with?*

—*With copper coins.*

—*But which type, escudos?*

—*No, it was money from outside.*

The barber gloated, self-satisfied, his chest puffed out. From time to time the old man breached the limit of their agreement and risked using his own initiative.

—*Then that man went in the market for to buy things.*

—*What things?*

—*Onion, orange, soap. He bought baccy leaf too.*

Baba Afonso leaped from his chair, pointing a chubby finger at him:

—*Now I've caught you: a man like that wouldn't buy baccy leaf. You've made that up. That category of fellow would smoke filter cigarettes. Jaimão, you're just telling lies, nothing more.*

Jaimão was taken aback by this sudden onslaught. Fearful, he looked at the barber and tried one last line of argument:

—*Ahh! It's not a lie. I remember even: it was a Saturday.*

Then there was laughter. For it wasn't a serious fight, their scruples were little more than playfulness.

Firipe pretended to be upset and advised the doubters to find another barber.

—*Okay, there's no need to get angry, we believe you. We accept your witness.*

And even Baba Afonso gave in, prolonging the game:

—*I expect that singer, Elvis Presley, was also here in Maquinino, having his hair cut . . .*

But Firipe Beruberu did not work alone. Gaspar Vivito, a disabled lad, helped him with the clearing up. He swept the sand with care, so as not to spread dust. He shook out the cloth covers far away.

Firipe Beruberu always told him to take care with the hair clippings.

—*Bury them deep, Vivito. I don't want the* n'nantché-cuta *to play any tricks.*

He was referring to a little bird that steals people's hair to make its nest. Legend has it that once the owner's head has been raided, not a single whisker will ever grow on it again. Firipe blamed any decrease in his clientele on Gaspar Vivito's carelessness.

Yet he could not expect much from his assistant. For he'd gone completely awry: his rubbery legs danced a never-ending *marrabenta.** His tiny head tottered lamely on his shoulders. He slobbered over his words, slavered his vowels, and smeared his consonants with spittle. And he tripped and stumbled as he tried to shoo away the children who were collecting crabapples.

---

*   A Mozambican dance.

At the end of the afternoon, when there was only one customer left, Firipe told Vivito to tidy up. This was the hour when complaints were received. If Vivito could find no way of being like other folk, Firipe paid more attention to jokes than to barbering skills.

—*Excuse me, Master Firipe. My cousin Salomão told me to come and complain at the way his hair was cut.*

—*How was it cut?*

—*There's not a hair left, he's been completely plucked. His head is bald, it even shines like a mirror.*

—*And wasn't it he who asked for it like that?*

—*No. Now he's ashamed to go out. That's why he sent me to complain.*

The barber took the complaint in good humour. He made his scissors click loudly as he spoke:

—*Listen, my friend: tell him to leave it as it is. A bald man saves on combs. And then if I cut off too much, at least he didn't have to pay.*

He circled the chair this way and that, then stood back to admire his work of art.

—*There you go, get off the chair, I've finished. But you'd better take a good look in the mirror, otherwise you might send your cousin to complain later.*

The barber shook the towel, scattering hairs. Then the customer joined his protests to those of the plaintiff.

—*But Master Firipe, you've cut off almost everything in front. Have you seen where my forehead reaches to?*

—*Ahh! I haven't touched your forehead. Talk to your father, or your mother, if you want to complain about the shape of your head. It's not my fault.*

The malcontents joined forces, bemoaning their double baldness. It was an opportunity for the barber to philosophize on capillary misfortunes:

—*Do you know what makes a person go bald? It's using another man's hat. That's what makes a man lose his hair. I, for instance, I won't even wear a shirt if I'm not sure where it's come from. Much less trousers. Just think, my brother-in-law bought a pair of underpants second-hand . . .*

—*But Master Firipe, I can't pay for this haircut.*

—*You don't have to pay. And you, tell your cousin Salomão to pass this way tomorrow: I'll give him back his dough. Money, money . . .*

And that's how it was: a dissatisfied customer earned the right not to pay. Beruberu only charged for satisfaction. Standing from morning to nightfall, weariness began to burden his legs.

—*Hell, what a dog's life! Ever since morning: snip-snip-snip. I've had enough! Living's hard, Gaspar Vivito.*

And the two of them would sit down. The barber in his chair, his assistant on the ground. It was Master Firipe's sundown, a time to meditate on his sadness.

—*Vivito, I'm worried you may not be burying the hair properly. It looks as if the* n'uantché-cuta *is losing me customers.*

The boy replied with choked sounds, he spoke a language that was his alone.

—*Shut up, Vivito. Go and see if we made much money.*

Vivito shook the wooden box. From inside there was the jingle of some coins. Their faces lit up with a smile.

—*How well they sing! This shop of mine is going to grow, mark my words. In fact, I'm even thinking of putting in a telephone here. Maybe later, I'll close it to the public. What do you think, Vivito? If we only take bookings. Are you listening, Vivito?*

The assistant was watching his boss, who had got up. Firipe walked round his chair, talking all the while, enjoying imagined futures. Then the barber looked at the handicapped boy and it was as if his dream had had its wings shattered and had plummeted into the dark sand.

—*Vivito, you should be asking: but how will you close this place if it hasn't got a wall? That's what you should be saying, Gaspar Vivito.* But it wasn't an accusation. His voice lay prostrated on the ground. Then he went over to Vivito and let his hand ripple over the boy's dangling head.

—*I can see that hair of yours needs cutting. But your head won't stand still, always moving this way and that, shaky-shake here, shaky-shake there.*

With difficulty, Gaspar climbed up into the chair and put the cloth round his neck. Agitated, the boy pointed to the darkness round about.

—*There's still some time for a scissorful or two. Now see if you can sit still, so that we can hurry.*

And so the two preened themselves under the great tree. All the shadows had died by that hour. Bats scratched the surface of the sky with their screeches. Yet it was at this very hour that Rosinha the market girl passed by, on her way home. She appeared out of the gloom and the barber stood hesitant, totally enveloped in an anxious look.

—*Did you see that woman, Vivito? Pretty, too pretty even. She usually goes by here at this hour. I sometimes wonder whether I don't linger here on purpose: dragging time until the moment she passes.*

Only then did Master Firipe admit his sadness to himself, and another Firipe emerged. But he didn't confide in anyone: as for the mute Vivito, could it be that he understood the barber's sorrow?

—*It's true, Vivito, I'm tired of living alone. It's a long time since my wife left me. The bitch ran off with another. But it's this barber's profession, too. A fellow's tied here, can't even go and take a look at what's happening at home, control the situation. And that's what happens.*

By this time he was masking his rage. He diverted the human grief from himself and imposed it upon the creatures of the earth. He threw a stone up into the branches, trying to hit bats.

—*Filthy animals! Can't they see this is my barber's shop? This place has got an owner; it's the property of Master Firipe Beruberu.*

And the two of them chased imaginary enemies. In the end they stumbled into each other, without a heart to be angry. Then, exhausted, they let out a chuckle, as if forgiving the world its insult.

❧

It happened one day. The barber's shop continued its sleepy service, and on that morning, just as on all the others, gentle banter flowed from one topic to another. Firipe was explaining the sign and its warning about the tax on sleeping:

—*Only those who fall asleep in the chair have to pay. It often happens with that fat one, Baba Afonso. I start putting the towel round him and he starts snoozing straightaway. Now me, I don't like that. I'm not anybody's wife to have to put heads to sleep. This is a proper barber's shop.*

At that point two strangers appeared. Only one of them entered the shade. He was a *mulato*, nearly white in colour. Conversation died under the weight of fear. The *mulato* went up to the barber and ordered him to show his papers.

—*Why my papers? Am I, Firipe Beruberu, disbelieved?*

One of the customers came over to Firipe and whispered to him:

—*Firipe, you'd better do as he says. This man's from the* PIDE.*

The barber bent over the wooden crate and took out his papers:

—*Here are all my bits of plastic.*

The man examined his identity card. Then he screwed it up and threw it on the ground.

—*Hey, barber, there's something missing.*

—*Something missing, what do you mean? I've given you all my papers.*

—*Where's the photograph of the foreigner?*

—*The foreigner?*

—*Yes, the foreigner you sheltered here in your barber's shop.*

Firipe was puzzled at first, then he smiled. He had realized what the fuss was about and prepared to explain:

—*But officer, this business of the foreigner is a story I made up, a joke . . .*

The *mulato* pushed him, silencing him suddenly.

—*A joke, let's see about that. We know only too well there are subversives*

---

* Portuguese secret police during the colonial era.

here from Tanzania, Zambia, wherever. Terrorists! It's probably one of those you put up here.

—*But put up how? I don't put anyone up, I don't get mixed up in politics.*

The policeman inspected the place, unhearing. He stopped in front of the sign and read it clumsily under his breath.

—*You don't put anyone up? Then explain what this here means . . .*

—*That's just because of some customers who fall asleep in the chair.*

The policeman's fury was already growing.

—*Give me the photo.*

The barber took the postcard from his pocket. The policeman interrupted his movement, snatching the photo with such force that he tore it.

—*Did this one fall asleep in the chair too, did he?*

—*But he was never here, I swear. Christ's honour. That's a photo of a film star. Haven't you ever seen him in films, the ones the Americans make?*

—*Americans, did you say? Okay, that's it. He's probably a friend of the other one, the one called Mondlane* who came from America. So this one came from there too, did he?*

—*But this one didn't come from anywhere. It's all a lie, propaganda.*

—*Propaganda? Then you must be the one in charge of propaganda in the organization . . .*

The policeman seized the barber by his overall and shook him until the buttons fell to the ground. Vivito tried to pick them up, but the *mulato* gave him a kick.

—*Get back, you son of a bitch. We'll arrest the lot of you before we finish here.*

The *mulato* called the other policeman and whispered something in his ear. The other one walked back down the path and returned some minutes later, bringing with him old Jaimão.

---

* Eduardo Mondlane, leader of the Mozambican Liberation Front (FRELIMO) guerrillas from 1962 to 1969, was educated in the United States.

—We've already interrogated this old man. He's confirmed that you received the American in the photograph here.

Firipe, smiling feebly, almost had no strength left to explain.

—There, you see, officer? More confusion. It was me who paid Jaimão to testify to my lie. Jaimão is mixed up in it with me.

—That he is, to be sure.

—Hey, Jaimão, admit it: wasn't it a trick we agreed on?

The old wretch turned this way and that inside his tattered coat, baffled.

—Yes. In truthfully I saw the man of which. In that chair he was.

The policeman pushed the old man and handcuffed him to the barber. He looked around with the eyes of a hungry vulture. He faced the small crowd which was silently witnessing the incident. He gave the chair a kick, smashed the mirror, tore up the poster. It was then that Vivito became involved and began shouting. The poor lad clutched the *mulato's* arm but soon lost his balance and fell to his knees.

—And who's this? What language does he speak? Is he a foreigner too?

—The boy's my assistant.

—Assistant, is he? Then he'd better come along too. Okay, let's go! You, the old man and this dancing monkey, get moving. Walk in front of me.

—But Vivito . . .

—Shut up, mister barber, the time for talking's finished. You'll see, in prison, you'll have a special barber to cut your and your little friends' hair.

And before the helpless gaze of the whole market, Firipe Beruberu, wearing his immaculate overall, scissors and comb in the left-hand pocket, trod the sandy path of Maquinino for the last time. Behind him, with his ancient dignity, came old Jaimão. Following him lurched Vivito with a drunkard's step. Bringing up the rear of this cortège were the two policeman, proud of their catch. Then the humdrum haggling over prices ceased, and the market sank into the deepest gloom.

The following week, two guards arrived. They tore out the barber's sign. But as they looked around, they were struck by surprise: nobody had touched anything. Instruments, towels, the radio and even the cash box were just as they had been left, waiting for the return of Firipe Beruberu, master of all the barbers in Maquinino.

Rosa Caramela

Our passions are kindled when the fuse to our heart is lit. Our most lasting love is rain, between the cloud's flight and the prison of a puddle. We are, after all, hunters who spear ourselves. And the well-aimed throw always carries with it a trace of the thrower.

L ITTLE, if anything, was known about her. Ever since she was a little girl, folk had known her as the hunchback cripple. We called her Rosa Caramela. She was one of those people who are given another name. The one she had, her natural name, didn't suit her. Re-baptized, she seemed to fit better into the world. Nor were we willing to accept other permutations. She was Rosa. Subtitle: Caramela. And we would laugh.

The hunchback was a mixture of all the races, her body crossed many a continent. Scarcely had she been delivered into life than her family withdrew. Ever since then, her dwelling was barely visible to the naked eye. It was a hovel made of haphazard stones, without measurement or care. Its wood had never been turned into planks: tree trunk, pure matter, was what remained. Lacking both bed and table, the hunchback didn't attend to herself. Did she ever eat? Nobody ever saw her with any victuals.

Even her eyes were ill-fed, having that scrawny look that conveyed hope of being gazed upon one day and the self-contained weariness of one who had once dreamed.

She had a pretty face, in spite of it all. Detached from her body, she might even have kindled desires. But if you stood back and glimpsed all of her, then her prettiness was cancelled out. We used to see her wandering along the sidewalk, her steps so short that her feet scarcely crossed each other. She found her diversion in the public gardens: she would talk to the statues. Of all her illnesses this was the worst. Anything else she did involved secret and silent matters, no one paid any attention at all. But talking to statues, no, nobody could accept such a thing. For the spirit she invested in her conversations was enough to give you a fright. Was she trying to heal the scars of the stones? She consoled each statue with a mother's inclination.

—*There now, let me clean you. I'm going to take this dirt of theirs off you.*

And she would wipe their limbs, frozen in stone, with a filthy cloth. Then she would go on her way, fleetingly visible when passing through the circle of light of a street lamp.

By day, we forgot she existed. But at night, the moonlight would remind us of her crooked outline. The moon seemed to stick to the hunchback, like a coin to a miser's pocket. And she, in front of the statues, would sing in a hoarse, inhuman voice: she would entreat them to emerge from their stony abode. She dreamed wide awake.

On Sundays, she retired, and was nowhere to be seen. The old woman would disappear, jealous of those who filled the gardens, disturbing the peace of her territory.

Nor did anyone ever try to explain Rosa Caramela's behaviour. The only reason that was ever given was the following: once upon a time Rosa had been left stranded at the entrance to the church, a bunch of flowers in her hand. Her fiancé, whoever that might have been, was late. He was so late that he never turned up. He had warned her: I don't want any fuss. It'll be just the two of us. Witnesses? God alone, if he's not too busy. And Rosa pleaded:

—*But what about my dream?*

She had dreamed of a reception all her life. A dream of glitter, a cortège, and guests. A moment that was to be hers alone, she a queen, pretty enough to inspire envious thoughts. A long white dress and the veil straightening her back. Outside, the hooting of a thousand cars. And now, there was her sweetheart depriving her of her fantasy. She brushed her tears aside with the back of her hand—what other use did it have? She complied. Let it be as he wanted.

The hour came, the hour went. He didn't come, much less arrive. The bystanders wandered off, taking their snickering and mockery with them. She waited and waited. Nobody had ever waited so long as she. Only she, Rosa Caramela. She sat there with only the step to comfort her, a stone suffering the weight of her disenchantment with the world.

A story people tell. Does it contain the sap of truth? What seems likely is that there was no sweetheart. She had extracted it all from her imagination. She had invented herself a wife-to-be, Rosita beloved, Rosa wedded. But while nothing happened, the outcome still pained her greatly. She was crippled in her reason. In order to cure her ideas, they put her away. They took her to a hospital and abandoned her there. Rosa never got visitors, nor did she receive any medicine from any quarter. She adjusted to her own company, dispeopled. She became a sister to the stones, so often did she lean against them. Walls, floor, ceiling: only stone gave her any size. Rosa landed, with the flightiness of those in love, upon the cold floor tiles. Stone was her twin.

When she was discharged, the hunchback set off in search of her mineral soul. It was then that she fell in love with statues, solitary and sure of themselves. She dressed them with tenderness and respect. She brought them drink, came to their assistance on rainy days, or when it was cold. Her favourite statue was the one in the little garden in front of our house. It was a monument to some colonial figure whose name was no longer legible. Rosa whiled away many an hour contemplating that bust. An unrequited love: the statued man remained ever distant, never deigning to give the hunchback any attention.

From our veranda we could watch her, we, under the tin roof, in our wooden house. Above all, it was my father who would watch her. A silence would descend upon him. Was it the hunchback's madness that caused our good sense to fly away? My uncle would joke, in order to save us from our state:

—*She's like the scorpion that carries its poison in its back.*

We shared our laughter among ourselves. Everybody, that is, except my father. He remained intact, solemn.

—*No one can understand the degree of her tiredness, you see. Always lugging her back around on her back.*

My father concerned himself a lot with other people's tiredness. He himself couldn't be bothered with matters of fatigue. He would sit there and make use of life's many tranquilities. My uncle, a man of diverse resources, would advise him:

—*Brother Juca, find yourself a way of making a living.*

My father didn't bother to reply. He even seemed to become more firmly ensconced, an accomplice of his old chair. Our uncle was right: he needed a salaried occupation. His only initiative was to hire out his own shoes. On Sunday, his team's supporters would pass by on their way to the soccer.

—*Juca, we've come because of the shoes.*

He nodded ever so slowly.

—*You know the contract: take them and then, when you come back, tell me what the game was like.*

And he would bend to take his shoes from under the chair. He would stoop with such effort that it was as if he were picking up the floor itself. He would lift the shoes and look at them in feigned farewell:

—*This is hard for me.*

It was only because of the doctor that he stayed behind. He had been forbidden excesses of the heart, rushes of blood.

—*My lousy heart.*

He thumped his chest to punish the organ. Then he addressed his shoes once more:

—*Look you here, my little shoes: make sure you come home on time.*

And he took his payment in advance. He sat with a set expression counting the notes. It was as if he were reading a fat book, of the type that like fingers more than they do eyes.

My mother: she was the one who stepped out into life. She would leave very early on her business. She would arrive at the market when the morning was still small. The world re-emerged through the sun's first rays. Among the piles of cabbages, her face could be seen, fat with sad silences. There she would sit, she and her body. In the struggle for life, Ma escaped us. She arrived home and left in the dark. At night, we would listen to her complaining to Father about his idleness.

—*Juca, do you think about life?*

—*Indeed I do, a lot even.*

—*Sitting down?*

My father spared himself in his replies. She, and she alone, lamented:

—*Me all alone, on the job, here at home and out there.*

Gradually, their voices would fade away down the hall. From my mother there were still some sighs to come, as her hopes swooned. But we didn't put the blame on our father. He was a good man. So good he was never right.

❧

And so life went on in our little neighbourhood. Until, one day, we got the news: Rosa Caramela had been arrested. Her only crime: venerating a colonialist. The militia chief explained the sentence: yearning for the past. The hunchback's madness concealed other, political motives. That was the commander's judgment. If it were not so, what other reason would she have to oppose, with bodily violence, the statue's demolition? Yes indeed, because the monument was a foot from the past dragging the present along behind it. It was a matter of priority that the statue should be circumcised, for the nation's honour.

Consequently, old Rosa was taken away, to cure her of her alleged mentality. Only then, in her absence, did we realize how much she contributed to the making of our landscape.

For a long time we heard no news of her. Until one afternoon our uncle tore open the silence. He had come from the cemetery, from Nurse Jawane's funeral. He climbed the little steps up to the veranda and interrupted my father's repose. Scratching his legs, my old man blinked hard, sizing up the light.

—*So, have you brought my shoes?*

My uncle didn't answer straightaway. He was busy helping himself to some shade, curing his sweat. He blew on his lips, tired. On his face, I noticed the relief of someone who has just returned from a funeral.

—*Here they are, good as new. You know, Juca, these black shoes were really useful!*

He fumbled in his pockets, but the money, always quicker to enter, was reluctant to come out. My father stopped him:

—*I didn't hire them out to you. We're of the same family, our shoes are related.*

My uncle sat down. He pulled over the bottle of beer and filled a large glass. Then, with the skill of knowledge, he took a wooden spoon and removed the froth to another glass. My father drank the froth from the glass. Forbidden liquids, the old man only indulged in fizz.

—*It's light, this froth. The heart doesn't even notice it go by.*

He consoled himself, his eyes looking straight ahead as if he were extending his thought. That self-absorption was nothing but a pretense.

—*Was the funeral full?*

While he unlaced the shoes, my uncle described the flood, crowds trampling on the flower beds, all there to bid farewell to the nurse, poor man, who had also died by his own hand.

—*But did he really kill himself?*

—*Yes, the fellow strung himself up. By the time they found him he was already stiff, he looked like a lump of starch on the end of a rope.*

—*But why did he kill himself?*

—*How should I know? They say it was because of women.*

They fell silent, the two of them, sipping at their drink. What pained them most was not the fact but the motive.

—*To die like that? It's better to pass away.*

My old man took the shoes and examined them suspiciously:

—*Is this earth from there?*

—*What, that there?*

—*I'm asking you if it's from the cemetery.*

—*Maybe.*

—*Then go and clean it, over there. I don't want the dust of the dead hereabouts.*

My uncle went and sat on the bottom step, brushing the soles. Meanwhile, he continued to talk. The ceremony was going on, the priest was saying the prayers, reviving their souls. Suddenly, what happened? Along came Rosa Caramela, all dressed in mourning.

—*Has Rosa come out of prison?* my father asked, astonished.

Yes, she'd come out. During an inspection tour of the jail, they'd given her an amnesty. She was mad, she'd committed no more serious crime than that. My father insisted, surprised:

—But she, at the cemetery?

My uncle went on with his account. Rosa, all in black from her back down. Like a raven, Juca. She came in like a gravedigger, glancing at each tomb. She seemed to be choosing her hole. You know, Juca, in the cemetery no one lingers when visiting graves. We pass by in a hurry. Only that hunchback, the old girl . . .

—Tell me the rest, my father cut in.

The story went on: Rosa right there, in the middle of everybody, began to sing. The bystanders stared at her in educated astonishment. The priest kept up his prayer, but people were no longer paying any attention. It was then that the cripple began to undress.

—You're lying, brother.

Cross my heart, Juca, may I be had by two thousand knives. She undressed. She began taking off her bits of cloth, at greater leisure than today's heat. Nobody laughed, nobody coughed, nobody did anything at all. When she was naked, de-clothed, she came over to Jawane's grave. She raised her arms and threw her clothes onto his tomb. The sight scared the crowd, which retreated a few steps. Then Rosa prayed:

—Take these clothes, Jawane, you'll need them. For you're going to be stone, like the rest of them.

Eyeing those present, she raised her voice, she seemed larger than a mere creature:

—And now: am I allowed to fancy him?

The onlookers fell back, you could hear the dust speak.

—What was that? I can fancy this dead man! He no longer belongs to time. Or am I forbidden him too?

My father left his chair, he seemed almost offended.

—Rosa spoke like that?

—It's the truth.

And my uncle, by this time in the spirit of the thing, imitated the hunchback, her twisted body: and this one, can I love him? But my old man didn't want to listen.

—Shut up, I don't want to hear any more.

Suddenly, he hurled the glass through the air. He wanted to get rid of the froth but, in a mistaken lapse, he let go of the whole glass. As if in apology, my uncle went and picked up the pieces of glass, scattered on their backs all over the garden.

That night, I couldn't sleep. I went and sat my restlessness down in the garden in front of the house. I looked at the statue, it was off its pedestal. The colonialist was lying with his whiskers next to the ground, it was as if he had climbed down himself, burdened by fatigue. They had uprooted the monument but forgotten to take it away, the job needed finishing. I felt almost sorry for Beardy, all soiled from the pigeons, covered in dust. I stoked myself up, and came to my senses: am I like Rosa, placing feelings in lumps of stone? That was when I saw Caramela herself, as if summoned by my ruminations. I sat frozen, stock-still. I wanted to run away, but my legs dissented. I shuddered: was I turning into a statue, becoming the subject of the cripple's passion? What a horrible thought, my mouth might escape me forever. But no. Rosa didn't stop in the garden. She crossed the road and reached the steps up to our house. She stooped and cleaned the moonlight away from them. She put her belongings down in a whisper. Then, tortoise-like, she withdrew into herself, perhaps getting ready to sleep. Or maybe sadness was her only intention. For I heard her weep, in a murmur of dark waters.

The hunchback was shedding herself, as if it were her turn to become a statue. I wandered endlessly in such thought.

Then it happened. My father, in painstaking silence, opened the door to the veranda. Slowly, he approached the hunchback. For a few seconds, he leaned over the woman. Then, moving his hand as if he were dreaming his gesture, he touched her hair. Rosa didn't react at first. But soon she began to emerge from herself, her face in the fullness of light. They looked at each other, both of them gaining beauty. Then he whispered:

—*Don't cry, Rosa.*

I could hardly hear, my heart thumped in my ears. I drew nearer, ever concealed behind the darkness. My father was still speaking to her, in a voice I had never heard before.

—*It's me, Rosa. Don't you remember?*

I was in the middle of the bougainvillaea, its thorns were tearing me. I didn't even feel them. Fear pricked me more than the branches. My father's hands sank into the hunchback's hair, they were like people, those hands, like people drowning.

—*It's me, Juca. Your sweetheart, don't you remember?*

Gradually, Rosa Caramela emerged from cover. Never had she existed so much, never had a statue merited such eyes. Softening his voice still more, my father called her:

—*Let's go, Rosa.*

Without wanting to, I had left the bougainvillaea. They could see me, I placed no obstacle between us. The moon even seemed to sharpen its shine when the hunchback got up.

—*Let's go, Rosa. Pick up your things and let's go.*

And off they went, the two of them, deep into the night.

The Bird-Dreaming Baobab

Birds, all those who know of no abode on the ground.

THAT man will always remain in shadow: no memory will be enough to save him from the dark. To be true, his star was not the Sun. Nor did he come from a country called Life. Maybe that was why he lived with all the caution of an outsider. The bird seller didn't even have a name to shelter him. They called him the birdman.

Each morning, he would pass through the white folks' neighbourhood, carrying his enormous cages. He made these cages himself, from such flimsy material that they didn't even look like a prison. What they did look like were winged cages, cages that might fly away. Inside them, the birds fluttered around in a twinkle of colour. A cloud of twitters enveloped the bird seller, so loud that they made the windows rattle:

—*Mother, look, here comes the dicky-bird man!*

And the children would flood the streets. Joyfulness was exchanged: the birds shouted and the children chirped. The man would take out a *muska** and put sleepy melodies to tune. The whole world was filled with stories.

Behind their curtains, the settlers tut-tutted at such abuses. They sowed suspicions among their children—who did that Black think he was? Did anyone know his credentials? Who had authorized those grubby feet to dirty the area? No, no, and no again. The Black ought to return to his proper place. But the birds, they're so cute, the children insisted. The parents took on sterner airs: enough said.

But the order was not destined to be greatly respected. One little boy more than all the others disobeyed it, and devoted himself to the mysterious birdman. That was Tiago, a dreamy child, whose only gift was to pursue his fancy. He would wake up early, put his nose to the windowpane waiting for the bird seller to come by. The man would come into view and Tiago would rush down the stairs, thirty steps in five jumps. Feet bare, he would go down the street and disappear among the swarm of birds. The sun would sink and there was no sign of the lad. At Tiago's home, people would start to give their worries a polishing:

—*Barefoot, just like them.*

The father planned his punishment. Only the mother's soft heart brought relief to the little boy's arrival, in the fullness of night. The father insisted on an explanation, even if it were but the outline of one:

—*Did you go to his house? But does that good-for-nothing have a house?*

His dwelling was a baobab, the empty hollow inside its trunk. Tiago told them: it was a sacred tree, God had planted it upside down.

—*See what that Black has been filling the child's head with.*

---

* A local word for a mouth organ.

The father turned to his wife, heaping blame on her. The lad continued:

—*It's true, Mother. That tree is capable of great sadness. The old men say that a baobab can commit suicide in despair by way of fire. Without anyone setting it alight. It's true, Mother.*

—*What nonsense,* the lady of the house soothed.

And she would draw her son away from his father's reach. Then the man would decide to go out, and join his rage to that of the other settlers. At the club there was clamour from all: the bird-man's visits had to be stopped. Measures could not include death by killing, nor anything that might offend the eyes of women and children. In a word, the cure would have to be thought about.

The following day, the bird seller repeated his joyful invasion. Even the settlers hesitated: after all, that Black was bringing with him birds of a beauty never before seen. No one could resist their colours, their chirping. The sight was like nothing else in this very world of ours. The bird seller bowed in nameless modesty, disappearing from himself out of humility.

—*These are truly excellent birds, these ones with their wings all a show.*

The Portuguese began to wonder: where in the name of magic did he get such miraculous creatures? Where, if they themselves had already brought the most distant bushland to heel?

The bird seller dissembled, answering with a chuckle. The whites began to fear their own suspicions—might that Black have a right to enter a world which was closed to them? But then they set about paring down his merits: the fellow lived in trees, among the birds. They were like creatures of the wild, was the general conclusion.

Whether because of the scorn of the powers that be, or because of the admiration of the meek, the birdman became a topic of conversation in the concrete part of town. His presence began to fill the length of a conversation, unsuspected empty moments. The more people bought from him, the more their houses were filled with sweet song. Such music fell strangely on the settlers' ears, proving that the area they lived in had little in common with the land around them. Could it be that the birds were eroding the residents' sense of self, turning them into foreigners? Or was it the Black who was at fault, that son-of-a-bitch who insisted on existing, unaware of the duties of his race? The traders ought to realize that there was no room for his bare feet in those streets. The whites were concerned at such disobedience, blaming it on the times. They yearned jealously for the past, when creatures could be tidied away depending on their appearance. The bird seller, by overstepping himself in such a fashion, was leading the world towards other awareness. Even the children, thanks to his seduction, were forgetting their manners. They were becoming more like children of the street than of the home. The birdman had even made inroads into their dreams:

—*Pretend I'm your uncle.*

And they all joined the family, all became related, relatively speaking.

—*Uncle? Have you ever heard of a Black being called Uncle?*

The parents were determined to arrest their dreams, their tiny, boundless souls. The command was issued: the street is out of bounds, you can't go out anymore. Curtains were drawn, the houses shut their eyelids.

Order seemed to rule once again. That's when things began to happen. Doors and windows opened by themselves, furniture appeared turned back to front, drawers were swapped round.

At the Silvas' house:

—*Who opened this cupboard?*

No one, no one had. Old man Silva got angry: everyone in the house knew that firearms were kept there. With no sign of having been forced, who could the burglar have been? Such was the indignant plaintiff's doubt.

At the Peixotos' house:

—*Who scattered grass seed among my papers?*

No one, nothing, not anyone, came the reply. The Peixoto supremo warned: *you know very well what type of documents I keep in that drawer.* He listed their secret functions, their confidential matters. Let the spreader of grass seed own up. *Bloody birds*, he mumbled.

At the mayor's residence:

—*Who let the birds in?*

Nobody had. The governor was unable to govern his temper: he had come across a bird inside a cupboard. Solemn municipal discussion papers covered in bird droppings.

—*Just look at this one: bird shit in the middle of the official seal.*

In the wake of all these occurrences, a general uproar gripped the area. The settlers held a meeting in order to try and reach a decision. They assembled at the home of Tiago's father. The lad slipped out of bed and stood at the door, listening to their grim threats. He didn't even wait for the sentence to be passed. He rushed off through the bush in the direction of the baobab. There, he found the old man settling himself by the warmth of the fire.

—*They're coming to get you.*

Tiago was gasping for breath. The bird seller was not put out: he knew, he was waiting for them. The little boy tried harder, for never before had the man meant so much to him.

—*Run away, there's still time.*

But the bird seller set himself at ease, in sleepy langour. He stepped serenely into the trunk and there he tarried. When he came out, he was wearing a tie and a white man's suit. Once again he sat down, clearing the sand underfoot. Then he paced up and down, surveying the horizon.

—*Run along, boy. It's nighttime.*

Tiago lingered. He glanced at the birdman, awaiting his gesture. If only the old man were like the river: still but moving. But he wasn't. The bird seller belonged more to legend than to reality.

—*And why did you put on a suit?*

He explained: he was the natural offspring of the land. It was his duty to know how to receive visitors. It was for him to show respect, the duties of a host.

—*As for you, go, go back home.*

Tiago got up, reluctant to leave. He looked up at the huge tree, as if he were asking it for protection.

—*Can you see that flower?* asked the old man.

And he recalled the legend. The flower was where the spirits dwelt. Whoever harmed the baobab would be persecuted for the rest of his life.

The settlers began their noisy arrival. They surrounded the place. The little boy fled, hid, and watched. He saw the birdman get up and greet the visitors. The beating started straightaway, with cudgels and kicks. The old man didn't even appear to be suffering, a vegetable were it not for the blood. They bound his wrists and pushed him up the dark road. The settlers followed behind, leaving the boy alone in the night. The child hesitated, now stepping forwards, now back. Then it happened: the flowers of the baobab fell, like stars of felt. Their white petals turned red on the ground.

Suddenly, the boy made up his mind. He dashed off through the bush after the procession. He tailed their voices and learned that they were taking the birdman to jail. When it became pitch-black behind the wall next to the prison, Tiago felt stifled. Was it any use praying, if the world around him had stripped itself of beauty? And in the heavens, just as in the baobab, no star glittered with pride anymore.

The birdman's voice reached him from beyond the prison bars. Now he could see his friend's face, and all the blood which covered it. Interrogate the fellow, squeeze him hard. That was the order which the settlers left behind them as they withdrew. The guard saluted obediently. But he didn't even know what secrets he was supposed to drag out of the old man. What madness could they prove against the old street hawker? And now, standing there all alone, the figure of the prisoner seemed free of all suspicion.

—*May I have permission to play? It's a tune from your part of the world, boss.*

The birdman put the harmonica to his lips and tried to blow. But he recoiled from the effort with a wince.

—*They beat me a lot around the mouth. It's a pity, otherwise I'd play.*

The policeman became suspicious. The harmonica was hurled out of the window, and it fell near where Tiago was hiding. He picked the instrument up, and stuck its pieces together again. Those pieces were like his soul, starved of a hand that might make it whole. The lad curled up in the warmth of his own roundness. As he set off into sleep, he put the instrument to his lips and blew, as if he were playing his own lullaby. Who knows whether the birdman, shut away inside, didn't hear the sound of such comfort?

He awoke in a kingdom of chirping. The birds! An infinity of them covered the whole police station. Not even the world, in its universal dimensions, seemed a big enough perch. Tiago approached the cell, surveyed the jail. The doors were open, the prison deserted. The bird seller had vanished without trace, the place had lost all recollection of him. He called the old man, but was answered by the birds.

He decided to return to the tree. There was no longer any other place where he might go. No street, nor house: only the baobab's belly. As he walked along, the birds followed in a twittering cortège, high in the sky. He arrived at the birdman's abode, and looked at the ground covered with petals. They were no longer red, having returned to their original whiteness. He entered the trunk, putting distance between himself and time. Was it any use waiting for the old man? He had vanished for sure, a fugitive from the whites. Meanwhile, he began to blow on the harmonica once more. He lulled himself in its rhythm, no longer with an ear to the world outside. If he had paid due attention, he would have noted the arrival of a host of voices.

—*That Black son of a bitch is inside the tree.*

Vengeful steps surrounded the baobab, crushing the flowers underfoot.

—*It's the fellow, along with his mouth organ. Play away, you scalawag, for you'll soon be dancing!*

Torches were put to the trunk, and the flames licked the ancient bark. Inside, the boy had unleashed a dream: his hair was growing into tiny leaves, his legs into timber. His wooden fingers dug rootlike into the soil. The boy was in transit to another realm: he was turning into a tree, consenting to the impossible. And from the dreaming baobab, there rose the birdman's hands. They touched the flowers, the corollas curled: monstrous birds were born and released, petal-like, on the crest of the flames. The flames? Where were they coming from, invading the remotest frontier of the dream world? That was when Tiago felt the sting of the blaze, the seduction of ash. Then the boy, a convert to the ways of sap, emigrated once and for all to his newfound roots.

The Russian Princess

"The rumour of the existence of gold in Manica, and the announcement of the building of a railway to transport it, were enough for pounds sterling to appear out of the blue in their tens of thousands, opening shops, establishing steamship lines, organizing overland transport, investing in industrial enterprises, selling liquor, seeking to exploit in a thousand and one ways not so much the gold, but the very exploiters of the future gold. . . ."

ANTONIO ENNES, MOZAMBIQUE,
GOVERNMENT REPORT, LISBON, 1946

FORGIVE me, Father, I'm not kneeling right, it's my leg, you know. This skinny little leg of mine which I wear on my left side doesn't hold my body up properly.

I've come to confess the sins of long ago, blood pounded in my soul, it frightens me just to think about it. Please, Father, listen to me slowly, be patient. It's a long story. As I always say: an ant's journey is never a short one.

You may not know, but this town was once favoured by another life. There were times when people came here from far away. The world is full of countries, most of them foreign ones. The heavens are so full of flags now that I don't know how the angels can fly about without bumping into a length of cloth. What did you say? Get to the point? Yes, I'm getting there. But don't forget: I asked for more than a little piece of your time. It's just that a life goes by slowly, Father.

Let me continue, then. At that time, there also came to the town of Manica a Russian lady. Nadia was her name. Rumour had it she was a princess there where she'd come from. She was in the company of her husband Yuri, a Russian too. The couple came because of the gold, like all the other foreigners who came here to dig up the riches of this land of ours. That man Yuri bought the mines, in the hope of becoming rich. But as the old men say: don't run after the hen with salt already in your hand. Because the mines, Father, were the size of dust: a single puff was enough and there was almost nothing left.

At the same time, the Russians had brought with them relics of past sustenance, luxuries from times gone by. Their house, if you were to see it, was full of things. And folk working for them? Why, there were more than many. As for me, being an *assimilado*,[*] I was head servant. Do you know what they called me? General Commissioner. That was my rank, I was someone. I didn't do any work: I told people to work. The boss's requests, it was I who attended to them, and they always spoke to me politely, with respect. Then I would take their requests and bellow orders at the domestic staff. Yes indeed, I shouted. That was the only way to make them obey. No one labours for the joy of it. Or could it be that God, when he expelled Adam from Paradise, didn't do so with a kick in the pants?

The servants hated me, Father. I felt that rage of theirs whenever I stole their days off from them. I didn't care, I even liked not

---

[*] Under the Portuguese colonial system, an *assimilado* was a Black African fluent in Portuguese and assimilated into European culture.

being liked. I grew fat on their anger, I all but felt like a boss. I've been told that a taste for giving orders is a sin. But I think that it's this leg of mine that counsels me in my wickedness. I have two legs: one of a saint, the other the Devil's own. How can I follow but one road?

Sometimes, I would catch snatches of the servants' conversation as I passed their huts. They would be ranting over a host of things, their talk bristling with teeth. I would approach them and they would fall silent. They didn't trust me. But I felt flattered by their suspicion: I commanded a fear that made them so small. They got their own back by making fun of me. They would forever be imitating my limp. They would fall about laughing, the rascals. I'm sorry for using oaths in a place of respect. But that old anger of mine is still alive. I was born with the defect, it was a punishment God had in store for me even before I took on a person's shape. I know God is good, without a fault. But Father, even so: do you think he was fair to me? Am I insulting the Holy Father? Well, I'm confessing. If I'm causing offence, increase my penance afterwards.

Very well, I'll continue. In that house, the days were always the same, sad and silent. Early in the morning, the boss would be off to the mine, the gold farm, as he called it. He would only return at night, in the thick of night. The Russians never had visitors. The others, the English, the Portuguese, never stopped by there. The princess lived enclosed in her sadness. She would dress formally even inside the house. You could even say she visited herself. She always spoke in murmurs, so that to listen to her, you had to put an ear right up next to her. I would approach her slender body, with a skin the whiteness of which I'd never seen before. That whiteness often attended my dreams, and even today I tremble at the fragrance of that colour.

She used to linger in a tiny room, gazing at a glass clock. She would listen to the hands dripping the minutes away. It was a clock from her family, and she only trusted me to clean it. If that clock were to break, Fortin, it would mean my whole life would break too. She would always tell me that, warning me to take care.

One of those nights, I was in my hut lighting the spirit lamp. Suddenly, I was startled by a shadow behind me. I looked, and it was the mistress. She was carrying a candle and came slowly towards me. She peeped round the room, as the light danced into the corners. I stood there tongue-tied, ashamed even. She was used to seeing me in the white uniform I wore for work. There I was in my pyjama trousers, devoid of a shirt and of decorum. The princess walked round me and then, to my astonishment, sat down on my mat. Can you believe it? A Russian princess sitting on a mat? She remained there a myriad of time, just sitting stock-still. Then she asked, in that way of hers when she spoke Portuguese:

—*So, you lyive herrre?*

I had no answer. I began to wonder whether she was ill, whether her head wasn't changing places.

—*Lady: it's better that you go back to your house. This room is not good for you.*

She didn't reply. Then she asked another question:

—*And forrr you, it's good?*

—*It's enough for me. All we need is a roof to shut out the sky.*

She corrected my certainties. It's animals, she said, that hide away in lairs. A person's house is a place to stay in, a place where we sow our lives. I asked if there were Blacks where she came from and she laughed her fill: Oh! Fortin, you ask some funny questions! I was surprised: if there weren't any Blacks, who was it that did the heavy work in her country? Whites, she answered. Whites? She's lying, I thought. After all, how many laws are there in the world? Or is it that misfortune was not distributed to people according to their race? No, I'm not asking you, Father, I'm just discussing it with myself.

That's how we talked that night. At the door, she asked to see the compound where the others slept. At first, I refused. But deep down, I wanted her to go there. For her to see that their adversity was far worse than mine. And so I complied: we went out into the darkness in order to see the place where those of the houseboy rank lived. Princess Nadia was filled with sadness at the sight of such living space. She spoke with so much expression that she began to switch her words, jumping from Portuguese to her own dialect. Only now did she understand why the boss never let her go out, or dispense favour. It was just so that I wouldn't see all this poverty, she said. I noticed she was crying. Poor lady, I pitied her. A white woman, so far from those of her race, there, in the middle of the bush. Yes indeed, for the princess, the whole place must have been bush, or the outskirts of bush. Even the big house, all clean and tidy in obedience to their customs, even her house was a bush dwelling.

On the way back, I stepped on one of those *micaia* thorns. The barb pierced deep into my foot. The princess tried to help me, but I pushed her away:

—*You mustn't touch it. It's this leg of mine, lady . . .*

She understood. She began to console me, saying that it was no defect, that my body merited no shame. In the beginning, I didn't like it. I suspected she felt sorry for me, that she was showing commiseration, and nothing more. But then I surrendered to her gentleness, and forgot the pain in my foot. It was as if that leg were no longer mine as it walked along.

From that night on, the lady began to go out often, to visit her surroundings. She would take advantage of the boss's absence, and tell me to show her the way. One of these days, Fortin, we must leave early and go as far as the mines. Those desires of hers scared me. I knew the boss's orders which forbade the lady to go out. Until one day, someone gave the game away:

—*The other servants told me you've been going out with the lady.*

The bastards had groused about me. Just to prove that, like them, I would bow before the same voice. Envy is the worst snake: it bites with the teeth of the very victim. Which is why, at that moment, I retreated:

—*It's not me who wants it, boss. It's the lady who orders it.*

You see, Father? There I was in a trice, informing against the lady, betraying the trust she had placed in me.

—*It's not going to happen again, do you hear, Fortin?*

We stopped taking to the streets. The princess begged me, urged me. Just for a little way, please, Fortin. But I didn't have the spirit for it. And so the lady was once again a prisoner in the house. She looked like a statue. Even when the boss arrived, after darkness had fallen, she just sat there benumbed, looking at the clock. What she saw was time, which only reveals itself to those in life who have no presence. The boss didn't even bother with her: he would march straight up to the table, and order drink to be brought. He would eat, drink, and then start all over again. He never even noticed the lady, it was as if she belonged to some lower form of existence. He didn't beat her. Blows are not the stuff of princes. Assault or murder are not things they carry out themselves, they hire others. It's we who are the workforce for their grubby whims, we who are destined to serve. I only ever delivered a blow, gave out a hiding, when told to by others. The only folk I ever beat up were those of my own colour. Nowadays, when I look around me, I have nobody I can call a brother. Nobody. These Blacks don't forget. It's an embittered race the one I belong to. You, Sir, are Black, you can understand. If God is Black, Father, I'm done for: I'll never be forgiven. Never ever! What did you say? I can't speak of God? Why, Father, is it that he can hear me down here, so far from Heaven, and me so tiny? Can he hear? Wait, Father, let me just make myself more comfortable. My devil of a leg, it never wants to obey me. That's better, now I can confess some more. It was as I said. Or rather, as I was saying. There was no ongoing story in the Russians' home, nothing happened. Nothing but the lady's sighs and silences. And the clock drumming away in that emptiness. Until one day, the boss hounded me with shouts:

—*Call the servants, Fortin. Quickly, everybody outside.*

I summoned the houseboys, the servants and also the fat cook, Nelson Maquina.

—*Let's go to the mine. Hurry, climb on to the cart.*

We got to the mine, we were given spades, and we started to dig. The roof of the mine had collapsed yet again. Beneath the earth we were treading on, there were men, some already stone dead, others taking leave of life. The spades rose and fell nervously. We saw arms appear, sticking out of the sand, they looked like roots of flesh. There was shouting, a confusion of orders and dust. Next to me, the fat cook pulled at an arm, summoning up all his strength to unearth the body. But blow me if it wasn't a loose arm that had already been torn from its body. The cook fell over with that piece of death gripped in his hands. Sitting back clumsily, he began to laugh. He looked at me and that laugh of his filled with tears, the fat man was sobbing like a lost child.

I couldn't stand it, Father, I threw in the towel. It was a sin, but I turned my back on that tragedy. There was too much suffering. One of the houseboys tried to grab me, insulted me. I turned my face away, I didn't want him to see that I was crying.

That year, the mine caved in a second time. The second time too, I abandoned the rescue attempts. I'm no good, I know, Father. But you've never seen a hell like that one. We pray to God to save us from hell after we die. But, when all is said and done, hell is where we live, we step on its flames, and we bear with us a soul full of scars. It was the same there, it looked like a field of sand and blood, we were frightened even to set foot on it. For death buried itself in our eyes, pulling our soul along with its many arms. Is it my fault, tell me frankly, is it my fault that I gave up when it came to winnowing bits of people?

I'm not a man given to rescues. I'm a person who is happened to rather than who happens. I was thinking about all this as I walked back. My eyes didn't even ask the way, it was as if I were walking in my own tears. Suddenly, I remembered the princess, I seemed to be listening to her voice asking for help. It was as if she were there, at the corner of every tree, on her knees and begging as I am now. But once again I refused to dispense life, I distanced myself from goodness.

When I got back to my hut, it pained me to hear the world round about, full of the beautiful sounds of nightfall. I hid myself in these selfsame arms of mine, I shut off my thoughts in a darkened room. It was then that her hands came to me. Slowly my arms, wilful snakes that they were, disentangled themselves. She spoke to me as if I were a child, the son she had never had:

—*It was an accident at the mine, wasn't it?*

I nodded without a word. She uttered some curses in her own language and went out. I went with her, for I knew she was suffering more than I. The princess sat down in the main lounge and waited for her husband in silence. When the boss arrived, she stood up slowly, and in her hands appeared the glass clock. The one she told me to take such care with. She raised the clock high above her head and, with all her strength, hurled it to the ground. The glass shattered and spread all over the floor in shimmering grains. She continued, breaking other pieces of china, doing everything unhurriedly and without a single cry. But those shards of glass were cutting her soul, I knew. As for the boss, he shouted all right. First in Portuguese. He ordered her to stop. The princess took no notice. He shouted in their language and she never even heard. And do you know what she did then? No, you can't imagine it, even I can hardly believe the events I witnessed. The princess took off her shoes, and looking her husband in the

eye, began to dance on top of the pieces of glass. She danced
and danced and danced. How she bled, Father! I should know,
I cleaned it. I got a cloth, and wiped the floor as if I were caressing the lady's body, bringing comfort to all her wounds. The boss
ordered me to go, to leave everything as it was. But I refused. *I've
got to clean this blood away, boss.* I answered him in a voice that didn't
even seem to be my own. Was I disobeying him? Where did that
strength come from that rooted me to the ground, imprisoned
in my own will?

So that's how it was, the impossible made true. A length of
time passing in a single flash. I don't know whether it was because
of the glass, but the next day, the lady fell ill. She lay there in a
separate room, she slept alone. I would make the bed while she
rested on the sofa. We would talk. The subject never changed:
recollections of her homeland, childhood balm.

—*This illness, lady, for sure it's caused by longings.*

—*All my lyife is therrre. The man I love is in Rrrussia, Forrrtin.*

I bustled around, feigning inattention. I didn't want to know.

—*His nyame is Anton, and hye is the only rrruler of my hearrrt.*

I'm imitating the way she spoke, but it's not to make fun of
her. That's the way I remember her confession of such a love.
Confidences followed, she forever yielding up to me memories
of her hidden passion. I was afraid that our conversations might
be overheard. I would hurry with my tasks so as to get out of the
room. But one day, she handed me a sealed envelope. It was a
matter of the greatest secrecy, no one should ever suspect. She
asked me to post the letter in town.

From that day on she never stopped giving me letters. One
after the other, first one, then another, and yet another. She wrote
as she lay there, the writing on the envelope shook with her fever.

But Father: do you want to know the truth? I never posted
those letters. Nothing, not a single one. That's the sin I bear and
must suffer. It was fear that inhibited me from the obedience

I owed her, fear of being caught with such frenzied proof in my hand.

The poor lady would look at me with warmth, trustful of a sacrifice that I wasn't even making. She would give me her correspondence and I would begin to tremble, as if my fingers were holding a flame. Yes, that's the right word: a flame. For that was the very fate that awaited all those letters. I threw them all into the kitchen stove. It was there that my lady's secrets were burned. I would listen to the flames, which sounded like her sighs. God bless me, Father, just telling you my shame makes me sweat.

And so time passed. The lady's strength deteriorated. I would enter her room and she would look at me, almost pierce me with those blue eyes of hers. She never asked whether an answer had arrived. Nothing. Only those eyes, stolen from the sky, looked at me inquiringly and in mute despair.

The doctor now came every day. He would come out of the room, shaking his head in nullified hope. The whole house lay in gloom, the curtains ever drawn. Only shadows and silence. One morning, I saw the door open just a crack. It was the lady peeping out. With a gesture, she summoned me in. I asked if she was feeling better. She didn't reply. She sat down in front of the mirror, and covered her face with that perfumed powder, so deceiving death's colour. She painted her mouth but took a long time getting the shade right on each lip. Her hands were trembling so much that the red smudged her nose and her chin. If I were a woman I would have helped, but being a man I just stood there, looking bashful.

—*Are you going out, my lady?*

—*I yem going shtation. We yarre both going.*

—*To the station?*

—*Yes, Anton yis arriving on next trrrain.*

And opening her bag, she showed me a letter. She said it was his reply. It had taken a long time, but it had arrived in the end, she waved the envelope as children do when they're scared you may deprive them of their fantasy. She said something in Russian. Then she spoke in Portuguese: Anton was coming on the train from Beira, he was going to take her far away.

She was raving, of course. The lady was feigning an idea. How could an answer have come? If I was the one who collected all the mail? If many a day had gone by since the lady left the house? And, what was more: if the lady's letters had been posted in the stove?

Supported by my arm, she started off down the road. I was her walking stick until we were near the station. It was here, Father, that I committed my worst sin. I'm very hard on myself, there are things I don't accept in me. Yes indeed, I'm the person I defend myself least from in everything. That's why this confession is such a weight off my conscience. I'm counting on God to defend me. Am I not justified, Father? Listen on then.

The princess's skin was right up against my body, I was sweating her sweat. The lady was in my arms, abandoned to me entirely. I began to dream that she was running away with me. Who was I if not Anton himself? Yes indeed, I cast myself in the role of the author of the letter. Do you think I was an intruder? But at the time, I agreed to it. For if my lady's life was devoid of any worth, what did it matter if I helped in her ravings? Who knows? Maybe this madness might heal the wound which was stealing her body away from her. But do you see, Father, the pretense I had taken on? I, Duarte Fortin, General Commissioner of all the domestic staff, was running away with a white woman, and a princess into the bargain. As if she would ever want someone like me, a man of my colour and unequal legging. There's no doubt about it, I have the soul of a worm, and I shall have to crawl around in the next world. My sins require many a prayer. Pray for me, Father, pray for me a lot! For the worst, the worst is yet to come.

I was carrying the princess along by a roundabout route. She wasn't even aware of the diversion. I took the lady down to the riverbank and laid her on the soft grass. I went to the river to fetch some water. I bathed her face and her neck. She replied with a shiver, and her mask of powder began to dissolve. The princess gasped for breath. She looked around and asked:

—*The station?*

I decided to lie. I told her it was right there, just nearby. We were in the shade only in order to hide from the others, who were waiting in the station yard.

—*We mustn't be seen. We had better wait for the train in this hiding place.*

She, poor soul, thanked me for my cares. She said she had never met such a kindly man before. She asked me to wake her up when the train came; she was very tired, she needed rest. I sat there looking at her, enjoying her close presence. I saw the buttons on her dress and imagined the warmth that lay underneath. My pulse gathered pace. At the same time, I was scared. And supposing the boss were to catch me right there in the middle of the grass with his lady? It would just be a question of pointing the dark muzzle of his shotgun at me and firing. It was the fear of being shotgunned that deterred me. I lingered there, just looking at that woman in my arms. It was then that my dream once again began to escape me. Do you know what I felt, Father? I felt that she no longer had her own body: she was using mine. Do you understand, Father? She had a white skin that was mine, that mouth of hers belonged to me, those blue eyes were both mine. It was as if her soul were distributed between two opposite bodies: one male, the other female; one Black, the other white. Do you doubt me? You can take it from me, Father, that opposites are the most alike. If you don't believe it, see here: isn't fire most like ice? They both burn, and in both cases, a man can only penetrate them when he's dead.

But if I were her, then I must be dying in my second body. That was why I felt weakened, listless. I dropped down beside her and we stayed there, the two of us, without moving. She, with her eyes closed. I, trying to stave off my slow drift into sleep. I knew that if I closed my eyes, I would never again open them upon life. I was already deep inside myself, I couldn't sink further. There are moments when we are very like the dead, and that semblance gives the dead encouragement. That's what they can never forgive: we who are alive being so like them.

And do you know how I saved myself, Father? By digging my arms into the warm earth, just as those dying miners had done. It was my roots that bound me to life, that's what saved me. I got up, sweating all over, full of fever. I decided to get out of there, without delay. The princess was still alive and gestured to try and stop me. I ignored her plea. I returned home, all the while with that same anxiety I had felt when I abandoned the survivors at the mine. When I arrived, I told the boss: I found the lady under a tree near the station, she was already dead. I accompanied him so he could see for himself. There in the shade, the princess was still breathing. When the boss bent down, she grabbed him by the shoulders and said:

—*Antoni.*

The boss heard the name that didn't belong to him. Even so, he kissed her brow lovingly. I went to fetch the cart and, when he picked her up, she was dead, as cold as stone. Then from her dress fell a letter. I tried to pick it up but the boss was quicker. He looked at the envelope in surprise and then glanced at me. I stood there with my chin on my chest, fearful that he might ask questions. But the boss screwed up the paper and put it in his pocket. We went home in silence.

On the following day, I ran away to Gondola. I've been there ever since, working on the trains. From time to time, I come up to Manica and pass the old cemetery. I kneel by the lady's grave and ask her to forgive me for I know not what. Actually, that's not true, I do know. I ask her to forgive me for not being the man she was waiting for. But that's only a pretense of guilt, because you know what a lie this kneeling of mine is. Because while I'm there, in front of her grave, all I can remember is the scent of her body. That's why I've been confessing this bitterness of mine to you, which has stolen my taste for life. It's not long now before I shall leave this world. I've even asked God to let me die. But it seems God doesn't listen to such requests. What did you say, Father? I shouldn't say such resigned things? But that's the memory I have of myself. Widower of a wife I never had. It's just that I feel so wretched. The only happiness that warms me, do you know what it is? It's when I leave the cemetery and go and walk among the dust and ashes of the old Russian mine. The mine is now closed, it died along with the lady. I go there by myself. Then I sit down on an old tree trunk and look back at the road I have trodden. And do you know what I see then? I see two different sets of footprints, but both issued from my body. One set is large, a man's feet. The others are the print of a small foot, a woman's. They're the princess's footprints, walking alongside mine. They are her prints, Father. There is no certainty greater than the one I have of that. Not even God can correct me of such certainty. God may not forgive me my sins and I may run the risk of having hell as my fate. But I don't care: there, in hell's ashes, I shall see the print of her footsteps, forever walking on my left-hand side.

The Blind Fisherman

—Each man's boat is in his own heart.

MAKUA PROVERB,
FROM NORTHERN MOZAMBIQUE

WE live far from ourselves, in distant make-believe. We vanish into concealment. Why do we prefer to live in this inner darkness? Maybe because the dark joins things, sews together the threads of separation. In the warm embrace of night, the impossible wins us to suppose we can see it. Our fantasies come to rest in such illusion.

I write all this even before I begin. Written with water by someone who wants no memories, which are ink's ultimate purpose. All because of Maneca Mazembe, the blind fisherman. It happened that he emptied both his eyes, two wells dried up by the sun. The way he lost his sight is a story that defies belief. There are tales that get harder to understand the more they are told. After all, many voices only produce silence.

It happened one fishing trip: Mazembe was lost in the endless deep. The storm had taken the little boat by surprise, and the fisherman drifted boundlessly, ad infinitum. The hours passed, summoned away by time. With neither net nor provisions, Mazembe placed all his faith in waiting. But hunger began to make a nest in his belly. He decided to cast his line, but without any hopes: the hook had no bait. And nobody has heard of a fish that kills itself out of choice, biting an empty hook.

At night, the cold ripened. Maneca Mazembe covered himself with himself. There's nothing more snug than one's body, he thought. Or can it be that babies, inside their pregnancy, suffer cold?

The week went by, full of days. The boat stayed above the line of the water. The fisherman survived above the line of life. As his hunger grew, he felt his ribs in the frame of his body:

—*I'm no longer myself.*

It's always like that: one's judgment grows thin more quickly than one's body. It was within that thinness that Maneca's decision took root. He pulled out his knife and held his face firmly. He took his left one out, and left the other one for other tasks. Then he stuck the eye on the hook. Disinterred, it was already a foreign body. But he shivered as he looked at it. That disinherited eye seemed to stare at him, hurt in its orphan's solitude. Which is why the hook, upon piercing his estranged flesh, hurt him more than any thorn can maim.

He cast the line and waited. He could already imagine the size of the fish, drowning in the air. Yes, for it isn't every day that a fish gets its teeth into such a tidbit. And he laughed at his own words.

At last, after many false hopes, the fish arrived. Fat and silvery. In fact: has anyone ever seen a skinny fish? Never. The sea is more generous than the earth.

That's what Mazembe thought as he avenged his hunger. He cooked the fish in the middle of the boat. Take care, for one day it will catch fire with you in it. That was his wife Salima's warning.

Now, with his stomach satisfied, he smiled. Salima, what did she know? Slim, her frailty was that of the reeds, which surrender to the lightest breeze. Nor could he understand how she was able to muster such strength upon lifting the mortar stick so high. And lulled by the thought of Salima, Maneca wilted into sleep.

But you can't tell the height of a tree by the size of its shadow. Hunger, obstinate as ever, returned. Mazembe wanted to row, but he couldn't. Strength no longer came to help him. It was then that he decided: he would pluck out his right one. And so, once again, he became his own surgeon. The fisherman was enclosed by darkness. The doubly blind Mazembe entrusted his fingers with sight. Once more he cast his line into the sea. He hardly had to wait before feeling the tug which announced the biggest fish he had ever caught.

In his provisional respite from hunger, his arms regained their competence. His soul returned from the sea. He rowed and rowed and rowed. Until the boat hit something, darkness meeting darkness. Judging by the waves, murmuring in infantile ripples, he guessed he must have reached a beach. He got up and shouted for help. He waited through many a silence. At last he heard voices, people approaching. He was surprised: those voices seemed familiar to him, the same as those from where he came. Could it be that his arms had recognized the way back, without the help of his sight? He was pulled by many hands helping him to get out of his boat.

There was weeping and bewilderment. All wanted to see him, no one wanted to look at him. His arrival spread joy, his aspect sowed horror. Mazembe had returned shorn of that which goes furthest towards making us what we are: the eyes, windows which reveal the light of our soul.

After that, Maneca Mazembe never again put to sea. Not that it was his desire to remain in such an unliquid exile. He would insist: his arms had proved that they knew the water's paths. But no one would let him go. Every time, his wife would refuse to give him his oars.

—*I must go, Salima. What are we going to eat?*

—*Better poor than a widow.*

She would put him at rest, they would catch clams, *magajojo*, shells you could get food from and sell. Like that, they would hold their misery at bay.

—*I can fish too, Maneca, in the boat . . .*

—*Never, woman. Never.*

Mazembe blew a storm: she was never to repeat such an idea. He might be blind, but he hadn't lost his male status.

Times passed. During the long morning, the blind man would stock up on the sunshine. As his mind rode the waves, his dreams fed their images to him. Until, when the day was at its height, his daughter would lead him to the caress of some shade. There they would serve him his food. Only his children were allowed to do this. For the fisherman had given himself over to one sole war: to reject the cares of his devoted wife, Salima. To accept her support was, for Mazembe, the most painful humiliation. Salima offered him tenderness, he shunned it. She called his name, he muttered an answer.

But as time deepened, hunger set in. Salima would creep out, more punctual than the tides, picking up the husks of wretchedness, too many shells for so little food.

Salima then announced to her husband: no matter how much it pained him, she was going to take the boat out the next day. She was going fishing, her body concealed powers unknown to him. Mazembe forbade it, in despair. Never! Where have you ever seen a woman fishing, ordering a boat about? What would the other fishermen say?

—*Even if I have to tie you to my foot, Salima: you are not going out to sea.*

With his word said and done, he shouted for his children. He walked down to the beach. All his skinniness was tautened by the bow of his body. The tide was low and the vessel was reclining lazily with its belly in the sand.

—*Come, children. Let's haul this boat up.*

He and his children pushed the boat up on to the dunes. They took it to where the waves never reached. Mazembe wagged his finger, slandering his wife.

—*Don't you try anything with me, Salima.*

And, turning to the boat, he declared:

—*Now you're going to be a house.*

From that day on, Maneca Mazembe lived in the boat, a mariner of dry land. He, along with his vessel, was like a turtle, turned on its back, incapable of returning to the sea. And in that lengthy solitude, Mazembe abandoned himself to neglect.

Until one random morning, Salima approached the boat and stood contemplating her husband. He was in a choice state of dishevelment, his face full of many a day's beard. The woman sat down and settled a saucepan of rice in her arms. She spoke:

—*Maneca, it's a long time since you gave me a good hiding.*

Who knows, she volunteered, maybe that bitterness of his was due to his abstinence? Perhaps he needed to feel her tears, lord and master of her sufferings.

—*Mazembe, you can beat me. I'll help: I'll stay still and not dodge at all.*

The fisherman silently ran along the paths of his soul. He knew women's traps. So he let the conversation drift rudderless:

—*I don't even know the time of day. Nowadays, I never know.*

Salima persisted, almost in supplication. Let him beat her. The man, after more than a few instants, got up. He stumbled over her, gripped her arm in an accusing clinch. Salima sat awaiting his conjugal violence. His hand came down, but it was to take hold of the saucepan. With a sudden gesture, he threw the food to the ground.

—*Never again bring me food. I don't need anything from you. Ever again.*

The woman sat among the rice and sand, the world dissolved into grains. She watched her husband returning to the boat and noticed how alike they were growing, man and thing: he deprived of light, it yearning for the waves. As Salima was turning to leave, she was stopped short by his calls:

—*Woman, I'm asking you to bring me fire.*

She trembled. What was the fire for? A deep foreboding caused her to want to say no. In tears, she obeyed him. She brought him a stick of burning firewood.

—*Don't do it, husband.*

The blind man held the log like a sword. Then he set fire to the boat. Salima screamed as she walked round the flames, as if it were inside her that they were burning. That madness of his was an invitation to disaster. Which was why she shook his ragged shirt, so that he would listen to her decision to leave, to take the children away with her to wherever that might be. And so the woman left, without even allowing her children to see their old father in his bewitched state as he unblessed their lives.

The fisherman was left on his own, the stretch of sand seemed vaster. In his pitiful design he allowed his night to fall, his fumbling fingers savouring the ashes. Touching the remains gave him a feeling of greatness. At least he had the power to undo, to destroy what was forbidden him.

The days went by without Maneca noticing. One night, however, Salima's presentiment was confirmed: that fire had flown too high and disturbed the spirits. For in the top of the coconut palms, the wind began to howl. Mazembe became agitated, even the ground shivered. Suddenly, the sky was torn apart and fat hailstones fell all over the beach. The fisherman ran through the emptiness in search of shelter. The hail punished him relentlessly. Maneca knew of no explanation. He had never met such phenomena. The earth has risen to meet the sky, he thought. Turned upside down, the world was letting its contents fall. With an orphan's anguish, the fisherman dropped to his knees, his arms wrapped around his head. He wouldn't even have heard himself if he hadn't noticed himself calling for Salima, amid his own sobs and the earth's lamentations.

That was when he felt a soft hand touching his shoulders. He lifted his face: someone was soothing his fever. At first, he resisted. Then he abandoned himself to it, turning childward towards a mother's embrace. He called out:

—*Salima?*

Silence. Who was that silhouette so full of tenderness? For sure it was Salima, her woman's body, so slender and firm. But this one's hands were like those of someone older, wrinkled by manifold sadnesses.

She brought him to a shelter, perhaps his old hut. There was a different silence about this place though, another fragrance. Out there, the winds were growing tired. The storm was dying down. Now, the hands were bathing his face, cooling his salt.

—*You, I don't know who you are . . .*

A comb tidied his hair. In the lull, Maneca was almost falling asleep. With a movement of his shoulder, he helped her to dress him in a shirt, freshly ironed clothes.

—*Whoever you are, I beg one thing of you: never use your voice. I don't want ever to hear your words.*

That woman's identity was bound to be lost in the silence. No matter whether those were Salima's hands, or the hut his own: in his ignorance he would acquiesce. For the rest, he was learning to take heed of women's cleverness in taming men, converting them into children, souls with insufficient confidence.

Maneca thus began to recapture time. He allowed himself to be succoured by the solace of that unknown woman. She respected his request and never uttered so much as a sigh.

Every afternoon he would go out into the bush. He was carrying out some secret task, his sole devotion. Until one afternoon, he appeared before his voiceless companion and said:

—Take these oars. Down there, on the beach, you'll see a boat which I have made for you to go out fishing.

And he went on: she should go out, impose her command on the boat. Nor should she worry about him. He would stay on the shore and concern himself with the jetsam washed up by the sea.

—Just take it that I'm looking for those eyes of mine that I lost.

From then on, each and every morning without fail, the blind fisherman could be seen wandering along the beach, stirring up the foam which the sea spells out on the sand. And with such liquid steps, he appeared to be seeking the wholeness of his face among the many generations of waves.

Woman of Me

The man is the axe, the woman is the hoe.

MOZAMBICAN PROVERB

THAT night, the hours ran all round me, like sleepless clock hands. All I wanted was to forget me. Lying there like that, the only thing I seemed to lack was death. Not the definitive one that takes us away with it. The other: the season-death, the winter subverted by guerrilla blossoms.

The December heat made me disappear, aware only of the ice melting in my glass. The cube of glass was like me, both of us were transitory, converting ourselves into the previous substance out of which we had been formed.

During this while, she came in. She was a woman whose soft eyes cast a moist film upon the room. She wandered around, as if she did not believe in her own presence. Her fingers travelled over the furniture in distracted affection. Who knows, perhaps she was walking in her slumber, maybe that reality held more in the way of fiction for her? I wanted to warn her that she was mistaken, that that was not her correct address. But her silence alerted me to the fact that a destiny was being fulfilled right there, at the meeting point of fateful providences. Then she sat down on my bed, arranging herself tidily. Without looking at me, she began to cry.

I didn't even guide myself: my caresses were already uncoiling on her breast. She lay back, emulating the earth in a state of gestation. Her body opened itself to me. If we had gone further in the moments that followed, we would have reached the realm of concrete fact. But in the course of my advances, I shuddered. Hidden voices held me back: no, I couldn't give in.

But this unknown woman was provoking me with the descent of her cleavage. Her bust peeped out at me, corrupting my intentions. Ancient legends were giving me their warning: a woman will come who will light up the moon. If you resist, you will merit the name of the warrior people from whom you stem. Not that I could decipher the storybook message very well. But what was certain was that there, in that very room, I was being put to the test, to see how much my powers were worth.

But thanks to the intruder's arts, I was disappearing, intermittent, from existence. I was unfulfilling myself. And when I appealed to myself to return to reason, I could not even get as far as that austere judge, my brain. All because of the woman's voice: it recalled the gentle murmur of a spring, the seduction of a return to times beyond, when there was no before. She sought to turn me into a child, to lead me back to a primitive quiescence. Birdlike, she nested in my breast. Was she seeking in me a mirror for the soft moonlight? I abandoned myself, without dignity. The dark circles of her eyes, round without end, aroused me like two sobs, it was as if they were part of my body yet gazed longingly at me.

She told her story, the episodes of her life. Variants of truth, they fed me the sweet taste of deceit. I wanted the infinite, just like children who always ask: and then?

But the stranger noticed an absence in herself. She had to go. She promised she would return straightaway. Presently, at the latest. From the doorway, she blew me a kiss, like a wife of many a year. She went out and blended with the shadows.

I don't know how long she took. Perhaps a night or two. Or a few scarce moments. I just don't know. For I fell asleep, anxious to extinguish myself. Waking up pained me, I cursed the morning. I understood the cause of such tribulation: waking up is not merely a passage from sleep to vigil. It's more than that, it's a gradual process of aging, each arousal adding to the fatigue of all humanity. And I concluded: life, the whole of it, is one extended birth.

Then I remembered the previous dream, conscious of the truth that she revealed herself only in a state of delirium. After all: the dead, the living, and those awaiting their birth make up one large canvas. The frontier between their territories can be summed up as fragile, moving. In dreams, we are all enclosed in the same space, there where time yields to total absence. Our dreams are no more than visits to these other past and future lives, conversations with the unborn and the deceased, in the language of unreason which we all speak.

The yet-to-be-born, those who are waiting for a body, are the ones we should fear most. For we know almost nothing of them. From the dead, we still go on getting messages, we take kindly to their familiar shadows. But what we are never aware of is when our soul is made up of these other, transvisible spirits. These are the pre-born, and they don't forgive us for inhabiting the light side of existence. They couple together the most perverse expectations, their powers pull downwards. They seek to make us return, insisting on keeping us in their company.

What are they envious of, these yet-to-comers? Is it that they have no name, that they do not breathe clear light? Or, like me, do they fear someone may be travelling through their lives before them? Are they scared that such anticipation will make them less possible, as if they might be worn out by some prior incumbent?

Well I, at that moment, envied both categories: the dead, because they seemed to resemble the perfection of deserts; the unborn, because they had an entire future at their disposal.

Seated on my creased sheets, I would look at the newly risen light of day, full of its restless particles of luminous dust. The sound of traffic reached me through the window, the city smug in its bustling disorder. I felt a yearning, not for supernatural beliefs but for the other, infranatural ones, our suppressed and silent animal convictions. It wasn't human nostalgia that afflicted me. For the longing of men is always for the present, it is born of a love that fails to fulfill its duties on time. My sadness was of another type: it came from having touched that woman. I felt burdened by the expense of remorse. What misdemeanours had I committed if desire had sprouted from my fingertips alone?

I got up, looking for some sign of negligence. But the room left me unprotected, orphaned. For in the final analysis, we spend our lives travelling from the uterus to our house, each house being but another edition of the womb. Like a bird that is forever weaving a nest, its nest, for its future births rather than for its offspring. This woman reminded me, after all, that the house offered me no welcome.

I glanced through the window, I saw the woman arriving. A suspicion, a certainty, came to my thought that she was no more than one of these yet-to-come creatures, dispatched in order to withdraw me from the kingdom of the living. Her temptation was as follows: to take me away into exile from the world, to migrate me to another existence. In exchange, I would feed her with bodily caresses, which only the living manage to possess.

I needed to think quickly: she enjoyed the advantage of not needing to consult reason. I had to find, in a trice, a possible escape. It came to me through intuition: somewhere there must exist the murderers of the dead, the defenders of the unborn. What I needed to do was to summon one such killer to extinguish not the life of that woman, but rather my suspicion of her. The question was: where would I find such a killer, how to provoke his immediate apparition? For it was urgent, she was coming, her steps were already climbing the stairs.

What to do, if I had no time left? Kill her myself, in body and in blood? That would only be of any use if we were both dreaming, something which I didn't seem to be. She had been sent expressly to fetch me, to take me there where everything is still futurely possible.

She came in, I shivered. This time, the intruder seemed even more beautiful to me, ever more like a goddess, demanding the total devotion of a believer. My deliverance arrived, a plank brought by a wave. I said to her:

—*I can imagine you still tiny, as you were in the yesterday of before. Do you remember?*

Startled, she became anxious. For a moment or two, her chest failed her, and she stood with bated breath. The unborn have no memory, their first cry is yet to blossom. Her fear inspired my cunning; I prepared myself while I watched her walk up to the mirror. The stranger contemplated herself as she got undressed, smiling in the petal of each gesture.

You just pretend, you don't even see yourself, I told, her, by now more in control of myself. She abandoned her self-attentions and came over to the bed and touched me. She called my name gently. She passed her fingers over my lips.

—*You don't understand.*

She smiled, hurt. My fragile artfulness had caused her offence. Nevertheless, I forgave myself. Her serene smile had returned.

—*Calm yourself, I haven't come to fetch you.*

What had she come there to do in that case? For the more she took possession of herself, the more concerned I became. The emissary went on:

—*Don't you understand? I have come to find a place in you.*

She explained her reasons: only she harboured the eternal gestation of springs. Without me being her, I was incomplete, formed only in the arrogance of halves. In her, I had found not a woman to be mine, but the woman of me, the one who, from now on, would light me in each phase of the moon.

—*Let me be born in you.*

I closed my eyes, slowly dousing myself. And so, lying there calmly, I listened to the sound of my steps as they became more distant. They weren't advancing in solitary march, but rather next to others of a female glide, as if they were hours that ran through me like sleepless clock hands that night.

The Flagpoles of Beyondwards

All we want is a new world: with everything new and nothing of the world.

R AIN is a jailer, imprisoning people. Constante Bene and his children, they were prisoners of the rain, shut up inside their hut. Never before had such water been seen: the landscape had been dripping for seventeen days. Scarcely taught to swim, the water hurt the earth. Fat raindrops, pregnant with sky, pattered closely on the tin roofs. On the side of the hill, only the trees persisted, without ever interrupting each other.

Seated in a corner of the old hut, Constante Bene measured the length of time. Ever since the beginning, he had been a guard on the estate of Tavares, the white man. He dwelt among the orange trees, in a place which had all but fled the earth. Up there, on the mountaintop, the ground behaved itself, good and proper.

—*Here, only the oranges have got a thirst.*

The thirst of birds, Constante might have been more right in saying. But he simplified life. To his two children, Chiquinha and João Respectivo, he taught the countless arts of tranquility. The children received cares from him, motherless orphans though they were. They alone looked after household matters.

Chiquinha, her body developed, exceeded her years. Her breasts already protested at the tightness of her blouse. Her father viewed her growth with pain. The more she grew into herself, the sharper Constante's sadness as he recalled his dead spouse.

His son, João Respectivo, remained small, oblivious to time. All were puzzled by his name. Respectivo? But that name had happened, independent of any desire for it. He had taken the infant boy to the town in order to register him. He presented himself at the government office with civilized intent:

—*I wish to register this child.*

And the clerk, his competence sluggish:

—*Have you brought the respective individual with you?*

—*No, sir. I've only brought my son.*

—*That's what I mean, your respective son.*

Constante Bene thought another name was being added to the child. And that's how the little boy, born from his mother's death, came to be called by that name. In the course of time, he made his entrance into the world led by only one hand, in the unequal half of his orphan's condition.

The guard gazed at the lofty parts of the world, the earth's shoulders, as unwavering as the centuries. As he did so, he thought: the world is large, fuller than fullness itself. Man believes he's huge, almost touching the heavens. But if he reaches places, it's only because he's living in a borrowed size, his height is a debt owed to altitude.

Why don't folk live within their means, just as they are? Why do they thrust themselves forwards in the arrogance of conquest? Constante Bene feared the dangers of desire. That's why he forbade his children to look beyond the mountain.

—*Never, not ever.*

The prohibition didn't need repeating. Many a tale was told about the other side of the mountain. It was said whites had never set foot over there. Who knows, maybe the earth there still preserved its indigenous hue, the aroma of times past? And, what's more, could it not be that such places were disposed to the exclusive pursuit of happiness?

That place: Bene called it Beyondwards. Many a time, during nightly fatigue, its secret calling encircled the hut. The guard allowed his dreams to wander, so much so that he could no longer trust himself to tell their story.

One morning, in the early hours, he took his courage in his own hands and set off in the direction of the heights. He scaled the rocks and reached the summit. He felt remorse, for he was disobeying his own command. He excused himself:

—*Today is today.*

Then he glanced in the direction of the forbidden side. A mist cushioned the moon, spread as pure as the light that envelops a woman's nakedness. It was so misty that the earth was able to free rain from its duty. He let himself sit there for some time. Until an owl issued him its warning. Such beauty was like fire: from afar it couldn't be seen, but once near, it burned. And he returned to the hut.

❦

Now, on the seventeenth day of the rains, Bene sensed the afternoon sighing. The light was already weary in its climb when the leaves saw the sign. The old man's pipe paused in mid-puff, the moment strayed.

That was when they saw the *mulato*. He was an arrival from afar, from the outer lands. He walked wrapped in his thoughts, under the teeming rain. He carried a haversack on his back. He passed the hut, unaware of the curiosity of its three occupants. João Respectivo went and peeped down the path. He saw the *mulato* scaling the heights, disappearing among the rocks further up.

What man was that, and where had he come from? Even without speaking, the three asked themselves. Love woes, guessed Chiquinha. A leopard hunter, João suspected.

—*That man is not a person to be trusted,* the father pronounced.

The youngsters defended the intruder, pleading his innocence. They needed someone to happen upon them, a fright in that feverless world. But Bene repeated:

—*That man is a runaway. If he wasn't a runaway, he'd stop here and receive our welcome.*

Then he tendered his threat: it was up to him to find out this new arrival's story. After all, that was his job. His children begged him; the *mulato* didn't merit such immediate suspicion.

—*Well, I don't trust him at all. He's a mulato. You don't know the ways of such folk.*

—*But the man passed by, he didn't even step inside our field.*

The father reflected: in fact, young João was right. The stranger seemed to be making for the high ground, there where men write no tracks.

—*You're right, son. But he must stay away from here.*

After the rains, the youngsters went out looking for the foreigner. They peered everywhere, among the stones on the mountaintop. They came across him on the topmost height, at the mouth of a cave. They watched what he did: the *mulato* had found himself a place to live. His hunger seemed to be for inhabiting the soil, deep among its lush green smells. He lived close to the ground, creeping around like an animal. Only a fire and a blanket eased his fatigue. João and Chiquinha watched from afar, lacking the courage to reveal themselves.

At home, their father chastised them for their snooping, saying,

—*Don't go there too often. I've always warned you: a fire is lit by blowing it.*

But deep down, Constante enjoyed hearing news. He asked about the things they had seen. The children replied with loose words, pieces of a torn picture. Then their father insisted: they shouldn't go there too much, he might be a dangerous madman. Above all, he was a *mulato*. And he explained himself: such a man is neither a yes nor a no. He's a maybe. White, when it suits him. Black, when it's to his advantage. And then again, how can one forget the shame they bear from their mother? Chiquinha broke in: surely they were not all like that. There must be as many good ones as there are bad.

—*It's you people who know nothing. Don't go there, and that's all there is to it.*

For awhile, his children obeyed him. But the girl. More than just sometimes, she began to climb the heights once more, pretending to look for firewood. Her old father, noticing her delays, suspected disobedience. But he said nothing, awaiting whatever fate might bring.

❧

One night, when the spirit lamp was all but out, Chiquinha was caught coming in. Her father:

—*Where have you been?*

—*I was there, Father. I can't deny it.*

Constante Bene chewed over her offence, pondered her punishment. But that daughter of mine has already got her late mother's body, he reflected. And he relented.

—*You know, Chiquinha, it's the bee itself that refuses its honey. Do you understand what I'm saying?*

She nodded. There then followed a slow wait. Bene blew out the flame, ushering in the dark. Now invisible, the two saw each other more clearly. Then the father asked:

—*Did he say anything?*

—*Yes, he did.*

—*At last? And what did this half-caste say?*

Chiquinha sat there as if she had heard nothing. Her father paused on the brink of his curiosity. But the old man, out of respect due to him, couldn't be kept waiting for an answer.

—*Listen, daughter: didn't you hear what I asked you?*

—*It's that I can't even remember what the man said.*

Her father fell silent. He rocked his chair, helping himself to get up. He was closing the windows when, once again, he asked:

—*Did you manage to find out whether there are other places out there in the world?*

—*It would seem that there are.*

The old man hunched his shoulders in disbelief. He took a turn round the room, stumbling into noises. His daughter asked why he didn't light the lamp.

—*For me, night has already fallen.*

Chiquinha adjusted her *capulana* round her shoulders. Then she sat down and remained still, as if existing were her sole function. They fell asleep. But they did so with their souls bared, which is an invitation to bad dreams. In his nightmare, the guard felt he was about to breathe his last. This is what he saw: the *mulato* was a soldier and was advancing through the orchard, in his guerrilla uniform. But what a fright: he was touching the oranges and they lit up in round balls of flame. The orange grove looked like a plantation of spirit lamps. Over the rustling of the leaves, singing could be heard:

> Iripo, iripo
> Ngondo iripo. *

Suddenly, lo and behold: Tavares. Furious, his musket in his hands. What was he firing at? At the ground, at the trees, at the mountain. The white man shouted at him:

—*You there, Constante, what sort of a guard are you? Pick those oranges before everything burns.*

Constante hesitated. But the gun barrel turned towards his chest caused his obedience to return. Tree by tree, he went reaping ardour until his fingers became ten flames. The old man woke up howling. His hands were burning. His daughter bathed his arms in copious waters. Relieved, he sat down in his chair and prepared his pipe.

—*No, Father. Don't play with fire again, let me light it.*

—*My daughter, I'm going to ask you to obey me one more time: never again climb the mountain.*

Chiquinha promised, but with false conviction. For, ever since that day, her tardiness had continued. Her father said nothing: he alone suffered the pains of premonition.

❧

---

* Song dating from the war of independence, heralding the approach of guerrilla forces.

One day, in expected surprise, Chiquinha presented herself, a picture of health, hands crossed on her belly.

—*I'm with child, Father.*

Constante Bene felt his soul fall at his feet. Chiquinha, still so much a daughter: how could she become a mother so soon? What justice was that, dear God, how could a little orphan girl be the mother of a child without due father? It was vital that the faceless progenitor should be found.

—*Was it him?*

—*I swear, Father. It wasn't.*

—*Then who is the owner of this pregnancy?*

—*I can't say.*

—*Look, daughter: you'd better talk. Who mounted you?*

—*Father, leave me alone.*

The girl sat down, the better to weep. Constante thought about beating her, tearing the truth out of her. But from Chiquinha's body there emerged the growing memory of his late spouse and his arm fell limp, vanquished. The old man returned to his room, lit his pipe, and smoked the entire landscape through the window.

The months passed by in a wide detour. Chiquinha's belly swelled, full and moon-shaped. In June she gave birth, helped by the old women of the neighbourhood. Constante wasn't at home at the time. He had gone out to do the rounds of his field. When he returned to the hut, the midwives were already preparing the meal. At first he was aware of the smoke-borne smell. Then the cry of a baby. He smiled, remembering the saying: wherever you see smoke, you'll find men; wherever babies cry, you'll find women. Now the sayings were getting mixed up. He paused in the doorway, his heart leaping. A cry in that place! It could only be one thing! His urge was to know how Chiquinha was, he felt like rushing in. But there was a deal of pride hindering him from becoming a grandfather.

—*That baby was born with too much presence*, he confessed inside his voice.

He went in, attentive to every noise and shadow. The women fell silent, tense. More than the others, Chiquinha sat stock-still with the bundle of life in her arms.

The father settled himself in a far corner. João Respectivo was the first to utter a word:

—*Father, have you seen the birth? A fat little boy child.*

Chiquinha's eyes yearned for her father's reply. Her gesture was almost one of repentance at showing the child, but then she corrected herself. The women began to file out. Now there wasn't much space left in the place.

Days went by, full of time, and still Constante could not accept his grandfatherly status. Many a time, the girl lingered by her father, in longing expectation of his blessing. Under her breath, she sang stealthy lullabies, the same ones she had learned from him. She sang more to lull her father than the child. But Constante avoided her, bedimming himself before his daughter's looks.

One night, when everyone was asleep, a trembling light crossed the room. It halted by Chiquinha's bed and stayed there, flickering like a beacon. Touched by the light, Chica awoke and saw her father, candle in hand. Constante excused himself:

—*That child of yours was crying. I came to see.*

Chiquinha smiled: he was lying. If the baby had cried, she would have heard it before anyone else. Later, João confirmed the truth: the old man crossed the darkness every night in order to peep at the cradle. Chica couldn't contain herself. She hugged her little son in blissful happiness.

On the following morning, with the sun already high, the guard was having his breakfast. He was chewing last night's leftovers, sucking his teeth with his tongue.

—*Listen there, Chica: isn't that son of yours ever so light?*

—*Babies are like that, Father. They only grow darker later. Don't you remember João?*

—*That's in the beginning, before their race gets to them. But this one here: so many days have passed, and it's time he got his colour.*

Chiquinha shrugged, at a loss. She peeled a sweet potato and blew on her scorching-hot fingers. At last, her son was a grandson. From now on, she wouldn't be alone in securing the little boy's life.

And so a new feeling was born in the hut. Even Bene seemed younger, warbling and weaving songs. Chiquinha rewarded her father with meals that lingered longer on his palate. Little João yielded himself to childhood fantasies, running along paths known only to the animals.

Constante did not require his presence, respecting his child's ways. Previously, he used to play with the boss's son. The children, on the curved pinnacle of their laughter, ignored the frontier of their races. Bene was pleased, seeing his little Respectivo receiving borrowed cares.

—*At least he gets fed there.*

Since the *mulato's* arrival, however, the boy had turned to loftier whereabouts.

Once, concerned at his son's lateness, Bene went out onto the mountain, in the direction of the wilderness which João had ventured into. Next to the well, he called his son. But it was Laura, the woodcutter's wife, who came out of the bushes. She carried a can of water on her head, as if she felt no weight at all. In the lull of her shoulders, the odd drop of water was spilled, wetting her back, her arms, and her breasts.

—*Constante, you're a guard, you should look after your life.*

—*And why should that be, just because I'm a widower?*

Bene thought Laura was trying to untie his widowerhood. He looked at the woman with many eyes, imagining her body beneath her *capulana*. He tried some sweet talk, but she diverted his words:

—*Do you know they're all talking about your daughter, and how she caught her child?*

She repeated the gossip to him: she'd been seen, nobody could say by whom, up there on the high ground. And then the unmentionable: a man had forced her, had tumbled on top of her. Constante muttered curses, his voice grew cold:

—*Was this man Black?*

—*No, they say he wasn't.*

—*I know who the rogue is. In fact, I've always known.*

Without taking his leave, he started back home. He didn't go into the house. From a box in the yard he took a cutlass. He drew it along his fingers, its sharpness his thought.

Then, unhurried, he climbed the mountain. Up on the summit, he searched for the *mulato*. He found him, bent over the fire, giving new strength to its heat. Constante didn't hide his intention, his arm hanging beside him, in full view.

—*I've come to kill you.*

The stranger showed no fear. Only his eyes, those of a cornered animal, sought an escape. With tightened throat:

—*Was it your boss who sent you?*

Constante ignored the question. For sure, the other wanted to distract him. He hesitated, unsure. Not an avenger by profession, he requested help for his hatred. He prayed within himself: my God, I don't even know how to kill! Just for a second, I beseech You, give this hand of mine certainty.

—*Why do you hate me so much?*

Once again, the other was diverting him away from his intentions; the guard queried:

—*Tell me: do you come from over there, from Beyondwards?*

—*From where?*

—*From over there, the other side of the mountain?*

—*Yes, I do.*

—*And has the new flag been raised there yet?*

The intruder smiled, almost in slow pity. Flag? Was that what interested him, to know about a piece of cloth and its colours?

—*You answer like that because you're a mulato. And mulatos don't have a flag.*

The other laughed scornfully. That laugh, thought Bene, was a sign from God. The cutlass glinted in the air and, hey presto, stabbed the stranger. Bellowing, he fell on top of him. He clung to him, a stubborn liana. The two danced around, trampling the fire. But Bene didn't even feel his feet ablaze. Another blow and the intruder lay twisted on the ground, like a pangolin.

The guard crouched next to his victim and with his hands checked to see if he was dead. He felt the blood, sticky to his touch. It was as if viscous fingers were pointing their blame at him. He sat down on the ground, tired. Where did such exhaustion come from? From killing? No. That deep despondency came from his feet, scorched by the fire. Only now did he feel the sores.

He tried to get up: he failed. His steps could barely touch the ground. He stared at the lights down there in the valley. It was a trackless distance away, an impossible return.

He dragged himself over to the *mulato's* haversack. He took out the water flask and drank. Then he emptied the bag: papers fell in the firelight. He picked up loose sheets, and slowly deciphered the letters. Beautiful dreams lay written there, promises of a more bounteous time. Schools, hospitals, houses: everything in abundance, enough for everybody. His pulse raced, mutinously. He shook the haversack again. It must be there, screwed up in a corner, he'd find it.

At that moment, like a silver wave, the flag fell out of the sack. It looked huge, greater than the universe, Bene was dazzled, he had never believed that he might one day have such a vision.

Meanwhile, he recalled the present pains: the flagpole at the administration block. There, his memory fell to its knees, the policeman's truncheon, *Don't kick up dust, you shit, don't soil the flag.* And he, dragging his feet, carrying his children, without raising his step. The boss, on the sidewalk, feigned concern with other attentions. Can a man lose so much of his soul in such a way?

But now this new flag didn't seem to be subject to any dust, as if it were made of the very earth. The colours of the cloth peopled his dream.

He was woken by his son, Respectivo. He looked around him, searching for the *mulato's* body. Not a thing, there was no body.

—*Did you bury him, João?*

—*No, Father. He ran away.*

—*Ran away? How could he if I killed him?*

—*He was only wounded, Father.*

A man of doubts, the guard shook his head. He had made sure of the other man's death. Could it be the work of witchcraft?

—*He was certainly alive. I helped him down the mountain myself.*

Furious, the guard hit the little boy. How could he? Help a fellow who had abused the respect of Chiquinha, of himself, of the whole family?

—*It wasn't him, Father.*

—It wasn't? Then who gave your sister her pregnancy?

—It was the boss, the white man.

Constante didn't even allow himself to listen. The *mulato* had taken a grip on those children's heads, had become their only faith.

—That son-of-a-bitch half-caste is from the secret police. I found a soldier's pack there in the cave. Do you think it was ever his? He's from the secret police, the PIDE, and he abused your sister and stole a guerrilla's haversack.

—It was the boss.

—Look, João, don't say that again.

—It was, Father. I saw him.

—Do you swear?

The boy asserted himself, with tears of conviction. Bene scarcely breathed. The size of that truth was beyond his grasp. His feet hurt him more, the blood asleep on his wounds. By now, flies were buzzing around, tainting the prestige of that sacred liquid. With his fingers, he crumbled a lump of sand. The earth submitted to him, reduced to flour. Such obedience between his fingers gradually brought him back to the serene breathing of one who has come to his decision.

—Don't cry any more, son. Look what I took from the sack.

And he held out the flag. João blinked, sluggish in his understanding. A flag, was it for a flag that the old man was rejoicing?

—Wrap the flag with the greatest care inside the sack. Help your father, pick up the haversack and let's go.

João offered him his shoulders. The old man jumped up on them, as if a child. He joked:

—We've swapped: I'm the son, you're the father.

And they both laughed. Secretly, the old man was astonished by the boy's strength: he didn't even pause to regain his breath.

—All right, son: enough is enough. Uncouple your body, I want to climb down from you.

They were near the house. They sat down in the shade of a large mango tree.

João turned his tongue loose, announcing futures:

—*This conversation is dangerous, my son.*

But little João was gathering courage, repeating the *mulato's* teachings. That land belonged to its sons alone, tired of bleeding wealth for foreigners.

—*Tavares . . .*

—*Leave the boss out of this.*

—*Father, you can't forever be a guard, guarding this land and pretending it wasn't stolen from us by the settlers.*

Father's temper was beginning to rise. The kid should keep quiet, he was talking through other people's mouths. The old man ordered them to get moving again. João tried to help his father, but he refused it:

—*I don't need you. Otherwise you might get a bit too big for your boots.*

They limped down the path. Now Constante supported himself with a stick, mumbling a procession of complaints. *At least a stick doesn't have ideas or vanities. It carries me along, that's all. As for men . . . Well, I prefer things, I have no axe to grind with them.* By the stream, after cooling himself, he changed his tone:

—*Listen, João. I always have this doubt in me: now I'm a white man's servant. What will become of me after?*

—*After, there will be freedom, Father.*

—*Nonsense, son. After, we'll be servants to those soldiers. You don't know about life, my boy. These gunfire folk, come the end of the war, they won't be able to get used to doing anything else. Their hoe is a musket.*

The boy looked away, denying such circumstances.

—*So why were you waiting for the new flag, Father? Why did you devote yourself to dreaming of the other side, the Beyondwards?*

—*It's just a dream that I enjoy.*

Respectivo gave up arguing. All his adolescence was opposed to was that such a clear sun should be condemned to such a summary sunset.

—*Don't deceive yourself, son: tomorrow will be the same day.*

They drew near the house and heard voices. They pricked up their ears: it was the white man who was shouting inside the hut. Constante, forgetting his limp, went in. The boss was embarrassed, and lost his bridle. But soon he calmed down, puffing out his shoulders, stretching his skin:

—*What's that you've got on your feet? Your paws are covered in blood.*

The old guard didn't answer. He shuffled up to the boss. Only then did he notice that he was taller: the white lacked heels. Taking his time, he lit his pipe. Tavares received the smoke of his affront:

—*Don't you want to tell me how you did that? Well then, I'll tell you what that is: a Black man's trickery. But you can be sure, you're not getting so much as a day off. I want to see you doing the rounds of the estate this very day.*

Impassive, Bene seemed not to hear. The boss came closer, as if to tell him a secret. There was big game in the neighbourhood, a terrorist. The administrator had alerted the farmers regarding a *mulato*, a dangerous, careless fugitive.

—*Keep those eyes of yours open, Bene.* Fungula masso . . .

—*Don't talk like that . . . Boss.*

—*Did you hear that?! And pray why not, Your Excellency?*

—*Because it's not even your dialect.*

Tavares laughed, preferring scorn. He took his leave. Before closing the door, however, he turned to Chiquinha:

—*We'll leave it at that then, do you hear?*

And he was gone. Not a single word coloured that space. Constante consulted the window, and received the silent messages of the landscape. It was as if the pipe were smoking him. After a long silence, the guard called his son.

—*You know where the mulato is. Go and tell him I want to speak to him, I need him here.*

—*But the night's so late.* Chiquinha shivered.

He caressed the girl's hair, mindful of her concern.

—*You go with João. Give the mulato my message, then climb the mountain and wait for me among the stones.*

—*Are we going beyondwards?*

Chiquinha opened her eyes wide with excitement. Her father smiled indulgently:

—*Go, accompany your brother. And cover my grandson with this blanket. Wait there fore me, I shall come.*

The children behaved obediently. They filled a basket with preliminary provisions.

—*You, João: leave the half-caste's haversack with me.*

The two children left, hurrying through the long grass. They avoided the mists which, according to legend, make your legs shrink. An owl hooted, inculpating times to come. In the dark, the world lost its angles and edges. Chiquinha followed where her brother's hand led her. Young Respectivo seemed to her, at that moment, to have been promoted in his years. He had already carried out his father's order, taking the *mestiço* his message.

They reached the rocks and sat down. Chiquinha hugged her baby with a mother's composure. She spoke:

—*You two don't like Tavares, I know. But in himself he's a man of good heart.*

Respectivo did not understand. The white had stained her, heaped abuses on her. What else did he deserve if not the fetters of vengeance?

—*Be quiet, João. You don't even know how it happened.*

Chiquinha got up, outlined in the moonlight. In her brother's eyes, she appeared like the moon through a cloud. Chiquinha lowered her voice:

—*Tavares doesn't even deserve punishment. It was I who provoked him.*

Her brother didn't want to hear any more. She wanted to explain, he wouldn't let her.

The mountain awoke, startled at their double shouting. Chiquinha's rage imposed itself:

—*I wanted to give him a father. Someone to get us out of this misery.*

That was when they heard the fearful crackle of flames. They looked down at the valley, it seemed like a fire suspended in mid-air, flying flames which did not need the earth in order to happen. Only later did they understand: the entire orchard was ablaze.

Then, on the red-stained horizon, brother and sister saw a flag being raised over the administration block. Blossom of the plantation of fire, the cloth fled its own image. Thinking it was caused by the smoke, the children wiped their eyes. But the flag asserted itself, a star's portent, showing that it is the sun's destiny never to be beheld.

The Waters
of Time

AND OTHER STORIES

Translated by Eric M. B. Becker

These stories originally appeared in *Rain and Other Stories* (2019), published in Windsor, Ontario, Canada, as part of the Biblioasis International Translation Series.

The Waters of Time

My grandfather, in those days, would take me down the river, tucked into the tiny canoe he called a *concho*. He would row, lazurely, barely scraping the oar across the current. The little boat bobbled, wave here, wave there, lonelier, it seemed, than a fallen, forgotten tree trunk.

—*But where are you two going?*

That was my mother's torment. The old man would smile. Teeth, in his case, were an indefinite article. Grandpa was one of those men who are silent in their knowing and converse without really saying a thing.

—*We'll be back in no time,* he would respond.

Not even I knew what he was pursuing. It wasn't fish. The net remained in place, cushioning the seat. It was a guarantee that when the unappointed hour arrived, the day already twilighting, he would grip my hand and pull me towards the bank. He held me like a blind man. All the same, it was he who guided me, one step ahead of me. I was astonished at his upright gauntness, all of him musclyboned. Grandfather was a man in full-fledged childhood, perpetually enraptured by the novelty of living.

We would climb into the boat, our feet a stroke on the belly of a drum. The canoe pulleyed, drowned in dreams. Before leaving, the old man would lean over one of the sides and gather up a bit of water with a cupped hand. I imitated him.

—*Always with the water, never forget!*

That was his constant warning. Drawing water against the current could bring misfortune. The flowing spirits won't be contradicted.

Later, we'd travel as far as the large lake into which our tiny river emptied. That was the realm of forbidden creatures. All that showed itself there, after all, invented its existence. In that place, the boundary between water and earth disappeared. In the unquiet calm, atop the lily-rippled waters, we were the only ones who prevailed. Our tiny boat floated in place, dozing to the gentle lull. Grandfather, hushed, observed the distant banks. Everything around us bathed in cool breezes, shadows made of light itself, as if the morning were eternally drowned in dreams. We would sit there as if in prayer, so quiet as to appear perfect.

Then my grandfather would suddenly stand in the concho. With the rocking, the boat nearly tossed us out. The old man, excited, would wave. He'd take out his red cloth and shake it decisively. Whom was he signalling? Maybe it was no one. At no point, not even for an instant, did I glimpse a soul from this or any other world. But my grandfather would continue to wave his cloth.

—*Don't you see it, there on the bank? Behind the mist?*

I didn't see it. But he would insist, unbuttoning his nerves.

—*It's not there. It's theeeere. Don't you see the white cloth, dancing?*

All I saw was a heavy fog before us and the frightful beyond, where the horizon disappeared. My elder, later on, would lose sight of the mirage and withdraw, shrunken in his silence. And then we would return, travelling without the company of words.

At home, my mother would greet us sourly. Soon she would forbid me from doing many things. She didn't want us going to the lake, she feared the dangers that lurked there. First she would become angry with my grandfather, suspicious of his non-intentions. But afterwards, already softened by our arrival, she would test out a joke:

—*You could at least have spotted the* namwetxo moha! *Then at least we'd have the benefit of some good luck . . .*

The *namwetxo moha* was a spirit that emerged at night, made only of halves: one eye, one leg, one arm. We were children, and adventurous, and we'd go out looking for the *moha*. But we never found any such creature. My grandfather would belittle us. He'd say that, when still a youth, he'd come face to face with this certain half-fellow. An invention of his own mind, my mother would warn. But, being mere children, we had no desire to doubt him.

One time, at the forbidden lake, Grandpa and I waited for the habitual emergence of the cloths. We were on the bank where the greens become reeds, enfluted. They say: the first man was born of these reeds. The first man? For me, there couldn't be any man more ancient than my grandfather. It so happened that, on this occasion, I hungered to see the marshes. I wanted to climb the bank, set foot on unsolid ground.

—*Never! Never do that!*

He spoke in the gravest of tones. I had never seen my elder look so possessed. I apologized: I was getting off the boat, but only for a little while. Then he retorted:

—*In this place, there aren't any little whiles. All time, from here on out, is eternity.*

I had a foot half out of the boat, seeking the boggy floor of the bank. I sought to steady myself. I looked for ground where I could put my foot down. It happened that I found no bottom— my leg kept falling, swallowed by the abyss. The old man rushed to my aid and pulled me back towards the boat. But the force sucking me downwards was greater than our effort. With the commotion, the boat overturned and we fell backwards into the water. And so we were stuck there, struggling in the lake, clinging to the sides of the canoe. Suddenly, my grandfather pulled his cloth from the boat and began to wave it above his head.

—*Go on, you greet him too!*

I looked towards the bank and saw no one. But I obeyed my grandpa, waving without conviction. Then something astonishing happened: all of a sudden, we stopped being pulled into the depths. The whirlpool that had seized us vanished in an immediate calm. We returned to the boat and sighed in shared relief. In silence, we split the work of the return voyage. As he tied up the boat, the old man told me:

—*Don't say a word about what happened. Not even to no one, you hear?*

That night, he explained his reasons. My ears opened wide to decipher his hoarse voice. I couldn't understand it all. He said, more or less: *We have eyes that open to the inside, these we use to see our dreams. It so happens, my boy, that nearly all are blind, they no longer see those others who visit us. Others, you ask? Yes, those who wave to us from the other bank. And so we provoke their complete sadness. I take you there to the marshes so you might learn to see. I must not be the last to be visited by the cloths.*

—*Understand me?*

I lied and said that I did. The following afternoon, my grandfather took me once more to the lake. Arriving at the edge of dusk, he sat there watching. But time passed with unusual sloth. My grandfather grew anxious, propped on the boat's bow, the palm of his hand refining the view. On the other side there was less than no one. This time, my grandfather, too, saw nothing more than the misty solitude of the marshes. Suddenly, he interrupted the nothing:

—*Wait here!*

And he jumped to the bank as fear stole my breath. Was my grandfather stepping into the forbidden country? Yes. In the face of my shock, he kept walking with confident steps. The canoe wobbled in disequilibrium with my uneven weight. I witnessed the old man distancing himself with the discretion of a cloud. Until, enveloped in mist, he sank into dream, at the margin of the mirage. I stood there, in shock, trembling in the shivering cold. I recall seeing an enormous white heron cut across the sky. It looked like an arrow piercing the flanks of the afternoon, making all the firmament bleed. It was then I beheld on the bank, from the other side of the world, the white cloth. For the first time, I saw the cloth as my grandfather had. Even as I doubted what I saw, there, right alongside the apparition, was my grandfather's red cloth, still waving. I hesitated, disordered. Then, slowly, I removed my shirt and shook it in the air. I saw the red of his cloth becoming white, its colour fading. My eyes misted until the visions became dusk.

As I rowed a long return, the old words of my old grandfather came to mind: *Water and time are twin brothers, born of the same womb.* I had just discovered in myself a river that would never die. It's to that river I now return, guiding my son, teaching him to glimpse the white cloths on the other bank.

Novidade's Flowers

NOVIDADE Castigo was the daughter of Veronica Manga and the miner Jonasse Nhamitando. She gained the nickname Castigo because, true to the moniker, she came into the world like a punishment. That much could be surmised shortly after her birth, from the blue that shone in her eyes. A Black girl, the daughter of Black parents: Where had this blue come from?

Let's begin with the girl: she was astonishingly beautiful, with a face to incur the envy of angels. Not even water was more pristine. Her one drawback, though: she was slow in the head, her thoughts never seemed to stay the night. She'd become that way—amiss—when one day, already a young woman, she suffered a fit of convulsions. That night, Veronica was sitting on the veranda when she felt insomnia's spider-crawl across her chest.

—*Tonight I'm going to count stars,* she predicted.

The night was already biting its fingernails towards dawn when, in one corner of the house, the young girl awoke in spasms and convulsions, as though her flesh were trying to break free from her soul. Her mother, predicting the future from the shadows, sensed a muted warning: What had happened? Light as a fright, she ran to young Novidade's bedside. In the houses of the poor all is well according to the degree of tidiness or disarray. Veronica Manga cut through the dark, dodged crates and cans, leaped over hoes and sacks, until she drew closer to her daughter and saw her arm, hoisted like a flag drooping at full-mast. Veronica didn't call for Novidade's father. It wasn't worth interrupting his rest.

Only the next morning did she relate what had happened. Jonasse was preparing to take off for his job on the eve of his descent into the belly of the mountain. He stopped at the door, reconsidering his intentions. Jonasse Nhamitando, all father-like, went to his daughter's room and found her lying still, her only wish to rest. Without removing his rough, worn glove, he tenderly stroked her face. Was he saying goodbye to another girl, the one who had been his little daughter? Then the young girl's father left the way a cloud parts from the rain.

The years passed in less than a blink of an eye. Novidade grew up, nothing new there. Her parents had acknowledged and assented to the idea: their daughter had sealed Veronica's womb. She wasn't an only child: she was a none-ly child, a creature of singular stock. Jonasse was a kind man, he refused to abandon Veronica. And the couple's daughter, in a pact with the void, showered her father with love and tenderness. Not that she put this into words. Rather, she did so by the way she would wait, suspended in time, for the miner's return home. For the duration of each of the miner's shifts, the girl remained apprehensive, neither eating nor drinking. Only after the father returned would the girl reassume her normal expression, and, in her voice like a stream, they discovered tunes that no one, save the girl, knew. And then there were the gifts she would pick for him: bizarre little flowers of no other colour than the blue found in her eyes. No one ever learned where she plucked such petals.

Many nights later, the family relived their earlier suffering. Jonasse was nowhere to be found. The miner was out digging the earth full of holes on the night shift. Back at the house, his wife's eyes rested over the rim of the light coming from the *xipefo*, their old oil lamp. She stitched together swaddlings of nothing, tiny clothes for a son who, as they well knew, would never come. Little Novidade dozed at the woman's side. The girl began to curl up, convulsing, her epilepsy an epic lapse. Her mother quickly tended to her. In her panic, she shattered the light to pieces, overturning the *xipefo* and its glowing light. As she calmed the girl, who was all lips and heavy breathing, Veronica Manga sought the matches above the chest. Only then did a muddy sound from the mountain outside call her attention. What was that? The mine exploding? Good heavens! She broke out in goosebumps. And Jonasse, her husband?

The woman zigzagged through the house in a run-or-die, moved from anxiety to alarm, a fly in a bull's tail. And then came even bigger explosions. Seen from the window, the mountain was transformed into a fire-breathing pangolin. Would boulders and bedrock tumble down upon the houses? No, the mountain, that one at least, had a tough constitution. And what about Jonasse? The woman knew she would have to wait till morning for news of her husband. But the young girl didn't wait for the morning light. In silence, she gathered up her tiny things in a basket and a sack. Then she arranged her mother's belongings in an old suitcase. Finally a few meagre words, in a gentle command, came from her mouth.

—*Let's go, Mother!*

Without stopping to think, the girl's mother abandoned her post, the spot where she'd nested for so many years. She let the young girl lead her by the hand, trusting in who knows what intuition. Along the way, the two of them crossed some others, like them, on the run. And Veronica asked them:

—*This thing we're hearing: What is it?*

It wasn't coming from the mine. Those were military explosions, the war was approaching. *And our husbands, where can they go to save themselves?*

—*There's no time. Climb onto the truck,* the others responded.

And up they went. Veronica situated her things better than herself, and made Novidade sit on top of the basket. The motor turned over, spinning more slowly than her eyes in their anxious search to find Jonasse emerging from the clouds of smoke and chaos. The truck pulled away, leaving behind only debris and explosions. Mother stood looking at her daughter, the composure in her expression, her dirty dress. What was she doing? Humming. In the midst of that whirlwind, the girl panned for bits of joy amid her quiet songs. Was she defanging that moment pregnant with disaster?

Between bombs and gunshots, the truck pulled forwards until it reached the front of the mine where Jonasse worked. And then the girl, disregarding the moment's developments, leaped to the ill-advised ground. She took a few steps forwards, ironing out the wrinkles in her little dress, turned backwards to offer her mother a sign of affection. Horrified, the vehicle came to a halt. Little Novidade resumed her path, crossing the road exposed to certain danger. The truck honked its horn in fury: the only thing that took its time there was death. The girl didn't appear to even hear. She stood in the road as if the way were entirely hers. In the dictionary of her footsteps, there was no sign of arrogance, nor any grand declarations. The fact that she was standing in the road, upsetting the chaos, wasn't an act of defiance but of distraction, plain and simple. She put the blue of her eyes to use. The driver, all nerves, called for her one last time. And the rest of the passengers screamed for her mother to order her to return. But Veronica didn't utter a word.

Atop a pile of sand pulled from the mine, Little Novidade leaned down to pluck wildflowers, the kind one spots on roadsides. She chose them at a cemetery pace. She stopped before some tiny blue petals identical to the colour of her eyes. The truck, tired of waiting, beset by the distressed clamour of its passengers, darted down the road. The mother refused to look away from her daughter, as though she wished to see her fate in its final form. What happened next, no one knows. Only she could see it. There, amid the dust: what happened was the flowers, the ones with a blue glimmer, began to swell and soar towards the sky. Then, all together, they plucked the girl. The flowers grabbed hold of Little Novidade with their petals and pulled her down into the earth. The girl seemed to expect this, as, smiling, she was swept away into the same womb where she'd seen her father extinguished, out of sight and out of time.

Blind Estrelinho

B LIND Estrelinho was a man of no moment: were it not for
his guide, Gigito Efraim, his story could be recounted and
discounted. Gigito's hand had led the unvisioned man for ages
and ages. That hand was separate yet shared, an extension of one
man into the other, siamesely. And so it had been almost from
birth. Estrelinho's memory had five fingers and they were those
of Gigito, gripped firmly in his own hand.

The blind man, curious, wanted to know everything. He didn't
make a fuss about life. For him, always was too seldom and everything insufficient. He would say, with these words:

—*I've got to live right away, or else I'll forget.*

Little Gigito, however—he described what wasn't there. The
world he detailed was fantasies and fine-lacery. The guide's
imagination bore more fruit than a papaya tree. The blind man's
mouth filled with waters:

—*What marvellosity, this world. Tell me everything, Gigito!*

The guide's hand was, after all, a manuscript of lies. Gigito
Efraim was as Saint Thomas never had been: he saw to not believe.
The aide spoke through his fingertips. He peeled open the uni-
verse, abloom in petals. His imagination was such that even the

blind man, at times, believed he could see. The other man would encourage him in these brief illusions:

—*Get rid of your cane, you're on the right path.*

A lie: Estrelinho still couldn't see a palm tree in front of his nose. Nevertheless, the blind man did not accept his sightlessness. He embodied the old adage: he was the legless man who was always trying to kick. Only at night would he become discouraged, suffering from fears older than humanity. He understood that which, in the human race, is the least primitive: the animal.

—*Does it trouble you that there is no light at night?*

—*Trouble is having a white bird spread its wings in your sleep.*

A white bird? In your sleep? The place for birds is in the heights. They even say God made the heavens to justify birds. Estrelinho tried to mask his fear of omens with subterfuge:

—*And now, Little Gigito? Now, looking up in this direction, am I facing the sky?*

What could the other man say? For a blind man, the sky is everywhere. It was with night's arrival and his guide fast asleep that Estrelinho lost his footing. It was as if a new darkness had appeared inside him. Slowly and stealthily he nested his hand in that of his guide. The only way to fall asleep. Is the clam's shyness the reason for its shell? The following morning, the blind man admitted:

—*If you die, I've got to die right after you. If not, how do I find the way to Heaven?*

It was in the month of December that they took Little Gigito away. Took him from the world to send him to war: they required his military services. The blind man protested: the boy could un-come of age. And the service the boy provided him was life-giving and lifelong. The guide called Estrelinho aside and calmed him down:

—*Don't go lonering around now. I already sent for my sis to take my place.*

The blind man stretched his arm as if hoping to hold onto their goodbye. But the other was no longer there. Or had he turned away on purpose? Then, with neither time nor tide, Estrelinho listened as his friend pulled away, engulfed, fargotten, inevitably invisible. For the first time, Estrelinho felt disabled.

—*Now, only now, am I one who turns a blind eye.*

In the minutes that followed, the blind man spoke loudly, all to himself, as if conjuring the presence of his friend:

—*Listen, my brother, listen to this silence. The mistake people make is to think that all silences are the same. They're not: there are distinct qualities of silence. It's like this. The dark, this snuffed-out nothingness that these eyes of mine touch: each one is unique, colourless in its own way. Understand me, brother Gigito?*

But a response from Gigito never came, and silence followed, this one, yes, repeated and the same. Dis-tended to, Estrelinho stood watching the in-sights, his eyes surrounded by sunspots and milky no-ways. It was a moonless night, its dark dye unending. Squinting, the blind man took in the darkness, its shapes and its fragments. The world bruised his uncoupled hand. His solitude hurt like a kink in a giraffe's neck. He recalled the words of his guide:

—*Lonely and sad is rheum in a blind man's eye.*

Fearing the night, he set off wandering, staggering along. His theatrical fingers played the role of eyes. Stubborn as a pendulum he went, choosing a route. Stumbling, snagging, he ended up falling down on the side of the road. There he fell asleep, his dreams zigzagging in search of Little Gigito's hand.

Then, for the first time, he saw the heron. Just as Little Gigito had described: the soaring bird, white like dawn. Its wings throbbing, as though its body occupied no space at all.

Anguished, he averted his empty gaze. It was a vision to invite misfortunes. When he returned to himself, it seemed as if he knew the place he'd stumbled upon. As Gigito would say: that was a place that snakes came to refill their venoms. But he couldn't muster the strength to leave.

He remained on the side of the road, like a balled-up handkerchief soaked with sadness, one of those that always appear at separations. Until the timid touch of a hand on his shoulders roused him.

—*I'm Gigito's sister. My name is Infelizmina.*

From then on, the girl led the blind man. She did so with great care and long silences. It was as if Estrelinho had, for a second time, lost his sight. The young girl showed absolutely no talent for invention. She described each snippet of the landscape with reason and factuality. The world the blind man had come to know dimmed. Estrelinho no longer had the lustre of fantasy. He stopped eating, stopped asking, stopped complaining. Weak, he wanted someone to carry him along, no longer just his hand but his entire body. At each turn, she pulled the blind man to her. He went along feeling the roundness of her breasts, his hand no longer sought only another hand. Until, at last, he accepted the invitation of desire.

That night, for the first time, he made love, intoxicated and overcome. In an instant, Gigito's teachings returned to him. What before had been scarce became abundant and the seconds surpassed eternities. His head swooped like a swallow and he let his heart be guided like bats: by the echo of passion. For the first time, the blind man felt sleep come over him without any anguish. And he fell asleep curled up in the girl, his body imitating fingers dissolved in another hand.

In the middle of the night, however, Infelizmina awoke, mugged by alarm. She'd seen the great white heron in her dream. The blind man felt a thud, as if wings had beat against his chest. But he feigned tranquility and began to soothe the girl. Infelizmina returned to bed, night-drowned.

The morning brought the news: Gigito had died. The messenger was brief, as a soldier ought to be. His message resonated infinitely, as the wounds of war ought to. It was strange the way the blind man reacted without the least surprise, as if he were already aware of the loss. The girl stopped speaking, orphaned of her brother. From that death on, she only grew sadder, withering away. And so she remained, unable to resume her life. Until the blind man approached and led her to the house's veranda. Then he began to describe the world, outdoing himself as he detailed the heavens. Little by little, a smile began to spread: the girl's soul was healing. Estrelinho befancied all manner of lands and landscapes. Yes, the girl agreed. She'd slumbered in such landscapes before she was born. She looked at the man and thought: I held him in my arms before this life. And when she had already shaken loose her sadness, she risked the question:

—*All this, Estrelinho? All this exists where exactly?*

And the blind man, confident in stride and course, responded:

—*Come, I'll show you the way!*

The Perfume

*T*ODAY *we're going dancing!* is how Justino announced himself, extending hands full of a package the colour of a gift. Gloria, his wife, wasn't sure how to accept it. He was the one who ended up untying the knots and pulling from the colourful wrapping paper a dress no less vivid. The woman, accustomed to living low, had spent so long waiting she'd already forgotten what it was she was waiting for. Justino oversaw the railway, one hour fused with the next, one enormous cloud of steam, a minute hand buried in his heart. Time, that stale thief of spontaneity, was an uninvited guest driving a wedge between husband and wife. What remained was a landscape of weariness, uninterest, and uh-huhs. Love—in the end, what was the point?

Which is why Gloria was so startled, leaving the dress dangling across her lap. What was she waiting for, why didn't she get ready? Her husband seemed to have played a joke on her. What had happened to him? He had always guarded her so jealously that she could barely appear at the window, much less anywhere else. Gloria stood up and dragged the dress along with her to the bedroom. Incredulous, she sleepwalked the comb sluggishly through her hair. In vain. Her untidiness had resulted in permanent braids. Gloria remembered her mother's words: an emancipated Black woman is one who knows what to do with her own hair. *But, Mother: First off, I'm of mixed race. Secondly, I've never known this thing called freedom.* She laughed at herself: free? It seemed like a word from another language. Just spelling it out caused her embarrassment, the same kind she tasted when putting on the dress her husband had given her. She opened the drawer, winning the battle with the stubborn wood. She grabbed the bottle of perfume, old but still in its packaging. It weighed very little, the liquid had long since evaporated. Justino had given her the perfume when they began seeing each other, she still a girl. It had been the only present she had received in her entire life. But now there was the dress. She squeezed the perfume bottle, milking the final drops. *What did I use this perfume on?* she asked herself as she tossed the bottle towards the void beyond the window.

—*I don't even know what wearing perfume feels like.*

She listened to the old bottle shatter on the sidewalk. She turned back towards the living room, her dress going one way, her body the other. The hem of the dress nibbled at her shoes. She dreaded what her husband would say, he was always pointing out when she went too far. This time, however, he had an unusual look, as though he didn't believe his eyes. He pulled her to him and adjusted her lines, lifting the dress a bit higher, until it was nearly nipping at her waist.

—*You're not going to put a little something on your face then?*

—*A little something on my face?*

—*Yeah, a little colour, a little polish or whatever.*

Gloria didn't know what to think. She turned around and headed for the bathroom, mouth agape. What had come over him, was he ill? Where the devil had that lipstick gone, the one that had spent years on the shelf collecting dust? She found it, hardly more than a stub, worn down by the kids' playing. She applied some to her lips. Lightly, only a shadow of colour. *Load some more on, put the red ones to use.* Her husband was talking to her in the mirror. She lifted her head, a stranger to herself.

—*Yes, we're going to the dance. Did you used to dance, before?*

—*And the children?*

—*I already made arrangements with the neighbour, don't worry about that.*

And off they went. Justino had to push the little truck. As always, she got out to lend a hand. But her husband refused: no, not this time. And he pushed the truck alone, where had anyone ever seen such a thing?

They finally arrived. Gloria's expression suggested she couldn't take in the reality. She sat there on the old truck's seat. Justino gently-manned the situation, hand extended, arm at the ready to hold doors. The dance had brought people from all around, full to the stitches. The music flowed throughout a dance hall swarming with couples. They found a table and sat down. Gloria's eyes did not do their work. They merely gazed bashfully at the table.

Then a man came up to them, his conduct respectful, and asked the brakeman if he'd allow his wife to take a gentlemanly spin around the dance floor. Her eyes, full of terror, waited for the storm to blow in. But it didn't. Justino looked at the young man and gave his consent. Gloria responded:

—*But I'd like to have the first dance with my husband.*

—*You know I never dance . . .*

As she stood there hesitating, he ordered her out on the floor, a command in the guise of tenderness.

—*Go, my Gloria, have fun!*

. And she went—slowly, still startled. As she twirled around the floor, she never took her eyes off her man, sitting there at the table. She looked deep into his eyes and saw there an abandonment she couldn't quite put her finger on, like the last of her old perfume. That's when she understood: her husband was offering her to the world. The dance, that invitation, they were a farewell. Her chest confirmed this suspicion when she saw her husband stand up and prepare to leave. She cut the dance short and ran to Justino.

—*Where are you going, husband?*

—*A friend called me, he's outside. I'll be right back.*

—*I'll go with you, Justino.*

—*Outside is no place for a woman. Stay, dance with the boy. I'll be back soon.*

Gloria didn't return to the dance. Sitting at the table he'd reserved for them, she raised her husband's glass to her lips and left her lipstick on it. She stood watching Justino disappear amid the smoke in the dance hall, bearing himself far away. Countless times she'd seen this retreat, her husband rendered faceless amid the steam of train engines. This time, however, she felt something in her chest, the arrhythmia of a hiccup. At the threshold of the doorway, Justino turned his head back for one more long look at his wife. In surprise, he saw an unprecedented tear glistening as it ran down her half-hidden face. Tears, after all, are water, and only water can wash away our sorrows. Justino felt something stumble in his chest, ash turning to ember in his heart. And the night came to an end, the door cut through that short-lived commotion. Gloria collected the tear from her cheek with the shoulder of her dress. To whom, within herself, was she saying her goodbyes?

She left the dance and set out into the dark night. She looked for the old truck. She held out hope she would still find it there, in need of a push. But there was no sign of Justino. She walked home to the sound of chirping crickets. Halfway home, she took off her shoes so her feet could feel the sand's warm caress. She gazed at the starlit sky. Stars are the eyes of those who died for love. They look down upon us from above, proof that only love can concede immortality.

She arrived home too exhausted to feel tired. For a second, she thought she saw signs that Justino was there. But her husband, if he had been there, had taken his tracks with him. Gloria lost her appetite to go on living there, their home wounded her like a portrait of the departed. She dozed off on the front steps.

She woke up early the next morning, in a daze between sleep and dream: she felt, inside herself, with only her soul's senses to guide her, the scent of perfume. Where could it be coming from? Could it be coming from her old perfume bottle? No, it could only be from a new present, a gift of the passion she began to feel once again.

—*Justino?!*

Leaping to her feet, she ran inside the house. That's when she stepped on the tiny bits of glass, scattered beneath her window. To this day, one can find the indelible tracks on the living-room floor from when Gloria shed the first drops of her bloody glee.

Rain

I'VE been seated at the window watching the rain fall for three
days now. How I've missed the soggy *rin-a-tin-tin* of each
raindrop. The perfuming earth reminiscent of a woman on the
eve of affection. How many years has it been since it last rained
like this? Having lasted so long, the drought had slowly silenced
our suffering. The heavens watched the earth's progressive decline
and saw their own death mirrored. We intirrigated ourselves: was
it still possible to begin anew, was there still a place for joy?

The rain is falling outside, melodic and divine. The ground,
this indigenous indigent, soon blossoms with various beauties.
I sit watching the street below as though looking through a
window onto the entire country. As the pools of water swell
and swell, Tristereza tidies up the room. For Aunt Tristereza,
the rain isn't a meteorological matter but a message from the
spirits. The old woman adopts a wide smile: this time, for
sure, I'll slip on the suit she insists so much that I wear. Such
a fine piece of clothing and here I am donning short sleeves
and blue jeans. Tristereza shakes her head back and forth at
my stubbornness: what justification could I have for such a
dishevelled look, for not attending to proper appearances? She
doesn't understand.

As she smooths out the sheets, she moves onto other topics of conversation. The elderly lady harbours no doubts: the rain is an answer to prayers, to ceremonies honouring our ancestors. In all Mozambique, the war is coming to a halt. Now the rain can fall once again. All these years, the gods reproached us with this drought. Deep underground, the dead—even those gone for some time—had begun drying up. Tristereza begins brushing off the coat I'll never use and offers up her certitudes:

—*Our land was full of blood. Today, it's being wiped clean, like these clothes here I'm washing. But not even now, you'll pardon this plea, not even now you'll give this suit of yours its turn?*

—*But Aunt Tristereza: couldn't it be all this rain is a bit too much?*

—*Too much? No, the rain hasn't forgotten how to fall,* says the old woman. And she explains:

—*Water knows how many grains are to be found in the sand. For each grain, the water forms a drop. Just like the mother who knits a sweater for her missing child.* Tristereza believes nature has its own ways of working, unfolding in simple ways just like hers. The rains were conferred on us at the right moment: the displaced who return to their homes will arrive to find the ground damp, just as the seedlings prefer it. Peace acts according to its own laws, free from the will of politicians.

Yet inside me a certain distrust persists: *Will this rain, my dear lady, not prove too long and too much?* Is the calamitous drought not being followed by a punishing rain? Tristereza looks around at the drenched landscape and shows me other meteorological insights that my wisdom cannot reach. You can always recognize a printed cloth by its reverse side, she's fond of telling me. God made us white and Black so that, on the backs of one and the other, He might decipher mankind. And pointing to the hefty clouds, she declares:

—*Up there, sir, there are fish and crabs. That's right, animals that always follow the water.*

And she adds: Without fail, these critters rain down during a storm.

— *You don't believe me, sir? They've even fallen right inside my house.*

—*Okay*, I say, pretending I believe her. *What kinds of fish?*

Negative: such fish can't be named. To do so, sacred words would be necessary and such words aren't fit for our human voices. And again she casts her gaze towards the window. Outside, the rain continues. The heavens are giving back the sea it had sheltered with lazy azure migrations. But it looks as if the heavens intend, in so doing, to overrun the entire earth, joining its rivers, shoulder to shoulder. I come back to my question: Won't the waters prove too much, falling with such malignant generosity? Tristereza's voice repeats itself in a diluvial monotone. She murmurmuses:

—*You, sir, you'll forgive my tongue, look like a creature in search of the forest.*

And she adds:

—*The rain is washing the sand clean. The dead will be pleased. It would be a show of respect your using this suit. To match this celebration of Mozambique . . .*

Tristereza holds her gaze on me, in doubt. Then, resigned, she hangs up the jacket, which seems to let out a sigh. My stubbornness dangles on a hanger. I glance towards the street; streaks of sorrow drip down the windows. What is it I'm always trying to escape? What reasons does the old woman have for accepting her confinement, all dressed for home? Perhaps for belonging more to the world, Tristereza doesn't feel, as I do, the lure to leave. She thinks the time of suffering has passed, that our land is being rinsed of its past. I have my doubts. I need to observe the street. Windows: are they not the place where houses dream of being the outside world?

The old woman finishes her work, says goodbye as she closes the doors, lingering and languid. Sorrow has crept into her soul and I'm its cause. I notice the plants outside sprouting from the earth. The colour green speaks the language of all the others. The old lady has already begun to repeat her goodbyes and is leaving when I call to her:

—*Tristereza, grab my suit.*

She suddenly gleams with surprise. As she undresses the hanger, the rain begins to stop. Only a few remaining drops of water fall on my coat. Tristereza urges me:

—*Don't brush them off, these little drops are good luck.*

And arm in arm, we both step out into the pools of water, carefree as children who see in the world the joy of a never-ending game.

Felizbento's Pipe

EVERY tale loves to masquerade as the truth. But words are nothing more than smoke, too weightless to stick to the present reality. Every truth aspires to be a tale. Facts dream of becoming words, sweet fragrances running from the world. You'll see in this case that it's only in the fiction of our wonderment that the truth meets the tale. What I'm about to report here took place in a peaceful land, one where Sundays outnumber the days of the week.

That land was still just beginning, newly born. The seeds there found a welcoming home, and green spread across the lush landscapes. Life was linked to time, the trees scaling great heights. One day, however, war landed, with its capacity for all manner of death. From then on, everything changed and life became much too mortal.

The nation sent workers in a rush. The representatives in the capital always act quickly when they're far from home. They told the living they must leave, converting them from home-towners to homeless. Security reasons. They called the residents one by one, in alphabetical disorder. It was Felizbento's turn. The old man listened, as incredulous as a frog that gobbles a snake. He consisted of nothing more than a sigh. He carried on as he had before, winding his soul. The others were condensed, packed up and bundled, on the backs of trucks. But Felizbento stood firm. An official took charge of the situation, ordering him to get to it. To leave, just like the others.

—*Didn't you hear the order? Now get to it.*

Felizbento applied a second coat of silence, rubbed one foot against the other, shining his shoeless feet. Or was he pointing at the earth, the only place he'd ever lived? He'd always silenced his suffering, armed with patience greater than his age. Finally, he pointed to the sprawling forest and said:

—*If I'm to leave here, I need to take all these trees with me.*

The nation's servant ran out of patience and told Felizbento that, a week later, they'd return to take him away, even if they needed to use brute force. And then they left.

The next day the man set to unearthing the trees, digging them up by the roots. He began with the sacred tree in his backyard. He dug in deep: there in the place he'd been hollowing out, total darkness had been set free. To continue his burrowing, he grabbed a Petromax lamp, the kind he'd got in Johannesburg. And day after day, he spent long hours at work.

His wife, disappointed, pointed out the unsuitability of his actions. It wasn't worth asking anything of Felizbento. The clothes of the dead no longer wrinkle. The obstinacy of old age doesn't bend. The wife remained perched in the window like a stopped clock. In the black of night, the old woman saw only the movement of the Petromax, which looked as if no hand guided it.

Her heart heavy, the woman sketched out a plan. She would offer herself, as in the times when their bodies believed they had no limits. She reached deep into one of the closets, where not even cockroaches dared to tread. She snatched the floral-stamp dress, some high heels. And she began her nocturnal wait, clothes and perfumes tantalizing. She remembered an old saying of Felizbento's, from times past:

—*If you wish to make love, nighttime is the best.*

Those who've loved time and again know the heat of the night, this bed of beds. At night, creatures change in value. The day reveals the world's defects: wrinkles, dust, lines—in the light, everything can be seen. At night, though we look more intensely, we see less. Each creature reveals itself only by the light it gives off. On this particular night, she emitted a soothing glow like that of the moon.

Felizbento arrived home from his toils, glanced at his wife. He was like a beached whale, the water that'd carried him there suddenly gone. His wife drew closer, touching his arm. She looked every bit her own woman, this was her irrefusable beauty.

—*Stay with me tonight. Forget the trees, Felizbento.*

Dizzied, the old man still hesitated. The woman wrapped her body in his, her fingers creeping across his skin. Felizbento felt like water in a fish. What could that be? Did that soul belong to this world? That's when, incidentally, she stepped on her husband's bare foot with her high heels. Her shoe was like a needle on a balloon. The farmer recoiled, determined. Machete back in hand, he went out to meet the blackness once again.

Then one day, Felizbento came back up to the surface and asked his wife to unpack his suit, get the proper clothes in order, to starch the fabrics. It had been more than thirty years since those clothes had been put to their use. His shoes no longer even fit. His feet had grown misshapen with barefootedness. In fact, there wasn't a shoe to be found that fit him.

He took the old shoes with him all the same, half-covering his feet, treading on his heels. He dragged them across the floor, lest his feet be separated from his footsteps. And off he went, as bent as a reed, in this youthfulness that's only to be found in old age. He began to enter the land and, only once, he turned back. Not to say farewell, but to rummage through his pockets for something forgotten. His pipe! He went through his clothes. He took out his old pipe and spun it in his fingers, beneath the trembling light of the burning lamp. Then, in a gesture of dejection, he threw it away. As if discarding his entire life.

There the pipe remained, remote and forgotten, half buried in the sand. It looked as if the earth gave it breath, smoking the useless utensil. Felizbento descended into the hole, disappearing.

To this day, his wife crouches over the hole and calls after him. Not yelling, but calling sweetly, as if to someone in his sleep. She still wears the floral dress, high heels, and perfume with which, in the midst of her despair, she attempted to seduce him. After awhile, she draws back, snuffed out. Only her eyes, roundly insistent, resemble those of an insomniac owl. What dreams beckoned that woman into existence?

Those who've returned to that place say that, beneath the sacred tree, there now grows a plant fervent with green, climbing an invisible arbour. And they give assurances that this little tree grew from nothing, sprouting from some old, forgotten pipe. And, at the sunset hour, when the shadows no longer try so hard, the tiny tree puffs out smoke just like a chimney. As far as his wife is concerned, there is no doubt: beneath Mozambique, Felizbento is smoking his old pipe in peace. As he waits for a capitalized and definitive Peace.

Jorojão's Cradle of Memories

My friend Jorge Pontivírgula, Jorojão to us, was telling me about the misunderstandings that plagued his life. Misfortunes that, to hear him tell it, had always come with a dose of presentiment. My friend revealed himself to be what he was: a pre-sentimentalist. But I'll get to that. First, however, I'll give a proper portrait of this Jorge's entire soul.

To sum up his life, Jorojão always had but a single desire: to stay out of trouble. But not even all his fears could stack up to him. His stature exceeded that of a giant. You would look to the clouds as you spoke to him. We used to joke: the man could only kiss sitting down! This Jorojão, in colonial times, circulated through politics like money in a beggar's pockets: changing place often and never finding a home. The din of the city made him ill. To escape to the bush, he offered his services as a safari driver. It's how he used to put distance between himself and the world's bad breath. But that wasn't enough, in the end. For one day he had to drive a delegation of the heads of the PIDE secret police into the forest to hunt. Savage men on a savage hunt: what could be worse? At the end of the day, one of the authoritarian policemen ordered him to clean their guns. Jorojão remembers beginning to tremble:

—*Guns?*

He didn't dare speak the word again beyond that moment. But he acted as if it was no bother at all, and scrubbed, cleaned, and oiled the weapons. As he was doing the last bit of shining, a bullet burst forth at full speed from one of the aforementioned unmentionables. One of the PIDE fell hard as a coconut on a blustery afternoon.

Thirty years having passed, Jorojão excuses himself: *It was just a little bullet, it was nothing at all. The fella really hit the dirt then and there! Aaah, but I can't believe he died from the shot. I think the fright must have given him a heart attack. Or maybe his head wasn't screwed on right.*

He fills his cup again, downs the entire drink in a single gulp. Then, closing his eyes, he clicks his tongue, sharpens his joy anew. Sadness already beginning to creep in, rising to the surface of memory, he feels the need to soak his soul in beer. Rocking his chair back and forth, he explains: it's this seesawing of his chair that transports him to bygone days. If not for the chair he would have already said farewell to all those memories.

The chair must have been rocking quite a bit, because he was retreating once again into the past: after the shot was fired, he was imprisoned for ties to terrorism. A good bit of luck, as it turned out: it was already January 1974. It didn't take long before the Fascist regime tumbled in April. That morning remains especially unforgettable for him. The masses stormed the prison, went straight to his cell, and carried him in their arms. It was only then that he took measure of his own stature: a giddiness overtook him. He was a hero, a defender of the people.

—*Imagine me there, eh, a guy who never gets involved in anything . . . If I were to receive an award it would be for keeping out of stuff.*

But the Revolution brought him distinction: he went on to lead one of the newly nationalized companies. Jorojão did his best to refuse. His refusal, however, led to an even bigger mess. So from that moment he performed his functions at the highest level of functionality. Jorojão arrived in the morning and didn't leave until late at night. Everything operated just so, the company coffers filling with profits. Everything was going so well that they began to get suspicious. Other state companies hadn't so much as a plate yet he filled up on soup? An inspection crew showed up, not even bothering to look at his papers. All they needed was to see the gun on the office wall.

—*This gun isn't in line with regulations.*

—*But this is the Glorious Gun, it's the one I used to kill that PIDE bastard, don't you remember, the one whose gun here I was given in a public ceremony?*

His explanation proved to be futile. How could they know if it was the same gun? Mounted on a wall, all guns look the same. They jailed him, charging him with stashing a suspicious shotgun. There he remained, making less noise than a pangolin. He still remembers these unhappy, inglorious times, of falling asleep to forget his belly. The memories still make him bitter.

—*Do you see now, sir? I don't do anything, it's these meddlesome troubles that always come looking for me.*

He stayed in prison for months. One day, through his cell bars, he saw a group of workers from his company enter the prison. He asked to speak to the warden, trying to understand the presence of his subordinates. The prison boss spoke to him with unusual deference:

—*Mr. Jorojão, did you not know that you were to be freed today?*

—*Freed?*

—*Yes, today, in commemoration of World Meteorological Day. However, now you're going to remain here awhile longer . . .*

Why had this been said and undone? The postponement of his release resulted from the following: the workers, longing for their imprisoned director, had performed a witchcraft ceremony to achieve his freedom. The authorities had interrupted the ceremony and arrested the participants, accusing them of arcane superstitions. The cause was now subject to the effect: Jorojão's release would have to be suspended lest the credit for it be given to the feudalist ceremonies. It's simple, the head of the prison explained at the time. *If you were to leave now they'd say that these superstitious rites produced their intended effect. And this goes against the principles of materialism. For this very reason, the district also postponed the celebrations for World Meteorological Day.*

Jorojão returned to his cell.

—*Have you ever heard such a thing? They kept me waiting there in prison on account of meteorological materialism!*

Months later he stepped into the freedom of the streets, at a time when no one could any longer tie his release to any stealthsly spirits. Bitten by the dog and left toothless by the thug, Jorojão lamented. To this day, you can't talk to him about the weather. Sitting in his old rocking chair, the immensity of each day weighs down on him. Work? For what? Work is like a river: even when it's reaching an end, what comes behind it is more and more river. Wearily stretching his legs, he asks me:

—*Who is it who's rocking: me, the chair, or the world?*

Lamentations of
a Coconut Tree

THE event was official and verified, it made the Nation's newspaper. The buzz about the coconut groves of Inhambane was worthy of headlines and much spilled ink. It all began when, seated along Inhambane's seaside drive, my friend Suleimane Inbraímo split the shell of a coconut. For the fruit didn't gush the usual sweet water, but blood. Exactly so: blood, certified and unmistakable blood. But that wasn't the only astonishing thing. The fruit cried and lamented in a human voice. Suleimane took no exaggerated measures: his wide-open hands dropped the coconut, and the red stains spread. He stood there, dumbfounded and overwhelmed, spent. The shock made his soul vanish into the low tide.

When I ran to help, he was still in the same position, head bent on his chest. Evidence of the incident had been removed, hands washed, amnesiac. Only his voice still trembled as he related the episode to me. I distrusted. Doubt, we know, is the envy that the unbelievable hasn't happened to us.

—*Forgive me, Suleimane: a coconut that spoke, cried, and bled?*
—*I knew it: you weren't going to believe me.*
—*It's not not believing, brother. It's doubting.*

—Go ahead and ask, among these folk around here, ask about what happened with these coconuts.

I filled my chest to let my patience breathe. I'm used to strange things. I even have a talent for stumbling on these inoccurrences. But this was not the right moment. We should have left that place long before. Our work had already ended a week earlier and we still awaited news of the boat that would take us back to Maputo. Not that the place wouldn't allow us some modest rest. Inhambane is a city of Arab manners, unpressed to enter time. The tiny houses, dark and light, sighed in the weariness of this eternal measuring of strength between the lime and the light. The narrow streets are good for courting; it appears that in them, no matter how much we walk, we never stray from home.

I watched the bay's feminine blue, this sea that makes no waves nor creates urgency. But my travel companion already had a flea in his ear. When I asked about the arrival of the next boat, Suleimane wobbled, one foot then the other, as prisoners do.

—Every time, it's coming today.

The man spoke in imperfect certainty. Because at that very instant, as if issuing from his words, breezes began to swell. It squalled. First, the banana trees fanned. Gesticulant, the leaves swayed listlessly. We didn't make the connection.

After all, only a hint of wind is needed to fan the fruitful plants. They should be called, in that case, fanana trees. But afterwards, other greens began to shake in agitated dance. Suleimane began with a stammer:

—This squall isn't going to abide any boat.

I sat there, listless a thousand times over, to show I didn't have an opinion. I unwrapped the little cakes I'd bought a short time ago from the ladies at the market. A kid approached. I thought: here comes one more cry-beggar. But no, the child stayed beyond a beggable distance. My teeth had already prepared for the taste when the kid's eyes grew wide, a shout rising in his throat.

—*Mister, don't eat that cake!*

I stopped mid-bite, my mouth in dread of who-knows-what. The boy renewed his sentence: I was not to stick my saliva on the flat cake. He didn't know how to explain, but his mother came at the child's gesticulation. The woman entered the scene with colossal heft, fastening a nimble *capulana*.

—*The child is right, I'm sorry. These cakes were made with green coconut, were cooked with* lenho.

Only then did I understand: they had offended the local tradition that held the still-green coconut sacred. Forbidden to harvest, forbidden to sell. The unripe fruit, *lenho*, was to be left amid the tranquil heights of the coconut trees. But now, with the war, outsiders had arrived, placing more faith in money than in the respect for commandments.

—*There are many-many displaced people selling* lenho. *One of these days they'll even sell us.*

But the sacred has its methods, legends know how to defend themselves. Varied and terrible curses weigh over he who harvests or sells the forbidden fruit. Those who buy it get what's left over. The shell bleeding, voices crying, all this was *xicuembos*, hexes with which the forefathers punish the living.

—*You don't believe it?*

The huge woman interrogated me. It wouldn't be long before she reeled off her own versions, applying the principle that two weeks of explanation aren't enough for he who half understands. Even before she spoke, those present clicked their tongues in approval of what she was going to say. In the good country way, each seconds the other. Exclamations of those who, saying nothing, agreed with the unsaid. Only then did the woman unwrap her words:

—*I'll tell you: my daughter bought a basket way over on the edge of town. She brought the basket on her head all the way here. When she tried to take the basket off, she couldn't. The thing looked like it was nailed down. We pulled with all our strength but it didn't budge. There was only one remedy: the girl returned to the market and gave the coconuts back to the man who sold them. You hear me? Lend me a bit more of your ear, for a moment. Don't tell me you didn't hear the story of neighbour Jacinta? No? And I add, sir: this Jacinta put herself to grating the coconut and began to see the pulp never had an end. Instead of one pan, she filled dozens until fear bid her stop. She laid all that coconut on the ground and called the chickens to eat it. Then something happened I almost can't describe: the little chicks were transformed into plants, wings into leaves, feet into trunks, beaks into flowers. All, successively, one by one.*

I received her reports quieter than a seashell. I didn't want a misunderstanding. Suleimane himself drank with anguish these stories of the common man, fanatical believerist. And then we were gone, leaving that place for a no-star hotel. We had the common intention to chase sleep. After all, the boat would arrive the following day. Our return trip was paid for, we no longer had to think about the spirits of the coconut groves.

Bags and suitcases tottering on deck, motors humming: that's how, at long last, we made our way back to Maputo. My animated elbow brushes Suleimane's arm. Only then do I notice that, hidden amid his clothes, he carries with him the cursed coconut. The same one he'd begun to split open. I marvel:

—*What's this fruit for?*

—*I'm going to send it for analysis at the Hospital.*

Before I could dissent from this logic, he countered:

—*That blood there, who knows in what veins it ran? Who knows if it was diseased, or rather, disAIDSed?* He rewrapped the fruit with an affection meant only for a son. Then he broke off, rocking it with a lullaby. Perhaps it was just this lullaby of Suleimane's, I could almost swear it, and yet he seemed to hear a lament coming from the coconut, a crying from the earth, in the anguish of womanhood.

Beyond the River Bend

WHAT I cite are facts from the newspaper. They went something like this: "A hippopotamus broke into the Centre for Typing and Sewing in the Munhava neighbourhood, leaving a path of destruction and sowing fear among residents of the most densely populated neighbourhood in the capital of Sofala province . . . . A night watchman present at the time said the animal wasn't your regular old hippopotamus, but a very strange specimen who busted down the door to the school, strode into the classrooms, and began to destroy the furniture. . . . Rumours have been circulating among residents in the area that the hippopotamus is in fact a former resident of the city who lost his life in the neighbourhood where the animal came from and that this old man had returned to proclaim the following prophesies: rain would cease to fall in the city and plagues were to kill people by the score. The prediction coincides with a surge in the number of epidemics in the metropolitan region. [End of citation.]"

The newspaper didn't cover the remaining events, those that occurred later. What I'm adding to the story here are the reports of those witnesses with faulty judgment, people versed in nocturnal apparitions. Luckily, in our world today, there are no sources undeserving of our trust.

Jordão—or Just J, as he was known—awoke that day in a fit of fear: what were those sounds coming from the school? He froze, tensed. He decided to sit still and face the consequences of doing nothing. But the racket grew louder. Someone had entered the school in a rage, looking for trouble. Thieves, they must have been. But was it really possible, this level of shamelessness? Was someone testing his courage? Jordão grabbed his gun and headed for the school. He rolled back on his heels, his feet in the opposite gear. The noise coming from the intruder was enough to set the daring running and make a coward of any hero. Fear is a river one must cross wet.

As Jordão drew closer, he called to the heavens for reinforcements:

— *May the xicuembos protect me!*

The moon lit the way. Its glow was strong, but not enough to pull a thorn from your foot. That's the reason Jordão can't be entirely sure of everything he saw; his eyes took in the events that followed but his thoughts found them difficult to grasp. When he looked through the window, he saw the enormous beast chewing through a sewing machine. The mammal's girth was unrivalled by anything he'd ever seen before. This wasn't some ordinary example of its species, this one. A more appropriate name for this beast was *hyper-potamus*. Just then, the giant beast saw the soldier peeping through the window frame. He looked straight at the man with the two sleepy eyes stuck to the roof of his forehead. Then he went back to nibbling on the furniture—the pudgy creature's picnic would not be stopped.

All sorts of ideas began to fly as swift as a flock of birds through Just J's head. How had the *mpfuvo*, as they called the beast in southern Mozambique, come to the school? Had he come in search of knowledge, to learn how to write, out of some thirst to transform from artiodactyl to artiodactypographer? Or had he come to improve his sewing abilities? No, that couldn't be. His fingers were stiffer than panhandles.

During those moments of hesitation, the soldier cast his thoughts back to the way things used to be: those who hunted the *mpfuvo*, in accordance with tradition, never set off for the river without first receiving the blessing of the mystic vapours. Husband and wife would bathe in the medicinal fumes for good luck. When the hunter stuck his prey with the first spear, a messenger would run to the village to alert his wife. From that moment forward, the woman was prohibited from leaving the house. She would light a fire and stand guard over it, without food or drink. Were she to break the ritual, her husband would suffer the wrath of the angry hippopotamus—the hunted turned hunter. Remaining cloistered bounded the beast's spirit, prevented the pachyderm from fleeing the spot where he would meet his end. The wife's confinement would end only when she heard shouts of joy coming from the river, heralding the hunt's success. In the village, everyone except for Just J would rejoice. It always seemed the spears had wounded his soul on that stretch of river.

But at that point, in the schoolhouse window, it wasn't jubilant refrains but the hippopotamus's rage that made the soldier stir. In truth, what provoked the beast's ire at the present moment was the scenery. Corners, doors, walls: this was uncharted territory for the brute. He snarled, gnashed his teeth. The soldier was made tiny by his fear, only his gun granted him any stature. Suddenly, without thinking, Jordão fired a shot. A flurry of bullets hit their mark. The nose, being in front of the eyes, never obstructs them. The beast, in all his girth, trembled and folded, collapsing to the ground. His pink belly lent him the appearance of a newborn. In his final moment he devoted a look full of tenderness to the hunter. As though, instead of resentment, he felt gratitude. Was it love at last sight?

Jordão recalled how, as a child, he'd developed a soft spot for the *mpfuvos* and their clumsy ways: such a large nape for so little neck! Fat as could be, they seemed to him suited to all sorts of dancing. And because the disaster-prone beasts, barely terrestrial, were his brothers: none of them was ever at home among others. Jordão often dreamed about the animals, which looked like upturned canoes riding the river's lazy current. In his dreams, he'd climb on their backs and ride just beyond the river bend. That was his greatest dream: discovering what lay up ahead of the human landscape and reaching the land beyond limits.

At that moment, however, gun in hand, Jordão hungered to lead other lives, to trample other creatures that he found inferior. He was flooded by an abrupt anger for feeling a certain kinship with such untamed creatures. Did this sense of superiority come from his rifle, or had age killed his capacity for imagination? Or do all adults commit this sort of adultery?

The sound of gunshots brought many curious onlookers. They launched straight into he-said, she-said, rage and outrage.

—*You killed the* mpfuvo? *Don't you know who this animal was?*

—*Just wait and see the punishment we'll get on your account.*

—*You won't need to wait until tomorrow. You're going to regret this finger of yours pulled the trigger.*

And off they went. Jordão sat on the top step of the school entrance with his thoughts. All that thinking had made him thinner. What could be done? He'd been accused of killing not some terrible beast but a man transfigured. How could he have guessed at the truth about the hippopotamus, his message-bearing role? He dropped his head into his arms and that's how he remained, more circumflex than the accent mark itself.

That's when he felt a nudge. Someone was tapping him on the back, as though to rouse him from sleep. He looked behind him and goosebumps rose across his entire body. It was a tiny *mpfuvo*, a baby hippopotamus. What could it want, this kid? Shelter is what it sought, the protection of a being greater than itself. He rolled around near the soldier's armpit as if seeking to stir an imaginary breast. Then he nestled up against his mother's giant body, grunting to call her attention. Jordão regarded the little animal with its mouth bigger than its snout. He rose to his feet and took the orphan into his arms. The little one wouldn't sit still, only making him heavier. Jordão stumbled, nearly dropping his cargo, before regaining his stuttering footsteps along the muddy riverbank.

When they reached the river, the young hippopotamus leaped up to join his herd. As he watched, Jordão felt the weight of his gun grow unbearable. His shoulder began to ache from the load. With an abrupt gesture, he threw the rifle into the river, as though casting off a part of himself. At that moment, he heard a human voice. Where was it coming from? It came from the young hippo he'd just saved.

—*Climb atop the capsized canoe.*

Canoe? That hefty thing cresting the surface? The voice repeated the invitation:

—*Come, I'll show you the place just beyond the river bend.*

Enthralled and disarmed, Jordão climbed atop the dewy dorsal of dreams and set off against the current to the land beyond limits.

High-Heel Shoes

IT happened in colonial times. I hadn't yet reached adolescence. Life took place in Esturro, a Beira neighbourhood not lacking for neighbours. In that tiny corner, the Portuguese set down their roots. The men there never amounted to masters of anything; even their dreams suffered from a lack of ambition. Their exploring only went as far as making the rounds of neighbourly quarters. If they robbed, it was so they might never become rich. The others, the true masters, not even I knew where they lived. For certain, they didn't dwell anywhere. Dwell is a verb one applies only to the poor.

We lived in this tiny neighbourhood of dust-ridden streets, where the sun set earlier than in the rest of the city. Everything carried on there without much fanfare. Our neighbour was the only intriguing figure: an imposing, whiskered man with a voice like thunder. But friendly, a man of refinement and good manners. Everyone called him Zé Paulão. The Portuguese man laboured at harsh altitudes behind the wheel of heavy cranes. He was like a rooster with its plume of feathers hoisted high, ruler of a vast roost, but living totally alone. Other men marvelled at his aloneness, the ladies cursed at such waste. They all remarked: such a human man, a man so blessed with manliness, such a shame he was living by himself and for himself. Never did anyone witness him in the company of another. After all, God doesn't dole out nuts to just anyone.

All that was known about him was this brief summary: his wife had run away. What reasons she had for deconsummating their marriage, no one knew. She was the model modest little Portuguese woman, the daughter of humble country labourers. Beautiful, of a flowering age. We saw her only once, when she was leaving the house, fearfully white. In certain and exposed danger, she was walking down the middle of the street. The cars screeched to a stop, fishtailing. The pale white woman didn't seem to hear a thing. Then I saw: the girl was crying, a true watershed. My father stopped our vehicle and asked her how we could help. But the young woman didn't hear a thing—she was sleepwalking. My father decided to accompany the creature, protecting her from the dangers of the streets, until she disappeared where the darkness came to an end. It was only then that we were able to confirm that the woman had left the house to make a most definitive departure.

From that moment on, only solitude was capable of comforting Zé Paulão. Or so it seemed to the neighbourly public. We, however, were the only ones who knew the truth. In the yard behind our house, where no others laid eyes, we could see, every now and then, women's clothing drying in the sun. Paulão had his ways of coping after all. But we kept our secret. My family wanted to be the only ones to relish that revelation. Let others pity the solitary man. We alone knew the backside of reality.

And there was another secret we kept to ourselves: at night, we could hear a woman's footsteps on the other side of the wall. In Zé Paulão's house, there could be no doubt, a woman's high-heel shoes ticky-tacked across the floor. They made the rounds through the bedroom, the hallway, and the sleepy rooms of our neighbour's house.

—*One hell of a scoundrel, that Paulão!*

My aunts approved of these naughty little comments, a snicker behind their teeth, their teeth covered by their hands. There was much discussion of the mysterious woman: who was it that no one ever saw arriving or departing? My mother bet: she had to be a rather tall lady, much taller than Paulão. The footsteps could only belong to a fat woman, my aunt countered.

—*Maybe she's so fat she can't fit through the door,* my father joked.

And then, still laughing:

—*That's why we never see her leaving!*

I used to dream of her: she was the most beautiful woman in the world, so beautiful and elegant that she could only come out at night. The world's eyes didn't deserve the sight of her. Or was she an angel? Paulão, seated high up in his crane, had nabbed her by surprise. What's for certain is that the mysterious woman next door filled my dreams, ruffled my sheets, and forced me out of my own body.

One night, I took advantage of my childhood, to play little games with myself, pretending I was an adventurer, a hero from one of those shoot-em-up movies. Climbing onto the roof, I escaped the manhunt for me, outwitting hundreds of Indians below. At the last minute, I leaped to my neighbour Paulão's porch. I could even feel imaginary arrows piercing my soul. I took a deep breath and a moment to grab my plastic pistol. Then a light went on inside the house. I crouched down, fearing I'd be mistaken for a common thief. Taking a few punches at the hands of my corpulent neighbour would bring no pleasure. I hunched down into a dark corner. I could neither see nor be seen. Just then, my ears stood up. The heels. The mystery woman must have been making the rounds through the adjacent accommodations. I couldn't resist catching a glimpse. That's when I saw a woman's long skirt. I was on full alert: finally, she was right there, within eye's reach, the woman of our mysteries. There stood the woman who gave form to my desires. Indians be damned! Paulão could go to hell! I drew closer to the light, defying all concepts of prudence. Now the entire living room was within view. The fascinating lady had her back to me. She wasn't so tall in the end, nor so fat as my family had supposed. Suddenly, the woman turned around. *Thud!* The earth opened in a huge abyss. Zé Paulão's eyes, adorned with makeup, locked on me. The lights went out and I leaped from the porch, my heart catacombing into the abyss.

I returned home, my head out of tune. I locked myself in my bedroom, giving shape to the silences. Hours later, at the dinner table, the same subject returned.

—*Our neighbour, the immortal lover—not long ago I heard those heels over there.* It was my father who spoke, setting off a wagging of tongues.

—*You all are just jealous you can't do the same,* my aunt announced. Everyone laughed at once. Only I kept to myself, silently fulfilling my obligations to melancholy.

Later on, when everyone had slipped into the release of sleep, I again heard the high-heel shoes. My eyes filled with a deep, inexplicable sorrow. I was crying for what, in the end? My mother, having suspected something in that way only mothers are able, rushed into my room, filling it with light.

—*Why are you crying, my child?*

I told her about the passing of an uncertain girl whom I'd loved deeply. She'd abandoned me, betraying me with another man in the neighbourhood. My mother pretended not to understand, a stroke of her maternal wand. Her smile was filled with unusual suspicion. She tendered her fingers through my hair and said:

—*Come, come. Tomorrow you can move to another room. You'll never have to hear the sound of those high heels again.*

Joãotónio, for Now

For now, I'm Joãotónio. I'll say it and then I'll unsay it: when it comes to women, I advance like the army. 'Cause my whole encounter with them feels like a battle. What I mean is the minute I look at a woman, I already start wondering: what's her voice like? It's not her audible voice that piques my interest, but the other, silent one, disembodied, capable of speaking as many languages as water. In other words: what I want to decipher is her moans, these wings sliding to the edge of the abyss, the chill that runs up the soul when it's lost its home.

You know what I'm talking about, bro: a person's voice obscures the sweet taste of her sighing. The voice conceals the way she sighs. I can already hear your question: what's this obsession with unravelling the secrets behind the way a woman sighs? It's the same desire a general has, bro. It's the taste of the enemy's surrender. It's the desire to hear in advance the way they make love, subdued and abandoned.

Sometimes, I stop to think: deep down, I'm afraid of women. Aren't you? You are, I'm sure of it. Their thoughts come from a place that's beyond reason. That's where our fear comes in: we're unable to make sense of their way of thinking. Their superiority frightens the hell out of us, bro. That's why we see them as well-versed adversaries in a battle. But let me get back to the beginning—just look at me, screeching like a hairpin turn, swerveering off into this pseudo-philosophizing. And start your listening over, too.

For the time being, I'm still Joãotónio. What I'm telling you now is the fiction of my unhappiness. Don't go telling this to everyone. I'm trusting you, bro. 'Cause it's not just anyone who makes his troubles public. What I'm about to write is cause for shame.

I'll start with Maria Zeitona, source of all urges. As I write the name of this woman, I can still hear her voice, smooth as a bird's wings. I already told you: a woman's voice is as important as her body. It whets the appetite more than appearances or seductions ever could, at least for me.

As I wasn't saying: Maria Zeitona seemed to be intact and untouchable. She gave off suspicion like an ember beneath ashes. Her body spoke through her eyes. And what crystalluminous eyes! We were married in an instant. I wanted nothing more than to suffer the promise of that inferno. I was marrying to consummate the ardencies swarming round my dreams. But the bad news, my brother: Maria Zeitona was ice-cold, frigelid! It was as if I were making love to a corpse. You could say we maintained asexual relations. And that's how she stayed more virgin than Mother Mary. I tried, I tried again, I used every technique from the whole of my experience. All the same, bro: for nothing. Zeitona was damp firewood: flames could not touch her.

I changed tactics, I gave her worthy surprises. I ran through all the preliminaries I knew. I even kissed the tips of her toes. Still no luck. A kiss is neither given nor received. It's life that does the kissing, and the kissing back. I'll say it again, bro: it's life that kisses us, two beings in an infinite moment. Enough with the family chat? All right, got it, bro, I'll get back to this subject of mine, Maria Zeitona.

At the end of these campaigns, I gave her a penultimatum: either she sweetened up or I'd resort to unfortunate measures. And that's what didn't happen. That, bro, is when I made my decision: I'd send Zeitona to a prostitute. That's right, my little Zeitona would intern with a pro of the romp and raze. That's how she'd learn to tangle in the sheets. At last she'd commit immortal sin.

It didn't take long for me to find the right instructor: it would be Maria Mercante, the renowned bacchanalian, with an innate talent for horizontal acts. Dark-skinned, deep-dipped Black. Possessor of savoury fillings. In this world, there are two creatures that use their rear to get ahead in life: the wild boar and Maria Mercante. I got straight to the point with that piece of tail:

—*Please, give my wife a lesson in nuptial twistings and turnings!*

—*Rest assured, sir. It's no use for a woman to be known for her qualities: she needs to have qualifications!*

And the able prostitute got to work. She held forth on irrelevant subjects—perhaps just to increase the price of these lessons. Zeitona would leave virginity behind with more regrets than the only one to have conceived without sin. Zeitona knew the math: the Virgin Mary had, in the end, turned down the visit of the Holy Spirit. She'd responded in these terms:

—*Bear a child without making love? Where's the pleasure in that? Go without food but get stuck belching anyway? I'll teach Zeitona. None of these platonics: sex at first sight.*

I interrupted her, directing the conversation to my more material woes. Advanced payment guaranteed, Maria Mercante accepted the job. I could rest assured: my wife would leave her tutelage hotter than the midday sun. We'd ruffle the sheets until the mattress begged for urgent repairs. And off Zeitona went to this place of ill repute. We might as well say it: an undressing room.

Weeks passed. The course ended, my wife came back home. She was, indeed, a changed woman. She had a different way about her but not in the way I'd expected. Man, I'm almost ashamed to admit it: all of a sudden my little Zeitona came on like a man! She, who usually sat back on her heels, was now leading the charge! That is and was: my Zeitona oozed manliness. And not just when making love. The entire time, in everything she did. Her voice, even. Everything in her had changed, bro, to the point I had to scratch my male parts just to be sure they were still there. I'm telling you: she was the one who pushed me to the bed—you better believe it. She's the one who turned me on, took my breath away. I lay there like a spectator, commanded and directed like a girl during her first time. And it's that way to this day.

The problem, bro, is this: I kinda like it. It's tough for me to admit it, so much so that I hesitate to write this. But the truth is that I'm enjoying this new position of mine, my era of passive initiate, being on the bottom, the embarrassment, the fear.

That's it, bro. Explain it to me, if you can. I don't know what to think. At first, I would make excuses: after all, there are several versions of the truth that can claim to be truthful. For example: when it comes to sex, there's no male/female. The two lovers join into a single, binary being. There was no reason to think I'd been given a lower position. You following, my brother?

But now, at the moment I write, I no longer have any appetite for explanations. Only for unreason. Every day the one thing I look forward to is nighttime, the quiet storms when I become Joãotónio and Joanantónia, man and woman, in my wife's virile arms. But for now, bro, I'm still Joãotónio. I'm saying goodbye, meanderly, to my real name.

That Devil of an Advocate

THE attorney rested his patience in the palm of his hand. Time was stretching on, the consultation had already exceeded its actual worth. He turned his head back to the woman seated in front of him. He'd stopped listening to her minutes ago. His distraction focused on the woman's legs, which she crossed and uncrossed. They had too much flesh for so little clothing. Resigned, the advocate returned to his duties as listener. The woman put forth her reasons for having left her husband.

—*My husband snores.*

—*And that's a reason? There are more people in the world snoring than sleeping.*

—*Yes, mister attorney, sir. But this husband of mine snores backwards.*

—*Snores backwards?*

—*Yeah, he only snores when he's awake.*

The attorney thought to himself: here is a woman of piss and vinegar. And he asked for more information, a firmer foundation. But his client continually wandered back to a story as useless as glasses in the hands of a blind man.

—*Now you look closely at me here, sir. You think I've gone senile? No, no—you don't have to answer that. The answer is clear as can be, it's in your eyes, mister attorney, sir. But this husband of mine is a big old soul. If you'd only seen him: towering, broad-reaching. But only from the neck up. Because on the lower levels, from the waist down . . .*

—I'm sorry, Miss. But these details . . .

—Details? It's exactly these details that result in children! You'll excuse me for saying so, sir, but you, sir, were born on account of a detail, mister attorney, sir . . . Intimacy doesn't intimidate me. We only call it trash because the smell twists our nostrils. But getting back to my husband, before the trail goes cold. If only you knew what a little Casanova he was. Night never fell, mister attorney, sir. How did he become like this? I've spent years asking myself, mister attorney, sir. You know what he says? That I don't turn him on because I spend my whole life crying. Now you tell me, is that a reason? Sure, it's true, I really do enjoy a good cry. I can't go a single day without spilling a little bit. But, for him, my former-ex-husband, this never used to be a problem. Before, he would clamber all over me, he never once slipped on my tears. It's only recently that he stopped visiting my body. And you know why? You know why he suddenly stopped? It was because he kissed me with his eyes closed. Yes, that's it, he would kiss me with his eyes shut tight. You, mister attorney, sir, you'll forgive the intrusion, but how is it that you kiss?

—How do I kiss? What sort of question . . .

—Don't tell me that you haven't been kissing, mister attorney, sir . . . Don't respond if you don't want to. But you, sir, know as well as anybody: a man can't ever kiss with his eyes closed.

—I know what it is they say about this, that you lose your way and your soul, that sort of thing . . . But I don't worry about such things. In fact, I don't close my eyes.

—And don't you ever start, mister attorney, sir. If you do, there's no way back.

The doctor of jurisprudence turned his attention back to the elegance with which the woman crossed and uncrossed her legs in her chair. The woman, all of a sudden, grew quiet. And stayed that way, on pause. Later, she scooted her chair closer to him and whispered:

—*Now, mister attorney, sir. Don't you start covering for my husband. Don't be a devil of an advocate* . . .

—*It's backward, miss.*

—*Backward? We'll see about that later. You know something, mister attorney, sir, I've been watching your eyes. Do you cry much, sir?*

—*Me? Cry?*

—*Yes, there's no shame in it. Tell me.*

And, having said this, she got up from her seat and sat on his desk. Her knees brushed up against the responsible attorney. The woman passed her fingers along his face and said:

—*I'll bet you don't know how to have a proper cry, doctor. There's a certain technique to it, you know. I'm quite an expert on the subject. I'm a graduate in sadnesses, I've done all the coursework. Suffering—what's suffering? Suffering is a road: you walk along it, forwards along its endless distance, to reach another side. This other side is a part of ourselves that we've never known. I, for example, I've already travelled far and wide within myself* . . .

The woman hopped down off the desk and made a spot for herself on the attorney's lap. The man, knowing he was in the wrong, didn't do a thing. He seemed to abandon himself to her. The woman continued her advances.

—*I'm going to give you a crash course in crying. Don't make that face. Men cry, yes, they do. They just have their own way of doing it. I'm going to teach you how to get the tears flowing.*

—*But miss, in all honesty* . . .

—*In all honesty, in all honesty. Listen up, learn something. There's no reason to be ashamed. First, do the following: gather up not that most recent and justified reason for sadness. It's not healthy to cry out each heartache one at a time. Each time we cry, we need to cry over every heartache from every life we've ever lived. We have to summon old wounds, bundle together every disappointment we've ever had. As if we were constructing a dike to stop the flow of water. Here, see what I mean? Let me rest my hand on your chest. Come on. Unbutton your shirt, mister attorney, sir. Yes, right here. This* is where all the rivers and their tributaries are going to swell until there's a flood. Suddenly, you're going to see, mister attorney, sir: everything bursts and the waters gush forth. Crying is a moment of torrid passion: when we finish, we're tired, like our bodies after making love.

The well-behaved lawman had already lain down lower than the sunset. His tie, unhoisted, danced in his client's hand. Inexplicably, one of his client's shoes rested atop the computer. The woman saw to the jurist's horizontality.

—Tell me, mister attorney, sir: would you like to cry with me now? Now, there's no reason to be afraid. And there's another, second commandment in the sobbing arts. You should never cry alone. It's very bad, it's harmful to your sadness. Crying alone invites evil spirits. If you want to shed a tear then cry together with someone else, two souls in tune.

She pulled his face towards her half-bared breasts. She herself unbuttoned her shirt even further. She felt the attorney's damp lips on her breast. But more than that, she felt his tears, abundant waters flowing forth. His tears were so large that they tingled as they ran down her body, tickling her. The two of them proceeded to follow the law that demanded that each body be a cup: turn it over and it spills across the floor. The two of them, were their lives to end at that moment, could be said to be not in an immoral but an immortal position.

And that's the scene upon which, to her great shock, the attorney's secretary opened his office door. The jurist and his client, in each other's arms, the two of them spilling tears everywhere. Why they were gushing tears as though a dam had broken, the secretary didn't understand. What astounded her most was seeing the way the doctor kissed: his eyes shut, closed tighter than the door the secretary shut to separate herself from that shocking scene.

The Deaf Father

I WRITE like God: to the point but without straight lines. Let whoever reads my words disentangle them. Only death is straightforward. Everything else has two degrees of doubt. Like me, a product of mixed lineage. My father, a Portuguese, light hair and light eyes. My mother was Black, black as coal. And so I was born with little shading in my skin but deep hues in my soul.

I speak of God with respect but without faith. As a boy, I never entered a church, not even to be baptized. That's my father's fault. Praying, he used to say, only serves to wear out pant legs. His skepticism told him that the church was an unhealthy place:

—*You barely walk inside, take two steps, and you're supposed to fall on your knees?*

At school, the priest's pointer singled me out: this must be the rain child. He never shows up at catechism and no doctrine has ever sunk in. He advised the other children to keep their distance:

—*Bad apples should be plucked from the bunch.*

They followed his advice and steered clear of me. Today I know that it wasn't out of obedience to the priest. I was alone on account of my colour. Like the word of God blotted by the rain. Yes, the teacher was right: I was a rain child.

And it's in the rain that I now look back upon my life. Each and every time, I begin with the blast that rattled my childhood. The bomb came wrapped in a book of postcards, and exploded as though tearing open the world. No blood was shed, save for mine. Scalding threads reeled down my neck. I wiped my face in search of the source. I discovered only with great effort: the blood had burst forth from my body, through my ears.

With all the commotion, no one bothered to notice me. There were cries, flames, my brothers. Days later, I complained about the buzzing: only then did they notice I'd stopped hearing. My ears were put to rest.

My mother blamed my old man. He'd been playing with fire, on account of addiction to kindness. We fled that town as if it were cursed, far beyond the world I'd known. My father feared more violence was yet to break out, wars born of the politics of those times.

Ever since, I've lost my reasons to enjoy life. The other children would play blind man's bluff. But what role could I play? Only the deaf man. In the beginning, I still could make out the shadows of sounds, the edges of sound-scratches. As I grew older, however, things became worse and, after some time, even the walls could hear better than I did. Recognizing my disability took some time. I was like a cripple convinced it's the world that's off-kilter.

—*Ah, so it's not you who's deaf? It's the entire world that's mute then?*

No one could convince me otherwise. Only the silence. I can't even describe this hollow abyss, this labyrinth of nothing. On I went, filling up with anguish, lone and lonely. And then one day, I'd come undone, at wit's end.

—*Dad: bring me a girl.*

I asked nearly voiceless. My father tried to toy around, but seeing the depth of my sadness, he took me by the hand.

—*Do you want to get married?*

I had read his lips, but acted as if I hadn't understood. He lowered his eyes, embarrassed. Did the girl I longed for exist?

—*I only want someone to listen to, Dad.*

I'd touched the man to his core. My father called local officials, appealed to tribal leaders, promised certain monies in return. For days, the search covered side roads and far-flung villages. Even today, I don't understand what guided their search, without so much as an image of this girl I longed for. Later, tired of looking, the scouts returned.

—*We found all sorts of girls. But this girl, the one he's looking for, we couldn't even catch a glimpse.*

Until one day they brought a girl of rare beauty to our house. She was, however, mute. My father turned her away, mindful of my request. Greater even than the desire to feel another's caress was my desire to hear another voice. They were about to turn the girl away when I appeared. I called to her and, in fear, she drew closer. I confessed my desire. My father tried to interrupt the entire time, aware of the girl's unimaginable voice but lacking the heart to reveal her disability. I took the visitor by the hands and asked her:

—*I only want you to tell me: where can I listen to the eagle's cry?*

The young girl whispered a secret. In reality, today I know that not a single audible word came from her mouth. But at the time, I basked in the illusion of her voice. My father looked on, caught by surprise, as my expression changed. I unbudded, deblossoming. Is it a miracle that in this world there aren't more miracles?

The girl was sent to the back room, where she was to spend the night. My heart was in such turmoil that no rest visited me. The next morning, my mother called me and, with gestures, explained herself.

—*The girl—we sent her away.*

—*Away?*

—*She's very dark, she's Blacker than black. Look at you: a mixed boy, nearly white. We can't set our family back.*

My father tried to calm things down: the girl's throat was maimed, she couldn't so much as grunt a vowel. But I'd already settled on a different fate. What did I do? I feigned I was a priest. I needed nothing more than to swipe a frock and cross. Then I hid in the forest, put the town far behind me, and reached the last bend in the horizon.

There was no place—on any map—more remote. The town was called NoWhere. I dedicated myself to rebuilding a tiny parish that already existed. In any event, there'd been another priest there before me, a man of generosity, who'd filled his pews with multitudes. An extra coincidence: like me, he too had been deaf. The result being that the people there believed deafness to be a prerequisite for the office of country priest. Now, thinking back on what I did, even I must admit: the Devil must be equipped with a terrible memory. There are so many things he can't remember.

In passing myself off as a man of the cloth, I'd discovered a way to live off the kindness of others. They looked after me, furnished the necessities. The poor folks—I made up prayers they found difficult to recite. Because with each recitation, I changed the words. Yet not even this caused the bewildered believers to waver in their convictions. Who knows, maybe it was my dedication to everything that, before, I'd never known. Nursing? I did that. Teaching? I gave it a try. Offering advice? I gave that a shot, too. In the end, in everything I did, I embodied kindness. Who knows if, as a result of having performed all these jobs, I filled the pews. On infallible Sundays, people poured in from the countryside to confess their sins. They themselves were serious. Only I stole the sacred stage. I'd sit in the confessional, dark as a turtle's belly. One by one, the faithful knelt outside the confessional and, at the top of their lungs, confessed their sins. In so doing, they knew what was in each other's hearts. That's how my predecessor had done things, and so it continued with me.

Yesterday, it rained so hard that the surrounding huts shook, threatening to collapse. The people came, seeking refuge in the church. At no other Mass had I ever seen so many. And then, from among the drenched villagers, I spotted a young woman, the very same girl my father had sent for to console me. Time had etched her face, her body. Each stroke to beauty's benefit. She concentrated on me with those same eyes that had turned me to a fool on my childhood porch. Then she went off in search of the heat of the fireplace. I thought I saw her talking to the others, coming to some agreement, exchanging words. I called the sexton over and gave him orders:

—*That woman over there. Go and see if she can speak.*

My assistant understood nothing at first. Off he went, getting closer and closer to her. He made a sign confirming that yes indeed, the woman plainly spoke. I was struck, a match lit in a volcano. My entire life came before me, in broken pieces, as if a bomb were shattering my memory. I climbed the altar, signalled for the dozens there assembled to quiet down. I know how to spot silence, I can read its arrival. I detect it in people's eyes. I knew, at that moment: only the rain could be heard, *tim-tim-ba-tinning* on the roof of the tiny church. Then I told them what I'm committing to paper now, the tenor of my dishonesty, my fake vestures, my apocryphal prayers. I confessed aloud, as they had done before me. I removed my frock, said my goodbyes, and left, making my way past unbelieving eyes.

Outside, as I'd surmised, the rain came down. My head spun, I hadn't realized how hard it was raining. Did the heavens threaten a flood? I took a few drunkard's steps, seeking the ground beneath the pools of water. Is it the blind man who never falters? A hand grabbed hold of me and turned me around. It was a young woman, that young woman. When she spoke, I lost my bearings completely. Will you believe me, now knowing of my treachery? Who do I swear to if I've lost even my ties to God? In other words, go ahead and doubt. But I heard her voice, indeed, I heard her without reading her lips. I listened to the woman's gentle voice, her words wrapping me in my own alarm.

—*Stay—please stay . . . dear Father!*

Square of the Gods

To Che Amur, whose version of these events served as the basis for this story.

1926: That was the year that marked the occasion. That's the year the personal story unfolded of the merchant Mohamed Pangi Patel, a powerful man who disbursed life and wealth on the Island of Mozambique. Accordingly, the years passed and Mohamed Pangi gave thanks to God for the beauty of the world and its marvels.

The Ismaelite grew rich off his own name, full of good cheer. His contentment only grew the day his only son came to tell him he'd decided to marry.

—You know something, son? Life is a sweet perfume.

Preparations for a wedding began. Such a celebration would never again be seen in such localities. Musicians came from Zanzibar, guests from Mombasa, peoples from Ibo and Angoche. The celebration lasted some thirty days. On every one of these days, the town square was covered with endless tables, boasting many a full spread. Day and night, foods of every variety and number could be found. The entire island turned up to help themselves by the belchful. In those days, not one of the poor felt the pang of hunger. And not a single family set foot in the kitchen: breakfast, lunch, and dinner passed the day in the town square. While the many mouths opened wide to make way for such delights, Pangi stretched out over a bench, wise to the warm weather. His only occupation was to perspire as he basked in the joy of watching so many jaws at work.

—*But Father, isn't this a bit much?*

Pangi's son began to worry about the mounting expenses. But Pangi responded with caution:

—*Better not a single bird in hand. Better to see great flocks spread their wings over the land. The heavens, after all, only came to be after the first bird's flight. And he smiled:*

—*Don't forget, son: life is a sweet perfume.*

And the old man began to explain:

—*We all carry this fragrance in our natural and congenital bodies. The fragrance, at first, bursts forth in all directions, strong, contagious. If anyone were to have smelled the world's first moment, they would have detected only their own perfume. But later, this fragrance thins. And then, in order to still sense it, people have to give their nostrils a workout: a headache for the nose. And that's how, from that point forward, with the smallest reminder of a shudder, even the surface of memories begins to evaporate . . .*

—*Father: how will we pay for all this?*

The question was an appropriate one. It wasn't long before the creditors arrived and Pangi's houses were foreclosed upon. Later, the goods from his stores were sold at public auction. Pangi's endless properties grew ever more scarce. Once a rich man, he was demoted to a de-minted man, suit pockets full of sand. All of this, though, took place out of sight. No one beyond the dispossessed Pangi knew of this settling of accounts. Silent as a dagger, the Ismaelite went on sitting on his bench, in a state of pure fascination, as he gazed upon the endless celebration.

Tired of calling attention to the situation, the groom resolved to leave the island. That night, he gave his aging father an ultimatum: either the festivities came to an end or he'd turn his back on his old man forever. The old man smiled, astonishful, firmer than the firmament. He pointed to nothing at all, singled out among the square-dwellers a nothing-nobody. And then he spoke:

—*Listen to this song. I like this song so much it hurts me each time I listen to it.*

With gale-force rage, Pangi's son burst away with a mind to luggage, ships, and one-way trips. His bride held back, seated on the selfsame bench as Pangi. The young woman soaked in charm, eyes fixed on her father-in-law. She adjusted her wedding garments and stepped closer to the patriarch in the sunset of his life. She took hold of his hand and opened her big eyes wide:

—*Father: would you dance this song with me?*

The old man stood up without a word and allowed the bride to lead him to the middle of the square. There, the two danced together, on a floor of a thousand tiny lights, silver insects stirring up the dark. As he twirled round and round, the old man took in the scent of the jacarandas. Jealousy is what he felt, for the eternity of the trees' perfume.

—*Tell me, my girl: do I still have my perfume?*

She smiled without responding. Instead, she took him by the arm and brought him back to the dance. As they rocked back and forth, Mohamed Pangi whispered an apology. Didn't she know? All of this wasn't for them, the naive newlyweds, and their benefit. In the end, the quantity had been expended to celebrate other happenings. All through these days, the island put poverty behind it, not a single mother stood measuring her child's cries, the men drank not to forget but to taste the sweet sap of the waters of time.

—*God must have loved to see a world like this. I'm offering this square up to Him, do you understand me?*

And he took leave of the bride with a kiss on her forehead.

—*You have the scent of fruitfulness, my girl—only the earth's aroma is as sweet.*

—*Tomorrow, in the wee hours, early in the morning, the festivities come to an end. Tell my son.*

—*Father, why don't you make your way home?*

What home? The square was his home now. He would live in the very square he'd offered to the gods. The bride shook her handkerchief—farewell—through the air.

The next morning, dawn broke on the town square without any celebration. The banquet tables had disappeared, the band had left, dance shoes and dust surrendered to repose. All that remained was absence in disarray, mere memory of cheer and melodies. Alone on a park bench, Mohamed Pangi Patel remained motionless in an unexpected pose, with a strange smile. Was it God who smiled through his lips? Had his life been written off, a sort of last lien against his debts?

The bride was the first to reach his side. She knelt down next to the body and plucked from his hair the many distracted petals that had fallen from the towering trees. But later, as they carried his body, she went back to gathering handfuls of the fragrant petals and returning them to her father-in-law. Mohamed Pangi Patel departed the square and its jacarandas dusted with eternal life.

Sea Loves Me

AND OTHER STORIES

Translated by David Brookshaw

The following stories have not been published previously in English.

The Tearful
Cook's Journey

ANTUNES Correia-Correia was a sergeant in the colonial
army in a time of war. If the name was doubly diffuse, the
man was singly diffused into two separate halves. He had stepped
on treacherous ground and shot up high into the air, to those
places where one leaves one's soul and brings back eternity.
Correia neither left nor brought anything back, incompetent even
when it came to dying. The mine that had exploded was for him
alone. But he, fat as he was, so well endowed with girth, would
have required two explosions.

—*Half of me is dead. I was only visited by half a death.*

He had only lost his life in one eye, one side of his face
defaced. This eye was like a kind of dead fish in the aquarium of
his visage. But the sergeant was so lethargic, so lacking in energy,
that people couldn't work out whether all of him was made of
glass or it was just his eye. He spoke with the impulse of only half
his mouth. He avoided conversation, so painful was it to listen
to him. He never shook anyone by the hand in order not to feel
his own emptiness. He stopped going out, obsessed with visiting
the antechamber of his own tomb in the darkness of his home.
Correia had lost interest in life: to be or not to be was neither

here nor there to him. Women walked past without any reaction from him whatsoever. All he could do was to repeat the litany: *half of me is dead.*

Now, alone and retired, wounded in war and incapacitated in peace, Antunes Correia-Correia took stock of his recollections. And the energy of his memory was a source of admiration. Even shorn of his other hemisphere, not a moment escaped him in his hunt for the past. *It's either one thing or the other: either my life was immense or it all took refuge in the right-hand side of my head.* For his memories to come to the surface, he would tilt his head to one side.

—*Like this, they can slide straight out of my heart,* he said.

Felizminha was the sergeant's Black maid. She had worked for him ever since he had arrived at the military quarters. Amid the steam of the kitchen, Felizminha would busy her eyes. She was always late in wiping her tears away, by which time a teardrop had fallen into the saucepan. It was as sure as night follows day: a tear was invariably one of the food's ingredients. So much so that the cook didn't even use seasoning or salt. The sergeant would taste his food and ask himself how she had managed to produce such refined flavours.

—*The food's seasoned with sadness.*

That was Felizminha's inevitable answer. The maid would sigh:

—*Oh, if only I were someone else, someone.* She was sparing with her merriment, as there was so little of it.

—*I want to save up my contentment so as to spend it later, when I'm a bit older.*

She lived shrouded in shadow, smoke, and vapours. She was so steamed up on the inside that she couldn't even make out what was happening in her soul. Her hand felt its way along the kitchen dresser. Her little space was dark, containing as it did irregular patches of penumbra. A kitchen is where the whole house is made.

One night, the boss stepped into the kitchen, shuffling heavily. He came face to face with the darkness.

—*Don't you want more light in this goddamn kitchen?*

—*No, I like it like this.*

The sergeant looked at her. The tubby Felizminha stirred the soup, tasted a spoonful, adjusted the salt in her tears. Fate didn't hold any more for her: merely this encounter between two half-lives. Correia-Correia knew how much he owed this woman who served him. Straight after the accident, no one understood the slurred thickness of his speech. A mother's attention was needed to lend support to that dishevelled white, that remnant of a person. The sergeant would blabber and whimper some sounds and she understood what he wanted. Little by little, the utterings of the Portuguese improved and became more like those of a person. Now, he looked at her as if he were still convalescing. The rustling of her *capulana* mollified old nightmares, her voice calmed the frightful incandescence emerging from the mouth of fire. It is a miracle one can find fellow feeling in times of frenzy and war.

—*You're thin, are you tightening your flesh?*

—*Thin?*

That would be a fine thing! What about a tortoise? Has anyone ever seen a thin one? Its eyes alone make it fat, bulging with goodness. The tubby Felizminha groaned so much when she bent down it was as if the ground were further away than her feet.

—*Tell me one thing, Felizminha: why all this weeping every day?*

—*I only cry so as to give my dishes more flavour.*

—*I've got good reason to be sad, but you . . .*

—*Where I come from, I just remember the coconut trees; the rustling of their leaves makes you think you're right down next to the sea. That's all, boss.*

The tubby Black woman spoke as she twisted the lid of her rusty old snuff tin. Her boss put his hand in his pocket and took out a new box. But she declined his offer.

—*I like old things, things that are rotting away.*

—*But you're always so sad, old girl. Do you want more money?*

—*Money, boss, is like a blade . . . it cuts both ways. When we count out the notes, our soul is torn open. What do people pay for with money? Life isn't just charging us for paper, but for our very selves. When a note leaves our hand, we've already said goodbye to life. You, sir, find solace in your memories. My sadness helps me to rest.*

Then the fat cook surprised her boss. She came straight out with it:

—*I've got an idea to help you salvage the rest of your time in this world.*

—*All I have is half a life, Felizminha.*

—*Life doesn't have halves. It's always one whole one . . .*

Then she elaborated on her idea: the Portuguese should invite a lady, one of those women used as escorts. The sergeant still had a body to match his age. There were even whores, cheap ones, women who were completely disposable.

—*But they are Black girls, and when it comes to Black girls . . .*

—*Get yourself a white one, there are also some of those you can buy. I'm telling you, boss. You came into this life thanks to a woman. Get yourself another woman to come back into life again.*

Correia-Correia gave one of his half smiles as he thought about it for a minute.

One day, the soldier left the house and spent the whole afternoon out. He arrived home in high spirits and headed for the kitchen. There, he declared grandly:

—*Felizminha, tonight, set another place at table.*

Felizminha's soul lit up. She took great care to tidy the living room, and placed a chair on the sergeant's right so that she could get the best possible view of the guest. In the kitchen, she perfected the tear with which she was going to season the meal.

But then nobody came. The place at table remained empty. On that and all subsequent occasions. There was only one change to the scene she had prepared: the chair reserved for the unadventful guest switched from the right- to the left-hand side, that side on which the world didn't exist for the sergeant.

Felizminha began to have her doubts: these women her boss was inviting, did they really and truly exist?

Until one night, the sergeant called the cook and asked her to sit down in the place reserved for his missing guests. Felizminha hesitated. Then, ever so slowly, she arranged herself on the chair.

—*I've decided to leave.*

Felizminha said nothing. She waited for whatever else needed to be said.

—*And I want you to come with me.*

—*Me, boss? I'm not leaving my shadow.*

—*Come and see the world.*

—*But what would I do over there, in that country . . .*

—*No one will do you any harm, I promise.*

From that point on, she began to prepare for the journey. Was she excited by the idea of seeing other places? Terrified at the idea of living in some unknown place, the place where whites live? The cook didn't bare her soul either by word or facial expression. The sergeant tasted her food and found no change in it. Always the right amount of salt, ever the same subtle flavour. On the appointed day, the soldier barged his way into the kitchen.

—*Come and pack your cases.*

They left the house, Felizminha, her head bowed, for all the neighbours to see. Then, in front of the onlookers, the sergeant took her hand. Their fingers hardly fitted each other's so plump were they, hiding themselves like shy toads.

—*Let's go,* he said.

She looked up into the sky, fearing that she would soon be up there in some celestial airplane, crossing worlds and oceans. She climbed into the old car, but to her amazement, Correia didn't take the road to the airport. He drove down lanes, round bends and along sandy tracks. Then he stopped and asked:

—*Where's that place with all the coconut trees?*

The Daughter
of Solitude

I n life, everything happens suddenly. The rest, that which
emerges peacefully, is what has already occurred without our
being aware. Some people let things happen without fear. These
are the living. Others put things off. These latter are lucky if they
come back to life in time before they die.

Girlie was the daughter of a Portuguese couple who ran a store,
and was always a level-headed girl. In the dim light of the shop,
she would serve Blacks as if they were the shadows of other, real
live people. The young girl's body was developing—the fruit
was growing ripe and its pulp was sweet. Thirst was invented for
imagining water. But in the vicinity of the shop, there were no
resident white men, the only kind she would share her syrupy
sweetness with.

The Pacheco family had been pioneers in the arid region of
Shiperapera, where even the original Blacks were scarce. Why had
they chosen such remote lands?

—*Here, beyond those high mountains, not even God can keep an eye on
me* . . .

These were the words of the Portuguese designed to discourage questions. No one understood why Pacheco had penetrated

so far into the desert dunes of Sofala, condemning his family to a life removed from folk of their own race. Dona Esmeralda, his wife, grew anxious as she watched her daughter grow. What man would she end up with, so far from human beings similar to herself? They gave her the name of Girlie in order to anchor her in time. But their daughter was following the path of the inevitable. In the immutable shadow of the shop counter, she would leaf through her well-thumbed photo comic. She dreamed of what lay in the comic strips . . .

—*Don't expect any comfort, girl: round here, all we've got is a bunch of Blacks.*

The young girl sought solace shut away in her room, between the sheets along with her magazine. Her hands shed their inhibitions in another's caresses. But this dousing of the flame brought her another, more acute torment. When, after sighs and perspiration, she lay back in her bed, a deep sadness descended upon her. It was as if a dead soul were being born within her. Similar sadness only befalls those mothers delivered of a stillbirth. Is it fair that we are able to visit such paradises and then be expelled from them? She found such farewells so hard to take that she started to avoid her own body. It was worthy of an exchange of fondles, receiving the saliva from someone else's belly. But around there, there wasn't anyone else for Miss Girlie.

—*Do you think that daughter of ours is going to get mixed up with a Black man?*

Her father snorted with laughter. There was a reason for his laugh: the Pacheco household was a nest of prejudice. They spoke of "the Black" in the singular. The others, those of another colour, were reduced to a word, uttered between the maxilla of fear and the mandible of scorn. Girlie fulfilled the teachings of her race. She would greet the customers without even looking up:

—*What d'you want?*

Massoco, their only employee, found the little boss lady's disdainful ways funny. He was young like her and carried sacks and crates, and drove their cart from the shop to beyond the horizon.

Girlie's fits of melancholia got worse. The pages of the magazine were falling apart from so much defoliation. On the day Girlie turned eighteen, she set herself on fire. She committed an act of self-immolation. But it wasn't one of those normal fires of conspicuous combustion. She burned in invisible flames, and only she suffered such fervours. She burned long and slow. Her fever opened the door to her delirium.

Her mother came and fanned her to provide a little fresh air. Her father came and administered some advice followed straightaway by threats. Nothing worked. The only way to douse her fire was with a male body, bathed in a double portion of sweat and caresses. Her mother tried to dampen any illusion of expectation:

—*My daughter, don't allow your body to be born before your heart.*

In her sickness, the girl stopped working behind the counter. She was replaced by the boy, Massoco, and the shop became a friendlier place. Girlie took to her room, emigrated from life, exiled from others. At the end of the day, Massoco presented himself, in solemn sadness. He even asked:

—*May I go and see the little boss lady?*

One day, a vet from the Ministry arrived at Shiperapera. She had come to inspect the cattle belonging to the natives. When the Pachecos heard the news, they decided to conceal their daughter's condition. She was in such a changed state! Pacheco went out onto the road to wait for his compatriot. He took with him his best manners and some dried fish cakes. He accompanied the vet to the guest house built by the administration in times gone by. When they had gone to bed, the Pachecos exchanged snide remarks.

—*Goddammit! That dame looks like a man!*

And they laughed. Dona Esmeralda was happy that their visitor had so little womanliness about her. In case her husband got sidetracked. One night, Girlie suffered a particularly severe attack. In despair, the Pachecos decided to summon the vet. Pacheco himself rushed to the guest house and begged the vet to come. On the way, he explained his daughter's condition.

Upon arriving at the store, they made for the troubled girl's quarters, maintaining a professional silence. In her fever, the girl took the vet for a man. She threw her arms around her, kissing her ardently on the lips. In their embarrassment, her parents rushed to separate them. The vet regained her composure, brushing imaginary hairs away from her cheek. Girlie, with a dreamy smile, now seemed to have fallen asleep.

Pacheco accompanied the visitor back to her lodgings once more. They walked the whole way without exchanging a word. As they said good night, the vet broke her silence and put forward her plan:

—*I'll play the man's role. I'll disguise myself.*

Pacheco didn't know what to say. The vet explained: the shopkeeper would lend her some old clothes and she would appear, in disguise, like a boyfriend fallen from the heavens. The Portuguese nodded vacantly and hurried home to tell his wife about the strange plan. Dona Esmeralda pursed her lips doubtfully. But so be it! It was for the good of their little girl. Then she crossed herself.

On the following nights, the vet would appear in her disguise. She would go up to Girlie's room and linger there. Downstairs, Dona Esmeralda would sit weeping silently. Pacheco would drink listlessly. After a few hours, the vet would come down, tidying a non-existent lock of hair from her face.

For whatever reason, the truth is that Girlie began to perk up. Some days later, the vet withdrew, a cloud on the road where even the dust was sparse. The following morning, Girlie came down to the shop, carrying her old magazine. She took her seat behind the counter and asked the shadow on the other side:

—*What d'you want?*

Massoco laughed, shaking his head. And life resumed, like a ball of wool looking for its end. Until one day, Dona Esmeralda shook her husband awake.

—*Our daughter's pregnant, Manuel!*

Insults, improprieties rained down. Windowpanes shattered, such was Pacheco's fury:

—*I'll kill that bastard of a doctor!*

His wife implored him: surely now this was reason enough for a visit to town. Her husband should break his promise and cross the mountains back into the world. At night, the couple set off on their journey, leaving their daughter a whole list of instructions on how to look after herself and other precautionary measures. Then they disappeared into the darkness.

From the window, Girlie peeped out at the moonlit cloud of dust on the road. Then she went up to her room, and opened her old magazine. Overcome by sleepiness, she settled down under the bunched sheets on her mattress. Before falling asleep, she squeezed the black hand that stood out against the white of the bed linen.

The Widower

A SHUDDER shows us how alike are a fever and cold. And it's with a shudder that I recall the Goan, Jesuzinho da Graça, born but unraised in Goa, still in Portuguese times. He came with his family to Mozambique, still in mid-boyhood. Just as happened to other Goans, he was branded a *caneco*.* As for him, he termed himself Indo-Portuguese. A practising son of Lusitania, he worked as head of funeral services at the town hall up until Independence. His was a gloomy office: life spared itself the trouble of paying it a visit. Was the Goan the ante-chamberlain of Death? He only allowed himself one moment of light-heartedness. As he left the office, the functionary would turn to his colleagues and invariably repeat the words:

—*Ram-ram!*

—*All this ram-rammery'll kill him*, his colleagues commented. And they shook their heads in disapproval: the caneco can't make up his mind what he wants to say. Jesuzinho Graça laughed at their incomprehension. "*Ram-ram*" was goodbye in Konkani, the language of his Indian ancestors.

---

* A derogatory Mozambican term for a Goan.

He lived in this constant state of self-effacement, as discreet as a creeper's embrace. For him, merely existing was an act of overbearing unseemliness. The *caneco* moistened his finger in time and turned the pages methodically and noiselessly. The nail on his little finger had grown so long that his finger was now a mere accessory.

—*The nail? That's for turning the papers,* was his answer.

That nail was the mouse of our present-day computers. The said appendage was a cause for conjugal irritation. His wife would warn him:

—*With that claw, don't even think of giving me a cuddle!*

Jesuzinho da Graça resisted all these protests:

—*If it weren't for its nail, a lizard would die!*

In all other things, he was as plain and brown as a fiscal stamp. Stolidly unsociable and solidly unemotional, too shy even to say excuse me, Jesuzinho witnessed the turbulence of history with a shrunken heart. Independence hove into view, the nation's flag was hoisted to the joy of many and to the *caneco's* fears. Terrified, he sat in the workers' rallies where they proclaimed the operation to "dismantle the State." He asked himself—does justice lie in the hands of the unjust? Unruffled and aloof, Jesuzinho attended to his demotion, his change of office. Yet his serenity was only superficial. Inside, he was alarmed by the sudden statements, understatements and overstatements issued by the Revolution.

From the silence of his office he could hear the world's crockery being smashed. He got home, and the same upheavals pursued him. He still managed the flicker of a smile when the speeches proclaimed *Victory is certain!* He would tap his wife on the shoulder and say:

—*See the extent of your certainty, my dear Victoria?*

If Jesuzinho was a shadow, his spouse, Victoria, was that shadow's dusk. On the third anniversary of Independence, at the precise moment when they were declaiming their revolutionary jargon, Victoria became certain forever. The light in the Goan lady's eyes extinguished. By the wall where the crucifix hung, he covered her with a sheet and smothered her with prayers. His one and only family had come to an end right there, Jesuzinho da Graça's only world.

In the months that followed, the widower's behaviour remained steady. Was Jesuzinho like the ant that never strays from its path? There was only one difference: he took longer to get from here to there. And as his solitude lingered, he began to give in to drink. His young house boy asked him apprehensively:

—*Do you not have any relatives?*

Jesuzinho pointed to the bottle of liquor. That was his relative from his father's side. Then he remembered and pointed to the crucifix on the wall:

—*That one there, on the wall, is on my mother's side.*

Life is as improbable as a drop dripping upwards. Little by little, the Goan began to show signs of disorganization: the hours escaped him. From being the most zealous of functionaries, ever observant of the regulations, he stopped padding his inky scripts with his blotter. Maybe he yearned for a time when the world was a gentler place, authenticated on a sheet of white paper?

But even in his discomposure he stuck to some routine. Tuesdays were when he got drunk, the only date he kept with time. He would go to the bar, and gradually drown his sorrows in the froth of his glass. He would arrive back home late, dishevelled but always taking great care with his white suit. He would sit on his settee and light a cigarette—what would his dear departed wife say?—and pull the tall ashtray towards him, his hands lingering on its smooth round ebony. Was he plaiting Victoria's hair? Then he would snap his fingers and call:

—*Piccaninny: come and loosen my tie, if you please.*

The house boy rushed forwards to relieve his throat. He unbuttoned his shirt and sprinkled some talc around the top of his singlet. With his knot undone, he was already in the mood for sleep. The boy's job was to supervise his boss's repose.

His slumber was punctuated with fits. After only a few minutes, the caneco was shouting for his late wife. His hand shaking, he would grab the phone and call the heavens. This was when Piccaninny's noblest function would come into play: he would play her part, imitate the dead woman's voice and sighs.

—*You must be paying for the call if you please, my dear Victoria. Up there in the sky, evereet'ing is being cheaper.*

His young employee tried to make his voice sound shrill, copying Victoria's screeching. When the conversation was over, he copied the old lady's ways, applying brilliantine to his boss's hair and making sure his parting was diagonal, just as it should be.

However, as time went by, the boy became terrified. He would ask himself: should I imitate the dead? Playing around with the spirits could only bring punishment. He went and consulted his father for advice. The old man agreed: leave the man, run away from all that. And he elaborated on his wise thoughts: how many sides has the earth got for a chameleon? As for the dead, do we know who they've got their eyes on? The other world is infinitesimally infinite: there isn't a dead person who isn't a member of our family.

So the lad returned, determined never again to get mixed up with apparitions. Come Tuesday, and the boss didn't go out bar crawling that night. He looked depressed, unwell. He lay on the sofa in the living room, gazing into nothingness. He called the lad and asked him to dress up as Victoria. The boy didn't answer. Surprised, Jesuzinho started to mutter to himself. A few moments passed, until the young servant noticed that the boss was weeping. He leaned over him and saw that he was whining the same name he always did:

—*My sweet little Victoria!*

The servant didn't budge an inch. The boss could beg as much as he wanted, he wasn't moving. The *caneco*, after all, was drunk.

His breath left no room for doubt. But how come, if he hadn't seen him drinking? Whether he'd been at the bottle or not, he was certainly overflowing with sighs and spittle. It was in the middle of his ranting and raving that he murmured the strangest words: he wanted to go and meet his wife with his nails duly clipped. Laying his arm across his servant's lap, he implored him:

—*Cut my nail, if you please, Piccaninny!*

The following day, they found the servant, motionless, next to the boss's seat. No one could believe what the boy said. It was like this: hardly had he begun to clip his nail than the boss vanished, like incense smoke.

—*So where's the nail, lad?*

The boy bent down over the floor and lifted what looked like a faded petal. He smiled as he recalled his boss. And he showed them the very last trace of his boss's human existence.

A Girl Without Words

(a second story for Rita)

THE little girl didn't say a word. Not a single vowel left her mouth, her lips only concerned themselves with sounds that didn't even add up to two or four. Was her language hers alone, a personal dialect of unrelayable and unreliable quality? No matter how much they applied themselves, the parents couldn't coax any understanding from their little daughter. When she remembered the words, she forgot the thought. When she constructed an argument, she lost her power of language. It wasn't because she was mute. She spoke in a language that doesn't currently exist among human beings. There were those who thought she sang. It must be said that she had an enchantingly beautiful voice. Even without understanding anything, people were gripped by her intonation. And it was so touching that some folk never failed to cry.

He father dedicated his affection and his affliction to her. One night, he took her little hands in his and begged, certain that he was talking to himself:

—*Speak to me, daughter!*

His eyes started to leak. The little girl kissed his tear. She savoured that salty water and said:

—*Sea* . . .

Her father was flabbergasted, both aurally and orally. Had she spoken? He leaped up and shook his daughter's shoulders.

—*You see, you can speak, she can speak, she can speak!* he shouted for all to hear.

—*She said sea! She said sea!* her father repeated from room to room.

The family rushed forwards and leaned over her. But she emitted no further comprehensible sound.

Her father didn't give up. He thought and thought and came up with a plan. He took his daughter to where she could see the sea, and where there was even sea beyond the sea. If that had been the only word she had ever articulated in her life, then it was the sea that would reveal the reason for her inability.

The little girl reached that expanse of blue and her heart shrank. She sat down on the sand, her knees interfering with the vista. And tears interfering with her knees. Was the world that she had wanted infinite, after all so small? There she remained, imitating a stone, with neither sound nor tone. Her father asked her to come back, they needed to return, for the tide was coming in menacingly.

—*Come on, daughter!*

But the girl was so still you would never have known she was sitting there. She was like an eagle that neither rises nor falls: it merely disappears from the ground. All the land is contained in the eye of an eagle. And the bird's retina is transformed into the vastest sky. The girl's father stood in awe, bedazzled: why does my daughter remind me of an eagle?

—*Let's go, daughter! Otherwise the waves will swallow us up.*

Her father circled her, blaming himself for the girl's state. He danced, sang, leaped up and down. Anything to distract her. Then he decided to take direct action: putting his hands under her armpits, he pulled her. But he'd never felt such a weight before. Had the girl put down roots or become the tip of a rock?

He gave up, exhausted, and sat down next to her. Does he who knows stop talking while he who doesn't know keeps quiet? The sea filled the night with silence, the waves already seemed to be breaking on the man's shocked heart. At that point, he had an idea: the only way of saving his daughter was to tell her a story! And so, there and then he made one up:

Once upon a time, there was a little girl who asked her father to go and get the moon for her. Her father got in his boat and rowed out far away. When he reached the line of the horizon, he stood on the tips of his dreams in order to reach the sky. Very carefully, he took hold of the star with both hands. The planet was as light as a ball of air.

When he gave that fruit a tug in order to pluck it from the sky, he heard a world-shattering pop. The moon sparked into a thousand shooting stars. The sea grew choppy and the boat sank, swallowed up into the abyss. The beach was bathed in silver, the strand covered in flakes of moonlight. The little girl started walking in the opposite of all directions, over there and beyond, gathering up those lunar shards. She looked at the horizon and called:

—*Father!*

Then a deep crevasse opened, a wound from the very birth of the world. From the lips of this scar, blood flowed. Was the water bleeding? Or was the blood turning to water? And that's what happened. Once upon a time.

At this point, her father lost his voice and he was silent. The story had lost its thread inside his head. Or was it the chill of the waters now covering his feet and his daughter's legs? At that instant, he cried in despair:

—*It's now or never.*

The girl suddenly got to her feet and walked into the waves. Her father followed, anxious. He saw his daughter pointing at the sea. Then he caught sight of a deep crack stretching the entire width of the ocean. Her father was alarmed at the unexpected fracture, a grotesque mirror of the story he had just invented. Fear struck him in the pit of the stomach. Were they both going to get washed into that abyss?

—*Daughter, come back. Please turn back, daughter . . .*

Instead of retreating, the girl waded further into the sea. Then she stopped and brushed her hand over the water. The liquid wound immediately closed. And the sea merged together and became one again. The girl turned and walked back, taking her father's hand and leading him back home. Up above, the moon recomposed itself.

—*See, Father? I finished your story!*

And the two of them, bathed in moonlight, disappeared into the room which they had never left.

The Very Last Eclipse

DOUBT gnawed at Justinho Salomão, willy-nilly, like a rat. The man was suffering for being a husband, weighed down by the icy shadows of suspicion. His wife, Dona Acera, was pretty enough to make your mouth water with night dreams. Devoured by jealousy, Justino was growing thin by leaps and bounds. Pitiably skinny and wasted away, he had to do a thorough search of the mirror just to catch a glimpse of himself. Justinho was so thin, it was he who scratched the fleas. One day, the priest warned him as he was leaving Mass:

—*Be very careful, Justinho: your soul is like a puff of smoke that won't fit anywhere.*

To hell with that priest who wouldn't talk straight. What the cleric knew was uncommon knowledge: Acera was too much of a woman to be a spouse. Justinho's doubts were raised more by argument than fact. Could it be that his wife was more unfaithful than a secret? The answer was a shadow with neither light nor object. On the eve of a journey, her husband's suspicions became more acute. On this occasion, a long series of visits necessitated his geographical absence. Acera was sad when he told her the news:

—*How long are you going to leave me all on my own?*

A month. The woman twisted her lipstick, shook her locks. Even a tear crocodiled itself onto her eyelid. Faced by such disconsolation, her husband became even more worried. Was it genuine or was it a convenient pretense? Who so young, so wet behind the ears, is capable of keeping themselves faithful?

On the eve of his departure, her husband decided to ensure her guaranteed loyalty. First, he went to the Church and asked the Portuguese priest for help. The man of the cloth twisted his hands reticently and, as was his habit, offered some cut-price philosophy:

—*Well, I don't know. To cross legs it takes two . . .*

—*Two what?*

—*Two legs, of course.*

And on he went, like water flowing down liquid paths. Justinho was expecting the cleric to put him at ease. To tell him, for example: go in peace, you're well married, with more rings than Saturn. But no, the priest rippled his brow with suppositions.

—*No, I don't know. Isn't the one who peeps most the sun itself?*

—*Explain yourself better, reverend Father.*

—*Do you want me to make myself even clearer? Answer me then: isn't the most unsullied ground in the house of the dead?*

Justinho didn't answer. He turned his back and left the church. He was still walking away when the priest's irate voice reached his ears.

—*I know where you're going, fellow. You're going to see the witch doctor! But you'll see what my powers, indeed my divine powers, are going to do to that tropical wizard!*

A shudder ran through Justinho. But he didn't slacken his pace as he headed for the witch doctor's, and he prayed that he would put his mind at rest. Was it heresy to knock on both sides of the door? If a man has more than one divine father, can't he have more than one belief?

—*I can't do anything about that. A woman's will is beyond my powers. What I can do is arrange for the abusers to be punished.*

—*How?*

—*I shall have to protect your house.*

And so the treatment was carried out: a small gourd at the entrance to his tin and timber abode. Anyone entering with disrespectful intentions would suffer serious consequences. The husband felt some concern:

—*Are they . . . are they going to die?*

The witch doctor laughed. Any guilty intruder would have his insides afflicted by bloating and wind. After his work had been carried out and the bill settled, the witch doctor hesitated for a moment as he took his leave:

—*Did you consult the reverend Father before me? And what did he say about me?*

Justinho shrugged, as if it were a matter that lay beyond his competence. The witch doctor turned his back and walked away, commenting as he went:

—*That priest is going to cry like a chicken, you'll see. Do you know the story of the chicken that ate the string of beads just so as to stop the other chicken wearing it?*

A few days later, and off went Justinho. The journey lasted longer than he intended. When he returned, his wife was waiting for him at the front door. She wore the dress he liked, her hairstyle was eye-catching, her body at her husband's disposal. Even her top button was out of a job, lying unused on her cleavage. Acera was completely at the whim of Justinho's yearning. They plunged into each other, their legs tangling with their sighs in a confusion of lips and sweat, lives and bodies.

Having taken his fill of his long-unfulfilled love, Justinho stretched out in bed, satisfied. He closed his eyes, like a breast-fed babe. Then he looked up and was astonished by what he saw: two men were floating up under the roof. They were rotund, inflated like balloons.

—*What's that, woman?*

—*What's what?*

He jumped out of bed in a flash and was even more astonished when he recognized the two unfortunates. And who were they? The priest and the witch doctor. Those selfsame men to whom Justinho had entrusted his wife's protection. There they were, pinned to the roof.

—*You? You, of all people?*

—*Hey, husband! Who're you talking to?*

Stuttering and blustering, her husband pointed to the ceiling. His wife thought he was having a religious fit, with his sights set on getting near to Heaven. Was Justinho going insane, epilectricuted?

Acera tried to run after her crazed husband. But the man had smelled a rat, and vanished into the darkness. He wasn't long: he came back with witnesses. He ushered a number of them into the bedroom and pointed at the perpetrators of the flagrancy. The others stood there, dumbfounded, without seeing anything at all. Only Justinho was able to see his wife's flying lovers. But they explained that it couldn't be the priest and the witch doctor there. They had been away in the city on a short visit. Everyone had seen them leave, everyone had waved them off on the bus.

The neighbours assured him of his wife's good behaviour. They took their leave, saying they would watch out for him, given the returning traveller's illness. It was even bad luck to have such a madman in the place. Even the retired nurse brought him some pills to cool his blood. Justinho agreed to lie down and take things easy. He would get his head together and adjust his thoughts to the here and now.

And they were all so insistent that he stopped seeing folk hanging from the roof. Gradually, he was freed from the visions that had made him so jealous. There were nights, however, when he would waken with a jolt and get up. He could hear laughter. Were the priest and witch doctor having fun at his expense? He listened more carefully: no, it wasn't laughter but sobbing, a cry for help. Unable to come down, the men imprisoned on the ceiling were begging him for a drop of water and a few crumbs to slake their thirst and keep their hunger at bay. By now, the poor men were no more than air and bone.

Acera's voice brought him back to reality:

— *Come to bed, husband. Calm down. Don't you want to sleep with me? Sleep in me, then. Don't you want to cross me? Use me as a pillow. That's it, relax, my love.*

And time passed, the weeks piling up on top of each other. Justinho wasn't getting any better. He spent more and more time listening to the lamentations of the two anguished men inside their dwelling.

Until, one night, he awoke with a fright. There were no longer the groans of the dying men, but a strange quiet gripped the place. He peered through the darkness and saw Acera wandering, her steps asking the silence to excuse them. Her husband didn't move, as he wanted to decipher his wife's mysterious movements. It was then that he saw Acera step onto a stool and attach a piece of string around the waists of the priest and the witch doctor. After this, she took them outside tied like a pair of balloons. In the garden, Acera wiped a tear from the priest's face and kissed the witch doctor on the cheek. Then she let go of the string and the two inflatables soared into the air, penetrating the clouds and disappearing into the heavens and into Justinho Salomão's astonished eyes.

That night, the inhabitants of the village watched the moon darken in what would be the very last, permanent eclipse.

The Indian with
the Golden Crotch

HERE comes Abdalah, the *monhê** from Muchatazina.
People knew it was him because of the tinkling coming
from his underpants. It was said the fellow carried gold in his
balls. Forgive me for using such a rude word. That's what they
say, but who knows for sure? Rumours travel at the speed of darkness. But let's give the gossips what they want: let's accept that
the *monhê* had had his balls stuffed. Let's suppose they weighed
a good few carats. Do I believe it? No idea. My belief is like a
bird. I only believe when the rain falls and drains away without
leaving any trace.

So I agreed to follow up this story about Abdalah. I like to
stick my nose in other people's business. I enjoy hearing what's
said and not said. I was assigned the incident so that I could
uncover its incidentals. How many lives does each deadly crime
conceal?

Whenever there's blood, folk give vent to invented versions.
People fabricate any number of explanations. The *monhê*, knowing

---

* A derogatory term in Mozambique for a person of South Asian origin, often used
  for traders from the subcontinent.

the Revolution was coming, had moved his wealth to his private parts. Where would he find a better bank? Another version: it was a case of witchcraft. Sarifa Daúdo was the main target for suspicion. It had been her, for sure. She was a strange woman, shut away between two walls, she was the origin of the Indian's deformity.

I was advised to begin with Sarifa, with whom the fellow had begun his love life. Sarifa was his cousin, upon whom he had first cast a honeyed look. They say our first love is always for a cousin. I also got on well with mine, my kissing cousins cosseted me too.

I headed towards the girl's house. She was still single, it was painful to see such beauty untried and untouched. I observed her sluggish movements as she poured me the tea that she had offered me as her guest. In some women, we are attracted by their shell, in others by the sea. Sarifa had forfeited her woman's charm, lost her taste for a gesture. Now, she was neither sea nor shell.

Eventually, I got her round to talking about Abdalah. At this point, even her eyes lost their glow, black spirals twisting inside a sea snail's shell. But the memory came back to her, expressed in a tiny, almost soundless voice. The romance had gone well. Love is like life: it starts before having begun. But what is good is in a hurry to end. The eternal shadow only lingers in the snail's conical shell. Was the girl loud-mouthed, a strumpet with a trumpet? Not at all, she was able to keep her thoughts to herself. The knotty problem was Abdalah himself.

—*But why, Sarifa? Why did his appetite become unwhetted?*

She wiped away a tear with the palm of her hand. Did the Indian hit her? Thrash her? No, at least he didn't behave like a man prone to violence. Does a man who bites not bark? Are you capable of burdening a woman with suffering, sir?

—*Let me put the question in another way: have you ever loved a woman, sir, with true passion and sworn commitment?*

I was unable to utter a word. I had gone there to ask the questions. When placed before the mirror of an interrogation, I felt like a lizard who thinks it's the other creatures who are animals. As I got up to leave, she spoke at last.

—*It was all because of the money.*

I took a step back. But she didn't say any more. She was washing the cups with astonishing torpor. Her hands caressed the glass out of which I had drunk. I felt as if she were touching my lips and I left, comforted by the illusion.

I headed home unwillingly. I paused here and there for no particular reason.

Then suddenly I came face to face with a bird of paradise. The florist got my attention by waving the flower's orange crest in front of me. Should I buy it? Why, and for whom? But, inexplicably, without knowing why, I paid the money. I felt ridiculous, holding the flower aimlessly in my hand. When I got home, the flower looked even more out of place. Never before had I stuck a flower in a vase.

I sat down with a beer and allowed myself to voice my thoughts: I needed a woman. I needed a birth-giving event, a flash of inspiration. I lacked a place to wait, free of time, free of myself. Shoulder should be a feminine word. Because that alone is what that woman's buttress deserved.

The next morning, I returned to Sarifa's house; whether moved by a desire to see her again or out of professional obligation, I don't know. The woman didn't raise her head: with her eyes on the ground, she told me about Abdalah. The man only made love after he had spread a wad of banknotes under the sheets. Sometimes they were meticais, other times they were rand. He would only get aroused when he had first fulfilled this ritual. He would lie there on his back, his hands caressing the sheet, his eyes taking the measure of infinity. Sarifa was left with the feeling that she didn't exist. With currency devaluation, his ardour varied. Sometimes, he took time to work up his manly vigour.

However, one night, he couldn't. He began to get irritated. He lifted up the sheets and inspected the notes. It was then that he began to get really suspicious: the notes were counterfeit. Someone had taken the genuine ones and spread fakes in their place.

—*Was it you, Sarifa?*

At first, his cousin didn't understand. Then a furious fist darkened her vision and ignited her understanding in a flash: there was some suspicion about the money. He beat her, and beat her again. Sarifa was knocked flat. She was bleeding profusely. It was Uncle Banzé, a man given to hot tempers, who picked her up from the floor. He patched up his niece, tended her wounds and ran to apprehend the Indian.

—*You went too far, my boy. Are you mixing love with dollar signs?* He jabbed his finger into his ribs and threatened him:

—*Well, I'm going to follow you in your dreams and see what comes out of them!*

This was his challenge: Uncle Banzé would visit the Indian's dreams over the next ten nights. If they contained more money than woman in them, then a curse would fall on Abdalah.

—*From Abdalah, I'll turn you into Abdilly-dally!*

It didn't take ten nights. On the seventh, the Indian already felt a weight in his groin. The fellow never visited Sarifa again, and he never loved another woman. And now that he no longer has access to romance, all he dreams about are women. Gold got into his goolies and the woman exited his daydreams. A dream's punishment is the one that hurts most. Ask Abdalah, the Indian with the golden crotch.

The Marine House

What man feels for a bird is envy.
Longing is what a fish feels for a cloud.

THOSE were the words of Tiane Kumadzi, the old man who lived isolated from people, far from the village, and out of his mind. I would follow him as he distributed his footsteps along the sand of the beach. My parents prohibited me from going on those wanderings.

—*That fellow's wrong in the head. You're forbidden.*

He was an unsuitable individual. And they added: That fellow is gathering the timber of a huge disaster. For what is the future, if we don't even have a word in our mother tongue for what is to come? The future, my son, is a country we cannot visit.

But I couldn't resist following in Kumadzi's damp footsteps when, in the early morning, he would look for signs of the world beyond. It happened in the half-light when the sun threw our shadows over the waves.

The old vagabond would teeter and totter like this, backwards and forwards, bent double as he muttered incomprehensible prayers. I was amused by that mumbo-jumbo of his, his head hunched below his shoulders, rummaging around among the seaweed, shells, and tree trunks brought by the ocean from distant storms.

I followed him silently, dying to find out where his search would take us. I preferred his company, as if Tiane were my childhood companion, more of a child than I.

—*How old am I? I'm the same as you.*

And then he would say: a child is a man who allows himself to fly. Sometimes he told me to run, to go beyond the endless beach. And that I should return breathless.

—*Take advantage of tiredness, son. There's wisdom in tiredness.*

Tiredness is a way of the body teaching the head. That's what Tiane said. That there were senses that only tiredness could arouse. Sleep and fatigue: they were hands that could open windows onto the world. It was through his tiredness that he managed to find what no one else dared find on the beach. On one occasion, I broke my silence and threw a question at him:

—*But what are we looking for, Granddad Tiane?*

—*This.*

And he tossed me a piece of wood. It was a stick like I'd never seen before: the edges were worn down, so that the roundness of the wood and the roughness of the bark were indistinguishable. I was struck: in what land did trees like that grow, so smooth to the touch of one's finger?

—*But what is this, Granddad?*

—*Find me more of these and I'll let you peep inside my house.*

I did nothing else for the next few days. While there was still a patch of daylight, I would tire my eyes out, rummaging through strange objects. I followed his advice: I exhausted myself out among the dunes, seeking the wisdom of fatigue.

At the end of the day, my feet were growing scales from spending so long in the water. My arms happily bore the weight of so many little pieces of wood. Old Kumadzi collected them all together in his garden, there where, in other people's houses, timber was piled up for firewood. At night, the old man devoted his time to making sense of that untidy heap. He examined each stick closely. By fitting them carefully together, each protrusion into a cavity, he gradually built a boat of some size.

The fishermen were astonished—a boat? That thing looked more like a house. And they gathered around, pricking the old man's peace and quiet with the blade of their curiosity:

—*Who taught you to make something that doesn't exist?*

Kumadzi shrugged. He didn't know, but the medicine man already had an inkling. That was a house that travelled on water, the work of a man-fish, a people no one had ever seen before. And the medicine man began to list the most frightful premonitions: times of ash and fire were coming.

—*It would be better if such times never came, it would be better if they never arrived.*

And he added his verdict: they needed to kill off the foreigners' journey as quickly as possible. He issued his order right there: on that very night, they would set fire to the alien construction. I was the only one to lend my support to the old man in his solitude. A heavy silence ensued until Tiane Kumadzi asked me to help him push the boat into the water. We were unable to nudge it even a centimetre. The boat was more fixed than a tree. Kumadzi breathlessly burst out:

—*Hey kid! Get into the boat!*

I pointed at myself in horror. Me? The old man nodded: I should be the one to sail it, to go out onto the sea so as to go and meet the folk who were coming. And he concluded:

—*That way, there'll be no one to boast that it was he who . . .*

I excused myself. I turned around and walked back through the darkness. I realized that the villagers were right in their advice: the old man was suffering the punishment of trying so hard to visit the future. I returned home but was met by a strange clamour. My father was at the head of an angry mob. Seeing me arrive, he ordered me:

—*Go back where you came from!*

And I was propelled forwards by their ranting and raving. They headed for Tiane Kumadzi's place. My old man pushed me forwards this way, that way and no way. I didn't even have time to gather my thoughts. By this time the boat was burning, swallowed up by a thousand torches, flames summoning yet more flames.

From one moment to the next, thick flecks of soot fluttered giddily. I watched the smoke rising and forming strange figures, monsters capable of swallowing entire worlds. I closed my eyes, but couldn't escape these visions. Then I heard someone saying to my father:

—*Careful, brother, this smoke is full of poison!*

Whether or not it was the poison, folk were thrown into drunken confusion. First, they started whooping, jumping, and dancing. Then, gradually, a party atmosphere prevailed and merriment intensified over the course of the night. Until their bodies lay spread-eagled on the ground.

Next morning, old Tiane shook me awake. The first thing I saw was the boat. That same boat that had been on fire but a few hours before. But there it was, fully intact. There were a few scorch marks, but nothing more. The old man anticipated my question:

—*It didn't get as far as burning, the wood was wet.*

In his hands, he held a chunk of half-burnt wood. He crumbled the ashes and mixed them with the sand. Then he added:

—*This boat was full of sea!*

He searched through the few ashes as if looking for something he had already seen. He was asking himself nervously:

—*Where is it, where is it?*

Finally, he bent over and picked up a wooden cup. He raised it. I walked over to take a closer look. It wasn't just a useful object. It was adorned with a beautiful design. Tiane pointed to the cup and declared:

—*See? The ocean wants to bring people together.*

He offered me the cup and asked me to drink.

—*Drink what?* I asked. I peered into it and saw that it contained some drops.

—*It's dew,* Tiane explained, to allay my fears. I raised the cup to my lips but was unable to drink. I mumbled an excuse:

—*I'll keep it, so as to drink along with the others . . .*

I hid the cup under the old marula tree. Then we went down to the sea to look for signs of the men-fish. The old man lingered in the water. By now, night had fallen and he refused to come out. He told me he would never again return to dry land. He remained there soaking up the sea. Did he want to become like the boat with its saturated wood? By the time he set off on his journey, he would have turned into salty timber. Already he had turned into a marine house, waiting for those destined to come.

Rungo Alberto
at Fantasy's Whim

I'M going to tell you a true story about my bosom pal, Rungo Alberto, lost on a dark night on the island of Inhaca. He was born next to the sea, in a place where land and water share their border. He would say: "my native water." Rungo never fuelled himself with any illusions: everything is sand without a castle. What he wanted was for Peace to come. He had his doubts about this. After all, the only way a war ends is if it never began. He had good reason. For he was a refugee from war. He was skinny: he paid no attention to his salient sternum. His hair was white, but because of his uncertain age.

This is what he would call me: Mio Conto, Mira Cuito, Miraconcho. Was he un-naming me? No, it was a mere inclination of his heart. Deep friendship made him invent all those names. One would not be enough on its own. I laughed: I had been in need of such an irregular identity for quite some time. I had long needed a certificate of indistinction. But I also trusted my friend's many visions. There were so many Rungos. But which of them was the real one? Well, the one I assumed to be Rungo Alberto announced one morning:

—*I'm going to build a boat!*

I had my doubts. Rungo Alberto was a very impulsive person, but he seemed to be biting off more than he could chew. As he wasn't a marine engineer and had no skills as a carpenter, where would he get the appropriate qualifications? Rungo turned his back, humming his own special song. Once again, he asked:

—*Don't you know this song? It's an anthem that's nearly national.*

The next morning, the man got down to work. He installed his workshop in a forest clearing, near the biological research station. He would go off there every day before the sun even rose. The blow of his hammer could be heard, causing the birds to cease their chirping. From morning to night Rungo Alberto would carve up the huge tree trunks. Had he turned himself into a jack of all joiners? In the improvised shipbuilder's workshop, one could see endless tree trunks on their way from being timber to becoming planks.

I wanted to take a peek, but he wasn't having it. No one was allowed to see his handiwork. That way, it would be protected from envy and wizardry. He was building his boat just as the sea made its coral, by turning its lacy spray into stone. The islanders would pass by and make fun of Rungo's declaration. Was that semi-urban man really adventurous enough to become a mariner?

Early one morning, Rungo rattled my window. With a pulsating heart, he led me down the secret paths that led to his workshop:

—*Feast your eyes, brother.*

He was pointing to a huge craft. I was astonished. That was a real boat, from bow to stern. It was over ten metres, and beautifully painted: blue, white, brown. Its mast, rose haughtily into the forest canopy. Rungo Alberto, discreet and circumspect, looked questioningly into my eyes. I couldn't refrain from expressing a doubt.

—*Tell me, my dear Rungo: how are you going to get the boat down to the sea?*

He had anticipated everything.

—*The students,* he replied, smiling.

—*The students?*

—*Yes, your students can give the boat a shove. Please speak to them.*

There wasn't a student who didn't want to join in. They rallied together their energy and their merriment. Four hours later, the boat was launched into the waters of the Indian Ocean. Rungo opened a bottle of Portuguese wine, poured a few drops on the boat, and some more onto the sea. Only then was the bottle passed around. Once blessed, the boat seemed better able to deal with the beating of the waves. When it comes to baptism, is it not the child who blesses the world?

The students returned noisily to their dormitories. He and I remained on the beach contemplating the boat as it rocked, lulled by its destiny.

—*So what are you going to do with it now?*

—*With the boat?*

He didn't know, nor did he want to think about it. He had built the boat, proved himself. The journey was another matter. Something undreamable.

—*This was my journey, I've finished it here.*

But in that case, what benefit was his work going to bring him?

—*Is it not in the desert that we gain a mirage?*

For days, he sat there on the beach contemplating the boat. He seemed anchored to his own triumph. Had Rungo taken leave of his senses, was his mind adrift? His wife got angry: Rungo wasn't giving her any help at home. In tears, she begged me to appeal to what remained of his senses . . .

—*Woman, I have no say in what he does with his timber. That man is wooden-headed.*

She fell silent. Rungo was so good that no one could stand being his enemy. It was some sort of a curse, a service commissioned from the other world. She knew it, people relied on the spoken word there. So that very afternoon, she went to see the witch doctor. She didn't have to wait long.

That same night, a storm blew up that threw the ocean into turmoil. The little boat loosened from its moorings and drifted off into the darkness. Rungo, so people said, set off after his creation.

Some days later, Peace came to the country. Even now, whenever I return to the island, I sit down on the seashore. Who knows of Rungo's story and his boat drifting towards the other shore? With its ever-shifting waters, the ocean doesn't let us see time. Whoever sees me gazing at the sunset, thinks I am absorbed in distant yearning. Sadness is a window that opens onto the back end of the world. Through it I glimpse Rungo Alberto, my old friend. Then a desert swallows up my soul. A foreign land is a place where no one awaits us.

The Dribbler

(No one can imagine how tiny my little town is.
But in it, there are folk who bid me good morning.)

WHEREVER I arrive is always somewhere. But I've never found greater shelter than in those places that lie in my memory. That's where my hometown can be found, emerging ever so slowly into the light, like a boat from the darkness of slime.

That place dominates my childhood as if time were the only territory. This other time flowed by, obeying the secret tenets of lethargy. News of world events always reached us late, crossing such great distances that by the time we got the news, the reality that had originally shaped them had already changed.

News from Europe reached us like the planks of ships wrecked beyond the endless mists. These items of news landed moistened in our hands, ready to be moulded by our minds. It was we who dictated the importance and gravity of events. Reordered in this way, the world was like a toy to us.

We became giants when our countryman, Eusébio, dribbled past the universe to run out onto the fields of the World Cup.

Wembley and Maracanã were transformed into the minuscule stadia of our childhood area. Our feet dreamed of soccer boots and each shot competed for headlines in the papers. At night, we imagined ourselves heroes from picture books.

At that time, the worldliest of wars was the one that pitted my area against all the others in the city of Beira. At the heart of this conflict was the soccer championship, which we went at hammer and tongs. This is where our honour was invested, and we would leave home just as warriors do when they bid their families goodbye.

It wasn't that soccer was the only area of contention. We had already fought a previous battle—basketball. But we weren't so good at it. This was a sport for rich folk. So out of step were we that, in the midst of a decisive match, our pivot stopped the game to ask the referee if he could head the ball into the basket.

We lacked tall players. Our tallest was Tony Candlestick, who had a dodgy heart—he didn't have enough valves for such a big ticker. The briefest run caused his face to assume a reddish hue similar to that of a water lily. We would request a pause for Tony to regain his vision and after a few seconds, he would catch his breath and mutter a *Let's get on with it!*

And on we went, invariably losing. The only time we won, we didn't even notice it. The effort had been so strenuous that we didn't care about the result. We were fanning Tony when our adversaries came over to congratulate us. Astonished, we retorted:

—*Did we win?!*

Having given up the elite sport, we returned to soccer, an activity more befitting our condition. That was when I found myself converted into a trusty centre forward. My fame emerged from a moment of confusion in the game—all games involved confusion as far as I was concerned—when someone unleashed a powerful shot in my direction. My only reaction was to protect my glasses, closing my eyes and turning my head to avoid being hit.

For a few seconds, I lost sight of the stadium. I felt the ball brush the top of my head. I later discovered that my reflexes had "ensured that the ball hit the back of our opponents' net." These words gave me a hero's status in the history of my neighbourhood. At the end of the game, I was carried around shoulder-high and awarded the lifelong captain's armband. With dubious merit, I had gained the status of commander of my team and the esteem of my neighbourhood.

However, the problem was that my team lacked players who could strike the ball. We would spend the match dribbling from one end of the field to the other, without ever summoning up the courage to shoot. We even adopted the tactic of sending high balls in to take advantage of Tony Candlestick's height, but he, with his valveless heart, would lose his vision the moment he jumped.

—*We need to score,* Senhor Herberto would say, our illustrious coach, a fifty-year-old Goan whom we suspected had never even seen a soccer match. This was his complaint:

—*All you do is dribble, you don't shoot.* Then he would sigh:

— *We're a team of dribblers.*

Between hard-fought draws and unintended victories, we reached the grand final of the inter-district championship. Senhor Herberto, who was always quiet, then came up with a solution— he'd heard that, in the town of Marromeu, there was a young man with a really strong shot. So strong that he was known as the "Marromeu Piledriver." With his vertiginous kick, the lad had already knocked down posts and trees and the mere mention of his name made goalies petrified.

He suggested we contract the "Piledriver," paying him to play for us as a forward. The idea was greeted like a stone hurled into a puddle. An immediate message was relayed to the mercenary striker. We received a swift reply: *I'll get there on the day of the final. Here's my price: 150 escudos. Paid, of course, up front.*

We were exultant. The money was a small fortune, but we would cover the cost, carefully pilfering from our fathers' wallets. We were so hopeful that we stopped training. The coach told us that immobility was a good counsellor and training sessions were only good for tiring our legs and wearing out our sports shoes.

On the afternoon of the final, the stadium was packed. Even the girls were there with their giggles and tittered secrets. We were all ready to run out onto the field and there was no sign of the famous "Piledriver." Marromeu was a long way away, could he have missed the bus?

But, lo and behold, at the last moment, our jaunty, magnificent forward appeared, fresh from the savannahs of Marromeu. To see him run out onto the pitch was like a balm for our anguish. There he was, kitted out differently from our team, in a light blue shirt with silver stars that glinted in the light of the sun. His hair slicked down to his parting, our precious reinforcement ran onto the field, giving those little jumps and skips that only the great professionals of the game indulge in to limber up and warm the spirits of the crowd. His cylindrical legs, as sturdy at the bottom as they were at the top, were his most astonishing feature. The lad wasn't for showing any bonhomie. Without even looking at us, and while still warming up, he muttered:

—*Have you got the money?*

Herberto replied that he had put it in the prearranged place.

— *And what about tactics?* our hired hand asked, still skipping about.

Herberto's tactic was the most straightforward possible:

—*To pass the ball immediately to the Marromeu Piledriver.*

And so the match started.

Not long after kickoff, I found myself with the ball, and in the glare of the sunlight, I raised my leg on a whim. The ball touched my knee and sped off over the heads of two opponents, in Tony's direction. He gave a leap and obviously, as he couldn't see it, headed the ball with his neck. The opposing team, the spectators, and above all we ourselves, were astounded by such well-planned exchanges. The ball came to me once more and our supporters screamed in frenzy:

—*Pass it to Piledriver, pass it to Piledriver!*

I gave the ball to our saviour. He didn't shoot straightaway. He allowed the ball to come to a standstill, and with the stylishness of a top-class ball player, took a couple of steps back to get his balance. Silence fell over the whole field of play, as if the entire universe were paying attention to the soccer player's virtuosity. Like a buffalo, Piledriver charged towards the ball. The thump of his feet and the dust they raised were such that I had to shut my eyes. I was waiting to hear the ball being given a hearty *thwack*. But all I heard was a timid *trrrr*, like a piece of cloth being shredded, stitching being ripped apart. When I opened my eyes again, I saw Piledriver's fat leg kicking the air and a suspicious brown stain spreading across his shorts. The hired hand had miskicked, but with such impulse that he had carelessly soiled himself.

What happened next was acutely embarrassing—our glorious striker leaving the field in tears, surrounded by us who seemed unaware of the brownish odours dribbling down his legs. As he was leaving, one of our team even stuttered:

—*Hey lads . . . what about our money?*

But our hired hand was already sneaking away through the bulrushes that surrounded the stadium. I can still remember the glitter of the silvery stars on his extravagant shirt amid the thick vegetation. As those stars faded, my own dreams of being a world champion soccer player were also extinguished.

Sentenced to Burn

—*Father: dissolve me my sins.*

Father Ludmilo didn't bother to correct him. If he were going to correct him, he said later, he would have to correct the man rather than the sentence. For his visitor muddled up his mixture of languages as he stumbled through his prayers:

—*Our boss who art in Heaven, your daily bread, braised be God.*

He was an outlaw, one could see it in his appearance. He displayed himself in the holy house of God, full of arrogance and disrespect. The priest studied the confessor as he spoke. And he noticed the machete strapped to the young bandit's boot.

But the sinner wasn't alone. At the entrance, one could see, against the sunlight, the silhouette of another fugitive. This other man's skin seemed lighter, and his frizzy hair was more that of a *mulato*. Father Ludmilo couldn't make out his face.

In contrast, the pronounced features of the man kneeling in front of him were distinctive. What he said, however, was certainly not:

—*God is pretty, Father, because we can't see Him. Even I refuse to go to Heaven so as not to suffer disappointment.* He uttered and then re-uttered the most disparate depravities. And on he went with his impious declarations:

—*The problem with God, with all due respect, is that He sleeps snuggled up to the Devil's backside.*

When all was said and done, what exactly did that ragamuffin, that bootlegger want? The priest didn't seem particularly interested. He yawned, tired. All you could say about that man is that he was a lover of disorder, a perpetrator of butcheries and massacres. His was an empty heart, not even his name had ever known a moment of warmth or affection.

—*Before, the Church made me scared, Father. It was a place that seemed to make you ill immediately.*

—*Ill?*

—*Yes, people go in and their legs go weak straightaway. They even fall to their knees.*

Ludmilo only pretended to pay attention. Nowadays, the only thing you need to do to pretend to be a priest is to know how to listen. In the end, the brigand was coming there to ask for undeserved forgiveness, even if he had to utter threats in order to get what he wanted.

—*Father: it's not entry to Heaven I want, no. I want a change of hell.*

For he could no longer stay in this earthly hell, alongside creatures of the wild, a dread-end existence. For he no longer knew what he was: was he a man outside the law, or a law outside the man?

—*I was even promised an ammunisty, or ministree, or amitree, or whatever you call it. I was promised one, Father. All I had to do was to give myself up with my weapon.*

The priest remained silent, his mouth expressionless, the epitome of a non-practising cleric, part-time servant of God.

—*Are you listening to me, Father?*

He signalled that he was, he was merely meditating, an unhappy cogitator in an exchange of secrets with God. He explained that the connection to Paradise was poor, because of the interference of gunfire from the war. The lad should continue with his confession, without omitting a single detail.

And so the bandit set off on his long list of crimes, a blood-sodden deluge. Not even the priest could imagine the extent to which evil could be so creative. For example, how it's possible to pestle an entire family to death: the old father battered with the stick, the mother forced to grind her own baby down and after all that, the mother raped to death. When the confession was over, the priest sat there, head bowed, as if he were dozing, indifferent.

—*Father?*

Ludmilo raised his head slowly: a tear glistened on his face. When he spoke, his voice had risen a few tones.

—*I can't forgive you, you filthy son of a bitch.*

At first, the reprobate was shocked. Then more insults rained down on him, the priest had lost all control. When he'd got over his surprise, the bandit took offence. He got up, and peered through the peephole as if to make sure that it was the priest speaking. Then he pushed the hatch of the confession box until its hinges snapped.

—*What did you call me? Repeat it!*

And grabbing the priest by the collar of his soutane, he lifted him off his feet. All of a sudden there was the glint of a machete in the air.

—*You're going to forgive me, or I'll turn you into cutlets.*

The priest stammered something in Latin. The bandit, his mouth jammed against the priest's face, asked:

—*What did you say?*

—*I spoke Latin, the language of the angels.*

—*Speak another language, all the angels are white, I don't want to share a language with them.*

—*Put the Father down or I'll shoot you!*

The voice came from the entrance; the other bandit had taken aim and was speaking. The Black man ceased his threats and put the cleric down. They stood there, looking at each other, in utter confusion. The visitor turned on his heel and walked slowly away, his rhythm falling in with the echo of his own footsteps. Suddenly, the priest called him:

—*Come here, my son. I have something to say to you.*

The bandit turned back, his hand on his belt. His gaze had regained its original arrogance, and he was once again the master of other people's fears.

—*What is it, Father?*

—*It's just that we don't have enough food to distribute here at the mission. We could do with a few sacks of maize. Do you think you could get us something?*

The robber was puzzled. Then he let out a guffaw: yes, sir, I can. Then he went over to the priest so that no one could hear what he said:

—*Just wait till the next truck passes by. One of the ones carrying gift aid.*

And off he went, along with his companion. The priest smiled, and turning his eyes heavenwards, said:

—*Forgive me, Father.*

The sacristan, who had heard the conversation, went over to the priest. He looked at him quizzingly. How could he associate himself with such folk, order a crime from a thief? Ludmilo didn't bother to explain, and instead made for the sacristy. The sacristan, weeping, clung to his gown.

—*Father, answer! How can you order stuff that's been stolen from the people?*

Ludmilo stopped and turned to face the boy. He seemed to want to answer, but maintained his silence. The priest pressed on again, passing the altar without dropping to his knees in devotion.

The sacristan wandered off, astonished, hemorrhaging the saddest thoughts. How could the priest have asked for the favour of stolen goods, fruits of the most heinous of crimes? No doubt some of the things he had used in the church likewise originated in such skulduggery. He spent the next few days ruminating: he needed to speak to Ludmilo, to ask him to be honest about his dishonesty.

But the priest avoided him. One afternoon, the sacristan was getting ready to say his prayers when the same bandit walked into the sacristy. He was on his own, and stinking. The boy shuddered with powerless hatred. The priest walked over to the visitor, and they greeted each other. The bandit gave him a sack.

—*Here are the things. See? I didn't forget!*

The priest thanked him and mumbled a few words. The sacristan couldn't hear what he was saying. For sure, the priest was overindulging in this unbelievable complicity with the forces of Evil. The killer then decided to withdraw. He wanted to take advantage of the paths being deserted, for he hadn't met a soul on the way there. The priest advised him to pay his respects at the altar before he went. The other man consented, his machete scraping along the floor with metallic stridency. Ludmilo walked towards the heavy entrance doors and opened them wide.

There was an earth-shattering roar. Voices and cries were unleashed in a split second. Outside, a huge crowd demanded that the miscreant should face justice. The sacristan crossed himself, faint with fear. The bandit squirmed with terror. He ran to the priest and begged him for protection. If left in the hands of the people, his life would be extinguished like a candle being snuffed out. The priest put his hands on the ruffian's shoulders.

—*Come with me, don't be afraid. I won't let them harm you!*

And crossing the threshold, leading the miscreant by the arm, the priest raised his arm in order to calm the crowd's fury. Silence fell. Ludmilo's words rang out as if to discourage their frenzy:

—*Brothers, remember the teachings of Christ, our redeemer!*

And advancing ever further into the human shell, he continued to remind them of the lesson of Jesus, and his example of noble justice. Then, all of a sudden, he pushed the criminal into the middle of the multitude while at the same time pronouncing his summary sentence:

—*Burn him!*

The furious crowd threw itself upon the condemned man, beating, kicking, spitting, and splattering on him. The priest went back into the church and closed the door behind him.

The Child's Heart and the Heart's Child

T HE kid was born with all his features in the right place. It was only when he started to try and walk that they noticed a defect, his little feet turned inwards, each one distinct from the other. Grandmother gave her verdict on his squinting footprints.

—*This child will walk into his own self.*

Then, there was another additional inconvenience: the boy muddled and chewed his speech. The others understood little more than splutters and whistles, and even his relatives only listened to him with a dopey smile that feigned comprehension. There's nothing scarier than when one human person doesn't understand the human in another person's voice.

The mother took the child to hospital. The doctor put his ear next to his chest and was deafened by his loud heartbeat. The child's pulse was on the surface of his skin. The doctor seemed fascinated by this unusual case.

—*We need him to stay for some more tests . . .*

—*No way! This child came here with me, and he'll leave with me.*

—*But, Madam, you must understand . . . we need to find a name for his illness.*

—*What do you mean, a name?*

—*His illness: I've got to find a name for it!*

—*But this name, is a name going to cure his illness?*

The doctor smiled. Ah, these simple folk, so accomplished at being thought so by others. And as his smile slowly faded from his lips, he watched mother and child walking away down the corridor. The child was carrying in his hand, drooping like a faded petal, a letter that he himself had written. He had wanted to give the doctor this little piece of paper that his inabilities had filled with writing. With careless concern, the mother took the paper from him and threw it in the trash can. The little fantasist and his obsessions! It must be one of the many letters the crazy little fellow pretended to write to his beloved girl cousin.

—*Are you still writing letters to Marlisa?*

The little boy was vehement in his denial. His mother shook her head. How hard she'd tried, but to no avail. Was it worth trying to teach someone things they'd never learned? It wasn't as if Marlisa, her niece to whom the letters were addressed, had ever deigned to open them. It wasn't even worth taking a peep at the moonstruck little chap's handwriting. Some folks live in the moon. In his case, it was the moon that lived in him.

Then the scribbler of all that scrawling collapsed into the bottomless pit of time. The little boy died, his skin all blue, as cold as if no light wanted to shine on him. The doctors rushed to take his body and carry out an autopsy. They pulled out his heart, the universatile muscle, vast like some fleshy planet. The organ was placed behind glass, on show for science and the news agencies. Cardiologists argued, in endless colloquia, over the appropriate term for such an abnormality.

The days went by, unnoticed. It was late one afternoon when his cousin Marlisa was dusting the house and came across the pile of useless letters. She weighed them in her hand before throwing them in the fire. She hesitated for a split second: had the little boy known how to write a single line of letters? She decided to take a peep inside the first envelope. And there she sat in astonishment, a single furrow on her brow, curling her hair slowly with a finger. She sat on the step for hours. They weren't letters but verses of a beauty that had no place in the present world. Marlisa's sadness flooded out, blotching the handwriting. The more the cousin became absorbed in her reading the more her thoughts rhymed with those of no other woman, so removed from her daily existence had she become. Was the girl falling in posthumous love?

But sprawled there across the stairs, not even Marlisa could imagine what was happening simultaneously to her cousin's heart that was being guarded by God and science. Indeed, behind the icy glass in the hospital, hardly had the first envelope been torn open than her cousin's heart bounded upwards in shock. Visitors let out an ear-shattering gasp. And as Marlisa, more than a thousand walls away, gradually leafed through the verses, the heart began to unravel even more, all glittering and shimmering. Until an arm could be seen emerging from that tight red ball, and then later a foot and the roundness of a knee and even more evidence of what was clearly occurring: the heart was flagrantly giving birth! And this was confirmed when a complete newborn child emerged from that cardiac uterus.

When the birth was at last complete, one could see that the newborn child was identical to his thoracic progenitor. It was scary how one was the carbon copy of the other. They were alike in every aspect except for the shape of the foot. The newly born infant's feet pointed outwards, as if it had come seeking people from other stories outside itself.

Bartolominha
and the Pelican

S H E lived on a windswept island, all alone. Her name was Bartolominha, and she was my favourite grandmother. Her place was breezier than the sky, exposed to distance and oblivion. Her husband, Bounteous António, had always been the lighthouse keeper. He shone his light out into the night, while never abandoning his lofty post. Even without receiving any salary for years on end, he remained devoted to his occupation. Those at the centre of authority, where money glitters and folk rot, forgot all about him. Impassive, without complaining or whining, Grandfather Bounteous imposed his own discipline upon himself, infallible in his mission to illuminate the coast's rocky cliffs. No ship ever foundered against the shoreline because of any lapse on his part.

All his diligence was worth little: Bounteous António died as he was climbing the huge spiral staircase. His body ascended more swiftly than his heart. In one second, that flickering inner light ceased to illuminate his breast. We only received the news years afterwards, when a rare boat put in at our city.

The whole family immediately set out to sea. We had to save Bartolominha. Grandmother couldn't be left like that, without any support, in the midst of such distant solitude. I went along with the other members of this mission to fetch our elderly relative. The one who was weeping the most was my mother, her favourite daughter. As we sailed along, she was disconsolate: who knows whether Grandmother had died in the meantime, without anyone there to bury her?

We disembarked with apprehension in our hearts, looking into every nook and cranny on the island. We breathed sighs of relief when Bartolominha came down to the rocks, wrapped in her *capulana*, the same one I always remembered her wearing. When we talked to her about leaving the place, she was angry. So we'd come to fetch her? Well, we should go back the same way we had come, because she wasn't moving. My father argued that she couldn't go on living there all on her own, in a place so devoid of folk. My uncle told her that no news reached the place from outside, nor did the outside get news of it. My mother added many a tear, her spirit stuck in her throat.

Bartolominha answered without saying a word, pointing at the burial ground next to the lighthouse. Then she walked off and turned, looking at the sea, her back to us. It was as if she were quietly summoning us. We lined up next to her, standing stiffly, facing the ocean. What was she trying to tell us, so calm and silent? Was she using the ocean to convey her side of the argument? My uncle still persisted:

—*Who will get you your food?*

It was then that she showed us the pelican. It was a creature she had reared ever since it was a chick. The bird had grown fond of her, and was more domesticated than any family member, to the extent of coming and going every day, with a fish for her meal.

—*I've got to stay here and water the lighthouse. It was my Bounteous who asked me not to let this lighthouse wither.*

We returned home, unable to dissuade her. The thought of her gnawed away at my sleep. I couldn't get any rest for nights on end. Should I leave things as they were? No, I mustn't give up.

So I went back to the island. I stayed there for a few days. I developed my arguments, and lured her with an invitation. If Grandmother returned with me, I would provide her with food and shelter in my new house. To no avail. The same haughty smile came to her lips. Then I suggested she come with me to travel through beautiful places.

—*I only want to travel when I am completely blind.*

I was puzzled. But I didn't answer, preferring to wait for her to give me an explanation. And sure enough, she did.

—*It's because I've led such a beautiful life that I only want to visit places within me.*

I gave up. The old lady's roots ran deep. To close the conversation, I told her that when I left the next day, I would also leave her a boat tied up to the trees on the beach. Just in case she needed it. She shrugged, repudiating my stubbornness once and for all.

That night, we dined in silence under the heavy shadow of an unsaid farewell. Bartolominha announced she was tired and was going to her room. She had made her living quarters inside the lighthouse. She mounted the first few steps of the spiral staircase and, before disappearing into the darkness, called the pelican. She would go to bed with the creature. They even slept in the same bed. The pelican would stretch its wings and she would fall asleep hugging the big old bird. She said that by doing this, her body would learn to fly.

—*One of these nights, I'll go with him, off into the distance.*

I lay back and gazed up at the stars like holes against the black background of the ceiling. I fell asleep, but then was woken by a strange nightmare. In fact, I wasn't dreaming of anything at all. I didn't even understand the reason for the impulse I felt as I got up from my sleeping mat. It was as if voices from the inner darkness were guiding me. I went to the burial ground and scratched at the earth with my feet. Then I discovered that the hole was in fact flat: the grave had no depth whatsoever. When I leaned over the mortal remains, I saw bones that were turning to powder. They were the bones of a bird. And a very bulky beak.

My heart pulsated chaotically. I ascended the stairs so quickly that I was almost stolen from the world by giddiness. I didn't get there in time. Near the lighthouse landing, I got as far as touching a fluttering white feather. I stood on the observation platform while the wind blew through my soul. At one point, I thought I glimpsed Bartolominha twirling around as if she were dancing in the lighthouse's fleeting, intermittent flash. Ever since that night, I have been the lighthouse keeper on Grandfather Bounteous's island. And I wave every time one of those great birds passes by.

Isaura, Forever Within Me

Isaura came into the bar as if she were entering through the very last door and we were the gods awaiting her on the other side. Outside, the sky was all blue, and the bazaar was buzzing with people.

The woman's arrival caused my heart to miss a beat, reined in by the shock. I listened to my inner turmoil, blood to one side, veins to the other.

It was because I hadn't seen Isaurinha for more than twenty years, more than half the time I had been accumulating existences. Suddenly, memories came to me as if images and sounds were tumbling chaotically into my heart.

It was in colonial times. Isaura and I were servants in the same house. She was a housemaid, and I worked outside. We were both kids, more of an age to be playing. At the end of the afternoon, when she stopped work, she would come and tell me all the news, the secrets of the lives of the whites. It was at the hour when I had to take the dogs for a walk. She would come with me, and we would walk around the block while she made me laugh with all her stories. She told me the boss would push her into dark corners and squeeze her up against the walls. There wasn't a wall she hadn't lain on while standing. All that made her sick, caused her stomach to churn. Who could she complain to? Would God listen to me? I used to dream that I plucked up courage to confront the boss. But I would fall asleep without even daring to complete the dream.

And now, here was Isaura interrupting my life, bursting into the beer hall. She had hardly changed, time hadn't reshaped her. She was as thin as ever. Her eyes gleamed like burning embers. A cigarette between her fingers rattled my recollections. As if the centre of my memory were a puff of smoke. Yes, the smoke from the cigarette that, twenty years before, she had brought through the back door of the bosses' house, where I was waiting for her. She would do this: she would pick up a cigarette end casually left in an ashtray in the lounge and take a few deep drags. She would fill her cheeks with smoke and then come and meet me in the yard. She had a clownish air about her, her face double its size like that of an owl.

She would come up right next to me, face to face. Then, mouth to mouth, my cupped lips would receive hers. Isaura would blow her smoke into me. I would feel my inner being warmed, my saliva at boiling point. Then, it wasn't just my mouth: my whole body heated up. That was how we smoked, sharing our breath, the mouth of one crossing the other's breast.

What is it that we were practising? Mouth-to-mouth fumigation? One thing was for sure: I dwelt in the heavens at those moments. Isaura exhaled eternities into me, her vaporous lips brushing my heart. And all that in the hut at the back of the house.

The procedure was a straightforward one: Isaura would clip off the ends of cigarettes, butt ends in their death throes. Isaura didn't seem to value our exchange of lips. What she loved was tobacco, gradually becoming addicted to the smoky vapours. As for me and the unloading of it into my chest, that was just a meaningless by-product of the process.

Until there came a time when the boss caught us in the act. Insults rained down on us, accompanied by blows. I immediately excused Isaura, and took all the blame. I made up my version of events: I had assaulted her and forced her against her will. I was expelled, given the sack that very day. I didn't even say goodbye to Isaurinha. I left with my belongings under a gloomy light. And I never heard from Isaura again.

Twenty years later, and Isaura was playing havoc with my afternoon, bursting into the bar. And what's more, she had a lit cigarette between her fingers.

The woman sat down at my table and, without looking at me, began to talk. She indulged her memories amid puffs of smoke and mouthfuls of beer.

—*I've got so many memories. One life wouldn't be long enough to talk about all of them.*

—*That's good, Isaura.*

—*But my favourite memory is you, my poor old Raimundo.*

—*Don't say that.*

—*I'm telling you: All that smoke I blew into you, do you know all I really wanted, and nothing else? It was a kiss.*

I quivered. Was that a knife blade lacerating me? But she went on, continuing what she had to say. Yes, indeed, she had once loved me. She'd never been open about it, for the sake of decency. She was so skinny that it seemed ill-mannered to reveal herself too much. But she had chosen the best aspects of her beauty for me, like someone who has gifts but doesn't know who to give them to.

—*Why, Isaura? Why didn't you look for me?*

—*Because I stopped loving you. It was because of that lie you told in order to protect me. That affected me really badly.*

From the moment I had defended her, her feelings had plummeted, the mere residue of a shadow. Why the offence? I shall never know. Sitting there, Isaura would never give me an explanation. As if it wasn't just time that had passed by, but a whole life. She got up, pushed her chair in as if tidying the furniture were the most important thing in this world. And she headed for the exit, while my anguish returned as if, for the second time, my life were draining away through that open doorway. I barely recognized my voice:

—*Blow me another puff of smoke, Isaura. Just another little puff.*

She looked at me, her eyes so distant they didn't even seem to focus. She took a deep drag, fought back a cough, and came straight over to me. When she stuck her lips upon mine, the following happened: the woman turned into smoke and vanished first into the air and then, ever so slowly, inhaled into my chest. That afternoon, I smoked Isaurinha.

Dona Elisa's Belch

WE were all going to listen to Dona Elisa belch. This happened on Saturdays, late in the afternoon. Elisa's house was on the very edge of town. Beyond that lay the highway, faraway places, the world. It was said that the universe began at the back of the grand old lady's house. The proof of this was displayed on the patio's stone floor—a footprint. It had been made by a human foot, but it was the subject of the most fabled stories. The owner of the footprint was the most ancient man, he who walked everywhere and still marches along inside us. That was why we would cross ourselves when we entered Elisa's yard.

Every Saturday, the same ritual was carried out in the lady's house. There was a long lunch with an unchanging menu: flatfish curry, soaked up with manioc and mealie flour. It was a heavy dish, enough to feed a garrison. She was given this food to stuff herself. Then they made a bit of money out of Dona Elisa's flatulent outbursts. Whoever wanted to listen had to pay. What did they expect? Misery provides a cup, need lays a spoon.

Her nephews took the money at the entrance: no paper money was accepted. It all had to be in loose change. One of the nephews on the door kept his eyes closed, for he was forbidden to look at the payment. He would check it by the tinkling of the coins in his cupped hands. Another lad next to him would give the go-ahead:

—*Go in. Don't forget to cross yourself.*

Dona Elisa would be sitting there, in all her vastness, in the middle of her backyard. She seemed to be in a trance, half-asleep, her eyes half-closed, like a crocodile in the shade. Her mouth was drooping, as if her jawbone had lost its solder. It was said that the lady was biding her time until the right moment. Her innards were fermenting, her soul hovering above her immense frame. We sat around her. The esteemed audience was requested to hush and remain silent out of consideration.

So there we remained, respectfully waiting. We were waiting for her to unleash her powerful belch, the one that folk said came not from her but from the world's intestines.

—*It's gas from the very depths,* was the guarantee.

I had already witnessed the spectacle once before. It was unforgettable. It was an eruption emanating from magma, a volcano summoning together its contents, like a train emerging from the bowels of the planet itself. For one second, we were convinced the end had come, the apocalypse.

On this occasion, I didn't go alone. I took the foreigner with me to witness the phenomenon. I had felt it my duty, and was inhibited. Generosity is so easy in such cases: providing what others don't even ask for. For the strange man had arrived in town full of credentials. He hadn't come to study plants, grasses, or animals. He had come to study us, folk used to their customs and accustomed to their uses. He had heard of Dona Elisa and her powers. Moreover, educated gentleman that he was, he had brought with him all the equipment to capture moments such as these: a camera, a recorder.

Once in the yard, after having crossed himself, the foreigner sat down like us, in the sand, pen and papers in his lap. Apprehensively, he asked me whether he might take a photo.

—*It might be better not to,* I suggested.

But what was the guy going to photograph? A belch? And I was even going to ask him not to press the button on the recorder when we were interrupted by the announcement of a sudden delay.

—*Mama Elisa is indisposed.*

Then I saw her pass by, supported by others. For a moment, she paused in the shade. She seemed to me to be peering at the visitor. I realized she was crying. Her relatives stood around her, shielding her from being seen. They sat the weighty lady down and fanned her thoroughly. Until a nephew came over and ordered the foreigner to take his shoes off. Barefoot, they crossed the yard, and I was told to translate the order.

—*Place your foot in the footprint.*

The man put his foot in the cavity in the stone. But his foot didn't fit the print. He was told to put his shoes back on. Someone said:

—*Mama asks you to go near her.*

We went over, the foreigner and I. Eliza seemed dozy. Had she been drinking? She asked the visitor to lean over her. She looked at his face for a long moment and then mumbled sadly:

—*No, it's not him.*

And there she remained, burdened by weight and years, until suddenly she sat up straight. Her triple chin quivered. Someone gave the alarm.

—*She's going to belch.*

But instead of the expected and now announced belch, she emitted a tiny squeak of a voice, the chirping of a little bird. This hiss was her final display.

A nephew gave us our money back on the way out. He excused her:

—*Those noises were never more than her heart in a state of collapse.*

In the end, Dona Elisa wasn't a case for scientific study. Neither geologists nor humanologists would understand her.

The only phenomenon she encapsulated was love, the passion that had long stolen away. And the footprint that, each Saturday, freed itself from the stony floor and trod upon Elisa's heart. That was the only reason for the sonic boom: stone freeing itself from stone, the buried past returning to this side of life.

The Blessing

IT happened during Portuguese times. The couple were the Esteves, distinguished folk, functionaries of the first order. They lived in a state of never-ending concern: their little boy had been sickly since birth, devoid of vitamins, lacking both hydrates and carbons. His skinniness was more visible than his body: he had a protruding sternum. And stranger still: he was assailed by fits of convulsive sobbing. During these attacks, the boy's breathing suffered, he seemed to be gasping for air, his chest escaping out of his mouth.

They contracted the Black woman, Marcelinda, to look after their only son. The mistress of the house, Dona Clementina, was overcome with motherly envy: the child would only calm down when he was sitting on Marcelinda's lap. He would lie back in the immense rotundity of his nurse, and grow as quiet as a fetus. The Black woman would carry him around, as if she were dancing, and would call him:

—Nwana wa mina!

No one in the house understood the language. Maybe that was why her words left a bitter taste. They didn't like the idea of Africa entering the intimacy of the home in such a way. As time passed, one certainty became apparent: the baby was jettisoning his biological mother. When he was ill, scared, or alarmed, only the maid was able to console the child. Disdain burrowed into his mother's heart.

—*I don't want her here. See about dismissing her.*

The father still tried to throw water on the flames. But Dona Clementina was unforgiving, she wanted to see the fat Black woman out of her life. Esteves knitted together his argument:

—*We should thank God that the boy gets on so well with her.*

But the mother's anger was implacable. Dona Clementina's nights were riven with nightmares. As she lay in bed, she would dream that her son was slipping away through a sudden crack, swallowed up by the damp gloom. She would rush off in a panic. There, in the dark background, she could hear Marcelinda's voice, singing a gentle lullaby. And her son was smiling at the maid, unable to see his mother's silhouette. The lady would wake up in a sweat, and creep down to her son's bedroom in order to hug him to her breast.

One evening, the Esteveses entertained some Portuguese guests. During the course of the evening, they compared their fantasies. The ladies assuaged Clementina's fears:

—*It's natural, Black women are experienced in rearing dozens of children.*

And another one added, ironically:

—*In Africa, they're all each other's children.*

Someone even asked:

—*How many does yours have?*

—*Actually, we've never asked Marcelinda . . .*

—*She's probably got loads. They're like that, I've never seen women have so many . . .*

And they laughed. Except for Esteves. That night, the Portuguese turned this way and that, unable to sleep. The following morning, the boss burst into the half-light of the kitchen and addressed the maid. He wanted to know about her children. Marcelinda hunched her shoulders bashfully, and smiled to herself.

—*Well, Marcelinda? Have you got so many that you lost count of them?*
—*Yes, boss.*
—*Seriously, you lost count?*
—*Yes, boss, I lost count.*

The Esteveses felt sorry for her. They gave her old clothes, things that were no longer going to be of any use for their friends' children. She accepted them with thanks. She wrapped them up very carefully, as if they were treasures that were going to be worn for the first time. Then, in silence, she withdrew, allowing herself to be swallowed up by each night's darkness.

One day, while she was dressing her son, Dona Clementina found a cotton thread tied round the little boy's midriff. She summoned the maid and demanded to know where this had come from. Marcelinda stammered:
—*It's a cure, lady . . .*
—*A cure?*
—*For the boy not to suffer so many coughs . . .*

They were her last words. When Esteves got home, the sentence had already been carried out. The boss lady had sacked the maid. The husband stood there, solemn and silent. Lacking the courage to say anything, he listened to his wife as she walked around the house, the offensive amulet dangling from her fingers:
—*I won't have it, I won't have it!*

Time passed, conclusively, while the boss lady became more and more desperate: the child wouldn't stop crying. His mother couldn't find a way of calming him down. She had no knowledge of how to ease his fevers, placate his weeping, control the boy's screams. The Portuguese woman could no longer sleep, and was at the end of her tether. The boss man came to a decision:
—*I'm going to Marcelinda's house this very day.*

In the middle of the night, he got up surreptitiously. He left the house without knowing where he was going. So where did that goddamned Black woman live? He was amazed someone should live in their house about whom they knew so little.

He wandered down lanes and alleyways, wearing out his eyesight and his shoes. The Portuguese fellow was embarrassed to find himself in such humble surroundings. Only the firmness of his decision made him go on. He asked around, made sure he had understood, corrected himself. After many a fright, he reached Marcelinda's little abode. He entered the yard and called out. In the darkness, he could hardly see the end of his nose. The Portuguese got a shock when he collided with Marcelinda's huge frame. He immediately delivered his desperate request: for the maid to return. For God's sake. Or, if she preferred, for the little boy's sake. Without uttering a word, Marcelinda retreated into the dark beyond the doorway. At this point, the vague outline of a man appeared, so thin that his undershirt looked more like an overcoat on him:

—*What's going on?*

Esteves explained the purpose of his visit, believing him to be the maid's husband. Marcelinda took no notice of either of the men but merely packed her things into a bag.

—*Hey there! You can't just do this. You turn up here, take her away, and off you go?!*

The Portuguese took some notes from his wallet. The man pocketed the cash as if he were putting it away in his soul rather than his clothes. Marcelinda squeezed herself into the boss's car. They drove off in silence. The boss wasn't sure whether the maid had been aware of what had happened as they left the house.

—*I paid an advance for your ... to that man.*

—*I didn't ask for money.*

—*What do you want then?*

—*I just want my little boy.*

My little boy?! The boss explained, as diplomatically as he could, that Marcelinda should avoid that expression. It's not important, but the lady doesn't like it. And he smiled nervously. He had never asked for anything like that from someone of another race.

Once in the hall, they advanced as stealthily as possible. Everyone was asleep. The boss pointed to the old room at the back of the house, and asked her not to make a noise in case the kid woke up. To no avail. Without their understanding quite how, the kid had heard them arrive. And without more ado, he rushed to hug the maid, unaware of the world around him. And there he remained, as if that were his first and only womb.

The following morning, Esteves overslept. The previous night had left him exhausted. He woke up to his wife's screams.

—*My son! Where's my son?*

One thought came to his head immediately: the Black woman had fled with the boy! He got dressed hurriedly and set off for Marcelinda's house. His wife, sobbing, sat in the passenger seat. They crossed the outskirts of town until they got to where he had been before. Dona Clementina remained in the car. Esteves went into the house but saw no sign of the maid. All he could see was the same man as the previous night.

—*Marcelinda? I haven't seen her since yesterday.*

Esteves was insistent, pushing him for answers as to where she might be. Then, right there by the entrance, he saw the bags containing the children's clothes they had given the maid. Unopened, just as they had arrived. So she hadn't distributed the gifts to her children?

—*Children? What children?*

—*Hers . . . her children.*

—*Marcelinda can't have children, she never had any.*

Esteves was dumbstruck. He hesitated, and began to retreat. He was leaving. But before he reached the door, he paused and asked:

—*What does* nwana wa mina *mean?*

—*Hey! That's our dialect. Are you learning it, sir?*

—*No, I just want to know what the expression means.*

—*It means: "my son."*

The Portuguese settled back into his car. His wife was waiting for him, wiping her tears with her handkerchief. The skinny man appeared at the door and shouted:

—*Don't say anything to Marcelinda.*

—*That we were here?*

—*No. Don't say anything about her never having had children.*

Suddenly, Dona Clementina stopped crying. Esteves glanced at her, before starting the car. He wanted to know what to do, where he should look. The skinny man then suggested they should go to the medicine man, two blocks from there. Marcelinda might have taken the kid there to undergo a ceremony. Esteves accepted his suggestion. He drove gingerly, lost, with only his wife's silence for company. He came across Marcelinda emerging into the street. The maid was carrying the sleeping child on her back. She seemed to be waiting for the boss, and she got into the vehicle without saying a word.

—*Shall we go?*

The sleeping kid was placed on the rear seat between the two women, the maid and the boss lady. The car moved forwards sluggishly. Dona Clementina's hands produced the blessed thread, the same one that had been the reason for her sacking the maid. The Black woman looked alarmed, her eyes fearful.

—*Do you remember this thread, the one to do with your spells?*

But the boss lady didn't seem angry. And she asked her:

—*Marcelinda, help me to put the thread around the boy.*

And in an act of symmetrical motherhood, together they tied the thread around the child.

A Last Look at Love

WHILE she dressed the dead man, her late husband, Dona Faulhinha preserved a single appropriate tear. It was always the same tear, the only one she had shed after Ananias Xavier had elected to pass on. If the tear did not merit any credibility, the death was no more trustworthy. The woman cast doubt upon Ananias, even after he had embarked on his final crossing. The man had invoked some strange illness. The truth of his motives now counted for little. What was certain is that suspicion now gnawed at her heart. In the half-light of the living room, Faulhinha received condolences. For the sake of her visitors, she exhibited her tear, the proof of her grief, glistening against the dark skin of her face.

When she was left alone with the corpse, Faulhinha truly wept. Not out of pity for the dead man, but out of despair at not having been taken herself. Regret that God's finger had not turned her page in the book of the living. What was there left for her to do now? To be the relic, the leftover of the non-existence that her life had been? During her marriage, she had never been happy. But at least she could feed on the hatred she felt for her husband, supreme womanizer and an expert in skulduggery.

After crying, something seemed to burst into flower within her soul. She felt drained but not empty. For her inner being strayed off-track: she had an insatiable desire to die. She had always been a shadow woman, dwelling in the quiet outskirts of her existence. If she had never felt life's pulse, how could she now have decided to put an end to herself? Surely she wouldn't have the courage for such a gesture of finality.

Faulhinha went to a corner of the bedroom and took the cage containing the late Ananias's pet bird. The grey-headed parrot had always irritated her, and she regarded tending it as lying outside her domestic duties. But she had promised to look after the parrot out of respect, after her husband's death. She placed the cage on the dining-room table, and gazed at it along with the clumsy creature inside. She noticed a sadness in the bird's eyes. A mere passing impression, for a parrot is a deceitful creature, well-suited to that rascal Ananias. Then the woman suddenly stopped still as if the most primitive decision in her whole life had suddenly blossomed within her.

At that point she fell to her knees, she who had never prostrated herself. She had problems with her bones and joints. *The day I kneel down, I'll never get up from the ground,* she was wont to say.

Now, however, she bent down slowly and with difficulty, her knees on the bare stone floor. And she asked God to arrange for her death. Let him take her, Dona Faulhinha da Conceição Dengo. For she would not cause any trouble. The angels wouldn't need to do overtime. She would die so modestly that no one would be aware she had left life. Death, that night, wouldn't even cause her any pain. She would swallow her last breath of air, and slip away from life into nothingness. No suicide, no blow, no author of the deed. Like a door closing by itself, without so much as a puff of wind. Absently. It wouldn't even be dying: there would be no verb to describe it.

It's worth hearing Faulhinha Dengo's words. She who had always lived in silence, now, in her final moments, launched forth into the most carefully worded oratory. Her aim: to charm the heavenly Lord himself, He who, poor thing, must yearn so much for the beauty of the word. So listen to Faulhinha's strange prayer, with the respect it deserves:

—*I'm asking God's permission to leave life today. Yes, I commend myself, for certain and forsaken. Let me cross to the other shore, God, Sir. Because over there, I'll be able to help Ananias get dressed, serve him his food, darn his clothes.*

All of a sudden, she was startled by a noise from the bedroom. A creaking of the bed, a cracking of joints, caused her to shiver. She took a sideways glance, for fear prohibited her from anything else. Her hands shot to her mouth to stop herself from screaming. There, on the bier, the corpse was adjusting itself in death by getting up and starting to talk:

—*Don't talk like that to God, my little flower!*

Was it an order? No, it was a plea. For the first time, he was asking her something in a humble fashion.

—*Don't do that, woman, don't ask to go.*

—*Stop interfering, husband!*

—*I need you to stay there, on the other side. I have no one left living to go on caring for me.*

But once Faulhinha had got over her fright, she went on saying her prayers, commending the little that remained of her soul. She was pondering with her whole body focused on the universe: how the world would be better if all the dead had been buried smiling. Folk would even hear the dead laughing out loud from under the earth when the moon was shining up above, nice and round. As things stood, the dead left unwillingly and were jealous of Life, now that they lacked substance.

Tired of having to listen, the dead man spoke more sternly. He was no longer making requests. He was returning to the ways he had when he was alive. He blustered and threatened. His wife, impassive, sighed:

—*Be quiet, Ananias. If you don't shut up, I won't be able to hear God's voice.*

—*Forget it . . . God isn't going to speak to you.*

His wife ignored him. Then she returned to her prayers. Ananias listened, his fury simmering. At one point, he even laughed. Once again, his laughter was aimed at belittling his wife. But then he became the boss once more, severe and controlling.

—*I've only got a moment, woman, listen to me. I've got some tasks for you to do over there.*

—*You can talk as much as you like. I listened to you too much when you were alive.*

—*In our race, who doesn't respect the dead?*

—*I don't.*

—*Are you pretending to be a white?! Let me ask you then: what God are you talking to? Our old ones, or the one that's all the rage now?*

—*Listen, Ananias. Haven't you died?*

—*Of course I've died.*

—*So get on with being dead.*

He should be quiet. Better still: he should no longer have a voice, no longer even leave memories behind him. For he had long ago caused her self-effacement. She who had been born with such hopes. When she had been born, she had thought it would be forever. One could never have guessed that Faulinha had once ruled her domains. It didn't seem so now, but she had been happy as a young girl, in the abundance of her childhood. This is what had been her salvation: to find strength in memories of a time that only exists outside Time. She had married in order to be two, but had ended up being no one. An abandoned wing, her soul had already forgotten the savour of flight. And it was his fault, Ananias's. So for that reason he should let her leave life, as she herself wanted.

The dead man listened to his wife's words in alarm. He never knew Faulhinha could speak so prettily. Before, she had stifled herself in silence. Now, as he listened to her elaborate prayer, he didn't recognize her. For example, these words of hers:

—*I want to enter the ground before the earth is all used up.*

Then, once again, Faulhinha directed her petitions to divine ears. That she should be buried, her face upwards to the ground. Her eyes gazing at the sky. It wasn't enough for her to love flowers: she needed to be a stem and petals, to blossom out there and finally justify her name.

All of a sudden, the dead man tried to accost his wife. He took advantage of her being on her knees, and grabbed her neck. But the woman reacted with fury and with brute force returned her late husband to his final resting place. When she spoke, leaning over the astonished Ananias, Faulhinha was spitting rancour:

—*Don't you understand, you son of a bitch? Don't you understand that I don't want to be your widow?*

Worse than being his wife would be the obligation to mourn him. She'd rather be any man's widow but his, saturated as she was by shadow, absence, and eternal waiting. The dead man, surprised, still had something to say:

—*But only a little while ago, you were asking God to let you look after me, here in the world beyond . . .*

—*Well, I was lying.*

The late Ananias climbed back onto his bed. He remained still, now categorically dead. The last syllable froze in his eyes. He closed his eyelids with his own hands. And he re-expired. Unresuscitated.

Without getting to her feet, merely dragging herself along on her knees, the woman pulled the cage towards her. She opened the door. The parrot didn't leave its enclosure straightaway. It waited for the woman's body to fall back onto the floor. Faulhinha collapsed, in the ground's embrace. The bird still waited a bit longer. Patiently, as if it were waiting for the ground to turn to soil. Or as if it were only concerned with its own problems. Then it flapped its wings while taking a last look at the woman. If Faulhinha were still there, she would have been puzzled as she recognized those eyes. Only then did the bird fly off deep into its first sky.

The Dead Man's Revelations

THEY say he made the most astonishing revelations on his deathbed. Only the nurse, Flávio Rescaldinho, was by his side. Flávio was the only person to hear the dead man's final confessions. After the inevitable outcome, the nurse positioned himself at the door of the room where the body was growing cold. On the wall hung a simple poster, on which the following could be read: HERE LIES THE RECENTLY DEPARTED SALOMÃO GARGALO IN HIS FIRST RESTING PLACE.

The weeping visitors were expected. First came his widow, who was still young, a tearful slip of a girl. Her name was Lisete Dwarves, a name that derived from a certain book she had read about a white girl who was made of snow and who had died because of an apple. Ever since the time of Adam, whites had miserable luck because of this fruit.

—*Flávio, tell me: what did he say?*

—*He talked a lot about love.*

—*About me?*

—*Well, I mean he talked about love.*

But weren't they synonymous, she and love? No, that was unlikely in this particular case, the nurse advised. The dying man had philosophized about passion and the universe. Love had always eluded him out of fear. Yes, feelings dreaded him. Only once, on one occasion alone, had he truly felt love in his heart.

—*Was I that once, me?*

Flávio stayed mum and dumb. In the clouds, goodness knows where, completely silent. But any cricket worth its salt is allergic to silence. And so Flávio Rescaldinho coughed and spluttered. And in his state of wheeziness, he mumbled into his handkerchief:

—*The dead man even wrote it down.*

—*Show me.*

He remained stiff and stone-faced. The widow rubbed her index finger and thumb together, suggesting payment. The nurse coughed again and reluctantly offered her a dog-eared piece of paper.

—*Here it is.*

The widow unfolded the message there and then. She read it to the end, and then returned to the beginning. She read and reread.

—*Is this all?*

The nurse nodded, denying any responsibility for it. He had not been present when the dying man had written it.

—*He wrote with a sinful pen, all you gave him as a nurse was the extreme punctuation.*

They needed a priest to resolve the poison of the dead man's speech, so as to give his soul a destination. What was Salomão Gargalo thinking while he was sighing? Where could he be found now in order to seek clarification? Only in Heaven, crammed into a star, all by himself. Or, more likely, frying in hell just like an egg.

And the widow withdrew, muttering curses and oaths. As for the nurse, he glanced sideways to appreciate her gait, her swaying rear end.

Next came the dead man's brother, all done up in his Sunday best: everything matching from his tie to his shoes. All in borrowed black and mourning. He spoke as if his voice was also located behind his dark glasses. He asked:

—*Did my bro talk about my situation?*

—*Bro?*

—*My* irmão, *my brother, my bro: it's an up-to-date term. Did he talk about me or not?*

The nurse, the guardian of the pharaoh's tomb, returned his English in kind: No! And he even translated it with a modulated, sarcastic *não*. Courteously curt in ceremony and protocol. Nothing, zilch, nix. All the departed had left by way of booty was a little piece of paper.

—*This piece here.*

The brother unfolded the paper eagerly. He read it quickly at one go. He seemed to be expecting more words, paragraphs, chapters.

—*Not so much as a crumb of an inheritance, nothing here for Quintonico?*

He waited for an answer in vain. And he set off down the hall feeling sorry for himself. Then came the mistress, bee-like, hunched over her stealthy feet. She came up to the nurse, rubbed up against him nice and snug. With a voice like the icing on a cake, she asked:

—*Out with it, Flávio: did he mention our relationship?*

Flávio swallowed his Adam's apple. The dead son of a bitch! Had Salomão taken advantage of this dame as well? That would explain the roguish smile on the dying man's final face. The nurse pretended not to understand. And he asked her to repeat the question. The girl stuck to him more tightly than a fiscal stamp and whispered the question right into his ear. Flávio was reduced to one simple gesture: he just handed her the piece of paper without uttering a sound. The lover opened the message like someone uncorking a bottle of perfume. She glanced over it and then stuffed the paper into the abyss of her bra. She was about to leave when a voice halted her in her tracks:

—*Now, now!*

It was Flávio, denying her intentions, his index finger swishing this way and that like a windshield wiper. The paper didn't belong there in those fleshy apertures, it should be returned to the safe-keeping of his fingers. The dead man's mistress now forsook all her flirtiness. She screwed up the paper and threw it on the floor.

At that precise moment, the mayor and his retinue arrived. Only he approached Flávio. The others, their cell phones in their belts like pistols, held back. The head of the local authority growled:

—*Did he talk of the money belonging to the municipality?*

The nurse failed to understand. You hear people talk about rain, not wetness. The leader of the council was pale: he seemed to belong more to the antechamber of death than to the council chamber. Yes, or rather no, there was just one simple question: had the dead man revealed any private dealings, the transfer of public funds to private wealth?

Flávio, with the utmost respect, made it known that he had heard nothing, knew nothing, suspected nothing.

—*If you will excuse me, and pardon the inconvenience, your most esteemed Excellency: all he left was that piece of paper, that one there on the floor.*

And he bent down to pick it up. With all due decorum, the nurse blew any intrusive bacteria away and then surrendered the document. The council leader took to rummaging through the pockets of his Italian coat for his glasses. But no sooner had he found them and put them on than he took them off again. The same fury caused him to screw the paper up again and roll it along the ground. The leader grabbed the nurse by the collar and whispered threats:

—*D'you know what a one-armed man has? One arm too many.*

And the retinue stood, looking straight ahead, awaiting his order. But the leader turned on his heels, his footsteps echoing down the corridor. The nurse looked at the screwed-up little piece of paper on the ground. One or two letters were legible. Flávio peered and made out the odd word: ... *you sons of* ...

Finally, when all the visits were done, Flávio Rescaldinho returned to the dead man's room. And when a solemn silence might have been expected, muffled laughter could be heard. Folk said it came from two breasts, two souls enjoying vengeance to the full. Thus confirming the adage: vengeance isn't self-serving. It just serves a purpose.

Ezequiela, Humanity

A CERTAIN young boy fell in love with a girl, whose name was Ezequiela. The boy was called Jerónimo. It was love that led to a ring and the altar steps. Before you could bat an eyelid, two destinies were joined, his and hers, both together.

Until one morning, Jerónimo woke up and saw another woman lying next to him in bed. She was white, with long blond hair. He pondered in alarm: who's this woman? Where's my wife? And he called:

—*Ezequiela!*

The white girl woke up, startled by the shout, and answered:

—*What's happened, honey?*

And he: honey honey, not for my money! Who the hell was she and how could she explain why she was there, in the middle of someone else's bed?

—*But I'm Ezequiela. I'm your wife, Jerónimo.*

He just laughed, flabbergasted.

—*How can you be if you're as white as can be and my wife is Black? How can you be if your hair . . .*

—*Calm down, Jerónimo, let me explain.*

And she explained. That's just the way she was, she changed her body every so often. Sometimes in size, other times in colour. Now beautiful, now ugly. At the moment she was white and later she'd be Black. She was very vice-versatile in the way she could change.

—*Do you love me like this, the way I am?*

—*The way you are, how?*

And that was the crux of the problem, her identity, the truly genuine Ezequiela. Saddened, he shook his head:

—*I can't. You're not the one I married.*

So Ezequiela suggested quite simply that they should just get on with life as a married couple, living under one roof, and then see what the future brought. And that's what they did. So it happened that one night, Jerónimo knitted his fingers through her silky hair. Then his fingers gradually ran over other parts of her body, until they dared to feel more hidden areas. And so they made love again, and their relationship was renewed.

He had already grown used to her lack of colour and the smoothness of her hair, when one night Ezequiela woke up as an Inuit, with yellowish skin, and eyes slanted at an angle. And on another occasion, she turned into an Indian woman, with coppery skin and jet-black hair.

But the strangest thing was that she never stopped being Ezequiela. And Jerónimo accepted her thus, ever in transit but untransmutable. At first, he found it hard to adjust and readjust. But later, he even began to enjoy this game of reincorporation. And he loved her in all her shapes, voluminous, slinky, large, and small. He even found it handy: he was the most monogamous of polygamous men in the universe.

Until one day he woke up next to a bearded, muscular man. Jerónimo shook himself as if ridding himself of some contamination: had he slept with that man? What else had he shared with the intruder?

—*Don't worry, darling. It's me, Ezequiela. I'm still me.*

But the fact is that Jerónimo had ungendered himself. His wife: a man? She had already turned into a white and a Black, short and tall, all of that, fine. But she had always been a woman. Ezequiela tried to calm him down, but he was on his guard. He even peeped at his wife in the bathroom. Could it be that she was a he in every way? And to his horror: she was. They started to sleep in separate beds, just in case he surrendered. After an afternoon of absolute silence, Jerónimo came to the point.

—*I'm sorry, but this has gone too far. For as long as you remain Ezequiel, I'm off . . .*

And he left, without taking any luggage with him at all. He slept goodness knows where, and ate whenever he could. One night, however, he felt ill, burning hotter than fire. At the height of his fever, he returned home, and found his wife still in her male phase. She supported him with her strong arms and brought him inside. He resisted, tense and as distant as convenience dictated. She placed him on the bed and brought him a cool towel and a welcome glass of water. Little by little, the husband became more subdued. And when he felt Ezequiela's lips kiss his brow, he even felt pleasantly sleepy. At that point he let himself go, even when he found it strange to feel the rasp of a beard brushing his neck.

The next day, Jerónimo awoke feeling revived and looked at himself in the mirror. He was puzzled by the asymmetry between his movements and their reflection. In fact, it wasn't a mirror: on the other side of the frame, it was someone else dressed in his own body. The person standing there, naked, in front of him, was himself. Trembling, Jerónimo asked hesitantly:

—Ezequiela?

And the voice emanating from the other side, shocked, shot back another question:

—*What do you mean, Ezequiela?! Don't you recognize your husband, Ezequiela?*

The Captain's Lover

I'M going to tell you about something that happened long ago in the very place where we live today. Once upon a time a boat loaded with Portuguese sailors arrived at our village. The ship wasn't suited to the beach. It remained away from the shore, hidden in the distance, there where the mists are born. The visitors stayed out there, shut away, doing goodness knows what.

Until, after some days had gone by, a little dinghy left the big boat, heading for the shore. In it were three fully clothed, bearded Portuguese. With them was a Black man like us. He wasn't one of our folk, but he spoke our language. This dark fellow jumped out of the boat and called to us, waving:

—*I want to speak to the human folk here*, he said.

And he gave us this message: the ship's captain needed a man urgently and right away. What service was this man required for? The service of love, replied the Black man who was accompanying the whites.

—*Of love?*

Yes, carnal love, a job requiring cloth-tearing, body-squeezing, sigh-stifling. The people tried to get the matter straight in their minds: that this captain of theirs needed a woman, one of the comely ones, full of pulp and juiciness.

—*No, what he needs is a man.*

—*A man?*

—*Yes, a man. Preferably one with a smattering of Portuguese.*

—*But, sorry again, a man?*

By this time, though, the delegation was already heading back towards the boat. They were left in doubt: could it be an error of translation? Were they to provide a masculine or a feminine person? The matter gave rise to serious disagreement. It didn't make much difference either way: either it was a mistake by the translator and they sent a masculine man, which would result in the Portuguese punishing them, or if the interpreter had been right and they were to send a comely woman, they would still be as angry. They didn't want to offend the whites. So the elders had a meeting in order to match the word with the intention. In the end, they reached a consensus: the request contained the right sex.

—*They asked for a male, we'll give them a male.*

What they needed to do now was to give the matter due priority. They didn't want to disobey the *tugas.*[*]

—*But which man shall we send?*

The villagers wondered among themselves. Until one of the elders suggested:

—*I know, we'll send Josinda.*

—*Josinda? But she's a female who's given birth to kids and all that . . .*

Yes, she was a woman, but so unfeminine that at first sight she could pass as a man. She was a strange fish, all muscular and boorish. If she hadn't had kids, you wouldn't know she was a female.

The elder who had made the suggestion pursued his idea. Josinda was just the ticket, the bee's knees: she was half and half,

---

[*]   Derogatory term for a Portuguese person.

both fish and fowl, prone to ambivolatility. And what's more, she spoke the white man's language.

—*We'll send Josinda with another name, shave her hair, and dress her up as a man. To be on the safe side.*

A kid was sent rushing off to summon the almost manly woman. He found the girl meandering along the beach in search of her widowed prince.

—*Josinda, come quickly: you're needed by the whites.*

—*Wait a moment, let me go and put on some better clothes.*

—*No, come just as you are, just like that.*

—*But like this, wearing my father's clothes, I look just like him.*

—*That's why. And by the way, you've got to say your name is Jezequiel.*

—*Jezequiel? Why Jezequiel, such an ugly, man's name.*

—*The Portuguese really like that name.*

Josinda presented herself before the elders. They gave her much advice, all very secret, mouth-to-ear stuff. They recommended that she put on an act, be coarser in her ways. Then at last she was ready and walked down to the dinghy belonging to the Portuguese. She spoke to the sailor who had come to fetch what had been requested.

—*I love that shiny uniform you're wearing, mister soldier.*

—*I'm a lieutenant.*

—*I'm sorry, I thought you were a soldier. My mistake, who doesn't make a mistake? Only a bird on the wing never stumbles.*

And off they went, swallowed up by the night. The elders stayed awake all night, fearing the outcome of any news. In the early morning, the soldiers' boat could be seen among the patches of mist.

—*So, how did it go?*

Josinda was standing erect in the boat, all wrapped up in clothes, only her eyes peering out. But those same eyes were full of tears: the woman was crying, something that had never been seen before. And so, weeping loudly, she disappeared into the darkness. The elders were shocked, and bade farewell to the Portuguese all the more respectfully.

Later, a delegation turned up at Josinda's door. They were burning with curiosity: what could have made the woman weep? They pressed her. But she stubbornly maintained her silence.

The next night, they saw a boat with soldiers approaching. The locals huddled together in groups on the beach, apprehensive.

—*They're coming to kill us all!*

But the Portuguese weren't disposed to violence. They asked for Josinda.

—*Our captain needs that Jezequiel again.*

And so some youngsters were quickly sent to look for the desired woman. They reached her house, and explained the demand. But Josinda shook her head and refused.

—*Tell them you couldn't find me.*

—*But the Portuguese . . .*

—*Leave me alone.*

Her tone of voice conveyed an assertive, unequivocal no. They insisted, threatened, begged. Nothing. The youngsters returned to the beach with an improvised lie. That ever since early morning no one had clapped eyes on the selfsame Jezequiel. The soldiers left behind them a promise: a reward for anyone who found her. And the boat set off, disconsolate, back to the ship, as if in mourning.

The next morning, two boats came: the soldiers disembarked and spread out, searching houses and vegetation. Folk made themselves scarce, frightened. They found Josinda's house but it was empty. There was no trace or even sign of her in the vicinity. By the end of the afternoon, they had finished their search and the soldiers returned to the great ship. They left behind one Portuguese, charged with finding information about the captain's so-called lover. He started off with bravado. Saying that he would kill, set things on fire, rape. Then he took on a gentler air, offering promises.

—I'll give money to whoever wants it. I'll give you all the money you want.

—All?!

—It's just that you can't imagine how much our captain is suffering. We've never seen him like this before.

It was in the early hours of the morning when the Portuguese captain was seen coming ashore, crestfallen and dishevelled. He jumped into the water and waded onto dry land, yelling like a madman. He was calling for Jezequiel, wandering in circles, his eyes agog. Then he collapsed, his shoulders hunched, worn out. He remained like this, befuddled and as still as a stone, for minutes on end. Around him, the soldiers waited, not knowing what to do. A whole day went by, without any decision being reached. Until the commander of the soldiers issued his order: They were to return to the ship, weigh anchor and leave.

—And what about our captain?

—I'm staying.

And indeed, he did stay. At first next to the sea. Later, he set off into the savannah looking for his lover of only one night. The last thing he did before abandoning the beach was to pick up a little stick and scratch away in the sand. No one there was able to decipher those drawings. But a Portuguese soldier who came back to the beach was astonished to see written in the sand the name: Josinda.

The Assault

Not long ago, I was the victim of an armed assault. It was on a street corner, in one of those alleyways where darkness is kept under lock and key. I couldn't even make out the shape of the assailant: all I could see, in a fleeting flash, was the weapon in his hand. I was already thinking beyond the normal limits of reflection: I'm done for! The pistol was next to my chest, showing me that death is a dog that obeys even before it's whistled at.

It was all muddle and panic, and I was preparing my accounts with life. Fear is a knife that cuts with its handle rather than with its blade. We brandish a knife, and the thicker the wrist, the more we cut ourselves.

—*Get back!*

I obeyed the command, stumbling until I bumped into the wall. My veins were frozen up, my heart turned to glass: I was in the antechamber of death, waiting for a single shot. I obeyed the assailant's orders absolutely mechanically. And as dopey as the cuckoo in the clock. What was I to do? Counterattack? Risk everything and, without a second thought, toss my life away without a care?

—*Say something.*

—*Anything?*

—Tell me about yourself. Who are you?

I measured my words. The more I talked and the less I said, the better. The guttersnipe was out to strip me bare. The best tactic would be a cautious silence. We fear what we don't understand. That much we all know. But in this case, my fear was even worse: I was scared because I understood. That is the function of terror: to transform what we cannot control into the irrational.

—Start talking.

—Talking?

—Yes, tell me things. Then it'll be me. It'll be my turn.

Then it would be his turn? But to do what? For sure, it would be to murder me in cold blood, with a shot at point-blank range. At that moment, as if from nowhere, there appeared a timid ray of light, almost nothing, more to foresee than to see. The fellow lowered his face and pressed his pistol against me menacingly.

—Any funny business and I'll . . .

He didn't carry out his threat. He was overcome by a cavernous cough. For a fraction of a second, he lowered his weapon while he got rid of his phlegm. For an instant he appeared defenceless, so vulnerable that it would have been bad-mannered of me to take advantage of the moment. I noticed that he was taking out a handkerchief and composing himself, almost unaware of my presence.

—Come on, let's go over there.

I took a few more steps back. Fear had given way to anxiety. Who could this scoundrel be? One of those people who turn to theft because of some greater weakness? Or someone who had been forced down this path by life? I should add that I was not concerned at that moment with the criminal's possible antecedents. After all, the earth feeds on what is rotten.

We walked towards the light. This was when I realized that my assailant was an old man. A *mestiço* of positively respectable appearance. But he was of the fourth age, his hair totally white.

He didn't look poor. Or if he was, he must have been one of those poor who are out of fashion, one of the ones from when the world was as old as we are. When I was a child, we took pity on the poor. They were part and parcel of that tiny place, destitute of everything, but without losing their humanity. Nowadays, my children are afraid of the poor. Poverty has grown into a monstrous place. We seek to keep the poor at arm's length, within the borders of their own territory. But this fellow wasn't one of those miserable wretches who had emerged from their inferno. That was when, now tired, I asked him:

—*What do you want of me?*

—*I want to talk.*

—*To talk?*

—*Yes, just that, to talk. It's because nowadays, at my age, no one wants to talk to me anymore.*

So this was what it was all about? Just a chat? Yes, that was the reason for the crime. The man had resorted to a firearm in order to steal instants, access a tiny fissure of attention. If no one showed him the courtesy of noticing him, he would acquire the right even if it had to be with the help of a pistol. What he couldn't lose was the last residue of his humanity—namely the right to meet with others, eye to eye, his soul revealing itself in another face.

So I sat down, without a care for time or expense. There in that dark alleyway, I told him about my life in all its complexion and untruths. In the end, he had almost fallen asleep over my stories, and I took my leave with one request: that the next time, he should dispense with his pistol. We would both willingly sit down together on a garden bench. To which, the old man immediately replied:

—*Don't do that. Let me hold you up, sir. I enjoy it more like that.*

And so that's what happened: ever since then I've been the victim of holdups, but without any fear whatsoever. Assaults without any somersaults. I've got used to it, and it's like taking a dog that's already died for a walk. In the end, what happens in crime is the same as what happens in love: we only know we've found the right person after we've met those who are right for others.

Bereavement

Tʜᴇ husband went to his wife, grieving, and burst out:
—*My wife has died.*

His wife quivered. She smiled in order to find light relief from his tasteless joke. But he, a tear seeping out of the corner of his eye, rammed the point home.

—*She has died.*

And he plodded off so as to give vent to his sadness. His wife, at a loss, thought her husband had flipped his lid once and for all. She went after him and touched him on the shoulder. Then she held back, realizing that her gesture was one of condolence.

That afternoon, dressed all in black, he went to the newspaper offices in order to arrange for the appropriate death notice to be printed. From there, he went on to the undertaker's. He returned home, woebegone. He collapsed onto the sofa, in front of his astonished wife.

—*I've seen to the formalities, everything will be taken care of tomorrow.*
—*Can I go to the funeral?*

He didn't even look at her, occupied as he was with his emptiness. He took his time in giving a negative answer, claiming that it would be better if she remained at home to look after the house. There might be visitors, and she should stay.

—I'll go on my own. I've never shared sadness. We only have a right to share happiness.

And next morning, off he went, wizened, among the drops of rain. His wife stood on the veranda, watching her husband recede, as if she didn't know this man with whom she had lived for more than thirty years. As the sun was going down, he returned, full of anguish. He was drained, his body hunched, his soul already migrating.

—Life has never been so empty for me as it is now, such a burden.

She let him be, out of respect for the depth of his solitude. The man looked at her, huddled in a corner, and asked:

—Are you going to stay around here for a few more days?

She stuttered an almost inaudible yes. He was treating her as if she were some distant relative, some unrecognized acquaintance from far away. And he showed her the bedroom where she could put some of her things.

—You can bed down here.

That night, by the light of the fire, he sat bent over like a question mark. He stayed there, his face hidden between his knees. He prayed, prayerless. She asked him whether he wanted some tea, who knows, it might help him forget a bit. She passed him a cup, along with the sweet aroma of the steam, which he breathed in before speaking.

—The woman I lost, there'll never be another . . .

And he related how they had met, explained how he yearned for those early days in their romance. What he remembered was decked with embellishments, so embroidered with tenderness that she was moved to tears. Did her husband love her so much after all?

The following evenings, she asked him to talk about that magnificent love, so that she could find strength in that other woman who, only he seemed unaware, was none other than herself. And so once again there was the unravelling of tender recollections.

On one occasion, the man became so emotional that his words stuck in his throat. And not even a sob proved able to unblock the road to speech. So then she decided to put an end to the whole episode. She knelt in front of him:

—*Husband, I am your wife!*

The man looked at her in astonishment. He examined her face, his brow furrowed slowly, and he smiled and said:

—*I know who you are . . .*

—*Well?*

—*I don't deserve this untruth, neighbour. It's very kind of you to pretend, but I have to accept the truth of my bereavement.*

And he continued: he was learning to be a widower. His neighbour should leave him be in his loneliness, a man needs to reinvent the earth after the flood.

—*Even so, I want to thank you for trying to pass as her.*

The lady, impassive, remained silent. And for many nights, she listened to his yearning as it unravelled like a rosary in her ears. The man was boundless in his memories of affection, discoursing poetically until morning broke on this sweetheart whose equal he would never be able to find, as long as the world turned and the nights rolled by.

And in this way, with endless recollections of love, he grew old and short of breath. Only she never grew old, ageless in both body and soul. Who knows? Perhaps because she had died before her own time was up.

Stop the Dance!

*T*o *erase love, you need to love.* Those were the words of my
Uncle Albano, retired but not tired. I was very proud of that
relative of mine: the lads in the street would sacrifice everything
to go and have a good chinwag with Uncle Albano. The old man
only had one subject of conversation: women. And always in the
plural. At least, if Uncle Albano was to be believed.

—*A woman is a cloud: there's no way of dropping anchor in one.*

And what he knew about women! He'd had hundreds of
affairs, he'd lost count. My father smiled condescendingly:

—*Your uncle's a recounter.*

But the lads were in no doubt at all. We were embarking on
our lives as macho men, and in order to give our mission an epic
meaning, we needed a hero, someone who could smother us with
stories and adventures. And the deeds of our retiree were enticing
to our heart and soul. Sometimes we pretended we didn't believe
him, but it was only to spice up his recollections. We were forcing
him to spill out a few more memories.

—*Uncle Albano, were there really so many of them that you lost count?*

—*Well, when it comes to women, we lose count even when there's only one.*

Questions jostled with each other. How was it that some
of them went and others came? Albano became serious and

responded without even pausing for reflection: The decision to start is made by the man, but it's the woman who decides to finish things. And he put forward the moral of the story.

—*Never let yourself get attached to one. She'll be like a liana seeking its soil.*

But that was at a time when there were no illnesses. People died because they did not give their bodies any pleasure.

—*It's not like with you people nowadays.*

Uncle shook his head, incapable of accepting it.

—*My patron saint is life, that's what it is,* he always concluded.

His guardian must have become distracted, for one morning, Uncle Albano died. He woke up lifeless, lying in his bed, dressed in his suit and tie. Well-dressed out of respect for his final transaction. *A man of my age always goes to bed well-prepared*, he would say. And that's exactly what happened. At his funeral, his fans, the local lads, were present in weight of numbers and range of sadness. Behind our disappointment, however, we harboured hidden expectation. We were hoping that the dead man's girlfriends would show up in their hundreds at the funeral mass. But there was no woman at all present at the ritual. Only when the graveyard soil began to be shovelled over the coffin did a lone, beautiful, leggy woman appear. She was wearing mourning clothes, and without more ado she reached up over her elegant slim lines and, rather than a flower, she tossed some screwed-up object into the grave.

Everyone left except for this strange *mulata*, who remained there in prostration. At first, she seemed to be praying. But in fact, what she was doing was singing. She was singing, almost in an undertone,

Cuando calienta el sol . . .

I withdrew with my father. On our way home, my old man stopped next to the park. There was no longer a garden, nor were there any flower beds. All this had been destroyed. Even the little green lake where geese swam was reduced to a stinking puddle. A swan with a broken wing still lumbered around in the mud. Was the creature dreaming of escape to a more watery lake? We sat down and my old man set off on long, silent ruminations. I didn't want the hand of sadness to summon him far away. That was why I asked him:

—*What was it that lady threw on top of the coffin?*

My father gazed at the mutilated swan and smiled. Then he ran his hand through my hair and for a short while seemed to forget his existence. He asked for my patience so that he could tell me a story. My father had never told me a story before. He was the opposite of his late brother, who had any number of tales to tell. And so I devoted all my attention to what he had to say.

The story began at a dance held at the Railwaymen's Club, sometime in the middle of the century. It was there that whites, *mulatos,* and one or two assimilated Blacks from the town would mingle. Dance nights were a well-known ritual around here. Many a love affair began at those parties. That particular night, the couples swapped partners and gyrated in a lively rainbow of colours.

Suddenly, an order was given for the dancing to stop.

—*Stop the dance!* boomed the emphatic command. Everyone paused in a climate of great expectation. Meanwhile, the master of ceremonies climbed onto the stage with a pompous, determined air. His voice rang out as he clung to the lapels of his white tuxedo:

—*We ask anyone who finds a lady's bra on the dance floor to hand it in to the management.*

Everyone stood still, dumbfounded, their spirits confused. Until a voice in the crowd cried:

—*A lady's bra? Is there any other type?*

There was laughter. At first timid and then noisy, like rain falling on a tin roof. People began to comment: many things were lost in the midst of a knees-up, but no one had ever allowed such an intimate item to escape them. While the raucous laughter spread, Uncle Albano came up to my father. He was horrified, shaking wildly.

They had to do something, for that bra must belong to the great love of his life, Maria Prudência. But the most important revelation—a discovery that came as a shock to my ears—was this: Albano had never had a girlfriend of any description. All he had was this obsessive, unsubstantiated passion, an affair that was doomed never to happen. For the girl was given to adventures, her body receiving more visitors than the Namaacha Falls. She took no notice at all of Uncle Albano because he was timid, better-behaved than a sacristan.

—*What if the bra is hers?*

If it was indeed hers, it would be the end for the girl, for her father was a bad-tempered brute, capable of pulling out his belt and delivering a beating. The big fellow couldn't stand such vexation. We had to do something.

—*But what's it got to do with you, brother? Forget it, end of story.*

But Albano was no longer there. He walked off, though not to his usual solitary corner. Until, not long afterwards, to everyone's bewilderment, he was seen climbing onto the stage and asking to speak. He half-squinted at the microphone. The sound of his shaking voice echoed through the room as he asked:

—*Is this metrophone switched on?*

There was general laughter. What was that skinny little fellow doing there, incapable of producing a shadow, lacking the gift of the gab or any presence whatsoever? The guy couldn't do anything right, he didn't dance, and he got all muddled up when he spoke to anyone.

—*I climbed onto this stage to announce the following . . .*

There he stopped. Blocked, his valves clogged. Their surprise was such that curiosity began to grow. They were waiting for what was to come: what was this "following"? And they egged him on.

—*Speak, lad!*

Then, after stuttering blankly, he eventually said:

—*It's mine!*

There was general agitation and incomprehension—what was his? And as people were already well and truly tanked up, they started booing, trying to hasten the outcome of his vagueness. The guy should get a move on, he was holding up the party. Albano held up his hands, asking for silence. His talking became a bit clearer. And the lad returned to the fray with this astonishing declaration:

—*The bra's mine!*

Not a hoot could be heard, not even the buzz of a fly. So the boy was confessing he was a pansy, camouflaging himself with womanliness? The humiliation was just too much. How could he subject himself to eternal badmouthing, condemning his name to the filth of tongue-wagging?

Only my father knew his brother's motive. He had sacrificed his honour to save the damsel he secretly loved. This was his secret, which was now being buried in the shape of an item of women's clothing next to his final wooden resting place.

Rosita*

IT was five days ago. They came and told me: get out of here, because all this is going underwater. They said the river was going to go berserk. I didn't know, but this river joined with another one and that one, in turn, joined with that part of the sky where the gods keep all the rain.

—*But what about this one here, do I leave him behind?* I asked, pointing at my old companion.

—*You choose. If you want to live, leave by yourself, right now.*

I didn't go. I talked to Makalatani while he was calmly eating. Both of us decided to wait. We couldn't take it: during the war they had separated us. We had both lost everything such a short time before. How many times can we lose everything in one life? It wasn't even ten years since we had fled the gunfire, each one of us fighting for our own survival. My companion, old Makalatani, where had he ended up during those years of war? I didn't believe he had survived. But when I returned to Chokwé, there he was

---

* I wrote this story based on witness statements I gathered during the flooding of the Limpopo Valley in March 2000. Rosita is a little girl who really was born in a tree. Her mother had sought refuge there because it was the only high point in that flooded landscape.

·305·

waiting for me. Loyal, right there where we had parted. The violence hadn't made him bitter. He was as sweet-tempered as ever, ready to start again, as always with so little against a background of nothingness.

Once again, the warnings to us to leave. Once again displaced? Were those people filling us with alarm so sure of the future? Do the poor abandon their poverty with such lightness of heart? But the truth is, it happened. Worse than happening, it followed pretty well immediately. And it was sudden: the sky became the colour of earth, like the Devil's spittle. The clouds were heavy as if made of mud. The sky grew so dense it ceased to be the dwelling place of birds.

We emerged from our houses. We looked at the sky. And we were suddenly afraid: because the sky was no longer wide. It was right there, at hand. The stars were countable, one family's fingers were enough to point at them.

Then came the rain, cascading to the earth. Huge, sluggish masses of water, each drop swollen and intense. On all sides, veins were born, every cranny turned into a stream. And the river filled, and burst its banks until it covered the vastness.

On the first morning, the rain had already filleted the road, swallowed up the bridge, chewed up the fields. God had lost control of the waters. Sadness smiled within me: I had always wanted to see the ocean. Now the ocean had come to see me.

Even so, old Makalatani only thought of eating, oblivious to the rain and to omens. But I wasn't. I looked at time, sniffed the river. I knew what they were like—time and water. Both had taken away children of mine, dreams, prosperity. I sat down on the banks of time. I stopped my life right there, resting on the edge. Later, I discovered there is no bank. Everything flows, the bank only seems to be still. That current of time was what had taken my wife, my children, everything.

The following night, the waters of the river rose. I was pushed to a shelter that I had thought exclusive to birds. I scaled the tree, climbed onto the roof of the storehouse. Makalatani climbed up with me. He seemed to be tottering, off balance. Then he lay down, as if there were nothing left to do. And there I was, quivering, gazing at the desolation all around. My belongings, my goats, the house: all were vanishing. My life flowing away. Just me and Makalatani on the roof.

Looking further away, I surveyed our surroundings, but could see nothing except for water. And I thought of our neighbour, Sofia Pedro. She was pregnant, almost about to give birth. Had she managed to escape? I called out to her by name. But the noise of the waters drowned out my voice. Only Makalatani looked at me, with those eyes of a naked woman. I was losing my appearance as a person. My skin was baked and cracked. It wouldn't be long before I turned into a fish, all covered with scales.

The following day, all I did was drink. I cupped my hands in the very waters of the river. What I drank was sick water. Makalatani drank with me, but he was never fussy about drinking. Now, both of us were bent double like animals, sucking up mud and dirt, our only nourishment.

I stopped drinking when I saw the bloated bodies of oxen and men float by on the current. I told Makalatani not to look. And I made a promise that I wouldn't allow death to contaminate my insides. Death is another river: every now and then it leaps over the bank and floods us like a vast ocean.

At night, I was mad with hunger. The water rose even higher, and the tin roof disappeared. My fingers were bleeding from clinging so hard to the wooden planks. I was witnessing my own death. I even got to thinking: I give up, I'll throw myself into the current. It was Makalatani who stopped me. There he was, so placid, knowing how to wait. Or ignorant of time? My companion expected me to show the same tranquility. He was teaching me tactics for survival.

On the fourth day, my eyes could hardly make out anything.

Everything was out of focus. That was when I heard a cloud descending noisily. It was a cloud with a motor. It hovered above us like an eagle. A white angel was lowered from the cloud and took hold of me. I was ready for anything. Except for leaving my companion behind. I shouted to the angel:

—*I'm only going if you take my Makalatani as well.*

The man shouted at me. The noise, the spattering of water, all suddenly woke me up. The angel was, in fact, a South African soldier who was opening his arms to me, hanging on the end of a rope. The cloud was a helicopter, its blade fanning us, over the shed where we were sheltering.

Everything was suddenly clear. And I shouted:

—*Come on, Makalatani, these people have come to save us.*

He turned his head away, fearful of heights. I started to push him but his weight was too much for me. I shouted to the soldier:

—*My ox! Help me to load my ox!*

It wasn't worth it. The soldier didn't speak Portuguese. He only spoke the language of soldiers: orders, immediate obedience. But I couldn't leave my old ox behind, my only treasure. Who would I have for company when I started my life over again? I shouted too, like soldiers do:

—*Hey, Makalatani, get into the helicopter, you lazy thing!*

The stubborn creature sat down on all four of its legs. And me, by now in despair: if you're not going, then I'm not going either. Fair enough, we'll both die, one without the other. And I sat down with the little strength left to me. At that point, the soldier's patience wore out and he put his arms around me. And up I went into the air, spinning around like a butterfly, dancing without any floor other than the body of the South African.

Taken by force, I was thrown into the helicopter.

—*What's all this now? Is a person rescued whether he likes it or not?* I spoke to the others, my brothers, who were huddled together in the belly of the aircraft.

—*Did you see that, folks? I was forced to leave behind my ox on the roof.*
—*What ox?* they asked.
—*My big old ox, Makalatani, that's the name I baptized him with.*

But the others who had been rescued like me were astonished. There was no ox next to me. And another even pointed out that he had seen my horned friend swept away by the torrent. He had seen that more than two days ago. The animal must have been already nearly lifeless, because all he could see was a horn pointing towards the heavens. So there had never been an ox on my roof, I must have been hallucinating because of the dirty water I had drunk.

I sat there as speechless as an orphan. I looked at my fellow travellers. They were all dripping with water, fear, fright. Until suddenly I caught sight of Sofia Pedro, my pregnant neighbour. She was holding a bundle in her arms, which made me wonder. She opened her *capulana* and showed me a baby girl, fresher than the dew.

—*Don't tell me you gave birth to that little girl on top of the tree?!*

I had never seen so great a fatigue in one body. But Sofia still managed to smile, and murmured:

—*This is Rosita, my Rosita.*

I fell silent in thought. I looked at the child, my eyes focusing on her. The girl seemed to be crying. But she couldn't be heard, everything was stifled by the engine. Sofia Pedro took the little girl and placed her on her breast. Rosita's squealing voice began to grow louder, superimposing itself upon the helicopter's engines. I assumed an inner calm, and my heart was flooded. And once again, I saw myself on a cloud, floating like a ship. I was travelling with my people, heading for those unseen fields where my ox was grazing the morning mist.

Yes, wherever we were bound, there would be land. Once again, the infinite territory of life. And Rosita was being born within me.

The Falling Man

WHEN they came and called me, I couldn't believe what they said.

—*It's Joey! He's falling from the building.*

And everyone there hurried to see what was going on. I joined the rush, the question buzzing all around: the man was falling? That gerund was a denial of the laws of gravity: whoever's falling already fell.

While I ran, my chest tightened. I foresaw my old friend lying smashed to pieces on the sidewalk. What had happened to make him commit suicide, fallen into the abyss? What lapse had brought his life tumbling down? It could be everything: present times are like bleach, leaving all the magic discoloured.

By this time, I was approaching the building and I was already pushing my way through the crowd. It was a sight that beggared belief: everyone was looking upwards. When I glimpsed the sky, I was even more perturbed: there he was, hovering like a great eagle, Joey Neto. José Antunes Marques Neto himself, like an aero-angel. Was he falling? If he was, then he was moving slower than a planet gliding through the heavens.

When had he thrown himself off? The previous night, but people had only noticed the following day. The whole world had then piled forwards and in a flash, explanations and epistemologies were being spouted. What had happened came from his having led an unblemished life: this was why he was given the necessary lightness. If he were a politician, he would have nose-dived straightaway from the weight of his conscience. Others argued differently: in his pelican's state, the citizen was escaping from his debts. No one demands payment in the air.

There was even a subtly Christian version. One onlooker, as thin as a stick insect, dressed as if he could fit into a single sleeve, bellowed, pointing to the firmament:

—*That, gentlemen, is the new Christ.*

The skinny fellow continued to shout: *What doors did Christ open for us? The doors to the sky, dear brothers. The sky.* But now, the aforementioned Joey was showing us the way to the stars. And he was doing so without having to die, which was an acknowledged advantage.

—*That, gentlemen, is Christ decrucified.*

He was told to keep quiet. Other more practical bystanders were busy with what might follow. And they were predicting a final outcome.

—*That guy is going to hang around like that for days on end.*

—*What'll happen is that he'll die of hunger and thirst.*

If you couldn't even eat properly on earth in the present conditions, it would be even worse up in the clouds. What rattled me was that we had to act urgently. Someone should do the right thing. And I shouted amid the buzz of conversation:

—*Have you called the firefighters?*

Yes, but they were on strike. Even if they weren't, it wouldn't make much difference: they had no fire engines, or ladders, or any willingness. In fact, they were distinctly unfiery firefighters.

It was getting late, people started heading for home. A scattering of onlookers stayed behind, in silence. I looked up at the sky again and focused better on my friend Joey. His face displayed such serenity that it was as if he were asleep. His legs were stretched out like a flamingo's, crossing at his ankles, his arms cushioning his head. He looked as if he were sky-bathing. What was going through his mind?

That was when I noticed a girl standing beside me, crying. She looked so young that I wondered whether she might be his daughter. I even asked her. Daughter? What daughter? She was his secret love, that's what she was. This was turning into the plot of a romantic love story, a drama without any cloaks or daggers. It wasn't even worth trying to find out. The girl had no explanation other than her tears.

Gradually everyone withdrew. Only the girl and I were left. She leaned against my shoulder as if she were asleep, if it weren't for the *drip-drip-drip* of her voice, mumbling away. Was she still crying? No. She was praying. She was praying for rain. At least he would drink a few drops from the sky rather than drying up like a shark pickling in brine. Whether the girl had invoked the right spirits or whether it was from natural forces, the truth is that in an instant, it began to rain. And it rained for the next two days.

Where nothing happens, anything can occur. And the crowds turned up in shifts. The space was packed with umbrellas, and people began to give voice to concerns.

—*If it goes on raining like this, the guy's going to get drenched, grow heavy, and come crashing down.*

Maybe the gods heard. It stopped raining. And over the next few days, it was as if the air itself had come to a standstill. Joey's flight became a city attraction. Various businesses were set up. Tourists bought tickets, guides to fantastic phenomena explained novel versions of how Joey had been born with feathers in his armpits and was the descendant of a family of secret flyers. The fellow had the trappings of a born trapeze artist. His own uncle hired a megaphone so people could send him messages of good-will and blessings. Even I paid to speak to my old friend. But when I found myself with the megaphone in my hand, I didn't know what to say. And I returned the instrument.

Then the appropriate authorities really did turn up, represented by the supreme chief of police, who made his voice heard by means of a loudspeaker.

—*Come down in the name of the law!*

The politician behind him whispered suggestions. The masses, the electorate, wanted a swift resolution.

—*Keep giving orders. Keep it up, but do so with firmness!* the politician encouraged him.

The spokesman obeyed, his voice become more strident.

—*Your behaviour, dear citizen, is truly undemocratic.*

It was against human rights, muttered the politician. It was against the image of stability the nation needed, the speaker even added. International donors would be shocked at such a non-state of affairs. But Joey didn't move an inch. He smiled roguishly.

Okay, so now let me get to the point. I won't go on so as not to prolong the deception. For everything that I've told you, Joey's flight and the crowd down below, it was all a dream. Let's breathe a sigh of relief. Reality is more lowly, made of heavier stuff, its feet planted firmly on the ground.

But next day, I couldn't be sure of my peace of mind. And I went to the place to satisfy myself that I had been dreaming. I found the city going about its daily routine. Up above was the sky, empty of flying humans. Only the blue as it should be, and the odd cloud. And the birds flying through the air. And the square, anchored to the earth, inhumanly human. All devoid of novelty and with few dreams to offer.

All of a sudden, I saw the girl. The same girl from the dream. Her, nothing more, nothing less. And what's more, she was still looking up at the sky. I went over to her and she, without turning her gaze from the firmament, muttered:

—I can't see him anymore. What about you?

—What about me?

—Can you see Joey?

I lied that I could. In the end, he was worth more as a bird. Even a pretend one. We should let Joey fly, for he had nowhere to fall. In this world, there's nowhere for birds like that to land. Wherever he is, there's another sky.

The Basket

Fᴏʀ the umpteenth time, I get ready to visit my husband in hospital. I hurriedly wash my face, comb my hair with my fingers, and tidy the same dress I always wear. It's been a long time since I've paused in front of the mirror. I know that if I look at myself, I won't recognize the eyes gazing back at me. I've visited the hospital so many times that I've even fallen ill myself. It wasn't from heart disease, for when it comes to a heart, I no longer have one. Nor was it from anything wrong in my head, for my powers of thought dimmed long ago. I live in a bottomless river, and at night I get out of bed and wander off outside my own body. As if, in the end, my husband were still sleeping beside me and I, as always, go to the other bedroom in the middle of the night. We didn't have separate beds but partitioned sleep.

Today will be like any other day: I'll sit next to his bed and talk to him, but he won't listen to me. The difference won't be there. He never did listen to me. The difference will be in the lunch box that will slumber, unattended, on his bedside table. Before, he used to devour the food I prepared for him. Food was the one area where I didn't feel rejected.

I look around me: the table is no longer laid and waiting for him, unfailing and appetizing. Before, I had no set time. Now,

I've lost all notion of time. Any moment now is for me to peck at something, hunched at a corner of the table, without a tablecloth or cutlery. It's not in the shadows that I live. It's behind the sun, where darkness fell long ago. The only route I follow is down the street to the hospital. I live for only one hour of the day: visiting time. My only occupation is to take my sick husband the daily basket containing his gifts.

They gave my husband a blood transfusion. As for me, what I'd like is a life transfusion, laughter entering my veins to the point of swallowing me up, a snake of blood leading me to madness.

Ever since last month, I've avoided speaking. I prefer silence, which suits my soul better. But the absence of conversation has created another bond between us. Silence has opened another line of communication between me and the dying man. At least now I'm no longer corrected. I'm no longer pushed around, told to shut up, to stop laughing.

I've even thought of exchanging talk for writing. Instead of this monologue, I'd write him letters. In that way, there'd be less suffering. Through letters, my man would gain some distance. More than distance: absence. On paper, I'd allow myself to say everything I'd never dared to before.

And I renew my promise: yes, I'd write him a letter made up merely of unbridled laughter, a revealing cleavage, made of all the things he never allowed me. And in this letter I would pluck up courage and announce: *You, husband, prevented me from living when you were alive. You're not going to make me waste more of my life by turning this into a slow, endless farewell.*

I return to reality, arrange the daily ration of food in the fateful basket, in this pretense that he will welcome me with an open smile and a healthy appetite. I'm on my way out on my daily routine as a visitor when, as I walk down the hall, I notice that the cloth covering the mirror has fallen off. Without wanting to, I notice my reflection. I take a couple of steps back and contemplate myself as I have never done before. And I discover the curve of my body, my bust still high. I touch my face, kiss my fingers, as if I were some other woman, some timeless, sudden lover of myself. The basket falls from my hand, as if it has come alive.

A hidden force draws me towards the closet. From it, I take the black dress my husband gave me twenty years ago. I walk over to the mirror and cover myself, swaying in some unmoving dance. My words are released, clear and succinct.

—*I only have one wish: that I should become a widow as soon as possible!*

My request surprises me, as if it were uttered by someone else. Could I express such a terrible desire? And once again, my voice affirms itself loud and clear:

—*The sooner you die, husband, the sooner I can wear this black dress for the first time.*

The mirror reflects back my timeless woman's vanity, born long before me and which I was never able to put on display. Never before had I been beautiful. But now I can confirm: mourning suits my dark eyes well. And suddenly, I notice something: I haven't even grown old. To grow old is to accept the flow of time, a way of being mistress of one's own body. And I have never loved enough. Like a stone, which waits for nothing and isn't awaited, I remain ageless.

And I rehearse my giddiness, demeanour, and tears. At the funeral, this is how I shall weep, my chin raised so as to slow the tear, my nose held high so as not to sniff. Like this, husband, I shall be the centre of attention, and not you. Your life erased me. Your death will cause me to be born. I hope you die, yes I do, and the sooner the better.

I drape the dress over the table in the living room, shut the door and set off in the direction of the hospital. I hesitate momentarily over the basket. I have never seen it before like this, so vulnerable. My triumph is to turn my back on this useless utensil. For the first time, there is sky over my house. On the edge of the sidewalk, I smell the scent of frangipanis. Only now do I realize I have never smelled my man. Not even my nose has ever loved. Today, I discover the street in all its femininity. For the first time, the street is my sister.

At the entrance to the infirmary, the same nurse as always is waiting for me. There is a shadow over his face.

—*Your husband died. It happened last night.*

I was so prepared, this had occurred so often that I didn't even need support. But after waiting for so long, I just wanted it to happen. All the more so after discovering in the mirror the light that had become entombed within me during my entire life.

I leave the hospital, waiting to be taken over by this new woman who has been announcing her arrival. However, instead of relief, I am struck by a thunderbolt that takes the ground from under my feet. Instead of the raised chin and the studied walk, I burst into tears. I return home, with faltering steps, in a solitary procession down this death-dealing street. Over my home the sky extends, more alive than I am.

In the living room, I return the mirror to its previous state by throwing a sheet over it, and then set about cutting the black dress into shreds. Tomorrow, I must remember not to prepare the basket for his visit.

The Deferred Grandfather

OUR sister Glória gave birth, and this was a reason for a family celebration. Everyone rejoiced except for our old man, Zedmundo Constantino Constante, who refused to go to the hospital to see the child. All alone in her hospital room, Glória sobbed and snivelled. All through the day, her eyes patrolled the door to her room. Our father's presence would be a much hoped-for blessing with regard to her newly born baby.

—*He must come, he must come.*

He didn't come. We had to bring the infant child back to our house for Grandfather to give him the once-over. But it was as if he were looking at nothing. There was no one there in the cradle. Glória burst into tears again. For her, it was like suffering the pains of a posthumous abortion. She begged her mother, Dona Amadalena. She should speak to her father and ask him not to inflict further punishment on her. Speak wasn't quite the right word: her mother was dumb, her voice had forgotten to be born.

The little boy said his first words and, straightaway, our father Zedmundo dismissed him:

—*Baah!*

He was contradicting everyone else's joy. Sister Glória was now shorn of any glory at all. She sighed impatiently. Such an audible sigh that the old man felt obliged to explain:

—*Learning to talk is easy. With all due respect to your mother. She's not dumb. It's just that her voice has gone to sleep.*

Our mother—the aforementioned Grandma Amadalena—shook her head. The man always shaded the cloud greyer than necessary. But Zedmundo, when it came to talking, had his reasons: we poor folk shouldn't open our mouth to speak, but to better bite our lip.

—*And that's why I'll say it again: talking is easy. The hard bit is knowing how to keep quiet.*

And he repeated the never-ending and incomplete memory, an episode we already knew by heart. But we listened out of respect and duty. Once, the Portuguese boss asked for his opinion in front of all the other labourers.

—*You there, fellow, what do you think?*

He thought of replying: a Black man doesn't think, boss. But he chose to keep quiet.

—*You're not speaking? You've got to speak, my old son of a bitch.*

Funny thing, that: a whole system built on not allowing the people to speak, and there he was warning him not to keep quiet. And this gave him such a sense of power that he gagged himself completely. Insults followed. Then there were blows. After that, he was put in prison. There he was among all those prisoners in jail because they'd talked too much: he was the only one paying a price for not opening his mouth.

—*I was so quiet that I was like your mother, Dona Amadalena, with all due respect . . .*

My old man finished his story and only my mother exhaled audibly to signal her saturation. Dona Amadalena had always spoken in sighs. But in tones so precise that her sighs had turned into a language. Amadalena sighed straight with crooked silences.

The days passed more swiftly than memories. More speedily than our sister Glória's tears. The grandson's first birthday came around. On that day, he took his first steps. There was applause, laughter, glasses were raised. Everyone put on a show of jubilation except for Zedmundo, who kept himself to himself:

—*I don't want him crawling around, he'll end up breaking something. Take him away, take him away . . .*

My father was unable to finish his remonstrance. Amadalena interrupted him by waving her arms around in addition to her lullaby sighs. Her husband was taken by surprise.

—*What's this, woman? Has the ant now got a guitar?*

His wife pulled him towards the bedroom. There in their own intimate, enclosed space, old Zedmundo explained himself. He had always said it: he didn't want grandchildren. He didn't want his children unloading their progeny on him.

—*I don't want any of that here. I'm not a grandfather, I'm me, Zedmundo Constante.*

Now, all he wanted was to enjoy the well-earned right to grow old. Folk die when they still have so much life!

—*You don't understand, woman, grandchildren were invented so as to yet again deprive us of the privilege of being ourselves.*

And he went on to explain:

—*To start with, we weren't ourselves because we were someone's children. Then, we delayed being ourselves because we were parents. Now, they want to eliminate us so that we can be grandparents.*

Grandmother threatened him; she was fed up, tired. This time, given the urgency of the matter, Amadalena resorted to scribbling on a piece of paper. In fat round letters, she decreed: either her husband softened his stance or it was all over between them. He was to leave, find somewhere else. Or she herself would leave. Old Zedmundo Constante replied serenely:

—*Amadalena, your name fits so snugly in my heart. But I'm not going to change. If I've got only a short time left, I'm going to take full advantage of it.*

He didn't leave, nor did she. It was Glória who left. She and her husband migrated to the city. And along with them, the little boy who was our mother's solace. She became even more devoid of speech, there in her silent corner.

After only a few weeks, we received news—their son-in-law had died in the capital. Our sister, our Glória, had been driven insane by her grief. She was interned, devalued as a woman, disqualified as a mother. And the little boy, even more of a grandson now, was arriving on the first bus.

The child walked in and my father walked out. As he was leaving, half-hidden in the darkness, he said:

—*You're right in all you didn't say, Amadalena, but I can't take it anymore.*

Where was it our father went? We even offered to go and look for him. But our mother told us not to. Old Zedmundo had never taken any particular route or had any lasting destination. The man was more unreliable than a ceiling. He returned a few days later, telling us he'd been attacked by some ugly wild animal, who knows, maybe a hyena, or perhaps some supernatural creature? He turned up at the front door and just stood there. There, inside that frame made only of light, the truth was merely confirmed: a door was made for a man to leave and a woman to narrow the time of her waiting. My old man had grown thin, while the fattest tears glistened in his eyes. Amadalena got a fright: Zedmundo was weeping for the first time ever. Had her husband really lost his self-assurance, had his soul been filleted of all its bones?

So then she became all gentle and motherly. She went to her husband and hugged him to her breast. And she sensed that it wasn't just a case of a tear being shed. Her man burst out crying. Seeing him like that, all snivelling and shrunken, my mother realized that the old man, her old man, just wanted to be the sole object of her attention.

Leading him by the hand, my mother made him come in and showed him his sleeping grandson. For the first time, my father contemplated the child as if he had just been born. Or as if both of them had just been born. With his clumsy hands, old Zedmundo picked the boy up and gave him a long slow kiss. And he lingered like that as if savouring his smell. My mother corrected his excesses and put the child back in the warmth of his bed. Then my father curled up on the faded sofa and my mother placed herself behind him as if she were rocking him in her arms until he fell asleep.

The following morning, when it was still early, I found the two of them still sleeping: my old man on the sofa, and next to him his deferred grandson. My mother had already gone out. All she had left was a scribbled note. I couldn't resist taking a peep at it. It was a message to my father, which went as follows: *My dear Zedmundo: have a good rest. And look after that little boy while I go to town.*

Between scribbles, corrections, and scrawls, the note was better guessed than read. It said that my father still had time to be a son. The fault was hers, for she had become forgetful: after all, my father had never been anyone's son. That was why he didn't know how to be a grandfather. But now he could once again become her son, without any fear.

Be my son, Zedmundo, let me be your mother. And you'll see that grandson of ours will make us be ourselves, less alone, better grandparents.

I folded the note and left it on the table. I waited on the veranda for my mother to arrive. I knew that she had gone to fetch my sister, Glória. Before, I had sworn to tell my sister this story. But now, I recall my father's advice about learning to keep quiet. And I decide that I shall never, but never, tell this story to anyone. I'll leave it for my mother, who is dumb, to tell it.

On that
Special Night

TWENTY-FIFTH, Christmas. *Quissimusse*, as they call it here. Mariazinha waits at the door for the annual visit of Sidónio Vidas, her occasional spouse. Here he is now, a conspicuous apparition, God bless him and his vainglorious vehicle. Never before had he arrived with such fanfare. He does so with the same effect as rain upon dried-up watercourses: by causing a flood after a long absence.

Mariazinha looks like a widow, standing with her two children in the doorway. She contemplates the bulky Sidónio, who resembles gelatin being pried away from the bottom of a glass cup. Mariazinha whispers awkwardly to her kids:

—*You know what to do: when I give the secret sign, make yourselves scarce!*

Her children peep at their mother out of the corner of their eye, scarcely recognizing her: a perfumed dress, her coiffure styled at the hairdresser's, her nails manicured. And they once again fear that this may be less of an encounter and more of a disencounter. It had been like that from the start: a night without a wedding, the husband a shooting star, and an oath of loyalty without a viable time limit.

The kids already knew: their father worked far away in a very foreign land, so distant that he could only visit his family on the night of the twenty-fifth. Every year, their father would turn up, always in a new car. He would bleep his magic remote control and, from the trunk, a whole array of presents would emerge, like a line of sledges, a chain of joyful excitement.

This Christmas, once again, the car has changed but nothing else. Their father opens the trunk of the car and pulls out packets in wrapping and Cellophane. It's more about decoration than contents, but isn't that what parties are all about: more illusion and glitter than substance? The kids, squealing with delight, fall on the presents. And they stay out in the garden, absorbed in their gifts.

Sidónio enters the living room with a governor's demeanour. His wife follows him, diminutively, as custom demands. The man surveys the room. On the dresser, there is an improvised nativity scene. Only the little bits of straw under the newly born child are real. The rest has been cobbled together in a hurry: the top of a Coca-Cola bottle, bits of wire, and some leftover trash.

The husband lounges around at the table in proprietorial fashion. He undoes the buckle on his belt, just in case he needs to. Mariazinha leans out of the front door and reaffirms her command: her children should keep away. The moment belongs to them alone, this night of all nights.

—*I fried some fish, the one you say you could die for.*

Sidónio smacks his lips and gobbles it up, bones and all. His wife eats while standing, her plate balanced in her hand, as she contemplates her husband. The gold chain glistens against his neck, both chain and neck more abundant than ever. The gold looks genuine. The wearer is the one who's a fake, without a hallmark or a guarantee of origin. Whenever he comes, he displays more and more chains and rings, lasting ornaments, so that Mariazinha shouldn't think that he left as a horse and came back as a donkey.

—*Be careful, husband, mind you don't get a bone caught in your gullet.*

—*A gullet is what poor folk have,* Sidónio corrects her. *People like me have a throat, understand?*

Sidónio belches to signal the end of the first course. Quieter than a god, distant and self-assured. His cell phone rings loud and clear, he grunts a few syllables in no particular language. And he turns it off, as if he were turning off his caller rather than the gadget.

—*Is there a dessert? A little pudding?*

—*I didn't have any sugar, but Alves, the neighbour . . .*

—*Ah! So that's it, sugar out of the kindness of Alves, the neighbour.*

There is irony, hurt, and suspicion in his tone of voice. Was Alves the neighbour too much of a neighbour?

—*Mariazinha, are you being faithful to me?*

—*Me? Sidónio, I . . .*

She is lost for words and bursts into tears. Could he, as a human being, doubt her?

—*Be quiet, woman. Don't say anything.*

All this commotion is upsetting his digestion. Sidónio is satisfied he is being obeyed. He strokes his belly with the same tenderness as pregnant women do with their coming baby.

—*I don't want your pudding.*

—*But, Sidónio, I made it especially for you, with so much love . . .*

—*Well, I don't feel like it, so there.*

Mariazinha gathers up the plate along with her tears. Back in the kitchen, she tidies herself, looking out at the husband's luxurious car through the cracked window. Those who go to war give as good as they get. But she had gone in peace, and had only been on the receiving end. There is his Mercedes, full of its own self-importance. But instead of envy she gets a happy sense of fulfillment. As if the car belonged to her, and she could display her curves from time to time on its seats.

She returns to the living room and stands leaning against the dresser. The furniture sways and the little figurines drop off.

Christ tumbles out of his crib. For the first time, Sidónio deigns to look at his wife. He seems to confirm the adage: a man is as old as his age and a woman is as old as she looks. He looks at her hands, and notices her nail varnish. Mariazinha draws her nails in, hurriedly concealing her vanity.

—*I did them this morning, I asked a neighbour to lend me a pot of varnish.*

—*I may have to review your monthly allowance.*

—*Ah! I haven't received your allowance for months . . .*

—*I've got my priorities, Mariazinha.*

With the meal over, Sidónio takes off his shoes, reclines in the armchair, and closes his eyes, absorbed in his own insides. Then something unexpected happens. His wife suddenly leans over him, all flirtatious, revealing expanses of her flesh.

—*I feel like dancing. Won't you play a bit of music, husband?*

—*What music?*

—*The music from your car.*

Sidónio struggles to his feet. Her eyes still glint, full of hope. But he's not getting up for her. It's time, he's off. At the door, she still murmurs:

—*Will you come back next year?*

—*I don't know, woman, I don't know. Things aren't easy, you know . . .*

—*But you can bring the others . . . your children's brothers and sisters. And you can bring . . . her, too. I don't mind, Sidónio.*

But the man's no longer interested in talking. He summons his children to say goodbye, and makes for his car. While he squeezes in behind the steering wheel, Mariazinha tells the kids:

—*That's one of the few good men left in the world.*

And the youngest one, squeezing his mother's hand, asks:

—*Is Father that man they call Father Christmas?*

A sad laugh vanishes from his mother's face as Sidónio disappears into the darkness of the highway. Mother and children stand contemplating the night, as if they have forgotten they have a home to go to. All of a sudden, the eldest tugs at his mother's skirt and says:

—*Look, Mother, here comes Mister Alves, the neighbour.*

Mariazinha hurriedly smooths her dress and smiling, murmurs:

—*You know what to do, children: when I give you the sign, make yourselves scarce!*

Isidorangela's Fat Name

ISIDORANGELA was that obese girl's name. A fat name at the whim of the pen. In the street and at school, she was an object of fun. And there was good reason for her to be teased: the girl spilled out of herself, her shapeless legs dragging her along in tiny, round, cushioned steps.

Like a stone thrown into a puddle, Isidorangela caused a wave of mockery. But no one could laugh out loud and openly, for the girl was the daughter of the mayor, Dr. Osório Caldas. As my father said, the man represented authority: "Our chief," was how he was referred to in our house. My father venerated Mayor Osório as if the fate of the world depended on him. My mother was all at sea with such deference, Mayor Osório this, Mayor Osório that.

—*Honestly, man, this devotion of yours is weird, anyone would think it was homosensual love . . .*

—*I feel sorry for him, Marta. Poor man, he must suffer with a daughter like that.*

At the end of every month, the mayor would take Isidorangela to the dance at the Railwaymen's Club, but no one ever invited her to dance. All the others danced, bodies twirled, hearts were giddily lost. Girls passed from partner to partner, all of them exhausted from dancing, light-headed. Only Isidorangela remained seated, nibbling at an endless piece of cotton candy. She even looked like cotton candy herself, in her huge hooped dress with pink folds.

As time went by, my father became more and more submissive in his manner, all unctuous and planning further flattery and favours. My mother's patience wore thin:

—*One of these days, you'll go and marry your mayor!*

And then she snapped:

—*I never thought I'd be jealous of a man!*

My old dad always gave her the same answer. As *mulatos*, we were lucky to be looked on with such favour by the chief. He'd even been promised promotion. The meek bide their time, while ever looking upwards. Not even I imagined the lengths my father would go to in order to please his chief.

That afternoon, quite unexpectedly, my father told me to comb my hair, and that I could even use his brilliantine.

—*But where am I going, Father?*

It wasn't explained. He put me in new clothes, brushed my jacket, and led me through the narrow lanes of our small town. At the door of someone's residence—the poor have a house, the rich have a residence, my father explained to me—he told me to take off my shoes.

—*Am I going to go in barefoot, Father?*

—*What do you mean, barefoot? What you're going to do is put these on.*

In one of his pockets he was carrying some new shoes, without a trace of dust on them. I had never worn such black shoes. Hardly had I put them on than I complained that they were too tight and uncomfortable.

—*Well, hunch up your feet, you've got a habit of stretching them out,* my father suggested.

Straight after this, he rang the doorbell so respectfully that his fingers scarcely touched the button.

—*You didn't ring it, Father,* I warned him.

Yes he had, I just hadn't heard it. Then he explained, speaking a Portuguese that I had never heard before: here, in elegant residences, the least sound makes a noise. That's why I should never make a racket when visiting the Caldas. And what's more, I should polish up my finest Portuguese.

We waited endlessly. My father refused to show any insistence. My shoes were squeezing my toes. At long last, there was the twitching of a curtain inside, the door opened, and Dona Angelina peeped out. We went in, full of bowing and scraping, my father speaking so quietly that no one could understand him. Angelina, the esteemed lady of the house, ushered us through rooms full of furniture and knick-knacks. Seated in an armchair, the mayor didn't prove much of a host. He waved offhandedly at my father and then returned to his newspaper. The lady of the house explained: Dr Osório was finishing a crossword, and needed to finish it before the electricity supply was cut off. Yes, evening would soon fall and the weak light of the oil lamp wouldn't be sufficient for the mayor to finish his favourite pastime. His Excellency had got stuck on a strange word: Kabala. With precisely six letters.

—*Kabala?!* my father asked, all clumsy and confused. Then, addressing me:

—*Didn't we come across that word only yesterday when we were going over your homework?*

And I replied, as if to no one in particular:

—*Of course, the feminine of cavalo, a horse.* I prayed that my father wouldn't oblige me to explain the meaning of the word.

—*Let's go to the lounge while we wait,* said Dona Angelina.

There in the lounge was the "Monument": Isidorangela, swathed in her pink dress. The biggest surprise I got was this: in her hand, she still held erect the little stick wrapped in spun sugar. That really got to me: cotton candy was my perdition. How did

Isidorangela manage to have that sweet in her home? Wasn't it exclusive to fairs and festivals?

—*Well, I'll put some music on to liven things up,* the mayor's wife announced.

Some kind of waltz filled the vast silence of the room.

—*Go on, invite Isidorangela to go for a twirl.*

The word sounded obscene to me: go for a twirl? My face must have presented the very picture of idiocy: brilliantine dribbling over my brow, my frown denouncing my painfully squeezed feet, my upper lip tightened as I coveted the sugary floss. A barely disguised shove from my old man propelled me towards the plump girl. Or rather, towards the "Monument's" arms. So that was it, my father wanted to butter up the chief and was using me in his psychiatric designs to free the fat girl of her complexes?

I was so infuriated that when I put my arm around Isidorangela, she almost stumbled and lost her balance. She nearly fell on top of me and the stick of cotton candy remained, like an unfurled flag between us. Temptation competed with my pains and I found myself saying:

—*I'm going to take a mouthful.*

—*Of me?* the fat girl laughed, tittering nervously.

My greed got the better of me and, sticking out my tongue, I demolished that castle of sweetness while I dragged the voluminous creature across the polished floor. Believing that I wanted her, Isidorangela closed her eyes and leaned in towards me, disposed to be at my disposal. My fear was that she might slip and collapse, unsupported, on top of me. I spun around the floor between the agony caused by my feet and the sugary delight melting in my mouth.

While on one of my turns, I was surprised to see my old dad and Angelina dancing as well. Farther away, in his huge armchair, the mayor sat dozing sleepily. Then, all of a sudden, what did I notice? My heart squeezing me harder than my shoes, I saw

Angelina's fingers, in furtive tenderness, intertwine with my father's. The record turning in the gramophone, the faded light caused by the oil lamp, the fat girl spinning around, it all made me feel giddy. And there was no longer any cotton candy left except on Isidorangela's face. On an irresistible impulse, I stuck my tongue into the remains of the sweet. The girl misunderstood my licking. As for me, I got the strange taste of a flavour of perspiration that was, in fact, my own natural perfume. I noticed her hair, which, underneath the apparent smoothness, was crinkly. And glancing at her almost fearfully, I saw, under her round face, a birthmark I thought exclusive to my biological family.

I wanted to disappear, to release myself from the world. But Isidorangela's fingers were already intertwining with mine, with the same voluptuousness as her mother's in relation to my father. In his darkened armchair, Osório Caldas was busy uncrossing words while sluggishly nodding off over his old newspaper.

The String and the Beads

I FIND JMC sitting on a garden bench. He is quiet, in deliberate solitude, as if he were only able to find due privacy there, on a public seat. Or as if it were the refuge where he had chosen to live for the rest of his life. All around him, time stands intact, each hour punctual in its passing.

He was never told his full name. I don't think anyone knows it, not even himself. People call him this, spelling out the initials: *jay emm cee.*

I greet him, with a slight bow of respect. He raises his eyes as if the light were too strong. There is a subtle movement of his fingers: he wants me to sit down and rescue him from his solitude.

—*Do you remember we sat in this same place a few years back?*

—*I do indeed, sir. It seems like yesterday.*

—*Yesterday is far too distant as far as I'm concerned. My memory only reaches as far as the olden days.*

—*But you're still young, sir.*

—*I'm not old, that's true. But I've accumulated a lot of wear and tear.*

And we sit in silence. I remember the times when this tall, thin man would enter this very same garden. It happened every day, in late afternoon. I remember the stories he confided in me. How he, while a respectably married man, would fall passionately in love with endless women. I don't have enough fingers to count them all, he would say.

—*Life is a necklace. I provide the thread, the women provide the beads. There are always so many beads . . .*

Every time he made love to one of them, he would never go back home straightaway. What he would do was to go to his old mother's house. He would tell her the intimate details of every new affair, the different varieties of sweetness of each new lover. Her eyes closed, the old woman would listen and even pretend to sleep on the tired old sofa in her living room. When he had finished, she would take her son's hands in hers and tell him to go and have a bath there and then.

—*Don't go back to your wife smelling of another woman,* she said.

So JMC sat in a hot bathtub while his old mother rubbed him down with a scented sponge. When he got out of his bath, she slowly dried him, as if time were passing through her hands and she were spiriting him away in the folds of the towel.

—*Go on, my son, keep spreading this great heart of yours around. Never stop visiting women. Never stop loving them . . .*

—*And what about Father? Was he always faithful to you?*

—*Your father, even though he was loyal, could never be faithful . . .*

—*Why was that?*

—*Your father never managed to love anyone at all . . .*

Now, after so many years, I barely recognize the tall, thin philanderer.

—*Forgive my asking, JMC. But do you still visit women?*

He doesn't answer. He is absorbed, contemplating his nails in their respective fingers. Did he hear me? Out of shyness, I don't repeat the question. After some time, he murmurs a confession.

—*Never again. I never visited another woman.*

His voice gains a sad hollowness. For his is a confession of a certain kind of widowhood. He breaks his pause and continues:

—*It was because my mother died, you know . . .*

My heart races in puzzlement. If only silence could be made by people not talking. But such a silence doesn't exist. And we both remain in this vacuum until Dona Graciosa, JMC's spouse, emerges from the dusk. She is unrecognizable, as if coming from a masked ball. She is full of radiance and flowers, her cleavage is larger than her blouse, her legs more exposed than her dress. I get to my feet to offer her my place on the bench. But she addresses her husband in a sweet, gentle voice:

—*Will you come with me, JMC?*

—*And who are you, my little flower?*

—*You can call me by my name, but only afterwards.*

—*Afterwards? After what?*

—*Come now, only after...*

The two walk off, arm in arm. Night envelops me in its misty embrace. And I hardly notice I am alone.

Entry into Heaven

I F nothing is repeatable, does everything repeat itself? That's the question I asked in catechism. And I pressed for even clearer answers:

—*Has life, whether saintly or godly, got another version to it?*

Father Bento didn't even want to listen: the merest doubt constituted disobedience. Firstly, once bitten twice shy. And then, a sin is hardly worth it if you can confess it. And Bento warned: you can't enter Heaven any old way. Up there, at the heavenly gates, due permission has to be granted. Then I asked: who does the choosing at the entrance to Paradise? A qualified doorman? A tribunal of venerable judges?

Years passed, doubts persisted. And I still need the matter clarified. That's why I've come back to you, sir, so that you can listen to me, even if it's only out of religious pretense. Please, mister priest, tell me this: this business of entry into Paradise, is it a question of race, or because we're not just any Tom, Dick, or Harry? Blacks like me, am I saved, do we get a license? Or do folk need to pay to grease some palms, get someone to put a good word in to whoever's in charge?

I'm a bigmouth, but it all stems from my doubts, my good sir. Questions leave my throat aching. For example: can someone go straight from their village to Heaven? Just like that, without having to pass through the capital or carry a travel permit, duly issued and stamped by the appropriate authorities?

And then there's this: I don't speak English. Even in Portuguese, I can only scribble things without sticking to the lines. I can just imagine seeing the sign there, like in the films: welcome to Paradise! And I won't be able to read anymore. They might well invite me to speak. It's like giving a loudspeaker to a mute.

My hope is that it'll happen like in the dance at the Railwaymen's Club. It happened so long ago that I need to journey beyond memory. It was the end-of-year dance. You know only too well, Father: the year isn't like the sun, which is born for everyone. The year ends only for some and begins for fewer people every time.

I knew they weren't going to allow me in. But my love for the *mulata*, Margarida, was greater than the certainty of my exclusion. And so, all bashful, wearing borrowed clothes, I lined up outside. And I was the only non-white in the vicinity. To my astonishment, the doorman didn't seem surprised. Placing his hand on my shoulder, he said:

—*Go on in, lad.*

He no doubt thought I was a barman. Who knows, maybe the doorman at the gates to Heaven will take me for someone else and let me in, thinking I'm going to work as one of the servants?

For what's happening, my most esteemed Father, is that I'm dying, leaking blood as my life wishes to let go of me. Do you see this dagger? It wasn't this that I stabbed myself with. For a long time now, I've picked it up by the knife rather than the handle. I've held the blade so much that my hands can now cut by themselves. I've turned into an instrument for slashing. In fact, you know this defect of mine, sir, these fingers that don't obey me, this hand that isn't mine, as if it only allowed my already dead soul the power to act. If I've killed myself this time, it's because of the sharpness of my fingers. Don't be like that, don't give up. Remember what I asked you, Father?

—*I want to be a saint, mister priest.*

And you laughed, sir. I couldn't be a saint. And why? Because a saint, you said, is a good person.

—*And am I not good?*

—*But a saint is a special person, more special than anyone else.*

—*And I, Father, I am especially unique.*

I didn't understand: a saint is someone who abdicates from Life. In my case, Father, Life has abdicated from me. Yes, I understand now: saints are sanctified by death. While I sanctified life, that's what I did.

Now, I'm reaching the end. A saint begins when he finishes. Yet I never began. But this isn't the first time death has revealed itself in me. My heart died on that faraway night of the dance. I got into the dance at the Railwaymen's Club, that's true. But I remained barred from the *mulata* Margarida's heart. The girl didn't even regale me with a cold, absent look from afar. She was a white girl among white men. But then she dropped a glass, which shattered on the floor. And I, to assuage her embarrassment, bent down to pick up the pieces, gathering them together in my hand. That was when the security guard, summoned by her young champions, grabbed my arm and forced me to my feet. The man pulled my hands so hard and squeezed me with such vigour that the splinters of glass cut deep into me. That was when I slashed my flesh, nerves, and tendons. And the blood of a Black man flowed like an illness staining the white men's immaculate domain.

What caused me the most suffering, dear Father, wasn't the blow. Nor was it even the vexation. It was Margarida watching me being ejected, without any kind of protest. I suffered so much because of her lack of interest that my soul imitated the glass: it fell, smashed to pieces. When they ejected me, I was no longer aware of myself, I had taken leave of myself for good.

Now that I've got so little time left, all my heart hears is the music from that dance where the *mulata* Margarida awaits me, her arms stretched out in justification of my postponed life. I'm entering the dance hall and, forgive any lack of respect if I take issue with you, but I no longer have the strength to say anything else. Only to dismantle that certainty of yours: life does have a second version. If love, contrite at not loving, so wishes.

Beggar Friday Playing in the World Cup

I AGREE with you, doctor: I'm the one inventing my illnesses. But what can I do, old and lonely as I am? Being ill is the only way I have of proving I'm alive. That's why I visit the hospital time after time, exhibiting my fevers. It's only on such occasions that I get attended to, doctor. Badly attended, almost always. But waiting in that endless queue, I have the illusion of being close to the world. The patients are my family, the hospital the roof over my head, and you, sir, are my father, the father of all my fathers.

This time, it's different though. For I, Friday by name, present myself with a genuine, serious complaint. I have come here all de-clavicled on account of a blow that nearly unshouldered me. It happened while I was watching a World Cup game. For some time now, I have been taking a look at the window display in the Dubai Shopping Centre, on the corner of Avenida Direita. It's a store selling televisions, and they leave the ones in the window turned on to encourage passing shoppers to make a purchase. I sit on the sidewalk, I've got my own spot there. Next to me sit all those beggars who invade the city every Friday looking for alms from the Muslims. Remember? That's how I got my name,

Friday. Think about this: I, who've always been such a weakling, got my weekday name.

There, on that sidewalk, I watch the soccer and gain the illusion of having a family. The sidewalk is a corridor in the infirmary. All us beggars lined up get ourselves a roof. A roof that covers us on this and other continents.

There's only one proviso in all this, doctor. It's just that I get a really ulcerous feeling whenever my eyes find themselves travelling to South Korea. What makes me envious aren't all those young men, all those feinting soccer players full of vigour. What I envy, doctor, is when the player falls to the ground and rolls over and over, making a big show of complaining. His pain causes everything to come to a standstill. A world full of real pain stops in the face of a soccer player's false pain. My troubles are so many and so real, and no referee makes everything stop so that I can be attended to, rolling around as I am inside me, laid low as I have been by others. If life were a soccer field, how many penalties would I have been awarded against my fate?

I know I'm stealing your time, doctor. I'll come straight to the matter of my shoulder. This is what happened: the owner of the shop ordered the sidewalk to be cleared. He didn't want beggars and tramps there. It scared away customers and he wasn't for spending screen time on poor folks' eyes. I refused to leave, doctor. Does the sidewalk belong to anyone? For me to leave, he had to call the police. They came and beat me up, and as I lay on the ground they kicked me as if they were beating their own poverty rather than me. I declared that I'd be back today to watch the game. That's because the Africans are playing and they need me among the spectators. They won't win if Friday isn't there. The owner of the shop told me that if I persisted, there would be a festival of fisticuffs. All I'm asking, doctor, is that you should intercede on our behalf. The sidewalk spectators of the Avenida Direita. The proprietor of the Dubai Shopping Centre won't say anything if the request comes from you, doctor.

So you can see that I came to the hospital not because of some cunning ploy, but because of genuine adversity. You look at me suspiciously, doctor, while you inspect my bruises. Now, concerned, he's placing me under the eye of an x-ray machine. I'm quite taken aback by such deference. Up until now, I've only ever had my photograph taken by the police. If I'd known, I would have got ready, doctor, polished my ivories and combed out my fleas.

But when they show me the photo, I'm overcome by shame at seeing the wretched, crude intimacy of my bones revealed. I almost shout: hide it, doctor, don't show me like this, for everyone to see. Not least because a momentary suspicion flashes through my mind: those innards aren't mine. I don't want to raise your hackles, doctor! But those things aren't just one or two bones: they're a whole pile of bones. I can't be so stuffed full of skeleton. That photograph would make a hyena's mouth water. I don't want to offend you, doctor, but please set fire to that film. And let me be, it's not worth wrapping me up in bandages and rubbing ointments into me. I'll just be on my way as quick as I can. Don't forget to phone the owner of the shop, doctor. Please don't forget. That's why I came. It was the request, not the wound.

And off I go to where the roads open out. I reach the television store and sit down among the beggars. Just imagine: they'd kept my place out of respect for me. I'm moved by all this. The doctor must have phoned after all, must have remembered my humble request. There are still good people in this world! My eyes gleam not because I'm watching the game, but because of the people looking in at the window display. Who said television doesn't give us our daily dose of magic?

What I saw in a soothing glimpse was the following, no more, no less: I and the Friday beggars are in the World Cup, we're a team kitted out in the most fabulous colours. And the doctor is our coach. At that precise moment, we are playing. I'm on the left wing and am controlling the ball, which is a way of dominating the world. Behind me, the crowd roars in approval. Suddenly, an opposing defender clatters into me. *Dangerous play*, thousands of voices proclaim. *Yes, a yellow card,* the doctor yells. But the defender continues his aggression, and the crowd protests even louder. *That's right, ref, a red card! Spot-on! Let's have justice in the game that we don't get in Life!*

But is the red from the card or is it my own blood? There's no doubt about it: I need help, I'm not putting it on, I'm really injured. They should stop the game, expel the aggressor from the field. But to my surprise, the referee himself starts attacking me as well. At that moment, it's as if I've suddenly awoken, as if I've emerged from the television onto the sidewalk. I can still see the policeman's truncheon come crashing down on my head. Then the lights of the stadium go out.

The Owner of
the Man's Dog

I'M going to tell you how I was betrayed not by my beloved, but by my dog. Left just like that without a word, without any consolation. There should be a hotel for the owners of dogs who've been abandoned by their animals. With networks of friends and solidarity groups and well-meaning ladies, allaying their conscience at charity sales. It's not a question of writing a conclusive work on canine ingratitude. Merely a word of warning to other loyal, dedicated pet owners.

I'm an ordinary member of the human race, with no proven pedigree, and if I have a place in any newspaper, it'll be in the unclassified advertisements. My dog, on the other hand, is of the purest race, a category proven on his birth certificate. The creature is thoroughly thoroughbred, full of ancestry. A retriever, son of a retriever, grandson of a great-grandson. In an unadulterated ancestral line, like the kings of genealogical descent. The clumsiest thing about him is the name he was baptized with. It's such a human name, I almost feel humiliated by it: Boniface. Is that a name for an animal? I'll get to the point and then lose it again.

Every day, late afternoon, I would take him for a walk. That is: he would drag me along on his leash. Boniface would choose what paths to take, where to stop, what speed to go at. And there were times when, so as not to cause inconvenience, I would bend down to scoop up his stinking poop. Did I show such a degree of deference to my own children? And on top of all these privileges, people would only ever talk about him:

—*Fine specimen, splendid animal,* they would say.

When they noticed me, it was by accident or as an afterthought. Me, humble little me, at the other end of the leash. I was the one being led, a mere member of the human race, without any proof of pedigree. My dog, my lord and owner, was above mere mortal animals. He didn't sniff: he merely inhaled the sophisticated odours on the trees. He didn't pee: he merely relieved himself with dignity, in the neatest of streaks. And if he soiled the street, he wasn't the filthy one: shame was directed at me and me alone.

My temper got worse the more of these injustices I had to face, to the point that I began growling whenever I put Boniface on his leash. This sense of vexation must have expressed itself in my face, for on one occasion I was asked:

—*Bite?*

I replied that they could relax and approach the animal, because he didn't bite.

—*I was asking about you, not the dog.*

That was the first warning. I was assailed by a sudden fear: one day, I might be forced to wear a muzzle. And to carry a vaccination certificate with me.

I started to avoid going out with the animal. Only when the city was deserted and when the noises of the nocturnal animals had died down did I dare take Boniface for a walk. And it was on one of these occasions that he, obeying his canine nature, assaulted a cat with a couple of bites. This produced a kerfuffle and accusations of responsibility. People asked me nervously:

—*Is there a vaccination certificate?*

—Who for? Me? I asked, by now at my wit's end.

There were no further retorts or altercations. Being the owner of a cat has great advantages: the person comes rapidly to the conclusion that he is the owner of a virtual animal, or that it exists only at certain times. But I was beset by an endless doubt: did they suspect that I was the one who had done the biting? I was doomed, unavailing of human rights. How could they suspect that, between me and Boniface, I was the one responsible for doing the biting? I'm only too aware that the human mouth contains so-called canine teeth. And on Boniface's snout there dwelt a smile of the purest innocence.

In order to put an end to the matter with the cat, I had to shoulder all the blame and claims for damages. As for Boniface, he remained in blissful disregard, ready for other assaults on innocent, civic-minded cats. That was the last straw. A dog is man's best friend? Well I, for my part, decided to run away from home, leave everything behind me, neighbours, friends, the losses and gains of a whole life. And I didn't come out of it too badly, such was my relief at not having to remain domiciliary and domesticated. I happily took up residence in a primitive hiding place, an empty shed in a public garden. I enjoyed a genuine dog's life. People would leave me a few leftovers. Sometimes, if I was lucky, a few doggy bags! Did I yearn for my own existence as a person? I no longer wanted to think about it. A man who barks doesn't bite, I barked, and the caravan passed by.

Until one afternoon my dog, none other than Boniface, emerged on the grassy horizon. He was dragging himself through the park, as gloomy as an autumn day. When he saw me, his tail almost detached itself from his body, so violent was its wagging. He bounded towards me and, jumping up, started to lick me. He seemed so happy that for a few moments my heart dithered and my eyes filled. Then I noticed he was carrying a lead in his mouth. He waved it around, suggesting that I put it on him so that we could once again walk the roads full of interesting smells.

—*Oh, how clever!* those present remarked, moved.

—*I was the one who taught him to do that*, I boasted proudly.

—*We were talking about you, my friend.*

That really was the last straw, the one that broke the camel's back. I didn't need to utter a word, that's what I should have added. But I didn't speak, nor did I bark. And it's in silence that I allow my pitiful fate to take its course. Just one last question: Is there a competition, by any chance, for fully-trained men? Don't give me an answer. The one who wants to know is Boniface, my old owner and master. That's what I always read in his eyes every time he passes, tall and haughty, through the park where I swap fleas with other members of the canine family, my colleagues in misfortune.

The Tearful Males

THEY met up for reasons of merriment. In the bar at Matakuane, the men would swap funny stories, manufacturing laughter. Their only motivation: they were celebrating life. Their spouses didn't tolerate such nonsense. After all, the womenfolk, they don't need a ritual to celebrate life. They are a celebration of life. Or life in celebration? For them, this masculine complicity was a tribal thing. Some atavistic wistfulness.

But the men didn't care. Whether it was atavistic or tribal, they kept the custom going. Any time one of them came to the bar, he would exclaim as he came through the door:

—*Have you heard the latest one?*

And no sooner had the stories been produced than they were consumed. Until one night when Louie Double-K, the leading light of such encounters, brought a gloomy piece of news. The moon was very much on the wane and there in the bar, for the very first time, the glasses remained full the whole night. For Louie gradually developed his story in a solemn tone of voice. Before reaching the crux of the narrative, perhaps some unambiguous death, Double-K burst out sobbing. And his friends, glass in hand, round the table:

—*Hey, Double-K, what's the matter?*

Even the silent, muscle-bound docker, Sylvester Stallion, tried to encourage the sorrower:

—*Straighten yourself up, man, at the verticals!*

But the weeper hadn't finished. And his whimpering grew into a professional mourner's wail. Amid his sobs, he released the threads of his baleful narrative. No one could understand a single word any longer, for his words came out all wrapped in snot. Someone in the room produced a handkerchief and it was passed from hand to hand collecting residues. It was too late: the flames of sadness had devoured Double-K's heart.

They gave up consoling him. Mollified, the friends gradually succumbed to their prolapsed spirit, induced by nothing more than the weight of slime in their soul. It must have been their sadness. And a dissembling tear even trickled down the bar owner's bearded face.

The following day, when they sat down in the bar, someone still fired off a joke:

—*Have you heard the latest one?* But the man regretted it immediately: what he was offering was an expression of his unhappiness. Melancholy had settled over them like a tablecloth on a table. Sylvester Stallion still attempted another joke. But no one laughed. Folk were more interested in hearing some more chapters of the sad story.

And so they asked Louie Double-K: disclose more details, tear down veils, undarken destinies. And Louie fell over himself to comply: the drama unfolded before the tearful gaze of his listeners. It wasn't long before they were all snivelling spittle by the spadeful.

And this went on night after night. One round of sadness followed by another. The regulars at the bar in Matakuane abandoned jokes and laughter and began to share lamentations, blubberings, and tears. And even Sylvester Stallion, the most macho and tight-lipped member of the tribe, ended up admitting:

—I would never have thought this, lads. But boy, is it good to cry!

To cry, but to cry in unison, the others added. And one even remembered to broach the idea of an association for weepers. They might even replace the female professional mourners at funeral wakes. But the others opposed this firmly. Among them there still remained, after all, a deep macho prejudice against tears in public, which were a womanish thing.

And so things developed so slowly that they hardly seemed to occur. But what did happen was that the one-time tellers of jokes changed the way they viewed the world. At the first sign of darkness falling, one of them would declare he was heading off back home.

—To give my folks a hand, he would admit, half-ashamed.

And another would decline the pressing offer of another drink:

—I don't want my old lady to get angry, he would explain.

—He who drinks a little too much drinks much too much, they all counselled.

And even Sylvester, who was always the last one out, urged them to keep an eye on the time. They should all make for home, the former free spirit suggested.

—Yes, let's go home. But not before shedding one last tear.

—Yes, let's have one for the road.

And so another little story was told to add some lustre to their sadness. The idea that crying was for sissies was something none of them remembered anymore. In the vicinity of the bar, night grew mellow as it listened to the lads gently blubbing away.

The women even got fearful when they saw so much change: their menfolk were inexplicably displaying more tenderness and consideration. Moreover, there were kind words, flowers, displays of affection: all these things they began to receive. Was this all down to being bitten by a fly, some sudden, age-related change? And they were right not even to ask. It was so good, so improbable, that the best thing to do was to let sleeping dogs lie.

Nowadays, anyone who passes by the bar in Matakuane can see for themselves: crying is about opening your heart. When you wail, you complete two journeys: one from a tear towards the light and the other from the man towards a greater humanity. After all, doesn't a person wail the moment he's born? Isn't crying the first expression of our voice?

And that's Double-K's verdict, expressed in other words: the world's problems can be solved if we take possession of a greater part of our being. And a tear reminds us of this: more than anything else, are we not water?

The Grandmother, the City, and the Traffic Lights

WHEN she was told I was going to the city, Grandma Ndzima voiced her worst fears:

—*So whose house are you going to stay in?*

—*I'll stay in a hotel, Grandma.*

—*A hotel? So whose house is that?*

How was I to explain? Even so, I tried: no one's, of course. A further doubt was aroused in the old woman: a house that was no one's?

—*Or rather, Grandma, it belongs to whoever pays,* I blathered in order to put her mind at rest.

But I only made matters worse—a place for whoever pays? So what spirits watch over a house like that?

I had won a prize from the Ministry. I had been chosen as the best rural schoolteacher. And the prize was a visit to the city. When I announced the good news at home, my old grandmother wasn't impressed by my pride. And she asked, frowning:

—*So when you get there, who's going to cook your food?*

—*A cook, Grandma.*

—*What's this cook's name?*

I laughed under my breath. But for her, this was no laughing matter. Cooking is the most private and risky act. Food is invested with tenderness or hatred. Into the pot goes seasoning or poison. Who would guarantee the cleanliness of colander and pestle? How could I allow such an intimate task to be undertaken by an unknown hand? It didn't bear thinking about, nor had such a thing ever been known to happen, to subject oneself to a cook whose face one didn't know.

—*Cooking isn't a service, my dear grandson,* she said. *Cooking is a way of loving others.*

I still tried to change the subject, distract her. But her questions piled up relentlessly.

—*Do folk there draw water from the well?*

—*Really, Grandma!...*

—*I want to know if they all use the same well...*

Wells, open fires, sleeping mats: there was a lot to explain. And I launched forth into a long, slow explanation that things were done differently there. But she wasn't satisfied. Not having a family over there in the city was something she couldn't comprehend. A person travels to be welcomed at the other end by our own folks' hand, folk with a name and a history. Like a bow seeking its two ends. As things were, I was going to some unknown place where names lose their colour! For my grandmother, a foreign country begins where one no longer recognizes a kinsman.

—*Are you going to lie in a bed made up by some unknown woman?*

In the village, it was all very straightforward: Everyone slept naked, wrapped in a *capulana* or a blanket depending on the climate. But over there in the city, the sleeper falls asleep fully clothed. And that's what my grandmother thought was too much. We're not vulnerable when we're naked. When we're dressed we're visited by witches and we remain exposed to their evil intentions.

That was when she made her request. That I should take a village girl with me to look after my daily needs.

—*Grandma, there isn't a girl like that.*

The next day, I went outside into the half-light of the cooking area, ready for a brief, hurried farewell, when I caught sight of her sitting in the middle of the yard. She looked as if she were enthroned, her seat the centre of the universe. She showed me some bits of paper.

—*Here are the tickets.*

—*What tickets?*

—*I'm going with you, my dear grandson.*

And so that's what happened, huddled in the old bus. We swallowed dust while the loudspeakers spread the sound of raucous dance music. Grandma Ndzima, rotund, spread across the seat, nodded off to sleep. On her ample lap, she carried a basket of live chickens. Before we had left, I had even tried to dissuade her: we should at least limit ourselves to carrying fewer fowls.

—*What do you mean, fewer? You yourself said there aren't any chicken coops there.*

When we entered the hotel, the management weren't disposed to allow an avian invasion like ours. But Grandma spoke so loud and at such length that they made way for her. Once installed, Ndzima went down to the kitchen. She didn't want me to go in with her. She took ages. She couldn't just have been handing over the chickens. Then, at last, she emerged. She was smiling.

—*Right, I've fixed everything with the cook . . .*

—*Fixed what, Grandma?*

—*He's from our area, everything is all right. Now all we need to do is find out who is going to be making up your bed.*

That happened later. When I got in from the Ministry, there was no sign of Grandma. She wasn't in the room, or in the hotel. I rushed after her in a panic, along the streets. Then I caught sight of something that would occur every afternoon: Grandma

Ndzima among the beggars, on the corner by the traffic lights. I felt a tightening in my chest: our respected elder begging?! The traffic lights whiplashed my face.

—*Come back home, Grandma!*

—*Home?!*

—*To the hotel. Come on.*

Time dragged on. Eventually, the day came when we were to return to the village. I went to Grandma's room to offer to help with her bags. My heart sank when I looked in: she was lying on the floor where she had always slept, her belongings spread around without any sign of preparation for packing.

—*Haven't you packed yet, Grandma?*

—*I'm staying here, Grandson.*

I was dumbstruck, and began to smile idiotically.

—*How are you going to stay?*

—*Don't worry. I've learned my way around here.*

—*Are you going to stay here all alone?*

—*Back in the village, I'm even more alone.*

She was so sure of what she said that all my arguments petered out. The car took its time leaving. When we passed the corner with the traffic lights, I didn't have the courage to look back.

Summer passed, and the rains hadn't given any sign of starting in the skies when I got a letter from Ndzima. I hurriedly tore open the envelope. Some crumpled old notes fell through my fingers onto the floor of the school. There was an accompanying letter that she had dictated to someone, in which she explained: Grandma was paying me for a ticket to go and visit her in the city. I felt my face slowly being lit up as I read the closing lines of the letter: . . . *nowadays, grandson, I sleep next to the traffic light. Those little yellow and red lights make me feel good. When I close my eyes, it's as if I can hear the open fire crackling away in our old backyard. . . .*

A Fish for Eulália

THERE had been no rain for years. Not so much as a drip, a
tear, the tiniest drop. People were puzzled by the harshness
of such a long period of drought. This could only be for the most
inexplicable of reasons. Nothing like this had ever happened
before in Nkulumadzi.

Sinhorito was asked for his opinion. He was a smelly young
ragamuffin incapable of solving any problem. Merely existing
was an insuperable difficulty as far as he was concerned. It must
be a joke their asking him to explain why the rains hadn't come.
But the fact was that they went to him to tell them the reason
for this untimely weather. Sinhorito had never been consulted,
not even in order to back up someone else's opinion. Much
less for him to give his own view. He remained self-absorbed,
a few points of light flickering inside his head. He didn't utter
a single word.

—*Be quiet, so that we can hear exactly what he's going to say!*

Laughter was put on hold as the crowd became tense. They
needed release from their fate. A scapegoat. Sinhorito was known
to have no knowledge whatsoever. His only specialty, according
to what folk said, was this: he had portable eyes that could be
removed and reinserted. He himself proclaimed it: whenever

he felt like it, he would pluck out his eyeballs and hide them in the palms of his hands. Whenever some painful moment was approaching or something ugly was in the air, Sinhorito would take out his eyes. A black owl would enter the darkness of night, windows through which the world left and drained away from the body. No one had ever seen this. It's what people said by way of a maybe. But then so what? No one is simply retarded: they must conceal other abilities in another dimension of their being. That's what we must assume.

—*Like that, without my sight, maybe I avoid the ugliness of this life.*

But no one believed in such prodigiousness. Only Eulália, the woman from the post office, declared herself a believer. And she asked him as he sat in the square:

—*Go on, take them out now.*

And he, with his eyelids shut, showed his closed fists. They were there, his two eyes, as alive as fish out of water. The woman smiled and ordered him to put them back. That she deserved to be seen, even though she was fat and somewhat the worse for wear. Then the young fellow squealed, which was his way of laughing. And he loaded his eyes back into his face.

So it was this Sinhorito they were now consulting on the antediluvian state of affairs. They crowded around, all ready to belittle him. They were seeking no other glory or victory. Idiocy and mockery were enough for them. The lad concentrated his expression, his eyes casting around in the emptiness, searching for the germ of an idea. At last, he dared speak:

—*Maybe . . .*

—*Maybe?*

—*Or who knows, maybe the sky is upside down?*

There were the first signs of laughter. Nonsense was beginning to take shape, in accordance with their expectations. The smaller the village, the more it needs a madman. As if the rest would be saved from madness by this one madman. But lo and behold, at that precise moment, with the palm of his hand, he demanded they listen to his answer.

—*Wait. Wait, the fellow's still got more to say. Go on, finish, Doctor Sinhorito.*

—*It's just that who knows* . . .

—*Who knows what?*

—*Who knows? Maybe the rain is falling on the other side of the sky.*

There were loud bursts of laughter. And some of them repeated the nutcase's absurd thought to one another. In the end, they dispersed. Only Eulália from the post office remained sitting motionless, next to the crackpot. Then she took his hand and begged him not to be sad. And by way of a first confession, she said:

—*I believe in you. I've already felt some rain of the type you describe, rain from another sky* . . .

And she kissed the lad's forehead. Then she curled up by his feet. The good-mannered Sinhorito tried to help her up from the ground. But Eulália frustrated his attempts.

—*Let me stay like this, in your shadow. I've never had anyone to protect me.*

Sinhorito remained motionless, so absorbed in providing shade that he fell asleep, innocent and defenceless. And she slipped away as subtle as a puff of breeze.

Many shadows passed, many a dream flitted by. Only the drought didn't end. Moreover, there was no longer any air, only waves of heat. Now, thirst competed with hunger. There was no greenery, no flesh, everything between the sun and the soil had been consumed. And the living grew weaker and weaker: the animals became devoid of vitamins, the plants shrivelled. Even Eulália fell ill. She was so skinny, you could count more bones in her than she really possessed. And she didn't even have the strength to suffer. She was in dire need of sustenance.

When the boy discovered Eulália's state, he became deadly serious and summoned together the whole village of Nkulumadzi. To a packed square, he declared:

—Gentlemen, I am going to become a fisherman! Who knows . . .

And he went on: people should no longer worry about whether there would be fish or not. Very soon, cooking pots would once again witness the arrival of this scaly creature, already cut up and filleted even before emerging from the waters.

—From the waters? Which ones?

There was more laughter. He might as well fish in his own sweat. For there was no river or lake left. Sinhorito pointed to the sky above his head.

—I'm going up there, up to the waters above.

He climbed into his boat and adjusted it vertically, its prow pointing towards the firmament. To the astonishment of all, Sinhorito started to row. The oars swished through the air and dipped into the emptiness. Mouths were agape in a multitude of exclamations of disbelief: the boat was moving upwards in an invisible current towards the clouds. The oars became more and more like wings. And the boat was turning into a bird. Until the clouds swallowed the vision in its entirety. At that point, someone shouted:

—Come and see. Look, Sinhorito is going up and up!

But he was almost out of sight by now, gradually drifting into nothingness. Then he vanished, a mere dot in infinity.

—Where is he?

He left and never came down again. They still waited for Sinhorito to drop helplessly to the ground, along with his boat. As nothing happened, the villagers returned one by one to their homes. Only Eulália remained, all by herself. There, in the square, she started waiting for something to happen. The woman gazed up into the sky when the sun was shining and when the stars were twinkling. But Sinhorito didn't come down. Neither he nor the rain he had set out to fetch. And much less any fish.

They came to get her. Her relatives came, the chief postmaster came. They pulled her, their strength against her will.

Eulália resisted all their attempts. She pointed up into the sky in distress.

—*He'll come, he'll come back . . .*

She had vowed not to abandon him there, where he had rowed so long ago. But her eldest brother-in-law forbade her: Sinhorito was mad. The girl should forget the fellow had even existed in deeds or in dreams. Eulália seemed to comply. But deep inside, she preserved a secret wish: she would build a boat, just like Sinhorito's. She surreptitiously collected together sticks and bits of plank.

—*One day, who knows, one day . . .* she repeated as she gathered material.

Then, all of a sudden, she was found out. Everything was set on fire in a fury. Wood was burnt as if some kernel of impurity were being eliminated.

In the meantime, Eulália regained her serenity. She seemed to have gotten over her delirium. Or had she gained some calm good sense? Only her large eyes scanned the clouds as she wandered through the fields. One day, however, she burst joyfully into the kitchen and announced:

—*Two drops of rain fell from the sky.*

They laughed. How was it that only two drops you could count on a chameleon's toe had fallen? The woman insisted, shouted, tugged at them. Once they were all on the veranda, she pointed among the blades of elephant grass to Sinhorito's two eyes. They had fallen from the sky like two fleshy fruits. And they were popping with wonder at all they had seen up there from where they had dropped.

The woman broke away from the arms that held her and ran to pick up what she had found. But as she was bending over, the skies opened in lightning flashes. And it rained thick and fast, a wild mesh of liquid hair draping itself over the lap of the universe. And shoals of fish tumbled out of the sky.

This is the story that Eulália now tells when her fellow villagers ask her to speak of the day when it rained fish. And they erupt and convulse with laughter as abundantly as those who are aware of the meagreness of their lives. It's good to have one's share of madmen. All next to each other on a rosary. Like beads lined up together on the thread of unbelief.

Sea Loves Me

First Chapter

God is a delicate subject of conversation, we've got to pretend he's an egg: if we squeeze him too hard, he breaks, if we don't keep a good grip on him, he falls.

ONE OF GRANDFATHER CELESTIANO'S SAYINGS,
REINVENTED FROM AN OLD MAKUA PROVERB

I'M only happy out of laziness. Unhappiness is harder to handle than an illness: you need to enter and leave it, sweep aside those who try to console you, accept condolences for a little bit of your soul that hasn't even got as far as dying.

—*Get up, mister lazybones.*

That's what my neighbour, the *mulata* Dona Luarmina, tells me to do. I reply:

—*Lazy? I'm just whitening my palms.*

—*That's the talk of a scalawag . . .*

—*Do you know something, Dona Luarmina? It was work that darkened the poor Black man's skin. And apart from that, living is all I'm good at . . .*

She laughs in that listless way of hers. The fat Luarmina smiles only so as to delude her sadness.

—*You, Zeca Perpétuo, are like a woman . . .*

—*A woman? Me?*

—*Yes, a woman sits on a mat. You're the only man I've ever seen sitting on a mat.*

—*What do you expect, dear neighbour? A chair is no good for sleeping.*

She waddles away, heavy as a pelican, shaking her head. My neighbour complains there's no man with as little sense as I have. She says she's never seen a fisherman let so many tides escape him:

—*You, Zeca, you just have no idea how life works.*

—*Life, Dona Luarmina? Life is so simple that no one understands it. It's like my grandfather Celestiano used to say when we started thinking about whether God existed or not . . .*

Besides, thinking produces a lot of stones and little by way of a path. So what's left for me to do, a retiree from the sea? Freed from fishing, I'm freed from thinking. One thing I learned over many years' fishing: time is carried along on the tide. We have to remain as sprightly as we can so we can always hitch a ride on one of those surges.

—*Isn't that so, Dona Luarmina? You know our folks' languages. Tell me something, my good lady: what's the word for future?*

Yes, how do you say future? There's no word for it in the language of this bit of Africa. Yes indeed, because the future, although it exists, never comes. So I'm happy to stick to the present here and now. That's enough for me.

—*All I want is to be a good man, lady.*

—*A good-for-nothing, that's what you are.*

The fat *mulata* isn't for beating around the bush. And she's right, as she's been my neighbour for so many years. She arrived in the area after my parents had died and I inherited the old family house.

At that time, I still went out on long fishing trips, weeks away out on the Sofala shoals. I wasn't even aware of Luarmina's existence. As for her, no sooner had she stepped ashore than she was sent to the Mission School, on her way to becoming a nun. She was shut away in the duskiness where God is addressed in whispers.

She only left this seclusion after some years. And she went to live in the house destined for her by her parents, right next to my dwelling. Luarmina was a seamstress, that's how she made her living. At first, she continued to keep herself to herself. Only the women who entered her abode had any dealings with her. As for me, all I got was the whiff of her shadow's perfume.

One day, Father Nunes told me about Luarmina and her nebulous past. Her father was Greek, one of those fishermen who cast his net along the coasts of Mozambique, on the other side of Saint Vincent's Bay. He had long ago gone to meet his maker. Her mother had died not long afterwards. Of grief, so folk said, not because she'd been made a widow but because of her daughter's beauty.

Luarmina, so it seemed, drove the important gentlemen who scavenged around her house crazy. The lady cursed her daughter's perfection. It was said that one night, in a fit of madness, she tried to strike Luarmina in the face. All in order to make her ugly and drive her suitors away.

After her mother's death, Luarmina was sent over this way to be set straight at the Mission, given over to prayer and the crucifix. The girl had to be trimmed on the outside and given a good ironing on the inside. And so that's how she came to devote herself to threads, needles, and thimbles. Until she moved to her present address on the fringes of my existence.

It was only after I gave up my life as a fisherman that I found myself taking a fancy to my neighbour. I began with letters, messages from a distance. Luarmina had already learned how to defend herself in a thousand ways as a result of my constant amorous approaches. She was always able to render my attentions useless by refusing me.

—*Leave me alone, Zeca. Can't you see I don't crease my bedsheets anymore?*

—*What a thought, lady?! Who said that was my intention, dear neighbour?*

But she was right. My visits have one purpose, which is to catch her off guard, to provoke a little tenderness. My dream is always the same: to wrap myself in her, carried away by the great wave that causes us to lose all self-awareness. She resists me, but I am always drawn back to her abode.

—*Dona Luarmina, what's the matter? It's as if you've really turned into a nun. One day, when love comes to you, you won't even recognize it . . .*

—*Let me be, Zeca. I'm old, all I need is a shoulder.*

To confirm this declaration of frigidity, she rubs her knees as if they were the cause of her weakness. Her legs, the way they swell up, make it hard for her blood to circulate. Her feet become icebergs: you touch them and they are frozen blocks. She is always complaining. On one occasion, I took advantage of this to make her an offer.

—*Would you like me to warm your feet up?*

With an expectant shiver, she got as far as accepting. Even I was left half taken aback, my heart galloping through my chest.

—*Will you warm me up, Zeca?*

—*Yes, I'll give you some heat . . . but from the inside.*

I was hoping she would drop her guard. But I got turned down. I was like the fellow who went to wash his hands and dirtied the soap. Or the one who wanted to clip his nail and cut off his finger. At my age, I should have known the correct way to proceed, the delicate tactics needed in one's approach. My late grandfather always said: *When we're young, we only get taught what's of no use to us. When we're old we only learn what's worthless.*

But it's a pity my neighbour and I can't pair up. For we're both semi-widowed: we've neither of us had a companion, but even so, that partner has disappeared. I'm younger than she, but we're both on the far slope where life only moves if it's in a downward direction.

Nowadays, I know how to measure someone's true age: we grow old when we no longer make new friends. We start dying the moment we stop falling in love.

And even Dona Luarmina, also known as Albertina da Conceição Melistopolous, was once beautiful enough to dazzle the menfolk. I know this because I once witnessed her good looks for myself. It was an occasion when I wasn't just confined to the veranda. I entered her house and sat in the big living room which looked out over the sea. That was when I saw the photograph. It was of a young girl of striking beauty, a body to bring water to the most tepid of mouths.

—*Who's that?*

—*It's me when I was young. Before I came to live here . . .*

I got to my feet and was about to touch the photo. But she abruptly blocked my vision, turning the picture over on the table. And that's where it remained for the rest of its days, that portrait lying there with its back to the light. I certainly tried to get a peep at the image of her former beauty through the window. But in vain.

I was left with the current vision of Luarmina, the fat, bloated one. The woman, through anguish, had allowed herself to swell, to pile on the kilos. I can understand: a good way of concealing sadness is to cover ourselves with flesh. Suffering is deathbound when it reaches our bones. When it gets there, sadness becomes increasingly skeletal. It is wise to give our body some cover, to insert some lardy borders.

Occasionally, there is some flicker of childhood in her. At such times, she tries to tease me, to spark me with a little jealousy.

—*A man once called me dolling.*

—*Dolling?*

—*Dolling or darling. It was a stranger from a foreign land.*

—*What's this darling business? I've got a lot of names that are much better than that. Would you like to hear them, dear neighbour?*

—*No. I'm sorry, Zeca, but I don't want to hear them. It's hard enough for me to have just one name, let alone lots . . .*

I've been prowling around the widow for years now. I even risk losing my plumage in my perseverance. But I'm chasing tail to no avail: my feathers brush nothing more than thin air. My strategy is to tell her about all the adventures I've had: I invent past deeds from my maritime endeavours. But they are not the type of adventures that bait her dreams. What Dona Luarmina asks of me are precise memories. And that's what I desire the least. They are scattered too widely throughout my being, even in the finger I lost while fishing. My body has become a cemetery where time is entombed, it's like one of those sacred woods where we bury our dead.

—*Tell me how it happened, I want to know what happened and how. Those things that make us yearn . . .*

As far as I'm concerned, my yearnings are never in a hurry. They take so long that they never get here. Once I start dancing I'm free of time—memories fly off and soar away from me. I should spend the whole time dancing, dancing for her, dancing with her.

—*Tell me about your past.*

My past is a burden for me: my childhood came to an early end, and I had to carry its effects in later life. When I was six, I took my grandfather's place on the boat; two years after that, my father lost his mind and left home, unseeing and deranged. Before she died, my mother put me into the care of the church. The Portuguese priest, Jacinto Nunes, educated me according to the doctrine of God and his book. But I wanted to return to the sea, and I soon swapped the book for the net, always unravelling much more than I got back in return. My grandfather Celestiano blamed my father for all this bad luck.

—*That son of mine, Agualberto, pig-headed as he is, went and joined the white men's world and didn't bother to bless his boat. He forsook his ancestors, and that was his punishment.*

I press Dona Luarmina not to ask me for my memories. I want to kill the past, and that woman must let me commit the crime. If not, then the past will end up killing me.

—*You, Zeca, are angry at the past, and you're jealous of the future: are you just going to live in the here and now?*

Having retired from fishing, I don't even have a present to fit into. As long as I was sailing out on the sea, lulled in my boat, I didn't suffer from time. For as I was rocked by the rhythm of the waves, it was just like dancing. And dancing, as I've already said, is the best way to escape time.

—*Come and dance, dear Dona . . .*

—*Dance? Me? With this body of mine?*

She laughs, ashamed. But Luarmina doesn't know this: those who dance lose their body. The tree is clever, for it doesn't move while its shadow dances all over the planet.

—*Dona Luarmina, don't you remember Maria Ballerina?*

And I recalled the girl who had lived in the area, a hot little number if ever there was one. She danced in a way that drove folk crazy, enough to make men's brains buzz and their eyes go askew. Her bare feet pummelled the ground like pestles, but they didn't raise any dust at all; the earth seemed aroused and to enjoy its beating. Maria Ballerina danced on request and for money. They would toss some coins at her and she would immediately set her body ablaze. Even the priest, Jacinto Nunes, would mumble into his cassock:

—*Heaven help me, even Archimedes would float!*

One night, as the dancer brushed past the open fire, her *capulana* happened to burst into flames. Maria Ballerina didn't stop dancing. The bystanders began to yell their warnings at her. The fire in her clothes began to blaze and grow thicker, but she didn't stop, and what's more, she allowed no one to get near her. She was in the grip of her own light-headedness, already dancing with death itself. Until she came to a sudden halt while still appearing whole and intact. When the first hand touched her she turned into ashes, a fine powder fluttering away, carried on the breeze.

—*Do you remember Maria Ballerina?*

Nothing. Luarmina doesn't reply. Had she even heard what I said? There's no two ways about it: my lady neighbour is suspicious of other people's misadventures. All she is interested in are the past times in which I featured. And I, by way of subterfuge, trick her with a few memories, improvise one or two thoughts. Until one day, I asked her:

—*Why only my personal memories?*

My neighbour didn't answer. Instead, she shot back:

—*Look, if it's so hard for you, tell me some of your dreams . . .*

But I never recall dreams that come to me while I'm asleep! We operate to a different timetable, me and dreams. So I warn her:

—*They'll be fake dreams . . .*

—*That doesn't matter.*

And I stood firm. For, apart from anything else, it brings us bad luck if we recall those who visit us during our sleep. So I was bound to introduce a few flashes of invention into my accounts. When it is not we who invent a dream, it is the dream that invents us.

—*It doesn't matter, Zeca Perpétuo. I would even pay someone to tell me their dreams today.*

A flicker of a smile crossed her face. But it was only moistened sadness. After that, I left my neighbour sitting where she was and crept back to my house with heavy steps. Luarmina had shut herself away in her world of fancy, as if she were unstitching some imaginary cloth:

—Sea loves me, sea loves me a lot . . .

This was Luarmina's ditty, her endless mumbling and jumbling. In the late afternoon, the *mulata* would sit down on the steps up to her veranda and forever unpick flowers. After a while, the whole yard would be lined with petals, the ground shimmering with a thousand colours.

Second Chapter

We launch the boat, we yearn for the journey: it's always the sea that travels.

ONE OF MY GRANDFATHER CELESTIANO'S SAYINGS

WELL, let me tell you something, my good lady. It's a pity you're going around tiring your eyes in front of everyone. What you should do, straightaway when you get up in the morning, is to wipe your face with a dream. That's what hinders time's advance and stops wrinkles from appearing. Do you know what to do? You lie out nice and flat on the sand, oblong fashion, stretching your mind diagonally. Then you just stay there, all quiet, right next to the ground, until you feel the soil embracing you with its love. I'm telling you, lady: when we keep still and quiet, like a stone, we start to hear the earth's ways of talking. At one point, lady, you'll hear a nautical voice coming from the ground, as if there were an ocean under the earth's skin. Make the most of this restfulness, Dona Luarmina. I take full advantage of these submarine silences. It's they that lull me to sleep even today. I'm its child, a child of the sea.

—A child, yes, for sure. You've long forgotten your age.

—Do you know what I'd really like? It would be for the two of us to get together, do you understand, Dona Luarmina?

—*Come to your senses, Zeca.*

—*Just think of us as verb and subject.*

—*I know your sort of grammar only too well . . .*

—*My dear good lady, you have no idea how much you enrich my eyesight.*

Luarmina doesn't favour me with a reply. And rightly so. Who am I? A hunter of fish who doesn't even have anyone to tell his adventures to. It's true, lady, I can't put lustre on my lies. And are they in fact lies? If I didn't really witness what I'm recounting but end up believing myself? It's all the sea's fault; all boundaries collapse there, everything is possible. At sea, there are no words, nor does anyone ask you to prove the truth. As old Celestiano used to say: where it's always noon, everything is night.

I turn my attention to the woman, Dona Luarmina. No one has ever been such a close neighbour. For at times when I can't see her, I dream of her. Always, without fail, that cushiony, flesh-filled woman. Her butt exceeds her buttocks. There was a time when she provoked men's attentions. But she has faded now. Not for me, as I'm fired up in her presence and ardent in her absence.

Late every afternoon, I walk over to her house. Her little place is funny: all it has is a backside. A bit like its lady owner: you don't have to beat around the bush in order to walk round it. You get there, and you're at its rear straightaway. I sit down on an old tree trunk and gaze at the woman unpicking herself:

—*Sea loves me . . .*

Then I think to myself: how I'd love to stick my hand inside her endowments! One night, as I lay on my sleeping mat, I even dreamed I walked up to where she was sitting and presented the following request:

—*Let me feel your buttocks; it'll be so quick you won't even have to put my brazenness out of your mind.*

—*Which one?*

—*What do you mean, Dona Luarmina?*

—*Which buttock?*

—*Either one, lady, they measure the same. Don't you remember your school geometry: the sum of the factors is always the same?*

While I was speaking, my hand was travelling over her lusty abundances, a crazy little train rolling over the contours of her seating area. My fingers tiptoed along her crevices.

—*What's going on? I haven't given you permission yet.*

—*This hand of mine belongs to the informal sector, Dona Luarmina.*

—*Every bit of you, Zeca Perpétuo, belongs to the informal sector.*

—*You know the saying, don't you, lady? Better a bird in the hand . . .*

—*You're an abuser . . .*

—*This is all a dream, just a dream. Do you know what I dreamed yesterday, Dona Luarmina? Well, I'll tell you, and don't interrupt me. You came with me to the Baixo da Nuvem nightclub and you were dancing with me. You were dancing all dressed in white, all very respectful. I closed my eyes and then, all of a sudden, you whispered in my ear: See: I'm as naked as a fish.*

I shivered. I didn't even have the courage to open my eyes. Her voice was buzz-buzzing next to my ear:

—*But take a good look: I've got a tattoo here on my belly. Feel it with your hand. Yes, right there. Now pass your finger over my hip, further down, yes there. That's it. They're tattoos to stop you slipping.*

This was all very pretty and a torrid tale to tell. But I was unable to pursue my memory of the dream any further. Dona Luarmina interrupted me, shaking me with her plump hand.

—*Be quiet, Zeca. You're an old codger. Why are you still having such dreams?*

—*Old, my foot! You, lady, who love birds so much: do birds' feathers ever wear out?*

—*But you, my dear sir, only fly close to the ground.*

—*Well, so what, Dona Luarmina? It's all the more fun down below.*

Luarmina wasn't the sort to laugh at jokes. She would allow herself a smile every now and then. For the rest, she shut herself away in sadness for not having had a child. When I called her a flower, she would return to the fray with a bitter retort.

—*Don't call me a flower, because it hurts. A seed is the only footprint a flower leaves behind. And I never left a child in this world.*

—*That wasn't your fault. The right insect never learned how to land on you. I wish I'd been there.*

—*Be quiet, Zeca.*

—*Listen to me: you're a flower, that's for sure.*

—*All right then, I'm a flower. But one of those that was never good for anything.*

—*You were good for beauty, Luarmina.*

—*And what is beauty good for? Good for nothing.*

—*Look, here's just one example: what lights up the sky most? Isn't it a rainbow? So tell me then: what's a rainbow good for?*

—*I've no idea.*

—*It's good for making itself look fancy, for teaching the sky how to dream.*

But she withdrew into herself again. She bade me forgive her. She had made up her mind she was a ruin. Here's what she said:

—*I frittered away my time, but time, it didn't forget me.*

That's what she said as she pointed to her neck and her aging skin. To which I replied, by way of comfort:

—*Well, time hasn't abandoned you, thanks and no thanks to God. Because it's me and time competing for you, Dona Luarmina. Let me be the winner. Please, Dona . . .*

—*Do you really want to taste me?*

—*Of course I do, lady!*

—*Well then, spin me one of your memories, a real one . . .*

Third Chapter

The dugout was launched into the sea, a speck of dust entered God's eye.

ONE OF MY GRANDFATHER CELESTIANO'S SAYINGS

I DON'T know why Dona Luarmina cried when I told her my old father's story. After all, it was she who asked for it! I had warned her of the sadness of this memory, but she was insistent. This was the only reason why I unlocked my recollections.

My father's name was Agualberto Perchance. He was a person in every way. Only one feature put his humanity in doubt: my old man had the eyes of a shark. It wasn't that he was born like this. It happened when he once jumped into the water from his boat in order to save his sweetheart. She was a very young girl he had met in other lands. He always took her with him in his boat, to keep him company on his fishing trips. At the end of the day, before he brought his fish back to the beach, my father would set course for beyond the horizon so as to leave the girl where she came from. Who was this girl, where was she from? This was a mystery that Agualberto kept to himself.

That afternoon, my father was fishing near to our beach. The sea was choppy. I was screwing my eyes trying to catch a glimpse of the girl who was with my father. My mother turned her back on the ocean.

—*Have you seen my father out there?*

My mother didn't answer. She was busy with her sticks of firewood and getting dinner ready. I stood there at the edge of the beach, looking at the little craft, now visible, now hidden by the waves. Until, all of a sudden, I noticed a figure falling into the sea. It was the girl. My father panicked and jumped in to rescue her. He plunged into the depths of the sea and stayed underwater for longer than his lungs would allow. Other boats put to sea to save him. We counted the seconds, minutes, the tears and the sighs. Only at the end of the day did my old man reappear on the surface of the water. No one expected him to re-emerge. But to everyone's astonishment and prayers, my father leaped like a dolphin between the waves, yelling as if the whole firmament had invaded his chest. The onlookers shouted:

—*He's alive! He's alive!*

The fishermen rushed forwards to go and get their re-emerged companion. They rejoiced, dancing and singing while the boats headed back to the beach. The women ululated. My mother advanced and came to a standstill in front of her man. What was going on inside her head? After all, that woman my father had tried to save was another, her rival, lacking legitimacy. Even so, she confronted my old man. Her eyes ascended from the ground until they stared into his face. And this was when she screamed, covering her face with her hands. The others approached my father and a murmur swept through them like an icy cloud.

—*His eyes!*

Yes indeed, Agualberto's eyes were no longer the same. No one managed to look my father in the face. For those eyes of his were the same colour as the sea: blue, marine in their transparency. His humanity had been washed away as if he were a fish. He had stayed far too long under the sea. And the rumour began to spread that Agualberto had the eyes of a shark, identical to those colossal, toothsome creatures.

From that day on, my father withdrew ever more deeply into himself, spending his time sitting on the beach contemplating the horizon. People came from afar to catch a distant glimpse of the Black man with eyes the colour of the sea. On one occasion, my mother tugged at my arm and whispered to me in an anguished tone:

—*That woman, that other one, can it be that she has really died?*

We all knew she had, that she had got lost in the deep, there where the coral blossoms into fish. Everyone knew except old Agualberto, who was bereft of reasoning. Every afternoon he would take baskets of food into the sea, along with supplies of fresh drinking water. He would dive and remain underwater for a long time. Then he would return to the surface at peace with the world, having paid his yearning its dues. However, every time he resurfaced, his eyes looked all the bluer. There would come a day when they would be rinsed of all colour, like those seashells that are bleached white. All this seemed like the fulfillment of some prophecy, a map of his thoughts: he was losing his sight in the same way he had lost his love. And this is what happened: Agualberto was left waxen-eyed, and he never visited the watery depths again.

When the blue left his eyes, my father also left home. Off he went. I was a child, and thought everything could be put right. My old man's departure introduced me to the belief that for certain things in this life there is no resolution. At the same time, I had to witness my mother's growing loss of sanity. She never accepted she had been abandoned. For long after my father had left, she would still tell me:

—*Wait, Zeca. Let me first ask your father.*

If I had been bullied or there were tears, she was always there to console me:

—*Don't worry, I'll tell your father.*

As if his not being present was no more than a delay in getting back from fishing. It is all part of the age-old custom: a child is never told they're an orphan. And so my mother dressed his absence in the garments of untruth.

—*Have you written him a nice little letter this week?*

I smiled sadly. But she gave me no time to reply.

—*Your father would be so happy to get a little note from you. He'd be so happy, he might even cry.*

—*But Mother . . .*

—*Do you know something? One day, a tear of his fell into the sea. And right there, at the point where the tear hit the wave, the tear turned into a piece of coral and sank to the bottom. Write to your father . . .*

—*But Mother, I don't even know what letters look like.*

—*That's why you're going to go and see the priest and attend the Mission. Your father will send you a bit of money later.*

—*All right, Mother.*

Then she would go back into our little house, looking as if she were walking right through the middle of a fire, surrounded by flames. She reminded me of Maria Ballerina in the way she seemed to regain her youth dancing with the blaze. But when my mother trod on the fire, nothing happened to her. I would remain out on the beach, escaping time, my gaze roaming over the night. My mother would come back some time later and tell me:

—*Do you see the stars, Zeca? Do you know what they're saying?*

—*No, Mother.*

—*You know, my son, the night is a letter that God writes in tiny handwriting. When you come back from the city, will you read me that letter?*

—*Yes, Mother.*

Fourth Chapter

If I built a chimney in my house, it wouldn't be to let out the smoke, but to let in the sky.

GRANDFATHER CELESTIANO'S WORDS

Day always starts with a lie. That is because the sun only pretends to be born. That morning awoke with heatful intentions and I decided to go for a stroll along the beach. This was when I came across Luarmina plunged in a pool of water. She was dressed, and her clothes clung to her body. I walked up to

her and asked her why she was taking a bath. She replied that she
wanted to warm up her legs.

—*Is the water nice and warm?*

—*I don't get heat from the water. What warms me up are the sea snails.*

And she explained: there were some snails that licked her legs,
grazing on those fat pastures of hers. The little creatures left
their trails of sticky saliva on my neighbour and all I could think
to myself was that my own mucus had been wasted, with all due
respect. Heaven forbid.

—*Do you mind if I join you?*

—*Join me where?*

—*In the water where you are having your bath, lady.*

I got in, and snuggled up alongside my neighbour. I lay back
in the water and closed my eyes just like she was doing. My
hands pretended to be snails, slimy slugs furrowing their way
over Luarmina's thighs. To my astonishment, the *mulata* didn't
push me away. My fingers continued, carrying out their duties,
fishing between her clothes and her body. I glanced at her out of
the corner of my eye: the fat Luarmina was floating, in blissful
subjugation, like a ship at anchor in a child's drawing.

Suddenly, however, she let out a cry. I ceased my capers and
hid my hands behind my back.

—*What a fright, lady! What's the matter?*

Luarmina pointed at something on the surface of the water.
They were dead fish floating.

—*Look, Zeca, they're fish without eyes!*

I shuddered. That was a sign. Someone on the world's other
shore was watching me. The dead are obstinate in their determination to be human. And right there, between me and Luarmina,
the message of the gods was plain to see. The *mulata* was more
terrified than I was.

—*What is it, Zeca?*

—*We'd better get out of the water. Come, I'll help you.*

Luarmina was trembling. To keep her alarm at bay, I kept talking non-stop. Do you know what fish are? How they first appeared? Well, sit down then and relax. Like that, yes. I'm going to tell you my grandfather Celestiano's version of the story. In olden times, there were no living creatures in the sea. Only on land and in the air. There were many birds, floating over the continents. The gods were happy enough to watch them flying over the forests, soaring up over the tops of mountains. Then, one day, a bird had the audacity to hover over the waters. And it was surprised by the beauty of its own flight, glimpsed in the water's reflection. It flew back and told the other birds:

—*I now know why we aren't allowed to fly over the ocean.*

And so off they flew in their thousands, flocks of them all anxious to see their image. Never before had there been so many clouds over the sea: all made of feathers, buoyant enough to sustain their weight. At this point, a storm broke out, the punishment of the gods. Lightning ripped through the birds like flashing knives. Thousands of birds fell into the waves and were swept along by the currents, as if they were pursuing their flight in liquid gusts. And so, from their wings, the swell was born, and from their feathers the spume.

—*The way I feel at the moment, Zeca, I'm not in the mood for listening to stories.*

Luarmina didn't want any distractions. She was being pulled under by the force of her own anxiety. It would be better if she did the talking.

—*So do you remember your family, Luarmina?*

But she didn't answer. Her past was like the future in our languages; it only began when it was over, like the lizard being eaten by its own tail. The rest dissolved in the mists of sadness.

—*For as long as I had a finger, I stitched cloth and dressed people.*

But she didn't find her life's fulfillment as a dressmaker. She wanted something else, she wanted to grow people inside her, to have children, be born again in other lives. But without such a gift, she no longer felt like entering her home, so alone was she. This was why she spent more time on her veranda than within the walls of her house.

—*That's why I like to hear stories about families. Go on, tell me about your home, your family.*

—*Don't ask that of me, Luarmina.*

—*You know something, Zeca: tonight, when the moon is up, I think I'm going to have a bath outside, in my yard . . .*

—*Will you be naked? I mean, undressed?*

—*Who knows, Zeca?*

—*And will you let me have a look, lady?*

—*If you tell me a story, I will.*

Fifth Chapter

The sea has one flaw: it never dries up. I almost prefer the tiny little lake in my village, which is very prone to drying up and we feel for it in the same way that we feel for a living creature, always in danger of meeting its end.

THE WORDS OF GRANDFATHER CELESTIANO

AFTER that incident, my old man was left with a mamba's moodiness. Any idea that nestled in his mind began to grow a fang. He was gone noiselessly at the crack of dawn, and took up residence there where we couldn't clap eyes on him, beyond the marshes where the ground brooks neither path nor building.

I only caught a glimpse of him every once in awhile. In such encounters, my heart always shrank. As a young child, I feared him, and fell over myself in my attempts to ingratiate myself in his presence. For the old man made a song and a dance out of everything and everyone: *suca, famba,** be off with you. Agualberto passed us with a stiff, slow gait. At first, we asked ourselves: is he blind? Impossible, the man pushed himself forwards as if he were pulling us towards him. Those vacant eyes of his stared into our soul rather than our face. The whole village was unanimous.

—*That fellow's got more sulphur in him than the devil.*

No matter how great our fear, we couldn't do without him. Why? Because my old man blessed the fish hooks. The fishermen would form a line and he would attend each one in turn. There would be complete silence while he closed his eyes. Agualberto Perchance would await the voices that would flow from his mouth. Somewhere out there, far away, the tide was turning, the ocean frolicked around as the tides raced. Until he received a signal that the tide was on the turn, he remained still and unblinking. He who knows, doesn't speak, he who is wise, keeps quiet. As my grandfather said: *Do you know the difference between a wise white man and a Black? The white answers your questions right away. For us Blacks, the wisest man is the one who takes his time before giving you an answer.*

And so my father waited in this state of immobility, while the fishermen who wanted to be blessed also waited. Until Agualberto raised his hand and wriggled his fingers as if he were summoning the invisible. He opened an old packet of cigarettes stuffed with a powder that bore some resemblance to tobacco. They had the appearance of cigarettes that had been chewed by time and sucked with the spittle of oblivion. The powders were sprinkled over the hook and luck stuck to it. Other times, he added various items to the bait: bits of glass, card, shells. All this was cast into the sea and the best possible good fortune invoked.

But how did this man, my father, survive? I asked myself that question from afar. My old man left home every morning, and

---

* —*Leave, go away.*

would eye the walls of the neighbourhood as if he were trying not to look at them. He would make for the quay. There, he would sit himself down on the wall, where he would receive the inevitable messages. Without fail, I would head for where he was, whenever I set off on my own fishing expeditions. Sometimes, he looked sad to me, his chest sticking out from his ribs. Was he shedding a tear on the landscape's shoulder? Was he being trodden on by his past? Or was he yearning for that extinct girl?

He sat on the edge of the quay, feeling the breeze off the Indian Ocean. The man didn't even articulate a word: merely loose sounds, little shards of speech. When he spoke, it was as if he were licking his own tongue. His body swayed like a tree in a gale. Was his body pondering different thoughts from his head? As far as I could see, he was praying, lighting the wick of some word, in a never-ending process of not wanting to forget or remember, absorbed in a yearning for other lives.

But he earned his money by blessing the fish hooks, the guarantee of a good catch. And every morning, the fishermen would wait by the wall while he unwrapped the same ancient cigarette packet and opened a bag full of offerings. I joined the hunters of fish. I would wait in the long line while gulls screeched overhead. When my turn came, I would be gripped by fear and slide away from the line. Countless times, I would line up again and wait. But when I came face to face with my old man, I would stumble over myself and leave the place.

Then one morning, my old mother died. She left life just as she had lived it, with neither history nor drama. She just complained:

—*The sun's pulling me too hard, I feel hot.*

She walked over to the water tank and dipped her wrists in as if she were looking to get cool. She leaned against the trunk of the tree and let her arms dangle in the tank. Without us knowing, she was dying, her veins diluting in water's eternity. We carried her away from there as if we were just putting her to bed. In silence, as if she had stolen away long ago. As if we were simply taking Mother for an afternoon stroll, like any other. Did my old mother die instantly? Or isn't all death instantaneous?

On the day of the funeral, the weather changed. Without any warning, the sky turned wintry. First thing in the morning, the cold filtered in through the cracks: no one would go out fishing in such weather. But in spite of this, I went. My mood matched the world, its winds and overcast skies. Who knows, maybe the quay would chase my clouds away? There I was, lost in my thoughts, holding the line as if my soul were attached to the submerged fish hook.

This was when I heard footsteps. I turned around apprehensively. The figure of Agualberto Perchance emerged from the mists and gave me a fright. There I was, my unblessed line drooping sadly in the grey waters. Had he recognized me, even though I had my back to him?

That would be impossible, because the old man was completely blind. Then he addressed me in his gravelly voice:

—*Is that how you're doing it? The fish won't bite . . .*

I didn't turn round. I stayed there hunched over with fear. For at that very moment, a sudden tug on the line indicated the presence of a fish brushing its lips over my hook. I didn't want to seem to be contradicting the soothsayer, so I pretended nothing was happening. But the quivering of the line then confirmed that I had had a bite from a large fish, endowed with both size and weight. As for me, in my cowardice, I neither moved nor made a sound. I don't know how, but my father noticed the quivering line.

—*Aren't you going to reel in the fish?*

And there was I without knowing what to do or say. I continued to look blankly in front of me, pretending I was dead. Fear was born along with us; it is the same fear that seizes us at the moment of our birth when we shed our first tears.

—*Go on, reel in the line!*

If he was blind, how did he see the tugging on the line? He seemed to guess my doubts.

—*After all these years, I don't need eyes to tell me when a fish is biting.*

He sat down next to me. Even sitting right on the edge of the quay, he swung his legs. I was trembling before his fierce gaze. His voice appropriated my own:

—*Where's your bait?*

Unable to reply, I pointed at my tin of worms. The man stuffed his thick fingers into the tin and took out a shiny, wriggling worm, turning it this way and that in the air.

He talked of fish and fishing in his own language. In the language of our area, there is no exact word for "to fish." We say "to kill the fish." There is no special word for "boat." And we call the ocean "the big place." We are people of the soil, the sea is a recent arrival.

—*It's not the bait I'm blessing.*

—*So what are you blessing?*

—*I'm blessing you.*

Did my father recognize me? Then he looked at me with that deep, empty gaze that I found impossible to return. And this is what he said:

—*I'm going to tell you this, lad: I'm blind when it comes to the living. But I can see death's shore clearly. And I can see your death . . .*

—*My death?*

—*You're going to die drowned in a bedsheet, as if the linen had become waves on the sea.*

—*Do you know who I am, sir?*

He nodded. It was because he knew who I was that he was there, sitting beside me. Then he asked me:

—*I came to ask you something: Do you know where the China Deep is?*

—*That deep gully out there in the middle of the sea?*

—*Yes, I want you to go there, every week. Take food and drinking water with you. Leave it out in the deep. Do it for me. Do you promise?*

—*Yes, I promise.*

Then he explained: this memory was his only reason for living. Down in the deepest depths of the China Deep, the woman he had loved, the woman he had eyes for, had met her end.

—*Do you know something? All these fish hooks I bless. It's all a lie. I only pretend to cast a lucky spell on them so that their bait, all those things I add to the hooks, will sink down into the depths and not come back.*

—*And what happens to those things you attach to the hook?*

—*They're gifts for the dead girl. They're for her. They're all for her. They're my gifts to her.*

Sixth Chapter

The snail is like a poet: he washes his tongue on his journey's path.

THE WORDS OF MY GRANDFATHER—
BUT I DON'T BELIEVE THEM

THAT afternoon, I was relaxing on my veranda, gazing at the ocean. It wasn't that I was taking in all that azure. It was the sea that was taking my dreams on a trip. And I was blind to memories, like someone eternally reborn. And so, on my veranda's old step, I wasn't talking—I was silence itself, lulled by the rhythm of the Indian Ocean.

Suddenly, the screech of a gull made me start. My nerves were as taut as a bow, and my reaction swift as an arrow. The stone left my hand in fury.

—*Hey, Perpétuo! You nearly hit me.*

It was my neighbour. Dona Luarmina always wanted to know the reason why I was so devoted to killing gulls. Poor things, she would say, they're birds full of whiteness, they adorn the sky with oceanic dreams. But why, Zeca, why are you so angry? As a man with such a brimming heart, how could I act so malevolently towards innocent creatures?

—*I can't explain.*

—*Why?*

—*Because it's a secret, Dona Luarmina.*

—*I thought only women hid their secrets.*

I smiled. That was a cunning blow designed to make my macho instincts teeter. What is a secret? A secret is an orange with only one segment. We eat that segment and are left with the peel wrapped around emptiness. I already knew that bitter taste of holding a fruit without any inside, while its peel turned to sand between my fingers.

I knew how much my persecution of the birdlife caused her to suffer. Do you know what she did, such was her pity of the gulls? She built a cage and put dozens of them inside. It was pandemonium, day and night. Not for Luarmina, who was a woman of little agitation. But for the children who would capture the birds and bring her kilos of fish for them to peck at.

At night, my sleep never hit bottom. Only bits of me slept; I was never completely asleep. That was because of the racket coming from my neighbour's birdcage. Until one night, in the midst of my sleeplessness, my darkened thoughts turned to gasoline, rage, and matches. Fire is passion: in an instant, it consumes everything. The imprisoned seagulls looked like white handkerchiefs flapping against the sunset. Their lives were extinguished. Wrapped in flame and light, too bright a light for them to keep flying. Until all that was left were ashes, and I slunk away before anyone saw me.

The next day, I went and paid my neighbour a visit. As I predicted, she was on her veranda. I placed my hand on her shoulder by way of condolence. She didn't move. She had already wept all she had to weep, and was exhausted. Only a solitary tear remained on the fullness of her cheek. I nearly offered her a handkerchief.

But then I remembered something she had said once before when she had cried. I shall never forget Luarmina's words.

—*You may have been comforted by a hand, a pair of lips, or a body, but no manner of caress will return your soul to you as much as a tear being released.*

—*How do you know that, Luarmina?*

—*A tear is the sea caressing your soul. That little speck of water is us as we return to the womb we came from.*

As I recalled her words, I put my handkerchief away. I let her tear roll down her cheek. And there we remained, without talking. Her silence was complete, more painful than a thousand sobs.

Suddenly, I got an urge to clean up what I had done and return the henhouse to life and the wing. But I was unable to carry out the task: if there was a broom, there was no ground to sweep. I decided to confess everything. And so I told her about Henriquinha.

Let me tell you, lady—I was once married, well and truly married. She was a girl full of body but soft in the head, one might even say mad as a hatter. At first, I didn't even notice her scattiness. Henriquinha seemed so composed, without any sign of either physical or mental dysfunction.

On Sundays, in the late afternoon, she would set off along the paths that led to the Church of Our Lady of the Souls. She wore her black dress, and made her way with a widow's step. As I watched that woman from the veranda, a shudder ran through me as if that walk of hers were tearing at the locks of my soul. Then, as I contemplated the way her backside shaped her skirt, I became reconciled to my situation. Such a beautiful and pious wife was a comely gift.

Until one day I was told that she wasn't in fact going to Mass at all. She was going to the top of the Red Dune, where she would get undressed for all to see, divested of all her clothes. The local folk would gather together to enjoy the sight. Even today, I can't remember how many times I failed to give in to such vexation. Was the woman playing a game of cat and no mouse? What should I do? I sat there quietly in the shade, pretending to be checking the state of the sea, searching my mind as hard as I could for an idea.

One not so fine day, I had an idea. I should follow her without anyone seeing. This is how I organized it: I played a trick with the calendar. I got hold of one from a previous year, and pinned it up on the kitchen wall. That morning, Henriquinha asked me what day it was.

—*I don't know, woman. Look at the calendar.*

She looked at it. Then I heard her voice exclaim in surprise from the bedroom:

—*Hey! Is it really Sunday today?!*

At first, she insisted there must be some mistake. It couldn't be Sunday. It is, I answered, all Sundays are like that, the same as weekdays except for the collar and tie. It's true, Henriquinha, we scarcely notice the week go by, and we're already in the next one. What a life it is for a fisherman, who doesn't think of days but of tides! And on I went, talking of this and that. I talked and talked so as to distract her.

—*At least you're lucky, Henriquinha. Your time begins at set hours, you get up and lie down, you go to bed and wake up. Whereas for me, my sun is the sea. Who knows what time that keeps?*

Henriquinha didn't even seem to hear. She went to the wardrobe and took out her formal black dress.

—*Are you going out?*

—*Have you forgotten that on Sundays I always fulfill my obligations to God?*

I smiled to myself. She'd fallen for it. For a few seconds, I even felt guilty. For a moment, I thought of dismantling the trap. But my soul was more powerful than sentiment. And off I went behind the woman, following her with utmost care, behind walls, thickets, and bushes. Until we reached the cliff of red earth. Henriquinha stopped on the edge, where the cliff drops into the abyss, right next to where the waves crash onto the shore. I stopped and watched.

At that hour, there was no one around. Maybe because it wasn't Sunday, and nobody expected a performance on that day. Then Henriquinha began to sway as if dancing to a music only she could hear. With her back to me, she shimmied pleasurably, as if some invisible rain were falling on her. She started pulling her dress halfway up her body, and her waist began to show between her hands and flashes of light. Then she shed her clothes. Every garment that fell to the ground was like a dead leaf alighting upon my astonishment.

Along with anger, I was filled with a fervent desire for her. As if I had never seen or touched her before, as if she were some unattainable woman. I even thought: I'll go over and ruffle my hair with her, initiate a little romance to cut our flesh to the quick. And I tiptoed over until I was standing behind Henriquinha, until I heard her gasps. The sound of that breathing of hers tricked me into thinking she had grown tired of me, that her body had been set ablaze in the fire of my blood. Suddenly, I felt a need to remove the source of my giddiness.

I pushed her. I didn't hear her scream or even the thump of a body hitting the rocks below. Only the screech of a gull as it brushed past the cliff. Had Henriquinha fallen? Had she died? Had she been swallowed up by the sea?

On the days that followed, I returned to the Red Dune, I searched every millimetre of cave and sand for any sign of Henriquinha's body. Nothing. Only absence. For me, this was more painful than a death, like those that involve a ceremony and burial. If I were a man in full control of my better judgment, I would still be torturing myself in an endless farewell to Henriquinha. But no. As far as I was concerned, nothing had happened. It's like the future: it exists, but there isn't any. If it had occurred, then at the same instant it had transitioned to another life, another memory that didn't belong to me.

There's only one more thing, Dona Luarmina: that seagull's cry, at the exact moment of Henriquinha's fall. That razor-sharp shriek rips the scars of a wound I never felt. You ask why I keep persecuting those birds, lady? Do you understand now, Dona Luarmina?

All that time, my neighbour had listened to me without moving, her face sunk in the shadow. When I finished, we remained shrouded in silence until Luarmina asked me:

—*Was that your secret?*

—*Yes, it was.*

Then she looked up and confronted me. Her expression wasn't even one of anger. Her eyes seemed empty, vacant. As if my words had induced in her some incurable blindness.

—*Go out to the backyard, and see what you did.*

—*I'm sorry, Dona Luarmina, I can't go.*

Then she struggled with her own body in an effort to get to her feet. The wood in her chair creaked in complaint. With Dona Luarmina, all chairs were rocking chairs. Without any help, she somehow got up, and then she held out her hand to me:

—*Come with me.*

I followed her reluctantly. Dispirited, I walked behind her as she made her laboured way to the cage. In front of me, Luarmina's back shielded me from guilt. Her bulk hid my vision of the world.

—*Look.*

I stood behind her, like a child awaiting a smack. She was insistent, but I stood with my head bowed, weeding the ground with my shame. Until all of a sudden, I heard the flapping of wings. That sound spattered my soul with memory, as if two worlds were colliding. I gradually raised my eyes, seeing first the chewed planks of wood, then the decaying remains of birds, their ashen feathers, all lying there as peaceful as the desert. The metal mesh remained intact. But out of that ash-grey mixture. I seemed to see a live bird, all white, its lacy wings in sudden flight. How had that seagull survived such a conflagration?

Dona Luarmina slowly withdrew. I was left there alone with the remains of the cage and a vacant memory that had drained away from me and from everything. My hands were shaking when I opened the cage door.

Seventh Chapter

The heart is a beach.

MAKUA PROVERB CITED BY OLD CELESTIANO

ON the first occasion, I felt moisture on my arm. I was in bed, awaiting sleep. Suddenly, I had a cold feeling on my arm: some sort of liquid that had got in through a crack was running down it. That was when I was gripped by the horror of the vision: water was coming from everywhere, from the floor, the ceiling, water was rushing to fetch me, its blue tongue ready to tear me away from this world. Soon I would be unable to breathe, hemmed in from the inside as well as the outside. I got up, and as I fled the room the floor got wetter. I was hallucinating, for sure. But the puddled mat was there as proof that it was true.

That was just the first time. This vision of drowning assailed me whenever I was on the point of sleep. Sometimes it was the sea that covered me, other times I seemed to be drowning in my own blood. Sea and blood, blood and sea. Where were these signs coming from? I recalled my days of yore, I remembered my old father telling me one day, when I cut my finger out in the boat:

—Suck a bit of that blood.

I obeyed, as I always did. My father studied my movements with an attention he never normally paid me.

—Tell me now: what does blood taste like?

I looked at the sea, without giving him any other answer. So what was my father telling me? That we had oceans circulating within us? That there are journeys we must undertake only within ourselves? I shall never know. The lessons old Agualberto gave me were always like this: vague and ill defined. Blood and sea, their similarities now came back to me like a punishment for some act of disobedience. Only then did I understand the real reason for those nightmares. When he sensed he was dying, my father addressed me with a request.

—Take me to see certain places.

By now, his eyes were completely white, like shells that had been licked by the sun over time.

—What are the places you want to go to, Father?

—Sit down, Zeca. I want to talk.

Agualberto Perchance never called me "son." On that occasion, he hesitated. But then he went ahead swiftly, and in a solemn tone:

—I'm more or less going to die.

—Don't say that.

—I know my hour has come. But I don't want to die in one place alone. I can't leave my whole self in only one place. I already know the places where I'm going to die, a little bit in each one.

This was what he asked: that I should lead him to those places where he wanted to scatter his little pieces of death. And so we set off, first in the direction of the baobab tree at Ritsene. By that time he was tired, and he leaned against the trunk. There he remained, catching his breath, until he spoke:

—Your grandfather Celestiano was right, son.

—What was it he said?

Grandfather had criticized Agualberto for surrendering to the white man's ways. The reason for his misfortune had been because he had turned his back against the older world.

—*This is our church,* my father said, pointing at the tree. *Do you hear, Zeca?*

—*Yes, Father.*

—*Tell Father Nunes that I came here to our ancestors' tree. Tell him I came here, that I didn't go and get down on my knees in his church . . .*

He took a piece of *konkuene* from his bag. He placed the black coral in a hollow of the tree trunk as an offering to the ancestors.

—*I'm the only one with a piece of coral like this; no one else has a piece like it.*

After that, we left, clambering along the riverbank. My father walked steadily next to me, as if he were able to make use of my eyes. Could it be that in spite of having lost the roundness in his eyes, he could still see?

—*I listen to the light on the water, and the direction it takes . . .*

—*So where are we going?*

—*Now we're going to the little forest where that boat of mine was born.*

I led him into a wood where he had prepared the timber for his first and only boat. The old man walked around the clearing, and felt the trunks of every tree as if he were caressing a woman's body. And he called every tree by name.

—*This one is called Hope, that twisted one over there is called Sunrise.*

He stumbled over shrubs, and tumbled to the ground. I made to help him get up. But he preferred to remain seated.

—*Let me die a little here. Pull me over there just a tiny bit. Yes, that's good, there's a little ray of sunshine here.*

He sat there for a time with his eyes closed. Once again, he took a piece of coral out of his bag and placed it on the ground. It was another offering to the gods.

—*Now what, Father?*

—*Now I'm going to the other side of the sea . . .*

—*I'll go and get the boat ready and I'll go with you.*

—*No. You stay, I'm going alone.*

I put him in the boat along with his old bag. I pushed him out as far as I could while still in my depth. I pointed it in the right direction and told him:

—*Keep going straight ahead, don't turn . . .*

—*I'm in the sea, my son, I don't need anyone to guide me now.*

And off he went. It was the only time he ever called me son. It was, I knew it, his farewell. Hearing that word from his mouth could have been my childhood being born. But it was his farewell.

Eighth Chapter

When my grandfather Celestiano sensed death approaching, he called his wife and asked her:

   —*Let me look at your eyes!*

   And he lay there enthralled, as if his soul were a boat floating on a sea that was his beloved's eyes.

   —*Are you cold? she asked, seeing him shiver.*

   —*No. It's you who are crying.*

   —*Crying? Me? It's started raining, that's what's happened.*

MY GRANDMOTHER'S RECOLLECTION
OF OLD CELESTIANO'S FINAL MOMENT

My illness has got worse: I no longer get out of bed. Even more serious: I cannot even sleep. The moment my eyelids close, the folds in the sheet turn into water, and the next moment everything turns red and I flow out into rivers of blood. If I sleep, I drown, if I remain conscious, I go mad. I need to dream, all I want to do is dream.

I can hear the door opening. It must be thieves, but I'm no longer bothered. Let them steal the nothing that I possess, let them take the little life left that I have. They would even do me a favour. But it's Luarmina peering round the door.

—*I've come to visit you, Zeca.*

—*Is that so?* I smile, in disbelief.

—*You always visited me. Today, I'm the one visiting you.*

Luarmina undoes a new sheet. She bids me help her to change the sheets on the bed.

—*These ones are soaking; how can someone sweat so much?*

I wanted to tell her it wasn't sweat but the sea itself punishing me. But I didn't hem and haw, and got straight to the point.

—*How good it is that you've come, Luarmina. It's because I'm about to die.*

—*Don't talk nonsense, Zeca. You'll live to throw a few shovelfuls on my grave.*

I made the same request as old Celestiano had made in his final moments: I wanted her to sit next to my bed just so that I could find pleasure in her eyes.

—*I beg you, dear neighbour: I want to swoon while looking into your eyes.*

Luarmina smiled indulgently, as if I had returned to my childhood once and for all.

—*If you go on talking like this, I'm going.*

—*Then do me a favour, lady. Tell me a story.*

—*A story? Me?*

—*Yes, neighbour, I've already told you so many of mine.*

—*But I don't have any stories, I've led such a sheltered existence.*

—*How is that possible?*

—*My life has been an uneventful one. I've lived so little that I haven't got long before I die.*

—*Make an effort, Dona Luarmina. It's shameful for a man, but I want you to lull me until I begin to dream. I need to dream, I need so much to dream!*

Luarmina got to her feet, bewildered. She wandered this way and that as if she were not so much seeking an idea but something that had been lost in the clutter of the room. Suddenly, she stopped next to the bed and uttered a strange order:

—*Get up, Zeca.*

She startled me. I refused, incapable of any movement whatsoever. But she persevered, pulled me, levered me up by my armpits.

—*But I can't stand. Leave me in bed.*

—*Stop babbling, Zeca, and help me to get you up.*

—*But what do you want to do with me, lady?*

—*What do I want to do? I want to dance with you, man.*

What an irony of fate! All my life, I had dreamed of dancing with that woman. Now she wanted to, but I couldn't. Luarmina still dragged me off as if I were a sack full of levity. I tried as hard as I could, but my feet couldn't keep up with the steps. Until she deposited me on the bed like a lifeless bundle.

—*I'm sorry, Dona Luarmina.*

—*You're ill. I shouldn't have forced you.*

—*It's not illness. For us, illness is something else, not what you whites . . .*

—*I'm a mulata, don't forget.*

—*You lady, for all intents and mispurposes, are white. The truth of my illness is this: I'm being punished by my father.*

—*Punished?*

—*Because I didn't carry out what he asked me to do.*

—*But that's no reason . . .*

—*No? I betrayed the promise I made. Don't you remember what I told you? I promised to look after that woman of his, I promised I would take her water, food . . .*

—*But you did all that.*

—*No, I didn't do anything at all.*

—*Yes, you did.*

I was puzzled by her insistence. What did that woman know about my life, what did she know about the lives of Black people?

I was getting annoyed at Luarmina's presumption. Maybe that was why I shouted:

—*I never did, lady. I never went back there.*

The *mulata* decided to sit down, bowed her head in her hands, sighed, and said:

—*That woman your father took around in his boat, that woman didn't die.*

—*What do you mean didn't die?*

—*She was carried away, clinging to a piece of wood . . .*

—*How do you know?*

—*Because I'm that woman.*

I lay there, gaping, my mind in turmoil. Was Luarmina joking, did she think I no longer had any sense at all? But she continued with a serenity that left me bewildered:

—*Yes, I'm that woman. And you comforted me with all your conversation, every time you visited me . . .*

—*It's not true . . .*

—*You fulfilled your pledge, Zeca. I'm telling you. You have no reason to feel ill.*

I was stunned. Could it be true, a story ending happily with such ease? I looked at Luarmina's face as if she had been there forever, as if this were merely another night in an entire life. Every time the fat *mulata* plucked the petals from a flower in that game of "sea loves me, sea loves me not," was it after all just my love making her do so?

—*But now, Luarmina, I have one illness left.*

—*What illness?*

—*You. You, Luarmina, are my illness.*

—*I promise you, Zeca, I'll come back later and cure your illness once and for all.*

—*But Luarmina, promise me you really are the woman from the boat!*

She kept quiet. Her head bowed, she murmured:

—*I'll leave the door open. Like that, you can listen to the sea . . .*

Listening to the sea, I fell asleep. But it wasn't all of me that slept. Just as my father had died bit by bit, I now fell asleep a bit of me at a time. First, it was my memory that fell into the abyss and was lost to existence. As if at last the sea were teaching my memories to sleep. As if my life were accepting the supreme invitation and leaving me for its eternal dance with the sea.

ABOUT THE AUTHOR

Born in Beira, Mozambique, MIA COUTO directed the Mozambican state news agency during the years following independence from Portugal. Since the late 1980s, he has worked as an environmental biologist and a writer. Couto is the author of more than thirty books, which have been published in thirty-five countries. He has won major literary prizes in Mozambique, Zimbabwe, Portugal, Brazil, Italy, and the United States, including the 2013 Camões Prize and the 2014 Neustadt International Prize for Literature. He was a finalist for the 2015 Man Booker International Prize and the 2017 International Dublin Literary Award.

Mia Couto lives with his family in Maputo, Mozambique, where he works as an environmental consultant.

ABOUT THE TRANSLATORS

DAVID BROOKSHAW'S many translations include Mia Couto's recent novels *Woman of the Ashes* and *The Sword and the Spear*, as well as earlier Couto novels such as *The Tuner of Silences*, *Sleepwalking Land*, *The Last Flight of the Flamingo* and *Under the Frangipani*. He has translated widely from the literatures of Lusophone Asia and the Azores Islands. Brookshaw is Professor Emeritus of Lusophone Studies at the University of Bristol, England.

ERIC M. B. BECKER is the recipient of a PEN Heim Award, a Fulbright Fellowship and a Fellowship from the National Endowment for the Arts. He has translated works by, among others, the Brazilian writers Lygia Fagundes Telles and Fernanda Torres and the Angolan-Portuguese writer Djaimilia Pereira de Almeida. He lives in New York City.